THE HUNGRY LAND

Also by Michael Mullen

KELLY
THE FESTIVAL OF FOOLS

For children
MAGUS THE LOLLIPOP MAN
SEA WOLVES FROM THE NORTH

THE HUNGRY LAND

Michael Mullen

BANTAM PRESS

NEW YORK · LONDON · TORONTO · SYDNEY · AUCKLAND

TRANSWORLD PUBLISHERS LTD
61–63 Uxbridge Road, London W5 5SA

TRANSWORLD PUBLISHERS (AUSTRALIA) PTY LTD
15–23 Helles Avenue, Moorbank, NSW 2170

TRANSWORLD PUBLISHERS (NZ) LTD
Cnr Moselle and Waipareira Aves,
Henderson, Auckland

Published 1986 by Bantam Press,
a division of Transworld Publishers Ltd
Copyright © Michael Mullen 1986

British Library Cataloguing in Publication Data

Mullen, Michael
  The hungry land.
  I. Title
  823'.914[F]   PR6063.U387

  ISBN 0-593-01138-4

02096454

Photoset by Rowland Phototypesetting Ltd
Bury St Edmunds, Suffolk
Printed in Great Britain by
Mackays of Chatham Ltd
Chatham, Kent

To the memory of my father and mother

1

WHEN PATRICK GILL lay in a ditch on a warm summer night or tried to sleep in a crowded mud cabin at the edge of a bog, he felt that there was a fatal curse on him.

'What is Gill but a spoiled priest and a drunken hedge-school teacher?' the peasants asked behind his back. 'He would sell his soul to the devil in hell for a drink.'

He would. Any dreams which he had once carried were now fragments. Time and poverty and the feeling that he was on the forgotten edge of Europe had destroyed all his hopes. He had sought refuge in drink; the raw poteen could set his spirit on fire. Sitting in a low shebeen, surrounded by illiterate peasants, he could be king for a night. 'Gill could blacken your name with that power of his to write satires,' they said of him.

A man who wrote satires could destroy the reputation of a family for ten centuries. Rioccard Barrett had written a satire on Owen Conway of Erris which was now recited in Irish all over Mayo.

With this power Patrick Gill could demand lodgings in any of the huddle of villages along the coastline. But in the towns he could not expect such hospitality; they spoke English there and cared little for a rhymer. They looked towards Dublin and London for their music and their songs.

In the mornings, after his bouts of drinking, when he set out along the tracks which were like a net across the county, he reflected grimly on his situation. He was growing old and careless. Large gaps were appearing in his memory; he could no longer recall passages from Greek and Latin which had once kindled self-respect within him. Even the words of Irish poems which he had learned as a boy were slipping from his memory. He was forced to substitute his own lines, which were both faulty and weak. 'I'll soon begin to forget my own poems,' he would remark in dry comment upon himself. 'And the day I begin to forget my own poems I better be on the look out, for it will be either death or the workhouse for me.'

Like all poets of his race, whose traditions had stretched back two thousand years, he had enjoyed patronage. He had been welcomed at the great house built by Michael Barrett in the woods of Eisirt outside Northport. The fact that this man, shipowner and landlord, had accepted him into his house once gave him a remnant of dignity. But now he was banished.

One night he had arrived drunk at the great doors and had beaten upon them demanding hospitality. He had cursed Michael Barrett from the lawn, calling evil down on him and his house. A sturdy servant had lit the lights in the great hall and opened the doors. Gill made his way up the steps, but the servant grasped him by his greatcoat and dragged him down the avenue.

'A poet deserves more respect!' he protested. 'He is entitled to traditional hospitality. It is his right! Tell Barrett that I'll satirise him. He won't travel the roads for shame! I have the power . . . I have the power and I'll use it. By God, I'll use it!'

The servant had pushed him through the gates and kicked him on the backside into a wet ditch. 'And I have the power in the top of my boot, Gill,' he said harshly. 'Michael Barrett thinks you have lost the great power and that you now compose only *rameis*.'

The final remark came as sharp as a knife. No greater hurt could have been inflicted upon him, and it quickened his mind. 'I'm banished from Paradise,' he said to himself. 'I have committed the great sin. My pride got the better of me.'

The great gates had closed slowly in the darkness, whining with rust. 'I might as well be as blind as Homer now. Barrett has torn out my eyes.' Lines from Greek tragedy had floated back through his memory as he left the road and staggered towards the sea-shore and its eternal sounds. He wept for the passing of patronage and middle age and for the great gift of poetry which he had once possessed.

He was cast upon a destitute landscape. The spectre of hunger haunted the small perished fields: men were muted by it, the women and children spare. The hungry and poor would be his patrons until he returned to the great house. His fate was to walk the endless tracks and roads of Mayo, moving from one miserable village to the next, lying at night among the populous stench of sweating bodies in one-roomed cabins. His food, like the food of the illiterate peasants, was simple. He ate potatoes and drank milk during nine months of the year, and meal from June to August.

With an insensible eye he regarded the changes in himself and in the countryside about him. Each year during the early 1840s the hunger increased. There was always the fear that the potato crop might fail, and when it did the people, undernourished, would quickly die. The landlords' agents and the gombeen men grew strong. They were middlemen, rapacious and cruel, and the peasants trembled at their names, for they held power over life and death. They could raise the rents at a whim; they could destroy the cabins and throw the peasants on to the roads. The dispossessed would have to make their way to the workhouses, large stone buildings and newly built. Here male would be separated from female; procreating stopped.

'I should leave this blighted place and go to America in one of Barrett's ships,' Gill would mutter as he stood at the quays of Northport and watched the families with their few possessions take passage to America. 'I might have better luck in New York, and Barrett might give me free passage.'

But he had neither the will nor the energy to emigrate. He was growing old and he would remain. 'Mayo has a curse on it, and part of that curse is upon me. Is there no God watching down on us at all? Is there an answer to any prayer, pagan or Christian?'

There was no answer to prayer. He often passed the great walls surrounding Michael Barrett's house, but pride forbade him to make his way up the avenue and apologise for his behaviour. 'I'd die or go to the workhouse before I'd ask Barrett's pardon,' he told himself, passing the heavy iron gates.

It was three years since he had approached the house, a green bottle of poteen in his hand. During that time Gill had felt himself growing thin and his memory failing by degrees. The people had grown too wretched to have confidence in themselves, and Daniel O'Connell had lost his great power to sway mass meetings. The people stared from small cabins or holes they had dug in ditches at a bleak and unpromising landscape.

2

FREDERICK CAVENDISH stirred heavily in the great armchair. He was silent for some time. He turned towards Michael Barrett and looked at the strong profile of the old man who continued to gaze into the fire, his fingers knitted together beneath his chin. The bright heart of the glowing logs seemed to hold his interest. The crackle of the flames and the firm ticking of the clock emphasised the comfortable tranquillity of the room, yet it was haunted by the memories of a dark past. They had been friends for more than half a century, yet it was only now, on the eve of his daughter's return from England, that Barrett confided in him.

'You think that I am an evil man?' he asked, continuing to look into the fire.

'It is a sinister story.'

'I am a murderer. I hear their screams at night, clear as a ship's bell. There were fifty in all. They cried out for mercy in their strange tongue. Fear almost burst their eyes. It was my decision. I condemned them to death.'

'And were there times when these images did not haunt you?' Frederick Cavendish asked, avoiding any comment.

'I banished them for a long time, confined them to some limbo inside my mind and battened them well down. Now in old age they have escaped. You sow the wind and reap the whirlwind. You do not have to die to be punished in some

11

inferno. You are punished here, you are punished here.' His voice grew strong as he repeated his final sentence.

A silence hung in the room again. Then Barrett said urgently: 'Am I a murderer or not? You have read the philosophers.'

'I will not stand in judgement! You force me into a difficult position.'

'You are Pilate. You wash your hands of this serious judgement.'

'You have been punished in your own way.'

'I built a house for a son who was born dead. My wife went insane, and now the fortunes of the house will be run by a slip of a girl who cannot be controlled. She should have been born male, and then I would end my days with some confidence in the future. I built up the fortunes of this great house. Blood was on some of the money, but the greater part was fairly gained. Now the fortunes of the family will be taken by a girl into the next generation and the name will fail.'

Frederick Cavendish watched Michael Barrett while he talked. He feared that his mind, looking only to the past, might eventually become unhinged.

'You are self-indulgent,' he told him.

It stirred the old man into immediate action. Anger sparked in his eyes. 'I have never been self-indulgent! I have endured all the hardships, and you accuse *me* of self-indulgence?'

'Yes, I do. You have witnessed the monarchy fail in France. Why should this house not fail? Is it of that great importance? The next generation will shift for itself. When you are buried in Eisirt wood, the line will continue.'

'Ah, you have me dead now!' Barrett exclaimed. 'I'll not die easily. I have a daughter to guide. She needs my advice.'

'She does not need your meddling advice. She is a woman now and belongs easily in three cultures. She has a dignity that you could never acquire. You are no longer responsible for the destinies of others – you are an old man like me. We cannot wish youth upon us. Will you accept mortality?'

'No, I will not!' he told him angrily.

'You are as stubborn as granite,' observed Cavendish wryly.

'I am, and that is why I survived,' retorted the other. 'Others went down, but I survived – and *you* would have *me* consigned to the vault in Eisirt wood?'

'Have some port; at least we can agree upon its quality.' Frederick Cavendish poured from the decanter standing on the small table beside him. The two men drank silently, looking into the fire, both given to their thoughts.

Barrett House stood among the woods of Eisirt. It had strong firm outlines, with its limestone walls, its roof of grey slate and channels of lead. The windows held classical proportions, oblong on the first two storeys, small and square on the third.

From the balcony on the second floor Michael Barrett had a clear view of Clew Bay and the sea. Now in his old age he often stood there looking out, knowing he would never sail in his three-masted ships again. He traced the journeys they made in the map room, large and spacious, which he had laid out when he built the house. The maps were rolled up in leather cylinders and stored like bottles in a large wine-rack against the wall. He would spread them on the large mahogany table and gaze down upon untroubled seas like an Olympian God.

More often now his mind was in turmoil. Sometimes he stared for hours into the great oak fire and considered the fortunes of his family. When he visited his earliest memories he knew that he was growing old. He was taking refuge in a past which was full of movement and colour, the sight of stately ships and the smell of the sea.

The Barretts had always belonged to the sea. People said that they had salt in their blood and that they were born with an uncanny knowledge of wind and tide. They could smell the approach of a storm or danger. But Michael Barrett, as he sat by the great fire and drank port, knew that there was more than salt in their blood. The blood had become mixed, and their allegiances were to many things.

'We are Irish and Spanish and English, Protestant and Catholic,' he told his sea captain, John Burke, as they sat together and talked of family matters. 'It is as important to have a Barrett in the House of Commons, in France and in Spain as to have one on the sea.'

'You might have all these mixtures, Michael Barrett, and you might have the polish of the English gentry, but in your blood is the sea, and your mind and your tongue are Irish.'

He had built the house for his wife on a hill overlooking the sea, its back to the mountains, in a sheltered place which was not exposed to the harsh north wind. The land was fertile here, and the growth almost Mediterranean: to subsidise the building he had sold his vineyards in Spain. He had supervised every stone which had gone into the construction. They had opened a quarry in the hills, and the masons had set up their awnings there. They carved the large blocks of stone which were drawn by teams of horses and set in place. When it was finished it seemed part of the landcape.

Michael Barrett was marked off from the penurious hard-drinking squireens, relics from the eighteenth century. They were a bastard race with their tally-women, their wild drinking parties, their domestic filth and their brawls. They were never invited to his house or his table; the old lusts, irrational as the Irish part of his mind, were now dead. Perhaps, he mused, it was his lusts which had unhinged his wife. He would never know. Perhaps there was madness in her blood-line and perhaps madness has crept into the family, he thought. If there is madness there, then it will take ten generations to dilute the stain. It was a thought that troubled him more than all others.

His wife had called his illegitimate children the 'bastard Barretts'. He had bought his women farms of land, and they had married men who were land-hungry, men who had little interest in the paternity of the first child. If it were Michael Barrett's child, then they were linked to him by a blood-bond. A Barrett bastard carried the handsome stamp of Michael Barrett upon it.

'He should have married one of his own instead of going to London for the lady of the house. Sure, what did she know of his or our ways?' the servants had whispered among themselves after they had discovered her body floating off Rinn Point. She was buried in the family vault in Eisirt wood. She had often slipped from her bedroom on windy nights, when there was sad music in the trees, and rushed in her nightdress through the forest paths. Throwing out her arms as she ran, she sang incoherent songs. She returned to the house in the morning, her feet soiled and torn, some delirium inside her deadening the cold and the pain. One morning, she did not return. All day they searched for her. Two days later she was found, her nightdress sodden and transparent. They carried

14

the body on a door along the five miles of sea-shore back to the house.

He had brooded over her death for several weeks, pacing through the pleasure gardens she had set out or walking by the sea, wishing he were walking through the streets of some medieval town in Spain or France. Despair sat in his mind for six months and only lifted gradually. He did not immediately settle back to his business but took command of one of his ships and sailed to New York four times in one year. He tested his courage against the sea and won: he exposed himself to the worst danger he knew and he survived.

He returned to his large office in Northport and sat before his ledgers, the desire for action now wasted within him. He became reflective and morose, and there were few whose company he enjoyed. The years passed sluggishly for him between his house and the offices. His large back became lobed with the passage of time, and he walked with a stoop.

'You are old before your time,' Frederick Cavendish would tease him as they sat before the blazing fire. 'Like Hamlet you are overburdened with thought – if it can be described as thought. You ruminate too much. You are dour company.'

''Tis my nature. I have a bad humour in my blood. You have neither chick nor child nor the heavy responsibilities of property or race. You are certain of your origins. I am not.'

'My origins are a matter of great doubt!' Frederick Cavendish referred to his paternity with no trace of embarrassment. His mother, it was rumoured, had been the mistress to one of the Georges.

'But you are British. You belong to the British earth.'

'I do not. I belong in Revolutionary France. I have always preached revolution.'

'Well, you no longer preach it. I read your editorials in the *Connaught Telegraph*. The fire has left you. You drink too much, and I'm told you sing in the taverns when you are drunk and you visit at the houses of merchants.'

'I still object to injustices and berate the landlords. That does not mean that I cannot share a glass of port with them. You are becoming insufferable.'

'Then, why do you make this journey to Northport to drink with me?'

'Because you have so few friends.'

15

'Friends are unnecessary.'

'Except the rake Gill and John Burke?' Cavendish asked.

'The rest I can well do without.' Michael Barrett spoke roughly.

'John Burke shares your deep attachment to the sea. Gill is a scrawny and drunken poet, and you're obsessed by him because of this mystical belief you have in the Gaelic language and the blood-bonds you have with the Barretts. Once we were young men in France before Napoleon crowned himself Emperor. You are complex in mind and emotion, Michael Barrett, never certain where your allegiance lies.'

'Well, it doesn't lie with the landlords and their agents and all they stand for! I have seen villages levelled and small fields turned into sheep ranches. If Kenrick is given a free hand, then the workhouse in Castlebar will be filled to overflowing and there will not be enough ships to take the emigrants to America or England. I sit here alone and watch all these things happen.'

'They are happening in Scotland and in parts of England, too. The peasants are right to leave their holdings. Let them take their chances in America. You have shown me the maps of that great continent. Part of it still remains unopened. There people own the lands; here the landlords own it by default, and by spurious rights.'

They were two old men alike in physique who could agree on few things. As they grew older they settled into their political positions and would not shift from ideas they had formed during the revolutionary turmoil in Europe. Their conversations always turned to the same subjects, and there was always division between them. Sometimes Barrett became angry with Cavendish and showered abuse upon him; Cavendish, on the other hand, always remained tranquil. Invariably after one of their quarrels, when they parted in bad grace, a letter of apology arrived at the offices of the *Connaught Telegraph*. These became more frequent with the years.

Frederick Cavendish began to feel old in the early months of 1845. It was not brought about by any sluggish humour in his blood but by the fact that he was approaching his seventy-eighth year. His feet were swollen with gout, and his heavy frame had shrunken. He had lived through disruptive events in history and had been in France during the Reign of Terror and the years which followed. He had been seduced by the ideas of Voltaire and Rousseau and he had thrown in his lot with those who undid a political structure shaped by a thousand years of history. He had seen blood on the guillotine platform, on the cobblestones of Paris and diluted in the waters of the Seine. And all this blood-letting had been justified by the youthful phrases they had bandied about in the taverns of Paris.

It was rumoured that he had shot a man in a duel or had fled from his debts, but it was all far away now and it had happened in another time. Was the blood still upon his hands or was it upon the hands of a young Englishman whom he did not recognise? He had acted in clear conscience then, but at seventy-eight he had become cynical about revolutions and his conscience was troubled.

At night-time he reflected on his present situation as he drank his port. In 1820 he had arrived in the town of Castlebar from England – no one was ever certain why – and set up the *Connaught Telegraph* in Spencer Street in 1828. He was a Protestant and known to have aristocratic connections, but his editorials were merciless and often libellous about the absentee landlords – and when he ended up in the courts, as he often did, he used the courtroom to be doubly libellous. Twice he had been imprisoned in Castlebar gaol. He had enjoyed the fishing and the shooting during several summers with Michael Barrett in Northport and decided to remain in this remote and bleak landscape, with its wide moorlands, its rivers teeming with fish, its casual ways. He had sold his property in Devon and uprooted himself from a controlled landscape. He would have preferred to move to France, but its political system was not in sympathy with his ideas.

Now he wondered if he had made the wrong choice. He was too old to pull up his roots and move from the garrison town of Castlebar. During the years he had watched people build rows of hovels at the end of the town close to the imposing workhouse. They had fled from the overpopulated countryside and settled here. The fever gestated in these dark and damp places during the spring and flared up in summer. The countryside became overpopulated in one generation, and small-holdings were subdivided into smaller ones. Men clawed

17

subsistence from impoverished fields while their children grew hungry, their women old. Each year there was a partial famine in some locality or other. The laughter had left people's faces, and there was a fear in government circles that this area of Mayo was the breeding-ground for an upheaval. Dublin Castle was prepared for trouble. A huge military barracks capable of housing two thousand stood above the town, and soldiers carried out their exercises on the great eight-acre parade-ground. There was also a police barracks close to the town green. A regular correspondence was carried on with Dublin, and very little went unnoticed.

Frederick Cavendish had forebodings concerning the future. It seemed inevitable that there would be a great famine and the whole country would be thrown into turmoil. There was little he could do to hold back the floodgates.

It had been reported that somewhere in England a blight had affected the potatoes. It had been carried from Canada, and he knew that at some date it would arrive in Ireland. When it did, a great disaster would follow.

The old men dozed now in the deep armchairs. The rich port and the warmth from the oak logs of the great fire drew off their anger, and they fell into personal thoughts. Presently Frederick Cavendish began to snore rhythmically, his mouth cast open, his purple eyelids drawn over his eyes. Michael Barrett watched his old friend. The passing of time had franked lines on his forehead, and there were bags of flesh, large as thumb knuckles, beneath his eyes, but in sleep the face was still controlled by intelligence. His mind had always been sharp, his writing clear and fine, and this was still so, but now he had come to terms with life.

Michael Barrett soon began to doze himself, his mind un-troubled by the recent images which had visited him. He reflected in a half-conscious way on his daughter Gráinne, who was now on her way from England. He wondered whether the years of training would have taught her to control the wild Barrett anger and independence. Could she be depended upon to carry the fortunes of the house into the next generation? He had built a house and a fortune, and he did not wish them to fail. Presently he, too, fell asleep.

Later the doors of the room were thrown aside and Gráinne Barrett, a wild red shock of hair falling to her shoulders, entered the room. The two old men stirred themselves from sleep and looked up, bemused at the beautiful woman who entered the room.

'I have returned from exile,' she declaimed dramatically in her silver voice. 'I have kept my promise to you, Father. I shall never return to England!'

Michael Barrett rubbed the sleep from his eyes and rose from the chair. 'But you are not expected until Wednesday! Had I known that the ship had entered the harbour I would have been on the quayside to greet you.'

'We had a following wind from the Blasket Islands,' the girl said excitedly. 'We sailed under full canvas.'

'And you took the wheel?'

'Yes! I felt the freedom of the sea in my hands and in my body. You cannot have known the loneliness I endured in that convent! It was good to be on the sea again.'

'Your mind is always on the sea,' her father said.

Frederick Cavendish had now risen from his seat and was a little uncertain on his legs. Gráinne rushed over to him and threw her arms about him. 'You have been sleeping,' she accused.

'Old age, Gráinne. Old age and ague. I humour a disposition to sleep.'

'And who defends democracy and the republics while you sleep?' she teased.

'Younger men, younger men,' he sighed.

'I prefer my Frederick Cavendish, with his fine phrases and sweet singing voice.'

'Ah, some day a young man will steal you away from me.'

'I have not met him.'

'You will.' He spoke gently to her and in a paternal voice.

'No man will have a wild sea-woman,' her father said brusquely, feeling a lack of the affection she had shown to Frederick Cavendish. 'Come and tell us all the news of London and of your voyage.'

They took their seats again and, sitting on a small stool between them, her arms binding her knees, Gráinne told them of her journey.

3

IN NATURE AND TEMPERAMENT Gráinne Barrett was very close to her father, and he was proud both of her beauty and of her free strong character. Her childhood had been free and easy at the big house. She had spent many hours in the servants' quarters and in the stables, and unconsciously she had picked up the language and culture of the people. Her nurse, Mrs Cassidy, was an Irish-speaker, like all the other servants.

Her earliest memories were of Captain John Burke bringing her presents from America. When she heard that his ship had arrived at the quay, she would wait breathlessly for him at the window of her father's map room. Then, when he emerged from the great vault of trees arching above the avenue, she would rush down the stairs and across the lawn to greet him.

'Captain Burke, Captain Burke, what have you brought me from the new country?'

He would sweep her on to his saddle and ride right up to the front door, her luxurious red hair flowing over his arm.

'Were you a good girl while I was in America?' he would ask. 'Mrs Cassidy will tell me everything.'

'I was a good girl most of the time, honest – except once or twice when I was bad, but it wasn't very often.'

'And will you marry me when you grow up?'

'I will, if you carry me across the wide sea.'

Her mother, always a shadowy figure in her life, objected

that she should be given free access to the servants' quarters where she would only learn a barbaric tongue and all the superstitions of the Celtic race. She further objected when Mrs Cassidy took her to her own village where Gráinne moved freely among the small two-roomed houses chattering with the people. Here she discovered a joyful chaos and tolerance which she would not discover at the great house or from the Protestant lady who taught her good behaviour and elementary music on the piano.

She became acquainted with Mrs McAndrew, the healing woman, who gathered herbs on the mountains; Festus the Amadaun, who danced a jig for her and was continually winking; but it was Dan, the Uileann piper, who was her favourite. On warm days he would sit on his stool in the sun, the bellows strapped under his arm, and having tuned the cantankerous instrument he would play for her.

When he played the music he became a mystical figure. He bent his large shoulders over the pipes, closed his eyes, and drew sad music from the chanter which would always haunt her. It was remote and lonely music which made her cry.

'Stop, Dan, stop! My heart is going to burst,' she often called out. 'I'll be sad all the day, and there will be strange people in my mind.'

'That's good, that's good. You have a good heart,' he had told her and did not explain further.

They were proud of Gráinne Barrett in Mrs Cassidy's village. They watched her grow, amazed at her great beauty. Gill had celebrated her in one of his better poems which was recited in cabins the breadth of Mayo. 'She could break a man's heart or lead him astray like the dream women of the poems,' they would say.

She was never far, within her mind, from the culture of the people and like her father found a tranquillity in its art forms. She knew the stories of her race: the sad story of the Children of Lir and their desolate existence on the northern seas beyond Belmullet; the story of Deirdre of the Sorrows; the intrigues of the ambitious war queen Maeve who brought about the wars with Ulster because she wished to possess the great bull of Cooley; the strange story of the Fool of the Speckled Coat; there was also the Fenian cycle of stories in her mind, more tempered by their love of nature and the hunt. She had listened

21

while men recited these stories beside turf fires, their memories never failing, the words carried on primitive chant. They had made their way down a thousand years through storytellers.

When she was six years of age Captain John Burke brought her to Northport and took her on board his ship. She still had a clear recollection of her visit to that part of the town which her father had built: the large warehouses with their many windows, men carrying bales of wool across the quay front to the boats which carried them to the ships. She watched the sailors smoking their pipes sitting on the bollards, their eyes towards the tides and the wind. 'Who is the pretty lady you bring with you, John Burke?' one of them asked.

'She is a sailor lady and some day she will be captain of a great ship.'

'Like the sea queen from Clare Island?'

'Like the sea queen,' replied John Burke.

'She has the O'Malley blood, and there is salt in it,' the sailors said amongst themselves.

They had rowed out to the great three-masted ship. It grew larger and larger as she approached it. There were rope ladders everywhere leading up to the platforms on the thick masts. The masts stretched up to the very sky. The furled sails were lashed to the yard-arms and beneath the yard-arms ran fragile ropes where men stood when they unfurled the sails. It was a strange, moving world where the wind sang in the rigging and where the timbers creaked under strain. The air was filled with the healthy smell of tar and rope. It was a clear free world, and one had only to follow the wind.

She climbed aboard and rushed excitedly about the deck. This was the world to which she belonged. Even at six years of age she ached for the ships. Captain John Burke had brought her into his cabin with its brass fittings, its small windows, its racks of maps, its bed carefully tucked away beneath the window.

'Can I come and live here in the summer-time?' she had asked.

'Of course, if your father permits.'

'It is much more interesting than our house, which always stands in the same place and never moves. Some day I will sail with you over the edge of the world.'

Later he had brought her down into the hold of the ship where the cargo was stored. It was a dark place, and he carried a lantern with him. He showed her the main ribs of the ship running from end to end, and he told her how they had been cut and shaped in Canada by men who were the best builders in the world. He explained how the large square dowels locked the timber beams together. It was a dark world, fetid with bilge water.

'It is alive like a horse,' she told him later, as they were going ashore.

'And spirited, too,' he told her. 'There is no ship but has some quality or other which makes them all different. Why, I have known lazy ships that barely moved under full canvas and fast ships which sped over the water with little canvas as if they had life in them. Such ships are like good racehorses.'

'And this ship?'

'My ship is like a good racehorse, and on a long voyage it will outpace all other ships.'

As she grew older her passion for the ships increased. She learned their tonnage and cargoes. Her father explained the maps and map-making to her, and he brought the seas alive for her as he told of a typhoon he had encountered on his way to Mauritius, how he had limped into Port Louis and watched racing on the Champs de Mars and slept on the spice islands. He told her of Commodore Anson's voyage into the South Seas by way of Cape Horn and how he captured the Manila Galleon with priceless treasures in her hold. His stories of the sea were endless. When he spoke to her in the library he was no longer a landowner and a businessman, he was a sea captain like John Burke.

By sixteen she was a fine horsewoman and could control the most fiery animal. Men watched her as she rode along the Great Strand, her red hair flying in the wind. 'She should have been a man,' they said, 'to take control of the ships.'

One day her father called her to his library. He was nervous when he told her to sit down opposite him.

'You must realise that you are no longer a child. Whether you like it or not, you are different to the other children with whom you play. I know that there is part of you which would like to stay here for ever, but you must some day be mistress of this house. I will not have you like a woman who talks and behaves like a fishwife and rides a wild horse. You have to learn the ways of society and how to behave properly. When friends' children come to dinner you do not know how to behave, and you have no mother to look after you.'

'I don't care for your friends' children,' she said, tossing her head. 'They are pompous and English, and their ways are strange to me. I know you detest them yourself. I know your mind.'

'Control yourself,' he told her severely. 'I have learned how to control my feelings, and you will have to do the same. You cannot always let people know what you are thinking. People say I am rearing a barbarian. You have a duty to the house and its continuation.'

'I prefer the ships and the sea. Why should I always be anchored here? I wish I could sail with John Burke.' Her tone was defiant.

'Well, you soon will, my lady. I am sending you to a convent in England. There you will learn how to behave properly and in a manner fitting your station in life.'

The sudden announcement took her by surprise. For a moment she was too stunned to speak. How could her father condemn her to prison? It would be a prison at the convent . . . she would be away from the sight and the sound of the sea.

'I'll fall into a decline, Father – I cannot live away from the sea! You are punishing me. It is very sudden and it is unfair!'

'You are expected in London. I have written letters to the convent.'

'Then you were plotting behind my back. I won't go! I won't go!'

'Go you will if I have to chain you to the deck.'

She was angry for a long time. Then she began to cry. She wished that her mother, that strange figure who had walked through the woods at night in her silk dress, was there to comfort her.

'I will make you one promise, however,' her father continued more gently. 'I am having a new ship built. I will name it after you and each year, until you have finished your education, it will travel up the Thames and bring you home to Northport.'

'You will name a ship after *me*?' She looked up through her tears.

'Yes, and it will be just as swift as you on your horse, but you will have to go to England for seven or eight months each year. I expect a lot from you. I have let you have your way, and you will never forget the people of this house or of the villages. This was part of your education. But some day you will have to defend them. It will serve you well to have polish and manners.'

'It's like transporting me to Tasmania, John Burke,' she told him when she went to board the ship for London.

'You need the finish. A wild horse is no good to anyone.'

'I'm not like a horse, John Burke.'

'Sometimes you behave like a wild one. It's time you said goodbye to those wild ways of yours.'

'You are against me,' she told him.

'I am at the moment,' he said and left it at that.

Her father had chosen the convent well. It was on the outskirts of London, set among pleasant trees, in a landscape of soft green hills. She went there in autumn when the leaves, brown and copper and curled, lay on the avenue leading up to the door. Her mind was filled with melancholy thoughts, and the world seemed in sympathy with her mood. She was fortunate that one of the sisters was an émigrée from France. The blood from some noble family ran in her veins, and she had fled before the revolutionary winds which had destroyed many great families and houses. A sympathy grew up between them in exile, and Sister Geneviève became her only close friend.

'You must be a diplomat,' Sister Geneviève told her. 'You must have a subtle and interested mind, like many of our French ladies. And you must always conceal your feelings. Do I not conceal my feelings? I long for France and its etiquette, but I shall never return there again. The world I belonged to has perished. I live in this horrid English climate with its beer-drinkers; the bad weather catches my chest, the sun does not shine, and I speak in English but I dream in French.'

During these years in London, Gráinne Barrett changed into a tall graceful woman. Her walk became elegant, and when she entered a room, with her red hair, her fine, almost fragile skin, her bright seafaring eyes and her laughter, men turned to look at her. She learned a pattern of behaviour which belonged more to a French château than to an English house.

But each summer Gráinne threw aside all that she had learned at the convent. Her father kept his promise. He did christen the ship *Gráinne*, and each year she sailed up the Thames and took her on board. She took the helm and brought her out of the harbour into the open sea.

'She is my ship,' she told John Burke, 'and look how she moves before the wind!'

It was a journey of some three days. They crossed the Irish Sea, moved round the coast of Kerry and up towards Clew Bay, the sails crowding the masts. John Burke taught her the names of the ropes and the riggings and the orders to call out to the men aloft reefing the sails.

'It is in your blood. You did not catch it from the wind,' Captain John Burke assured her. 'Some day I will bring you to America.'

'Would you really take me to America?'

'It is a rough journey.'

'I do not mind. I have to know the hardship. I'll go as a member of the crew.'

'Well, what would your father think?'

'I do not care. How can I know everything about a ship if I cannot climb aloft?'

'We will see.'

Her last year at the convent passed rapidly. She was presented to the Queen, her father standing beside her dressed like an English gentleman. He felt proud of her, for she stood out amongst all the other women. Queen Victoria stopped to speak with her. When she discovered who she was she said: 'And so you are related to the Sea Queen, who stood as an equal before Queen Elizabeth?'

'Yes, there is a relationship between us, Your Majesty,' Gráinne said demurely.

'Then I must be careful of my throne' – and she passed on down the line of waiting ladies.

'She has no need to fear for her throne,' she whispered to her father. 'I'm far more interested in her colonies!'

Her father refrained from laughing. 'That is treasonable talk,' he told her, with a wink.

They left the palace, and when they entered the carriage they began to laugh.

'I will admit that she's no beauty,' Michael Barrett said.

'She looks like Mrs Cash who takes in the washing,' Gráinne retorted.

When the time came for her to leave the convent she went to see Sister Geneviève for the last time. Geneviève had grown frail in the last year and walked with a silver-topped cane. She could no longer walk in the damp cloister and spent most of her time in a deep armchair in front of the fire.

'It is this horrible English weather which has weakened me,' she told Gráinne as she sat before her. 'I must be getting very old, for I am visiting the past a lot. I wish I had some French wine to drink! It would warm my old bones and make my exile happy, but you know the rules of the convent. . . .'

'I could always have some smuggled in, Sister Geneviève. That would make it taste sweeter.'

'No. I will keep my promise. I shall not drink wine. But some advice before you go. Use your wealth well. Those who are rich and privileged have their obligations. The world is changing. That fire which kindled in France will blow through the world. It can be a terrible destructive fire. Remember your French and practise it. It is a fine and delicate language, not like the language of the beer-drinkers. English is not a good language. Too heavy, too heavy. . . .' Her mind began to drift away from exile, and Gráinne knew that it was time to leave. She waited until the old nun fell into a comfortable sleep, and then left the room.

A coach was waiting at the door of the convent to carry her to the ship. She looked towards the sky as the coach made its way down the avenue; soon she would be sailing the seas.

4

THE HUGE SAILOR took Myles Prendergast and lifted him over his shoulder. His body, drugged with the tavern wine, was listless and his arms swung foolishly as Brian Burke carried him up the steps of the tavern and out into the narrow street, lit here and there with a brothel light.

'Where do I go, John?' he asked the sea captain.

'I am never certain of my direction on land,' John Burke called out to the group of men who poured out of the tavern behind him. They formed a confused mass and took account of their position.

The tavern-keeper was at the door, rubbing his hands. 'I can promise you heavenly delights; the women are from North Africa, brown of body and passionate. They are sweet as red grapes.'

'Pox-carriers,' John Burke roared. 'At this time of night all women are from Africa and they are all beautiful, and tempted as the men may be to indulge in sweet pleasure I'll castrate them if they don't return to the ship.' He turned to his crewmen. 'Are you all here?'

'We are,' they called out.

'I hope so. I can't return to Michael Barrett and tell him that one of his sailors went missing in the brothels of Bordeaux. And what would your mothers say?'

'That we brought shame on them.' The sailors clutched each other for support.

28

'You can die where you like for Ireland, but don't die for yourselves in this pox-ridden spot. I'll lead the way and, Brian, you take up the rear with the Frenchman.' John Burke, squat and wide, moved forward, his pistols in his hands. He sang the marching song of his ancestors, which was taken up by the men. They felt confident in the narrow streets filled with thieves and pimps.

Myles Prendergast, still unconscious, was unaware of the dangerous journey through the alleyways and side-roads. On one occasion they were confronted by a group of mulattos carrying machetes, who formed a wall in front of them. John Burke discharged a pistol directly into the ground before them. The lead pellets cut into their legs. They howled in pain and ran before them. 'Lead the way, lead the way!' he roared in Irish. 'I have drowned your kind without compassion.' His eyes were filled with the mad anger of hate. It stirred easily in his mind, which was pagan and instinctual. He was feared even in Bordeaux, where he had once killed a man in a brawl. He had torn out his throat with the neck of a broken bottle. Had Myles Prendergast been more aware of his savage reputation, he might not have made his acquaintance so easily.

Eventually they reached the sea-front, where hundreds of ships and boats were moored to the bollards along the quay. They made their way on board *Ann Marie*, and Brian Burke carried Myles Prendergast down to the sailors' quarters and heaved him off his shoulder on to a rough bunk. Myles Prendergast was not aware when the ship hoisted its anchor and sailed out of the narrow port. Neither was he aware that his journey to Bordeaux had been noted.

Four days previously Prendergast had boarded the coach in Paris. He had chosen to take the long route through Orléans, Tours, Poitiers and Angoulême to Bordeaux. He watched the landscape change from the carriage, for it was a pleasant journey, and when he grew tired of the forests and the vineyards he read from a book. The old lady who sat in the corner irritated him. She said nothing during the long journey but continued to knit a shapeless stocking. The knitting-needles clicked upon each other for four whole days. Once he tried to engage her in conversation, but she indicated that she was dumb. She became an irritant during the long journey, and of all the passengers who had boarded the coach in Paris she was the only one who continued to Bordeaux.

He had taken the journey south because he knew that the British spies kept a close eye on the northern ports and his departure to Ireland would be noted. His military training had made him conscious of the fact that a network of British spies was spread out across France, with a hard core in the capital city. Even during the bloody turmoil of the Revolution spies had mingled with the crowd about the guillotine, making mental lists of those who had been put to death.

'They are like woodworm in every level of society,' the Revolutionary Circle in Paris had told him. 'You think you have got rid of one pest and then another takes its place. They are in the government ministries, they are in the houses of the rich, they are in the streets and even in the brothels. Eventually everything they discover ends up in London. Always watch for them.'

He had watched for them at the beginning of the journey but he had failed to notice any one of the passengers behave suspiciously, and after the third day of the journey he no longer worried.

The old lady with the knitting did not stay at the inn with the other travellers when they arrived in Poitiers. Instead she took her travelling-bag and made her way towards the suburbs of the city. Her pace quickened when she was well removed from the coach stop. Finally she reached the address given to her in Paris. It was a secluded house surrounded by tall hedges. She was brought to a large room and questioned by a softly spoken Frenchman, who sat behind an ornate desk and took notes. She described Myles Prendergast in detail but she could not give any further information. She told the French gentleman that Prendergast was on a journey to Bordeaux, but she could not indicate if he were going on a sea journey. She was instructed to follow him to Bordeaux, and before she left the next morning she was given an address in the city. She must immediately contact a British agent when she arrived there.

She knew the name of the passenger but she knew nothing of his background. She was an English spy who made long journeys in coaches and passed her time knitting shapeless stockings.

Myles Prendergast was the son of a Galway merchant who had thrown in his lot with General Humbert in 1798. He had fled the country with his wife after the insurrection had failed, and his property and business had been confiscated after his departure. Now, as an old man, he sold books in Paris. Behind his shop the Circle gathered each Sunday evening to listen to reports from Ireland and to make plans for the future. They now looked to America for support. Already they had formed cells in New York and were in constant communication with them. Emigrants were pouring into the eastern cities of America, and they realised that their new strength lay there. Here a force could be raised which some day might make Ireland free.

He reached Bordeaux as the sun was setting behind the city. He could make out La Tour Pey-Berland, rising two hundred feet above the ground. It had survived the ravages of the Revolution, when it had been converted into a shot tower. He knew that in another church, Des-Feuillans, lay the remains of Montaigne. Once this city had had an Irish college, which had been suppressed during the Revolution. Ysabeau and Baudot had brought their portable guillotines to this city, and a tribunal had been set up there. Martyn Glynn, superior of the college, had been guillotined before the Fort Du Ha. Others might have suffered the same fate but for James Burke of Killaloe, who had them released and placed on board ship bound for Ireland.

James Burke, a priest, had been the most intemperate of men. He took the Revolutionary oath, pillaged his own church and others and sold the chalices. He had drunk wine with Ysabeau, another clerical reprobate, and toasted the Revolution. With the wealth he acquired from the pillaged churches he settled down to farming. But in October of 1793 news was brought to him that priests and students of the Irish college had been flung into the Carmelite prison. He left his farm and rushed into the presence of Ysabeau, freshly back from Cadillac, where his portable guillotine had been busily employed in ridding the country of the enemies of the Revolution.

Burke called out as he entered the prison: 'Ysabeau, preserve the lives of my countrymen held within the confines of this convent!'

Ysabeau, who had seen the sacred vessels profaned during

31

the Festival of Reason, who had watched as an ox was adored in the Cathedral, and who cared nothing for human life, was moved by the voice of this clerical reprobate turned farmer, and he ordered their release. James Burke accompanied them to the docks, and watched them as they waved from the ship's deck on their way to Ireland.

That had been many years ago, and Myles had listened to his father tell the story of Abbé James Burke many times. 'Oh, he was a strange man, Myles, and damned in hell no doubt. But he was caught up by the flame of the Revolution as we all were. There were many priests who carried the same flame within them when they arrived home from France. I marched side by side with them through Castelbar and on to Ballinamuck when Humbert sold us out. We took a gamble and we lost.'

'And you lost your property in Galway for your troubles,' Myles reminded him.

'And I would do it again,' the old man said stubbornly. 'I still hear the revolutionary songs singing in my ear, and we gave them a good race for it, but Humbert sold us out.'

His father never deviated from his love of Ireland. Night after night he remained up, when Paris slept, printing and binding pamphlets which were carried to Ireland to be distributed secretly in taverns and at fairs. And as some friend set out for Ireland from the shop he would recite the poem of Donnacdh Rua McConnemara, 'Bring the Blessings of My Heart to Ireland'. The poem, composed in Newfoundland, suited the melancholy qualities of old Mr Prendergast's heart. As he crated his pamphlets into small boxes he would remark: 'Each box contains an army. These pamphlets will be read in cabins and in town houses. They will spread the French fire. The day will come again when we will rise out, and not with pikes and forks but with quality guns; for you must always be as good as the enemy.'

He had watched the political development in Ireland from his exile in Paris and followed the fortunes of Daniel O'Connell with great interest. He knew the history of the O'Connells and their patronage of the Irish poets during the penal times and of their proximity to the sea. They drank wine smuggled from the Continent at Derrynane House and listened to the famous lament written by one of the O'Connell women which he himself often recited in his exile.

He had watched O'Connell drag the nation up from its knees. In 1829 Catholic Emancipation was granted; it was the first of the freedoms. Myles remembered his father rushing into the shop as soon as he received the news from London. 'O'Connell has broken the first link, God bless him! We are half-free. The country is behind him now. He has only to raise his finger and everyone in the country will rise up in arms! We will break the final link. You'll see the House of Parliament opened up in Dublin. Rush up to the Irish college and tell Father O'Halloran that we are half-free. Tell him that Catholic Emancipation has become law!'

Myles ran through the streets of Paris repeating to himself: 'It's a great day for Ireland. Catholic Emancipation has become law!' He ran across the quadrangle and up the stairs to Father O'Halloran's room.

'Father,' he called out. 'The Catholic Emancipation Bill has gone through the House of Commons and we are free at last!'

Father O'Halloran bent down and wrapped his arms about the boy. He hugged him so hard that he thought he would break his heart. Then he felt the priest's body shake with sobs. Large tears rolled down his cheeks. 'For three hundred years we were run to ground; for three hundred years they suppressed our church; and for three hundred years we had to make our way down every dusty road in Europe until it seemed that God had forsaken us. You bring great news, Myles, the greatest news we will hear in one hundred years.'

Myles ran from the room and down the corridor with the news, and soon the bell was ringing out over the college. From the balcony he looked down at the quadrangle, at seminarians who like children were throwing their books and papers into the air. Somebody called out 'Three cheers for Daniel O'Connell!' and cheers echoed through the cool arches. This was the exultation which must have greeted men's hearts when they heard the Liberty Bell ring out in Concord or watched the Bastille put to the torch, and he wondered at the power this strange land of Ireland exercised over its exiles, a land where poets had seen visions in a language which had been maturing for two thousand years.

He watched the jubilation for a full hour. The news had by now spread out into the streets, and many Irish exiles poured into the college through the great gate.

Suddenly, he felt a hand upon his shoulder. He looked up to see Father Jennings, a very old priest, his cheeks criss-crossed with dark furrows.

'You brought the news, my son?'

'Yes, Father.'

'You are Eoin Prendergast's son?'

'Yes.'

'Then, you have fine blood in your veins. Your father will not be satisfied with religious freedom alone.'

'No, Father.'

'Oh, no, he won't! We put up a fight for more. I was with him in '98. From the garret in Northport I saw men hanged in the square below me. They were hanged in front of my eyes. I was lucky. I was saved. I escaped through Clew Bay in a Barrett ship as did many others. It seems a long time ago now. . . .' He looked down at the figures dancing in the quadrangle below. 'Well, it is a young man's fight now. I don't know where it will take them or what blood will be spilt on the way. We have a most unhappy history, a most unhappy history, and we will not win political freedom as easily as we won religious freedom. O'Connell has done as much as he can.' With these words he departed. Myles watched him shamble along the corridor, his bent head swaying loosely from side to side.

The years passed pleasantly in Paris. Myles followed the course of Irish history through the papers and the visitors who arrived at their printing shop. He spent two years in a military academy but then joined his father in the shop. They printed a newspaper each month which was read by all the exiles in Paris and northern France.

In 1840, Myles noticed a new departure in Irish life when a young barrister called Thomas Davis founded a paper called *The Nation*. They read the first edition avidly in Paris, and the paper spread to every corner of Ireland, in cabins and in taverns. Children learned the poems of the *Nation* by heart; it had a fresh confident spirit.

Daniel O'Connell in the meantime continued to draw great crowds to his monster meetings. People gathered at Clontibret, Mullaghmast and Tara to hear the great orator. Myles and his father were amazed at the great numbers which gathered for the events.

'If O'Connell would organise them into an army, then the British House of Commons would quickly repeal the Act of Union,' Myles suggested.

'It will never happen. O'Connell hates the shedding of blood. He believes that he can change things through due process of law. He will never succeed,' his father answered.

His father was right. At a monster meeting assembled at Clontarf, the scene of the historic battle, army guns were trained on the place. O'Connell's men rushed among the advancing people to tell them that the meeting was called off, and half a million people turned for home. It was the end of an era. Nothing could be achieved by peaceful means; it was time for another attempt at a revolution. Daniel O'Connell had served his purpose well. He had brought his people out of the dark eighteenth century and lifted them up from their knees.

Beside the tranquil Seine and in a city where revolutions were hatched, it seemed as if 1847 or 1848 might be the year of change. A new generation of Irishmen might rise as they had risen in '98. Already there were rumours of secret societies forming in the towns and countryside, and there was evidence that guns were being smuggled in from America. Myles decided to visit Ireland for six months and discover if the country was ripe for rebellion. He would go ashore in some quiet harbour along the western coast and visit the land of enchantment from which his father had been exiled. His mind was excited at the prospect of setting foot in Ireland, for all his life he had been in exile from his own land.

The quayside at Bordeaux stretched for two miles along the river. Ships from all over the world, with furled sails and intricate riggings, were anchored here ready to take on the casks of brandy and wine, and bales of hemp, flax and cork. There was the confused babble of tongues from Spaniards and mulattos from the colonies of Réunion and Mozambique. The siesta hour was now past, the oppressive summer heat departing from the day, and a slight breeze came up from the river.

Myles had been advised by Bernard Tracy of the Circle that the Barrett ships were the safest in which to take passage and that the Irish sailors usually gathered at Le Juge, tucked away in the brothel area. It took him a considerable time to find it among the narrow streets. The passageways were almost dark, with their overhanging balconies; here a man could disappear without trace, and he felt uncomfortable in his city clothes. He was aware of eyes looking at him from blank windows, figures passing behind him and disappearing into the shadows, and his forehead broke out in sweat as he grasped the handle of his pistol. He felt as if he had entered the underworld of Bordeaux and there was no way out.

At last he rounded a corner and saw the sign of Le Juge above a tavern. He entered cautiously, his eyes adjusting to the semi-darkness. Candles dribbled wax over fat bottles, giving a small insecure light to the faces gathered about the tables. The tobacco smoke, thick and rough, caught his throat. Everywhere was the smell of caked sweat.

'Ah, fine gentleman,' the tavern-keeper said insolently, arriving almost immediately in order to cut off his entrance. 'I'm afraid that I do not serve rare wine here. Strangers are not welcome.'

'If I judge from the voice, they are all strangers here,' Myles remarked curtly.

'They are men of the sea, and the sea is its own republic.'

'Well said, sir. I'm from Paris and I seek a Captain John Burke. I'm told I would find him here.'

'There is no John Burke here, and we are not accustomed to shaven men. It makes people uncomfortable, very uncomfortable. Men with Parisian French have been found floating in the river, their throats cut and their pockets empty.'

Myles Prendergast was now certain that John Burke was somewhere in the tavern. He looked at the tavern-keeper, with his large pocked nose and massive body, and felt uncomfortable in the clothes he wore. 'I'm not a French gentleman. I am Irish and I wish to speak to an Irish sea captain.'

'Well, where did you pick up your fancy accent?'

'In Paris.'

'How long have you been in Paris?'

'All my life.'

'Well, then, you are a Frenchman!'

'My father was an Irish émigré.'

'That's a fancy one for you! As far as I am concerned you could be a government agent. We have had some visits from

36

them. They have never returned.' The tavern-keeper continued to stare at him, blocking his passage.

Myles Prendergast looked past him and called out in Irish so that his voice filled the long dark room: 'Is there a bastard of a sea captain here called Burke from Mayo? If there is, would he get this stinking French dog out of my way, for he smells of horse piss!'

The effect of the remark was instant. There was a wild roar from inside and the sound of a bottle breaking on the stone floor as a figure rushed up the passageway between the tables. 'Who dares call me a bastard on French soil and in Connaught Irish? I'll wrap his guts around his neck!' The man stopped when he saw Myles Prendergast. 'Who insulted me? Who insulted me?' he asked in fragmented French.

'This gentleman from Paris,' the tavern-keeper told him.

'He's not from Paris. He's after insulting me in Galway Irish!'

'Well, he speaks fancy French.'

'Well, he doesn't speak fancy Irish!' The man turned to Myles. 'Who are you?'

'I'm Myles Prendergast from Paris. I had to flush you out of the darkness. This man barred my way.'

'You are lucky you got this far. You should have stayed at the docks. This is a dangerous place. By now you should have a slit throat and empty pockets.'

'So the tavern-keeper told me.'

'Well, come with me. Don't stand there – let him by, tavern-keeper.'

'I do not understand you Irish,' the tavern-keeper said, shrugging. 'Once somebody speaks that doggerel tongue of yours he seems to be able to get through enemy lines!' With that he went off to serve some sailors who were shaking empty bottles at him and calling for more bad wine.

'Dante's hell doesn't compare with this place,' Captain Burke said as he led the way to the end of the room.

'Here is the man who insulted me,' he told his companions. 'He says he is Myles Prendergast.'

'And well he did it! He has the control of the tongue,' said one man.

'Only a native could string words together like that,' another agreed.

John Burke introduced them as his crew members, and then turned to Myles. 'And what do you want from me?' he asked.

'Passage to Ireland. I will pay well for it.'

'And why a Barrett ship?'

'The north is watched by the British spies.'

'And what is your reason for going to Ireland?'

'I'm going to visit Galway and see the city my father had to leave after the rebellion.'

'Good. We will take you – and the passage money can buy drink, so place your money on the table.'

Myles Prendergast placed several gold coins in front of them.

'Four will do. Keep the rest. We will ask no more questions. At the moment we are pleasuring and we have no intention of being interrupted, even if there is another revolution and the head is taken from some king or other. Now, Tom Clancy, sing a dream poem for us.'

They all fell silent, and Tom Clancy, after ridding his throat of phlegm, commenced the song and the poem. Myles Prendergast listened to the strange music which was different from anything he had heard in Paris. It was sad and bleak without the comfort of harmony or accompaniment. When he finished there was a moment of silence.

'It was well sung,' John Burke announced in verdict, and they all agreed. They then talked about the qualities of poetry as if talking about such matters was as natural as talking about the sea.

'We'll have a merry song now,' John Burke told them. 'We can't always be sobbing and following sad and lovely women through dream woods. I'll give you a song, half-Irish, half-English and half-French, which a sailor I knew wrote in this very room.' He started immediately into the song without making any apology for his ability to sing it. It was a rough tavern song and they all joined in the chorus.

The light deserted the narrow streets outside the tavern. The smoke thickened and the air became dense. Myles Prendergast drank too much, and much later in the night he fell asleep. The last thing he remembered was Brian Burke lifting him over his shoulder as if he were a child.

5

THE SHIP SAILED almost directly north out of the harbour of Bordeaux. It was a journey not without its dangers, and John Burke was constantly vigilant, avoiding the islands and sandbanks, until they reached Pointe de la Grave. The channel to the open sea was about a hundred miles long and barely a mile wide. They moved slowly under limited sail, tacking carefully. The tide had been full and favourable at the early light when they weighed anchor. Only with a full tide could they be certain of avoiding hidden submerged shoals.

John Burke looked at the gentle controlled landscape now emerging from the grey light that would soon be filled with the warmth of the sun. Grapes grew easily on the light sandy earth. When he grew tired of the hard weather on the Atlantic crossings he often thought that he might settle here and make journeys to the Mediterranean.

The men were busy in the rigging, dropping canvas or drawing it up as the wind changed its strength. The fresh air filled his lungs and cleared his mind. One of the men had brought warm tea to him, which he drank from a large mug. It filled his body with well-being.

The stranger, Myles Prendergast, was unaware that they were passing down the narrow channel to the sea. He was lying in a heavy sleep in the sailors' quarters. John Burke considered the position of his guest. He was almost certain that Prendergast's story was correct. The very fact that he spoke perfect French and Irish was of itself sufficient to prove this. However, there was always a slight doubt lurking in his mind; one was never certain whom the London spy network employed. John Burke was also nervous that the twenty guns which had been smuggled aboard might have attracted the attention of the English interests in Bordeaux. He would have to make sure that Myles Prendergast had not been planted in his ship.

When they reached the open sea he handed over the ship to his first mate and went down into the sailors' quarters where Myles Prendergast was still in a deep sleep. Searching through the pockets of his coat, Burke found some money and a map of Bordeaux. He examined the map. It was an ordinary street-map which could be bought in Paris. He felt the lining of the coat and the trousers but could detect nothing hidden there. Quietly he drew off the large leather belt. It was made from a double course of leather and had been recently stitched. He took his knife and slit the stitching open and took out three sheets of paper. Two of them contained lists of names in Irish, many of which he recognised. Some of them had taken part in the '98 rebellion and were now old; some were even dead. His own name was on the list, but he did not find that strange. He was, however, surprised to see the names of Michael Barrett and Frederick Cavendish. They had no direct connection with the '98 rebellion as far as he was aware, yet they were high on the list.

Myles Prendergast woke from his sleep with his temples throbbing. He opened his eyes. Just as he made an instinctive move to get on to the floor of the cabin he noticed the barrel of a pistol aimed directly at his face. He looked up. John Burke's expression was hard.

'We have some talking to do,' he said directly. 'Who are you?'

'I told you at the tavern. I am Myles Prendergast and I am making a visit to Ireland.'

'What is the purpose of the visit?'

'I wish to visit my father's family in Galway. I wish to observe the customs and the manners of the people.'

'And for this reason you came to Bordeaux to avoid the English spies?'

'My father is known to them, and I am sure I am on their lists. Could you take that pistol from my face – it could go off.'

'It has gone off before at close range,' John Burke answered curtly. 'In fact it blew the ear off a British spy.'

'I am not a British spy. If I were, I would have travelled to the north and taken a ship there.'

'You could have done that. But then you would have had to travel from Dublin to Connaught. Sailing in a Barrett ship brings you directly to the western coast. What do you know about this ship?'

'I know that it is a safe ship. I know that in the past it has taken men in and out of Ireland.'

'You could have obtained that information from your British contacts.'

John Burke noted that even under hard pressure Myles Prendergast continued to talk Irish. 'Now, what do these papers mean?' he asked and held out the papers he had taken from the leather belt. His concentration was broken for a moment, and Myles Prendergast sprang forward and grasped the hand carrying the pistol. He turned it towards the roof and then with surprising strength forced Burke back on to the bunk.

'Now, listen very carefully,' he said. 'I do not talk with a pistol in my face. If you call out for help, you will be dead in ten seconds, so listen. I am what I told you. I have been sent to Ireland by the Revolutionary Circle because I have some military experience. The purpose of the visit is to establish contacts there. The lists were made out by the Circle, and the letter of introduction was written by my father. If I were a spy, I would not venture on board this ship.'

He eased his grip on John Burke, and the captain put away his pistol. 'You are stronger than I suspected. Nobody has ever done that to me before. I must be getting old,' Burke said, dismissing his humiliation. 'I believe you now.'

Myles smiled grimly. 'It was the only thing I could do to prove my innocence. Now can I go on deck and get some air?'

'I did not realise we were so far out to sea,' he told John Burke later, when the latter had joined him to watch the coast of France disappearing below the horizon. 'Otherwise I would not have been so foolhardy. I thought for a moment I would swim ashore.'

'It would have been a long swim! Come to my cabin and we will talk more.'

They settled down in the captain's cabin, and Burke poured two glasses of rum. 'Here's to your health,' he began, raising the glass. 'I hope your mission prospers.'

'And what do you think of its chances?'

'I do not know. No revolution starts in the countryside. They must begin in the towns and they begin with thinking men. Sure, there are men in the towns who still believe in a cause and there is a group of men in Dublin who preach revolution through their papers, but I do not think the country is as yet ready.'

'Then the mission is already a failure,' Myles Prendergast said bleakly.

'I would not say that. As I say, there is a patriotic feeling in the hearts of the people, but with Catholic Emancipation the Catholic middle class and the Catholic professional people are now good servants of the Crown. They wish things to remain as they are. And so the country is divided.'

'And what of our American friends? We have contacts with them in France.'

'They have not visited the country. You see at present there is a famine threatening. The potatoes have been planted and there is an expectation of a good harvest, but if it fails, then everything fails, mark my words. The starving never fight, and the barracks has been brought up to full strength.'

They sat in the cabin throughout that afternoon and discussed many things. For Myles the discussions were both important and disappointing; the Circle in Paris had a false view of the state of matters in Ireland.

Late that evening John Burke suggested to him that he should join a secret society. To violate the oath meant death. 'Anyone who breaks the pledge risks the chance of being killed,' he told him.

'Tell me more about it,' Myles asked, alert.

John Burke explained to him the aims of the society. He did not tell him how strong it was but he intimated that guns were being brought into Ireland and stored for the revolution.

'I will join it as soon as I reach Ireland,' Myles said decisively.

'Do you wish to join now?'

'Is it possible?' Myles was puzzled.

'Do you *wish* to join?'

'Yes.'

'Very well, then.' John Burke went outside and called two of his relations. Two candles were lit on the table, and in the presence of the three men Myles was sworn into their secret society, solemnly repeating the words after John Burke:

'I, Myles Prendergast, do swear to form a brotherhood among Irishmen and I will serve to obtain equal and full representation of all the people of Ireland, that neither fear nor reward nor punishment shall ever induce me to give evidence against any member or members of this society. I will take up arms to defend these principles when called upon by an appointed officer.'

When he had finished the words they shook his hand and for the first time he felt that he was caught up in something greater than John Burke had at first intimated.

The sailors left the cabin, and now John Burke felt that he could be more free in his talk. He took out a large map of Mayo and explained the geography of the area. He pointed to the positions of the military barracks and told him the number of soldiers in each town.

'You see, they are preparing for us. There is talk of rebellion in the air. It is vague, but they wish to defend the most unprotected flank of Ireland. If an invasion comes, it will come from the west coast. Now, it could not only come from France, for there is the danger it might come from this direction – America. We will not look to France the next time, we will look to America. Already our society is strong in New York; the emigrants carry bitter memories with them.'

He was a man who had considered many possibilities. He had an expert knowledge of guns and ammunition. 'We must never go into the field again ill-prepared. They were fools to take on the British with pikes. Good only for close fighting if you can get near enough. New guns are being made, and we must have them. You wondered why I was suspicious of you? I will show you.' John Burke went over to the oak panel of the cabin and drew it open. Behind it stood a rack of new guns gleaming in the light. He took one out and threw it to Myles.

'Do you recognise it?' he asked.

43

'No.'

'It's American. The British soldiers have nothing to compare with them. They are accurate within four hundred yards. No more pikes. With four hundred yards between you and the enemy you have a good chance of slipping away.'

Before Myles had departed from Paris the problems of Ireland were tinged with a mythical quality. Now, listening to John Burke, he felt that he was facing a new truth. His father's recollections of Ireland were of a time that had departed. He now felt a mature enthusiasm in his blood and a sense of adventure; his visit would be attended by dangers.

'It is night now; let us go above,' John Burke said, leading the way on deck. 'I will take the wheel and you can stand by me. I am never happy in a room. The sea braces me.' It was a clear night, and the sky was filled with stars.

'You never see stars as bright as this in a city,' Burke said, looking up.

'They are like diamonds,' Myles remarked wonderingly.

'More like buttons on a soldier's uniform,' Burke rejoined, and they began to laugh. They fell silent for a while and listened to the sound of waves breaking before the prow of the ship and the occasional creak of timber under strain. The wind was even and the sails were set for the night.

The rest of the journey was uneventful. Once they came in sight of a British ship, but they quickly changed their course. During the voyage Myles learned many things from John Burke. To begin with, he would have to change his clothes: his French ones were too obvious. He would be disguised as a merchant buying wool for a Liverpool company, and John Burke gave him some information about the wool trade between Northport and Liverpool.

They sailed up the western coast, far out to sea and away from the sight of land. Then, when they were in a position about thirty miles out from Galway Bay, they drew in their canvas and waited for darkness.

'Tonight you disembark,' Burke announced. 'You can travel with me to my village tomorrow. I will join you after the ship is safely anchored in Northport. Wait for me at the O'Hares' cabin. They will take care of you.'

Some time after midnight they noticed lights flashing in the darkness. 'They are ready for us,' one of the sailors called.

'We have been expected for the last three days. Signal three times and then put out the lantern,' instructed Burke.

An hour later Myles heard voices at the side of the ship as men greeted one another in the night. He could barely make out the black shapes of the curraghs bobbing below him on the sea, but there must have been at least ten of them. Men climbed aboard and greeted the crew familiarly. 'I brought a young man from France,' John Burke explained to the man who seemed to be in charge of them. 'He is one of us. I'll stand bail for him. Give him lodgings and direction at the O'Hares' tonight. He will tell you who he is and why he is here.'

'Will you have more guns after your next voyage, John?' someone asked.

'If you can sell the brandy and tobacco in Galway and bring me the money, I can buy them. Our next voyage is to America. I believe I will have something of interest to show you when I return.'

The men continued to load barrels of brandy into the small boats. It was difficult work as the curraghs bumped about in the darkness beneath them. When they were finished and ready to depart John Burke took Myles's hand.

'May good luck go with you. We fight in a good cause. Take care of yourself. Tomorrow you will see the hills of Ireland in their bright glory.'

Myles Prendergast made his way down into one of the boats. 'Watch out,' they warned him. 'Don't put your foot through the canvas or we are done for.'

The fleet of small boats cast off from the great dark ship. They moved with great rapidity, the men arching forwards and backwards in rhythm. Soon he could make out the vague outline of cliffs and hear the sound of the waves pounding at their base. The sea was now erratic, but with feathery strokes of the oars the men reacted to each change. Then the sound grew louder and he could see the waves rising high against the cliff walls. There was a gap in the cliff face, and here the sea was churned and agitated as the waters rushed through the opening. The men were calling to each other, lining up the boats behind the leader and turning their heads towards the phosphorescent opening. They waited for the opportune wave, and rising on the crest they rowed swiftly and accurately through the gap. Myles could see the waters boil and foam on either side of him as the waves were torn on the rocks. Then they were through and in a quiet bay, and soon he was standing on the shore of Ireland.

6

JOHN BURKE waited for his cousin to bring the horses which would take him to his village. He had not been there for six months and he had certain points of business to clear with his relations.

He looked again at *Ann Marie*, now at anchor in the bay. Some of the crew members were making her ready for the voyage back to Bordeaux. She had not aged with the years. Her timbers had settled together, but she was still swift and subtle and she was his woman. She had beauty of body, grace of movement, and when she was under full sail his heart ached with pleasure as she rose to the great waves and cut through their crests, slicing them evenly.

His thoughts were disturbed by the sound of hoofs on the cobblestones behind him. He looked about and saw his cousin, leading two horses towards him. He rose from the bollard upon which he had been sitting and put his pipe in his pocket.

'It's a fine day for a journey,' Brian Burke called to him.

'Yes,' he said, looking at the sky. 'Only a light wind in our faces and no rain towards the south-west.' He had a seaman's eye for the weather.

They made their way out of Northport and rode south, John Burke looking intently on the harsh brown landscape through which they were moving. His anger had been growing as he made his way towards Croagh Patrick, the sacred pilgrim mountain, which rose like a huge cone from irregular hills. The pilgrim's path, like a cicatrice on the grey hide of the mountain, was clear from the base to the summit. He had often climbed there and looked down on the islands in Clew Bay, small and snug like a school of basking whales, snouts facing into the Atlantic. But he did not raise his eyes to the mountain today. He looked at the small mud cabins close to the earth and thatched with rushes. They were windowless and without chimneys, fit only for animals.

The O'Hares were an old couple without family, and Myles was shocked by the small cabin in which they lived. He slept on rushes close to the animals, who kept the room warm. Before he slept his hosts offered him cold potatoes and milk, which he accepted through politeness, though he thought that he would vomit the unpalatable food. The cabin was filled with heavy smoke from the turf fire, and the low rafters were black and crusted with soot. The smell of turf smoke was pungent and new to him.

He slept fitfully and when he woke in the morning he was again offered potatoes and milk for his breakfast. A thin light entered through the open door, making him all the more aware of the squalor of his surroundings.

The animals were driven out to the sea-pastures to nibble at impoverished grass by the old man, who had a sad stoical face. He and the old woman spoke only in Irish. It was a sweet and rich language, and Myles wondered at the bright images that the old woman so easily used. Her mind was sharp and alive. He had spoken with the French peasants, but their minds were as servile and limited as their circumstances; this old woman spoke in poetry.

'John Burke is our protector. He will not see us without. If the potato fails, sure there is the bag of smuggled meal and my man is never without his tobacco. Others have known the pangs of starvation, but never either of us, and we have lived through the bad times.'

'Do you speak English?' Myles asked, curious.

'An odd word. The English is spoken in the towns and by the gombeen men and the quality. They look down on us for our ways and the manner in which we live.'

Their conversation was suddenly interrupted by the old

48

man, who came rushing in from the field. ''Tis Gráinne Barrett, woman, riding along the beach on her white horse! Put on your scarf and straighten your skirts, for she may call to see us, and the stranger must not be seen! He's to be hidden until John Burke arrives.'

They waited at the door, while Myles stood in the shadows. He heard the sound of hoofs on the flat beach stones and then the heavy breathing of a horse close to the door of the cabin. 'You come like the lady from the legends, Gráinne, with your hair flying and the sea-foam at your feet,' the old woman said.

'You speak richly, Sorca,' Myles heard the stranger reply. 'I find freedom on the sea-shore. The air is filled with the scent of the sea. The house is like a prison, and the rooms are small spaces.'

'We hear that you will be with us now and that you will no longer return to the great school in England.'

'I am finished with England. When I was there I had dreams only of the sea, and I could not sleep there at night because the pulse of the sea was not beating about me. Look – I must return to the shore; the horse is warm and restless. But I shall see you again.'

Myles could hear the sound of the horse's hoofs on the beach. He stood by the window and watched as the figure of the woman, with her grey cloak gathered about her and her red hair falling on her shoulders, reached the foam line on the beach. As she urged the horse forward, her hair was carried back by the wind. He watched her until she became a small speck on the beach.

'Who was that?' he asked the old woman when she returned.

'Gráinne Barrett, the daughter of Michael Barrett. She will rule the great house when her father dies, but she should be mistress of the ships. The sea is in her blood, and they say she can handle a ship like any man. I watched her grow to womanhood. She is one of our own. She speaks the tongue and knows our ways. Her ancestor was queen of the islands and had many ships under her command.'

'And why did she travel to England?'

'Her father wished to make her a lady after the English manner, but she was always a lady after the Irish manner.' The old woman chuckled.

49

Later, from his post by the window, Myles observed the figures of John Burke and his cousin making their way along the beach.

'You have been well looked after?' John Burke asked Myles, who came out to greet him.

'Indeed I have,' Myles replied, smiling at the old couple.

'Oh, he speaks sweet Irish,' said the old man, almost in explanation.

'Well, then' – John Burke looked towards the surf – 'if you are ready, you can use my cousin's horse and he will make his way to the village in his own time.'

Brian Burke handed Myles the reins, and he mounted the horse. He bade goodbye to the old couple and followed John Burke along the sand, with the sound of Gráinne Barrett's voice ringing in his ears.

When they reached the sea they galloped their horses along the sand close to where the long even waves were coming ashore. The breath of the sea air in his lungs and the expanse of the sea itself exhilarated John Burke. He kneed his horse and sent him into a canter, then he raced him over the ribbed sand, forgetting the hunger and the poverty about him. Soon he would be on board his ship again, bound for France, and he would forget the brown bogs and miserable fields, numerous as meshes on fishing-nets.

They moved up from the shore on to the dusty road and continued their journey. They approached Louisburgh, a place beaten by winter storms which moved in from the Atlantic and set upon the houses and howled among the bent trees in the Protestant graveyard; the grey rains fell out of a leaden sky, making the landscape introvert.

They moved out of the town and on towards the village of Cashel. It was set in a scoop of mountain, facing the sea, and was isolated, remote and difficult of access. The British soldiers would not venture into the village unless they were certain of the weather – or the escape route, for it was set in a defile. The place had been chosen well by the Burkes in the seventeenth century.

John Burke knew that his approach to the defile which led to the village had already been noticed. A sheepdog had been let loose from a cabin by the side of the road. It carried news to the village that John Burke was approaching.

He had been brought up here, and it was here he learned about the sea. At twelve he could manage a curragh and at fourteen, using a rough sail, he made his way in the canvas boat to Galway. He had seen the great sailing ships along the sea-front, and they made him restless. He could never be happy until he sailed in them across all the seas of the world.

They passed through the defile. The path was narrow, and a rough stream made its way down to the sea. During heavy rains, when the stream was charged and querulous, the village was cut off from the outside world. The defile opened out, and beneath them lay the village with its white-walled cottages and thatched roofs. The houses were at angles to each other, not regularly positioned as in English villages, and close to the village was an L-shaped pier, its arms protecting a hooker. On the strand were several curraghs, backs up like beached seals. Each year they were drawn up and patched, then rubbed with animal fat to make them watertight and swift on the water. Only those who had handled a curragh knew how resilient it was on the sea and how it could ride the highest wave. It answered quickly to the slightest movement of the awkward timber oars.

They came up the stony path to greet him, men, women and children calling out: 'You are welcome to the village, John Burke. Your coming is a great surprise, and you bring a stranger with you.'

'These are strange times, John,' said one man. 'We have the police and the soldiers snooping into our business, for we are told they dispatch reports from the Barracks to the Castle in Dublin and Queen Victoria gets to hear about all that's going on.'

'Then, if she is well informed sitting on her backside in London, she must know that you are a rogue, that you are all smugglers and that you have buried sovereigns up in the hills!' John called down at them. 'You'll all swing for your roguery from the hanging-tree in Castlebar or you'll go to Botany Bay.'

'Imagine saying unreasonable things like that to small sheep-farmers trying to keep hunger from the door!' his cousin Angus said, handing up a bottle of whiskey. John Burke, feeling secure from the thoughts of famine and now in the security of his own village, put the bottle to his mouth and took a long draught. Tonight he would sing for them in the kitchen during a ceilidh.

They carried on the banter until they reached the centre of the village, then he swung down from his horse and went to meet the old men and women. There were cries of delight when he threw his arms about the old women and slapped them on the backside. 'I'd have you in the ditch any day to the young ones! Sure, the sweetest music comes from the old fiddle. . . .'

'Go on out of that, John Burke, but it's picking up the pox from you we would be, and you carrying God knows what from the black women of Africa and Spain!'

Myles, who had spoken very little to John Burke during the journey, looked at the group of men who gathered about him. He could see that they formed a tight communal group and he felt a stranger in their midst.

'Myles Prendergast is one of us,' announced John Burke, sensing his discomfort. 'He has taken the oath at sea and he knows the price he will have to pay for breaking it. Now, while this man is lodged in the best house in the village and has some decent food to eat, we will go to the pier and talk of important matters.' And he walked with the men down the twisted village street, while Myles was led by the women and children to his lodgings.

It was midday now. The sky was February blue, and beyond them the mountains had taken on a purple colouring. The tide was full and without tension, the curraghs pulling sluggishly against stone anchors. On the sea-meadows beside the small bay sheep grazed. John Burke sat with his villagers, their backs to the pier wall, smoking their pipes. Here they held the 'court', as it was called, where all village business was discussed openly. John Burke's troubled mind was suddenly filled with content: he had no greater ambition, when he was finished at sea, than to return to this village and grow old as these men did. He would look towards the sea, his arms resting on the pier wall, and remember his voyages. But he did not know whether this could be.

'Has the whiskey been brought to Galway?' he asked.

'Yes,' Angus told him, 'and a good profit it yielded. It was carried at night and the coastguards sleeping in their quarters. Harrington will take all we can give him as well as the American tobacco.'

'Then, we have enough for the guns?' John Burke asked directly.

'Yes.'

'I will bring them aboard at Bordeaux. If we are intercepted by the coastguards, then I'll open up on them. You never know what informer is planted in France. Once we have them, we are protected, and if there is a rising, then we won't go into a fight with pikes as they did in '98. They tell me that there is a new weapon called a revolver invented in America. They say that you can have five shots in the barrel and it's deadly at close range. It is something we could well look into.'

They passed round the bottle of whiskey and reflected on what John Burke had said. For many years Michael Barrett's ships had carried illegal whiskey and tobacco which were taken at night-time in the curraghs from the ships before they passed into Clew Bay, and later sold in Galway. They paid a coastguard for information concerning the movement of the government vessels. In this way they could carry on their illegal business.

For five generations the Burkes had lived in Cashel. They had once been merchants in Galway who had been dispossessed. With a few belongings and little money the families had made their way to this valley and had taken to the sea as common sailors and built up their fortune. They had their money in America and London, but they had an abiding hatred of British rule in Ireland and the dominance of an Irish culture by a foreign one. They spoke in Irish. Their secrets and their hates were communal, and the decisions they took in a casual way on the pier were firm and binding. They were bonded by blood renewed by men and women from outside the valley who married among them. The valley gave them protection from the land, and the sea was a safe escape route. All Michael Barrett's ships were crewed by men from Cashel or their relations along the sea-coast.

When the main business was finished, John Burke set about arranging for the next voyage. It would be a dangerous one, and he wanted only men from the village. 'I trust only my own and I'll not have loose-tongued men with me. The British have agents everywhere, even in France, and some of them, believe it or not, know the Irish language. If we drink, we drink together, and I'll take a whip to any who strays,' he said firmly. 'And now we'll talk no more business. Tell me about the sheep and the fishing and how you are all doing, for tonight I'm going to enjoy myself. There is hunger beyond the mountains, and I have a bellyful of it. Only a good dance or a song will cheer me up.'

Myles, despite his knowledge of Irish, felt that he was not part of the communal dancing and singing that night in Vinney Burke's house. He sat beside the fire in conversation with an old sailor. On one occasion he was drawn on to the dance-floor by a young woman who tried to teach him some of the wild steps, but he could not grasp the movements and his mind and body were too rigid. Later, on the plea of tiredness, he returned to the room set aside for him and slept soundly in the feather bed.

John Burke, on the other hand, sang all his songs and danced until morning, when they all made their way down to the pier to watch the sun rise. He carried a bottle of whiskey with him and drank to the health of all about him, clapping the old men on the back and reminding them of the first time they took him out in their curraghs.

'It was a long time ago, John Burke, a long time ago, and we were all young and foolish. . . .'

'And now you are all old and foolish as ever,' he told them.

He would have spent the whole day drinking with the men, but a horseman came through the pass and rode down the valley. It was Thatcher Donaghue. He rarely visited Cashel, and at once they knew he carried some important news.

'What is it, Thatcher?' Angus Burke called out, before the man had time to descend from his horse.

'It's bad news from Castlebar!' Donaghue was breathing heavily from his ride. 'You know Widow Kenny's son, the half-idiot, who joined the soldiers? Well, he was flayed alive in the Barracks there. I don't know if dead he is, but if he's not dead he's near it!'

'What bastard did that to him?' John Burke asked, sobering quickly.

'I don't know. Some new colonel or general, I heard. They say it was something fierce the way his back was flayed and his bones showing. McEvelly, the publican, sent word this morning.'

54

'Then, this colonel or general will pay in kind for what he has done,' Angus said fiercely. 'No bastard will get away with that.'

7

NED KENNY, the half-idiot, lay on his stomach on the rush pallet, his eyes still bulged with pain. It was now two weeks since his back had been harrowed and torn open by the cat-o'-nine-tails. He had slept little during the two weeks. He wept at his humiliation. His screams had been heard in the town as he cried out for mercy. Twice he had fallen unconscious and twice he had been revived on the orders of Colonel Spiker. The soldiers in the ranks had hissed as they watched the back of Ned Kenny shredded by the soldier brought in from Castlerea.

Ned Kenny had joined the 29th Regiment in Castlebar in 1841. The regiment had led a wandering life, posted at one time to Mallow and at another time to Dublin. He was a simpleton who loved horses: even the most skittish horse was quiet in his company. Colonel Richardson, the old colonel who travelled with them, told his officers that Ned Kenny, despite his simple ways, could talk to horses in their own language. His life was ordered. Each morning he made his way to the stables to comb down his charges and polish their harness until it was bright as silver. He oiled the leathers until they were supple and carried a brown lustre. He led a contented life following the cavalry from barracks to barracks, standing at the square and watching the cavalry manouevres with a constant delight.

He was also batman to Colonel Richardson, at seventy a bloated figure who had to be helped on to his horse. Richardson drank too much whiskey, and each night Ned Kenny undressed him and saw him to bed. Each morning he changed the bandage on his gouty foot, cleaning out the raw suppurating wound which never healed. This was one of the many wounds the colonel had received during the Peninsular Wars and he was respected by the men under him for his courage in former battles.

'I don't know what I would do without you, Ned,' he often told him as Ned eased the heavy body into bed. 'I don't know what I'd do without you. Wellington himself couldn't have a better man at his side!'

'You mean the Iron Duke himself, Colonel?'

'Yes, Ned. The very Iron Duke himself. The very best soldier who ever drew on a pair of trousers.'

'He'd have been a queer soldier without them!'

'Now that I think of it, Ned, he would.'

The fortunes of Ned Kenny changed suddenly. The colonel had been drinking all day and complaining of his wound. Before going to his bed he sat before the fire and Ned poured him a large glass of whiskey.

'It's too much you had, sir. It can't be good for you. My mother told me that drink is no good for anybody, even if it's coloured.'

'It warms me, Ned. It deadens the pain and it helps me to sleep.'

Ned was pouring him another glass when the colonel's face turned purple. He tightened his hand over his chest and cried out, 'I'm done, Ned. It's the end!' and slumped sideways on the chair.

'Are you all right, Colonel Richardson? Are you all right? I've another drink for you.' Ned shook the heavy military figure until it struck him that the colonel was dead, and he began to sob for the passing of his friend.

The next day he polished the harness and combed down the horses for the burial service, weeping as he worked. He refused to leave the stables until it was time for the funeral. He was proud of the magnificent way in which the cavalry performed; he had sent his master off to the hereafter (of which he had always been dubious) in the best fashion he could.

Colonel Richardson died at a convenient time for his military masters in Dublin. Already they had intelligence that there were signs of unrest in Mayo; no place in Ireland was more densely populated, and in the event of a famine it could become rebellious; precautions must be taken in time. Colonel Spiker had all the qualities needed to put down such a rebellion: he was ruthless with his enemies and could set up a proper spy system to keep him in touch with all that happened. He was a harsh disciplinarian, and men feared and hated him.

'If Spiker has a heart, then it is made from gunmetal,' his associates remarked. 'He may be able to put down rebellions but he can also cause them. . . .' Some doubted his suitability.

When Colonel Spiker first rode into the Barracks square and looked at the condition of the buildings and the men, he knew that he would have to make an example of a common soldier in order to tighten discipline. His eye detected disorder everywhere.

When he was shown his quarters he called Ned Kenny. 'Do you expect a colonel of Her Majesty's Army to live in a pig-sty?' he roared at him as he looked at the rooms. 'When was the last time these floors were scrubbed, or the mattress aired? It smells of stale urine!'

'What's that, sir?'

'Piss,' Spiker said with a sneer.

'Oh, I'm sorry, sir. Colonel Richardson was inclined to wet his drawers. He couldn't make it to the pot under the bed.'

'I wouldn't keep a pack of hounds here. Fetch a new mattress and blankets. I am not going to sleep on the bed of an incontinent old man. I expect it to be ready in two days.'

'But, Colonel, I will not be able to comb the horses down. It takes a power of time to comb the horses down and prepare the harness.'

'What do you mean? Do not the soldiers attend to their own horses?'

'Some of them do, sir, now and then, but they say I talk to the horses.'

'You are an Irish fool,' said Spiker contemptuously. 'I come to a filthy barracks and I am served by a fool! Get me the officer in charge. And knock before you enter my room.'

Kenny rushed from the room, confused and ashamed. He had not been called a fool before. He began to feel uncertain of his surroundings; something was going to happen to him, and he was afraid.

He listened at the door while the officer in charge received a dressing-down. 'And get rid of that fool who attended Colonel Richardson. He smells of horses and horse manure. You have let things slide here. This is the worst barracks I've ever been in! By God, sir, by the time I'm through with the men they will know what discipline and order mean! Discipline and order keep an army ready – now get out of my sight and have the cavalry drawn up for inspection.'

Three days later, Ned Kenny was replaced by a young soldier. He was not permitted to touch the horses, but was ordered to clean the stables and dispose of the dung which had been heaped behind one of the buildings. His humiliation was increased when he drove the dung-cart through the town to the estates of Lord Lannagh. He felt that all eyes were on him, that people were pointing at Ned Kenny, the dung-man. Anger passed through his mind in heavy surges. He would take a pistol to Colonel Spiker and blast his head apart at close range.

To kill his sense of humiliation, he began to drink. He had a bottle hidden in the stables, and he would start on his work with a swig of whiskey and continue working and drinking until dinner-time. He missed the company of the horses and his control over them. From the corner of the square he watched them put through their manoeuvres. He no longer belonged to the movement and noise of the cavalry.

Then one day he made a fatal mistake. Colonel Spiker had a company of friends in to see the cavalry go through its paces. They sat on a low platform and watched the horses wheel and turn before them with the precision of marionettes. Suddenly Ned Kenny could bear it no longer. He staggered out from the corner of the barracks and stumbled in and out amongst the cavalry, crying out: 'They are my horses and they have been taken from me! Colonel Richardson would not have taken my horses from me. . . .'

Instantly the rhythm of the horses was broken. The ordered movements fell into disarray. Horses whinnied and shied.

Colonel Spiker was livid with rage. The very order and discipline of which he had spoken to his invited guests were shattered before their eyes by a drunken soldier. Kenny was quickly whisked away to a cell. Colonel Spiker promised himself that he would take full revenge on this soldier and make an example of him.

The court martial was precise and formal. Ned Kenny, now sober, was brought before the colonel and some officers. He felt insignificant as he stood there. He looked at Colonel Spiker's face, charged with hate. He cried out in a childish voice that he was sorry and that he would never touch a drop of whiskey again. The officers, sitting on either side of Colonel Spiker, seemed nervous in the company of this man.

The offences were read out by an officer, and the sentence was handed down instantly by the colonel. No one was prepared for its severity: Ned Kenny was to receive a hundred lashes of the cat-o'-nine-tails. On receiving the sentence, Ned Kenny vomited on the floor. The officers were stunned, though one of them had the courage to intervene on his behalf.

'But, sir, he may not be able to withstand the punishment. It is very extreme. We have had no whipping in the barracks for the past ten years.'

'And that is why the discipline is so weak – the barracks rooms like stables and the soldiers drunk coming home from the town.'

'Less would achieve the same purpose, sir. If it is fear you wish to instil into the men, half the lashes would have achieved your aim.'

'I'm afraid, *sir*, you have lost your taste for hardship and endurance,' Colonel Spiker shot back. 'Do you realise that at this precise moment the French are in possession of detailed maps of this province? They know exactly how many buildings constitute this barracks, they know how many rooms are in each building and they know how many soldiers occupy these rooms. You know what happened in 1798 – well, it will *not* happen in my command! The sentence will be carried out in three days' time. Send for an outsider to carry out the punishment – I'm sure nobody in the barracks has the belly for such work.'

He left the court martial and went to his quarters, deep satisfaction glowing inside him. He took delight in the expression on Ned Kenny's face. The very fact that he vomited in fear would help secure the discipline he wanted. By the time his term in Castlebar was finished, he would have the most orderly barracks in Ireland. He examined himself in the mirror, proud of his fine body and his colourful uniform. He was unmarked by any campaign, and his skin was soft and white.

Ned Kelly was marched out of the courtroom between two soldiers. He collapsed at the door and had to be dragged to his cell.

'Oh, God! Oh, God, but I can't take a hundred lashes on my back, lads,' he cried. 'I can't take a hundred lashes on my back! Sure, if I'd known, I'd have kept away from the drink – not a drop would have wet my mouth. If only he gave me one chance or a warning. I can't take it, lads.'

The news of the harsh sentence was soon carried through the barracks. Gloom settled on the stark rectangle and the grey buildings. Many wept at the severity of the sentence. 'Did he not know that Ned Kenny was a simpleton?' they asked each other. 'He's not to blame for his mistakes!'

Ned Kenny sat on his sleeping-pallet. He was too dazed to lie down. His head throbbed in pain when he thought of the swish of the cat on his back. He had seen horses marked by whips, and it had invoked pity within him. The palms of his hands were wet with sweat, and he tried to dry them on the rough surface of his trousers. But they could not be dried. They immediately broke out in sweat again.

The soldiers came to him in the cell and tried to give him comfort. Many of them felt that he would die during the whipping. They told him that he would not feel the final strokes.

'Oh, I'll feel them. I'll feel them all right. I'll feel them on my back. I've seen a horse whipped – it brought welts out on its back.'

He broke down several times during the three days in the cell. 'I wish my mother were here, or John Burke. I'm lonely here. I wish I were over at the sea cropping the seaweed or fishing. I only came into the Army for the horses. If Colonel Spiker didn't treat me like dirt, I would never have taken to the drink.'

Fury burned in the common soldiers. They sat on their bunks in the darkness and planned the murder of Colonel Spiker. 'He picked the weakest. Even a Justice would grant a fool a pardon. Ned Kenny never did harm in his life. He has the innocence of a child. He's making an example of him.'

61

'May the whore shrivel in hell or, worse still, may he be paid back in his own kind. . . .'

'I have seen a man die under the lash. It would be better to shoot him and be done with it.'

'It's too easy – he wants to hear Kenny cry out. He was not satisfied that the man vomited in front of him and has been pissing in his trousers ever since. He wants him to cry out so we'll all hear.'

'We should turn the guns on him.'

'Then we would all have it. . . .'

'If only there was a bloody war to fight! Here we are the Colonel's toy soldiers doing his bidding. *He* was never under fire like Richardson – if he had been, he might have had some feeling for a common soldier.'

'We better dose Kenny with rum tonight. The whipper from Castlerea will arrive tomorrow. They say he's half-mad.'

That night they brought rum to Ned Kenny. They waited while he drank the whole bottle by a weak candle-light. They spoke in whispers and tried to bring him some comfort, and later he fell into a drunken sleep. It was a sleep broken by nightmares. The sentry heard his screams as he stood at his post beside the main gates.

It was a bright morning for the whipping. The sun caught the limestone barracks with light and cast shadows on the square. The soldiers went about their duties in a mechanical manner, aware of what was going to take place at twelve o'clock, and a brooding silence weighed over them all.

At twelve o'clock the bugle echoed through the square. The soldiers and the cavalry drew themselves into their positions about the whipping-post hastily put together from three beams. Ned Kenny, dazed with drink and fear, was dragged from his cell. Two soldiers put their arms about him and brought him to the whipping-post. The toes of his boots made light marks on the dust.

'Christ and Mary save me! Christ and Mary save me!' he cried out in Irish, his voice broken and childish. The voice filled the silent barracks with its strange foreign intonations. It was muffled when he was dragged into the rigid square of soldiers and cavalry. Still crying out, he was tied by leather thongs to the crossing made by the timbers. His back was exposed. It was white and unhealthy.

'He has only the skin of a child,' one of the soldiers whispered. 'God, I feel like crying.'

'Commence,' Colonel Spiker called in a firm voice. He sat on his horse, a snarl of pleasure on his face, his uniform stiff and colourful.

The soldier from Castlerea shook the cat-o'-nine-tails free, and set out the thongs in a fan shape on the ground. With a quick flick of his wrist, they stung the air behind him and came down on the white back, tearing it like five fingernails. Ned Kenny screamed out in a high-pitched voice, which carried across the barracks walls to the town. All work ceased. Cry after cry followed. The people of the town counted each scream.

The soldiers looked on helplessly as the skin was shredded, sprays of blood falling over their faces. At fifty-six the screaming stopped and Ned Kenny's feet collapsed. He was suspended by his hands. It was now an easier stroke for the soldier from Castlerea: the body did not resist; the shoulders no longer kicked back at the strokes.

'The bastard has killed him,' the soldiers whispered in Irish. 'He could go easier.'

'Who is he?'

'I don't know. He was brought from Castlerea last night – they say he's half-mad.'

'He'll suffer for this. . . .'

The soldier stopped whipping after seventy strokes. He knew that the last thirty were now worthless.

'Continue,' the colonel ordered.

'He's had enough!' the soldiers called from the ranks.

'Silence,' a sergeant-major cried.

There was a mutinous silence amongst the men as stroke after stroke descended on the inert body until the hundred had been delivered. The back was shredded flesh. The shoulder-bones were exposed. Blood flowed down the split in his backside and was absorbed by the top of his trousers.

'Cut him down,' Colonel Spiker ordered. 'Men dismissed.'

The soldiers returned to their quarters in silence. They felt sick in their stomachs and ashamed that they had not rebelled.

Ned Kenny was carried to the infirmary and placed on his stomach. The old debauched doctor looked at the shredded flesh and the exposed bones.

63

'Worst I've ever seen, and I've seen everything in the Peninsular Wars,' he told the soldiers.

'Will he live?' they asked.

'I don't know. Keep him dosed with drink for a week if he revives. For himself it would be better if he died. No, he'll never sleep without nightmares after this. You see how torn his skin is – well his mind is also torn. He'll never be the full shilling – not that I believe he ever was, but I'll do what I can for him.'

There was a deadness in the body, but a shallow breathing indicated that there was a small flicker of life there. Ned Kenny's mind was comatose. The body now functioned by a deep instinct.

It was semi-dark in the Black Horse tavern in Castle Lane. Candles stuck in the mouths of wide bottles lit up the rough tables and shed half-light on the faces about them. It had a low ceiling, and the beams were black and blistered with tobacco tar. Men sat about the tables drinking whiskey from pewter measures, conspiratorial, suspicious of anybody who opened the door and came down the two worn limestone steps. At the end of the tavern was the tap room, cut off from the rest of it by a wooden partition. Behind the porter-barrels was a door which led into a backstreet.

It was through this tavern that information from the military barracks came to the Whiteboys. The tavern lay directly beneath the barracks in a lane that looked like a gully. Several soldiers in the barracks had sympathy with the Whiteboys.

Jeremiah Egan was a hedge-school teacher. He spent his summers in some country house teaching the children reading and arithmetic and his winters in Castlebar. He was a tall man with fine fingers and blue eyes. A soldier entered the tavern and made his way down to the tap room. Jeremiah Egan put a large whiskey in front of him.

'I heard the screams today,' he said. 'There were over fifty of them. I counted each stroke.'

'There were a hundred of them,' the soldier told him bitterly. 'He fainted after the first fifty, I think. I'm still sick after it. A mist of blood came from Ned Kenny's back and fell on my face. I'll never forget it. There was no mercy shown, and Ned Kenny was half-simple.'

'Is he alive?'

'He's between life and death. It's in the balance. It's hard to see how he could live. His back was ploughed red – you could see the bones. Several soldiers pissed in their trousers during the whipping.'

'Why didn't you rebel?'

'This Colonel Spiker is not like Colonel Richardson. He's a tyrant!'

'Did you find out who Ned Kenny was?'

'He's a relation of the Burkes from Cashel, I'm told, on his mother's side. He was calling for her like a child for three nights.'

'Who carried out the whipping?'

'A madman from Castlerea. They say he was given ten sovereigns for the job. He was whipped away from the place immediately it was over.'

The soldier did not realise that he had made a foul pun. Jeremiah Egan gave him a sovereign for his information and told him to report to him both on the condition of Ned Kenny and the movements of Colonel Spiker. He would be paid well for his information.

When the soldier left the tavern, Jeremiah Egan took pen and paper and wrote a letter to the Burkes of Cashel. He expressed a wish to meet them for a secret military trial.

Three days later the Burkes arrived in Castlebar. It was a fair-day, and the town was crowded. They went unnoticed. Late that evening they drifted into the Black Horse and made their way up the rickety stairs to a small back room. There were five men present: Jeremiah Egan, Sean McHale, John Burke and two of his relations. They were in an angry mood: by now they had a clearer picture of what had happened in the barracks.

'Ned Kenny's action did not merit the whipping,' Jeremiah Egan began, after he had given them further information about Ned Kenny and Colonel Spiker.

John Burke looked at him in anger. 'Well, that's a cold type of start to a meeting, Egan! When you wanted guns in the past you knew where to come for them. There is not much fire in your voice.'

'I'm only stating a fact,' the other said.

65

'Well, I'll restate it for you. No soldier should be whipped, and the man who orders a soldier to be whipped a hundred times deserves what's coming to him. And if the man he has whipped is a simpleton, then the action is the work of a fiend.' Burke looked at the schoolteacher. His eyes were as emotionless as fish. 'Now, in what way can Colonel Spiker be made to pay for his crime?' John Burke waited silently for his answer.

'I suggest that he should be assassinated. We could lay in wait for him, but it would have to be planned to a detail. They would scour the country looking for us, and we would hang for it. Sean McHale is of one mind with me in the matter.'

John Burke looked at the two men. The only action they had engaged in so far was an attack on a small police barracks which had failed. They had cut off the tails of a landlord's cattle and maimed his horse. John Burke had not travelled to Castlebar to take orders from two Whiteboys.

'The Burkes will deal with the matter in their own way. While you plan your assassination, Ned Kenny is probably dying in the barracks. We want information – as much as you can get. We want him out of there. You have the ear of the soldiers. Get Ned Kenny out of the barracks in a coffin. We want him pronounced dead. If he recovers, he will be half-mad and he will be placed in an asylum. We'll have none of that.' His mind was clear. The Burkes had laid out their plans before they had arrived at the tavern.

'That will require money,' Jeremiah Egan told him.

'There it is,' John Burke replied sharply, and he placed a purse of sovereigns on the table and pushed it over towards the schoolteacher. 'We want value for money. You owe us more than one favour, Egan, and I swear if you don't get Ned Kenny out of the barracks I'll come to Castlebar and shoot you myself. You have not suffered at the military's hands as we have.' He took out a pistol and placed it in front of him. It was directed at Jeremiah Egan's chest.

'There is no need for threats, John Burke,' the man said nervously.

'I am protecting myself. If this tavern is attacked, I intend to shoot my way out of it.' He watched the Adam's apple in Sean McHale's neck move. He was afraid.

'We will do as you suggest,' Jeremiah Egan said.

'Are you going to leave Colonel Spiker free to take his revenge on another common soldier?' McHale asked.

'I see you have a voice, McHale. Well, you find out the movements of Colonel Spiker. We want to know when he takes his pleasure or what company he keeps. That should not be difficult to find out. Then we will deal with it in our own way. You have got your money and your orders. Good night.' With that the three Burkes rose and left the room.

'They don't want us in on it,' Jeremiah Egan said. 'They have their own plans. I'm damned if I should take orders from John Burke. What has he ever done for the cause?'

'I think we'd better follow his orders. They are a savage breed and strange in their ways.' Sean McHale was still shaken.

'Leave me to think about it,' Egan said, and the other left the room.

Egan was angry at the direction the meeting had taken. He knew that the Whiteboys were ineffectual and was angry that John Burke also knew it. He realised, too, that if he ever wished to escape from the country it would have to be in one of Michael Barrett's ships. However, there was one advantage in it: he could now let the Burkes deal with the matter – it was no longer in his hands. He had no taste for battle but he had a taste for intrigue. Now he must set about getting Ned Kenny out of the barracks.

Colonel Spiker looked out the window of his quarters as the plain coffin on a cart was trundled across the barracks square and through the archway at the sentry gate. No great pity stirred within him. He had restored the discipline of the barracks with this death, and the discipline of the Army was above all other considerations. A common soldier was of little matter, especially when the common soldier was Irish, and the Irish were numerous and filthy vermin. He had seen them swarm about the streets of Castlebar since his arrival. A plague or famine was necessary to thin them out; they could not be sustained by the land. He continued shaving when the sound of the wheels on the cobbled path died away.

Within the coffin, Ned Kenny, half-conscious of the rawness of his back, lay on his stomach, aware of the wheels bumping on the stones. He drew air through the auger holes in the bottom. He wished to cry out but he knew that he must remain silent until they were outside the town. The cart made its way around the Mall and the police barracks, then turned at the Protestant church and headed west.

Later Ned Kenny heard a knock on the coffin lid. 'I'll open it now, Ned, and you can breathe some fresh air. We are out of town.' The lid of the coffin was slid back. The fresh air on his body was like the touch of cool velvet or ointment. 'You are all right now, Ned. If I see any soldier, I'll cover you up.'

'Thank God and His mother. Thank God and His mother,' he moaned. Then his mind became confused again and he was visited by nightmares. He began to rave.

It took three days to get to the valley. The coffin was destroyed at one of the safe houses where they had rested, and Ned Kenny was placed on soft wool and his back covered with cool seaweed to hurry the healing. The story of the whipping had moved before them. When people looked at the flayed back of Ned Kenny they grew angry at the manner in which Colonel Spiker had destroyed the simpleton.

Myles Prendergast had not moved from the village. He had followed the sequence of events from a distance. John Burke suggested that he should not leave Cashel until the Ned Kenny matter was settled. Fury was gathering within John Burke at the description he received of the whipping. 'I tell you, Frenchman, I will not rest until I have my revenge. I will take it when Ned Kenny is safely here. You are one of us now, bound by oath, and you are part of it. You are no longer an observer but part of the fight and, remember, it is a fight and it has been going on a very long time. We need your French Revolution here and we need it before it is too late. In the meantime, while we wait for it, there is a score to settle with Spiker.'

'Is it wise to reveal your hand?' Myles was cautious. 'Is personal revenge a suitable motive in the present case?'

'Yes,' John Burke had roared. 'You will see what the brave Colonel Spiker has done to a half-idiot who never did any harm to anyone in his life. Spiker like all his ilk thinks we are vermin, a peasant race with a barbaric language. He will learn a lesson, let me tell you!'

'Very well.'

Four men were waiting for the cart at the valley mouth. They lifted Ned Kenny on to a pallet and carried him through the defile. Then they brought him to one of the cottages and placed him on a bed. The seaweed was removed, and John Burke and Myles Prendergast stared in horror at the lacerated back. It looked like pulped meat with small shreds falling loose.

'It's better for a man to die quickly in battle than to have that done to him,' Myles cried out.

'Colonel Spiker may have forgotten what he has done to this man, but you do not flay a Burke relation and get away with it.' John Burke was grim.

'Spiker deserves to die,' Myles shouted angrily.

'No, Myles. He deserves to half-die and half-live, and that is the way it will be.'

Myles Prendergast planned the night campaign. It was obvious to him that they should move rapidly through the dark countryside and attack close to woods where they could immediately take refuge if the effort failed. The raw weals on Ned Kenny's back had hardened his resolve, and he agreed with John Burke that they must take immediate revenge. He now understood the anger of the old men in Paris when they described the scenes they had witnessed after the failure of the rebellion. The sight of Ned Kenny, half-idiot and now on the edge of madness, broke the detachment within him. He was part of the Brotherhood, sworn to rebellion.

'Four of us will be sufficient to carry out the work,' he told John Burke. 'Pick a night when there is a full moon. Once we have fixed on our plan we move rapidly – the action must be over in one hour and we must have a wide margin of time for our escape. We could hang for what we are about to do.'

Each day Ned Kenny's back was covered in cool sea-wrack, and the iodine and salt cauterised the rawness. Soon patches of scab began to form on his back and the long process of physical healing began.

'We won't be able to heal his mind so easily,' one of the women said. 'It is full of wild shapes.'

'Do your best for him,' Angus told her. 'We will take care of him in the village. We'll get him a dog, and he can mind the sheep on the hills. He can fish off the pier and maybe take a curragh out into the bay. We'll see. . . .'

Colonel Spiker felt comfortable of mind and body as he said good night to Henry Massingham on the steps of the eighteenth-century house. Behind them stood the large open door showing the hall and the wide hunting-table. When the family had retired to bed the two men sat in the library in front of an oak fire, swapping stories of London.

The moon was full and marked a path on the trout lake below the lawn. They had spent a pleasant day shooting by the same lake.

'Were it not for houses like this and days on the lake I would find this wilderness stranger than India,' the colonel remarked.

'We keep the barbarians at bay!'

'Do you think they will rise up?'

'I don't think so. They are hungry and they are subservient. We were well served by the '98 rebellion – it flushed out the rebels. This is a country without leaders. I do not think the Queen has any fear of rebellion in this corner of her empire.'

Colonel Spiker, warmed with wine and a little uncertain, made his way down the steps of the house to his carriage. His whole body felt pleasant and slack as the carriage set out on its journey to Castlebar. He could hear the crunch of gravel under the wheels as they went down the dark avenue and was lulled into a light sleep.

It happened at Moneen Wood. The horse shied, and the movement jolted him awake. He looked out of the window of the carriage at the hideous white masks with their black eye-slits. No word passed between the men. They moved expertly. He was pulled roughly from the carriage and his clothes torn from him until he was naked. He had no time to feel embarrassed. A fear gripped him which he had never experienced before. He was dragged to a tree and his arms lashed about it; he could feel the rough bark tear his chest. Then, silently, one of the figures raised a whip. His eyes started from his head as the lashes fell on his sensitive back. He screamed for mercy as the leather thong cut his flesh. Beside him somebody counted the strokes in Irish; they were slow and deliberate,

70

coming at painful intervals. His screeches echoed through the wood until he collapsed, but the strokes went on by lantern light, counted out now in firm, angry French, until the back was flayed. The driver, who had been forced to watch, was released and ran blindly into the wood.

Two hours later the sentry heard Colonel Spiker's coach approaching. It stopped halfway down the avenue. The horses began cropping the grass on the soft, green margin. He decided to investigate. He was surprised that there was no driver sitting on the driving-seat. When he opened the door and peered inside he took one look, then turned from the carriage and retched into the grass. Colonel Spiker lay on the floor in his own blood, his back and buttocks in shreds.

The night had gone well, and the bright moon casting dull light on the landscape helped them in their journey through the small roads. As dawn edged into the eastern sky they reached the opening in the mountains which led to the village.

'How did it go?' Angus was waiting for them when they descended from the sweating horses.

'Well,' John Burke told him.

'Not well enough. We should have killed him. I should have put a bullet through his head,' Myles said angrily. He had not suspected his own fury until he had grabbed the whip from John Burke and meted out the final strokes.

'No, let him suffer. Let him cry out at night like Ned Kenny does. A quick death would be too good for him.'

'I made one mistake,' Myles was bitter.

'What?' asked John Burke.

'Like a fool I counted the final fifty strokes in French.'

'I thought you counted them in Irish!' John Burke was surprised.

'No, in French.'

'Don't worry. He was unconscious after forty strokes. The deed is done. The military in Castlebar now know that they have not crushed all the rebels.'

Later that day, after an exhausted sleep, John Burke walked down to the pier with Myles. His admiration for the Frenchman had increased, and he realised how important he could

71

be to the organisation. Myles understood military tactics and he was ruthless.

A plan was forming in John Burke's mind. 'Would you sail to America with me, Myles? I leave in about four weeks' time. I am to meet several gentlemen in New York who are interested in our cause. They provide us with money and arms and, if necessary, men. But I wish to bring someone with me who can explain the military situation to them.'

'Is four weeks sufficient for me to study the military installations and write up a report?'

'You can write it up on the way.'

'Let me consider it.' Myles looked out to sea, his mind still on the events of the previous night.

'Very well.' John Burke was impatient to move on. 'I will meet you in two days' time in Northport. I think that you would help the cause greatly if you met the members of the organisation in New York. Many of them are highly placed in the American Army.'

'You place your hope in the Americans,' Myles remarked drily.

'No one else will come to our assistance. Think about it.'

8

THE HUDDLE OF HOUSES seemed small and insignificant as Liam Joyce looked behind him. About them lay the patchwork of fields from which they drew their sustenance. Beyond the fields lay the bog and beyond that again the mountains. Liam Joyce knew every crevice and cranny in the mountains. He had gathered wild birds' eggs there to sustain the thin diet of the village.

He was a man of exceptional strength and appearance. His eyes had a sharpness which showed a quick mind. He was fortunate that he had had a good basic education: he had attended a hedge-school where he had picked up the rudiments of reading and writing, so he could read the papers which not only gave local news but also news of what was happening in the outside world.

Each week the village gathered in his kitchen where by candlelight he laboriously read the paper to them. Night after night he read out the reports of what was happening in the House of Commons and in America. 'It's important to know what's happening in the wide world,' he told them. 'There is no virtue in ignorance.'

He was thirty years of age and had accumulated both cunning and wisdom from the soil and the politics of the time. 'We must survive. We must learn to survive and never give in. Remember, we owe nothing to anybody. We are the slaves for the moment but we can throw off the ropes and chains if we are bright.' He knew that Kenrick was due. He had read of the application of the court orders in the *Connaught Telegraph*. It was inevitable that the village would be levelled.

All that January day he made his way by narrow paths to Castlebar. He had eaten a large plate of gruel in the morning, and inside his shirt he carried a half-circle of rough bread to kill the hunger. Two small pigs grunted in the baskets on the donkey's back. They were active in the small squares of osier. The night previously he had gathered with the other men in his one-roomed cabin and decided to buy meal. They could live longer on meal than on bacon, and a pig yielded good money. They had been hungry during the winter, but it was not deep starvation; it was the whittling away of flesh and energy. In the other villages they had also been hungry. It had been a hard decision.

'Let them fatten. They will pay Kenrick's rent,' his father advised. 'The pigs have always been our salvation. They have kept the hunger away from the village.'

'I tell you, Father, Kenrick has set his eyes upon this place as he has upon others. I read it in the papers. He will not rest until he has cleared us out. There is a better yield from fat sheep than from the rents we pay him. Kenrick will bleach the land.'

'And what will we do, Liam, when the gale day comes and we have no money left aside?'

'I do not know. I only know that we are hungry and the children and women need feeding. Hunger weakens a man's body and a man's intent. The day we succumb to hunger is the day we lie down and die.'

'You do not know the ways of the world, Liam. You decide to venture into Castlebar with two pigs. Who do you know there and what will it all yield?'

'It is better than staying here,' he replied vigorously.

'You are leader of the village,' they agreed. 'If you think that this is the proper decision, then make it.'

That night as he lay in his wife's arms on the reed bed he told her: 'I hate this tyranny of place and I hate this poverty. I know that we were born for better things. My grandfather was a schoolmaster and he had the great racial poems in his head. We were not always land agents' curs and slaves. We come from rich ancestry. We must get away. This bog is not going to be our graveyard.'

'But how will we get away, *allanagh*?' she asked him. 'I have been always by your side, and for a time things went well for us, but now with the high rents and the bad times we are being beaten into the earth.'

'I was not born to be beaten. There must be a way out.'

'Would you have us go to England?'

'No, not to England. To America. I have read in the papers about America and the great city of New York and the lands that lie to the west. No plough has ever been put to them. There is land there to sustain us. I will not be beaten into the earth. I am not vermin.'

He loved this woman who had shared his life. Their sexuality came easily to them out of the Irish phrases.

'Declare would the children hear! Declare would the children hear!' she called to him in comfort as the anguish left his loins and he cried out in primal moans.

'I will not have you go hungry, woman. I will not have you go hungry,' he told her, his face on her shoulder.

'I know, love. You would go without for me.'

'I will bring you to a safe place. The land is poisoned. Here the grass is thin, the sodden earth miserable. I will not break my back wrestling with it.'

Her fingers ran through his hair as he spoke. She soothed him with the short idiomatic phrases of love which came to her like a litany.

As the village disappeared in the wide expanse of bog he thought of his wife and two children and his relations. Left alone in the bleak bogland they could be happy, but always there was the fear of the land agent, Kenrick.

'May Kenrick roast in hell and may the fallen angels chew the marrow of his skull for the affliction he has brought upon people,' he said to himself as he thought of the fear under which the village lived. 'And may all his seed, breed and generation never have luck until time cracks.'

The curse upon Kenrick had come from the anger within him. The catechism had told him that he should love his enemy, but he felt that it was faulty in its thought and theology. The bishops had advised that they should accept the heavy burdens placed upon their backs. 'Ah, the bishops are far away and in towns,' Liam had argued against the village elders, 'and they call upon us to follow a law which is not God's law. Let them eat plates of gruel morning, noon and night and soon they will change their ways of thinking. Anyway they all talk English and have English ways.'

'We must follow what they say,' he had been told.

'Well, I won't. I want to live and I want to be free.'

They respected his independence. He had brought some confidence to the people when he took his father's place as the village leader.

Calling out poems, he made his way across the bleak expanse of land. He loved their music. Sometimes he sang them to himself. They were noble poems and they gave him inward respect. 'Little does Kenrick know of the wealth inside the Irish language and the great poems that the peasants carry within them.'

His journey took five hours. He stopped at a stream and drank the cool water and ate some of the bread. He ate it slowly. It brought warmth to his stomach. Then he washed his face and hands and continued.

In the distance he saw the smoke rise from the chimneys of the garrison town of Castlebar, drifting across the blue empty sky. He could just make out the military barracks, high and formidable. It made him feel insignificant against the British power over the great towns. He wondered if he could ever break away from its control.

He passed by the hovels that had been carelessly thrown up. Children dressed in rags played in the filthy street with the glazed look of hunger in their eyes. Old women sat at the doorways smoking clay pipes, their faces rutted with age. A black residue of dirt and smoke filled the ruts. There was a stale smell of urine hanging over the street. Here and there some gombeen man or other had set up a shebeen. It was midday; many men and women reeled drunkenly past him. Now at the centre of the town, he looked in wonder at the three-storeyed buildings facing the Green, each big enough to house a whole village. Some people left one of the houses and entered a carriage; they were comfortable and well fed, oblivious of his presence. Straight in front of him was the most important building he had ever seen, the Court House with its slate steps, its Greek columns and the half-lit entrance. Men had been brought from the Court House prison which was below ground level to be hanged on the Green. He passed the Protestant church which stood on a platform of earth and looked at the tables of stone which stood above the graves. Further up the hill and a little removed from the town stood the prison, which housed not only criminals but also the insane.

He wondered that shops could be so large and contain so many articles. Clearly the desires of the rich for possessions were limitless. He looked at the women's clothes. They were fine and elegant of line. The price of one dress could have kept his village in meal for a fortnight.

Everywhere he witnessed the presence of soldiers and policemen. He had a natural fear of men in uniform and cast his eyes down as he passed them, certain that they looked at him suspiciously.

He arrived at the market-place. Huge crowds moved among the stalls. There was a continuous babble of talk in English and in Irish. Hucksters called out from their platforms to the sea of people beneath and waved their articles in the air. He took his place, an anonymous figure, among the small farmers at the end of the market. Like himself, the men looked poor and shared the communal humiliation of their poverty standing together in a huddled group. Liam Joyce infrequently attended the markets but he knew that in this corner he could gather valuable information. He needed to discover as much as he could about Kenrick.

Soon he was engaged in conversation with the others. They talked in Irish and in low voices. They were all certain that the lands were going to be cleared. Sheep and cattle could yield more from the land than the rent of tenants.

'Mark my words, before the year is out many of us will have nothing to sell at this market. If Kenrick won't get us, it will be the rents; and if it is not the rents, then it will be the hunger. Every year things get worse and now they say that there is a curse upon the land for our sins and our drunkenness.'

'And what about the sins of the rich? They live by a different law. They lie in soft beds, and the rest of us on clay floors with our feet towards the fire.'

77

'They deserve to be evicted,' Liam Joyce said.

'Keep your voice low, for that is treasonable talk and even the police know the Irish. Beware, there are spies everywhere. But look – there's Kenrick himself, riding past. Observe him closely, for you will see him again.' The small farmers were hushed.

Liam Joyce watched Kenrick on his horse. He had a large savage head and a purple nose. There was a sneer on his face as he looked down at the farmers, and Liam shuddered involuntarily and a cold sweat broke out on his back. Kenrick carried a coiled bullwhip in his hand. He had brought it down heavily on the backs of many men but never on a beast; beasts were more valuable than men. Kenrick went out of view, and the small farmers began to talk amongst themselves again. Liam Joyce was ashamed of his fear. Would he ever be free of this poisoned land?

It was late in the evening when he sold the two pigs to a buyer. He was not satisfied with the price he obtained, but the market was now almost empty. He had to accept the offer. He left with despair in his mind. The evening was cold, and it penetrated his clothes. Lanterns burned in the public houses, and men lunged forward as they staggered up and down the street. Liam Joyce was tired, and his mind had lost the early sharpness of the morning. He was hungry, and when he tied the donkey behind Molly Ward's public house he took the remainder of the bread from inside his shirt and ate it. When he had satisfied his hunger he took the money he had received for the pigs and bound it in a piece of cloth which he hung about his neck. He then counted twelve pence on to his palm. That would pay for the drink in Molly Ward's and for his accommodation in some loft or other.

In the public house the soldiers were raucous. Their voices filled the long dark room which smelt of stale drink and tobacco. They smoked their clay pipes and cursed freely at each other. He came to this place because his father always spoke with respect of Molly Ward. He told him that she had hidden men in her house when they were on the run. He bought a drink of whiskey and sat in a corner. It warmed him against the cold. He rarely drank. He was conscious of this waste upon himself. Money was a precious gift: it bought food and should not be wasted.

He drank slowly and later he allowed himself the luxury of

a second drink. He thought of his wife. They would sleep apart tonight; he would not bind himself to her. But he could not banish the thought of Kenrick from his mind – he was the most feared and hated man in County Mayo.

It grew late, and he did not notice the crowd thin out. The soldiers had to return to the barracks early. They rolled out the door calling to each other and slapping each other on the back.

'Are you lost in your thoughts?' a voice asked him. He looked up. Molly Ward stood before him.

'I didn't feel the time passing. Are you closing?'

'Not for the moment. I'm having my nightly drink; not that I don't have my daily one. They say it will kill me. But, then, something is killing us always. Aren't you one of the Joyces?'

'Yes.'

'I knew your father. How is he keeping?'

'Old and cannot move out as much as he did.'

'You must be the oldest. What's your first name?'

'Liam.'

'Yes, that's right, Liam. And what brings you to Castlebar?' By now she was sitting beside him, a whiskey-glass in her hand. She looked old to him.

'To sell pigs.'

'And did they yield much?'

'Not enough.'

'I suppose that you did not sell them until evening when you felt like giving them away for nothing.'

'That's right.'

'That's the way the buyers work. I know them of old. They have a hold on you like the gombeen man.' She drank her whiskey and called to the servant girl to fill up two glasses. When the drinks were placed before them, Liam Joyce offered to pay.

'Keep your money,' she said, waving his coins away. 'It's hard-earned, and thanks to the great thirst of the resident army I will not go without.'

'It will lighten my head,' he told her.

'Then, it's food you want. Did you eat today?'

'I did, but only half a cake of bread.'

She called to the servant girl to bring bread and cheese from the kitchen. 'Eat that now,' she directed when the large plate

79

was placed before him. She watched him savour every mouthful.

'Why do you sell pigs in January?'

'We are going hungry in the village.'

'And the rents?'

'They are due in three months' time. Something might turn up.'

'And what do you think will turn up but Kenrick on his horse? You know what is happening. Soon everyone will be on the road to Castlebar and the workhouse.'

'Then, what can we do?'

'Emigrate,' she told him. 'Things will get worse.'

'How can I get enough money to buy the passage for them all?'

'Do what has been done before. Send the two healthiest; let them earn the passage money for the rest.'

'We have little money.'

'Well, sell what you can to raise the money, but do not leave it too late. I have seen children left in the workhouse by their parents who went to America and later sent back the money for their passage.'

'Do you think it could be done?'

'It could if you are careful, and I'm sure that you are a careful man. But let no one be a party to your thoughts until you are ready to make the first move.'

'You are *certain* it could be done?' Liam questioned her anxiously.

'It is a chance you will have to take and it will take courage, but you'll need to act quickly.'

He felt excitement growing within him. Perhaps he would be free of the miserable earth that grudgingly gave him nourishment. Perhaps he could breathe the free air of America. Perhaps some day he would buy a fine dress for his wife. 'I must think about it.'

'Then, I will leave you to think. And tonight you can sleep in the barn at the back. It will save a few pennies.' With that she left him to his thoughts.

That night in the dark barn, lying on hay, he felt exhilarated. He tossed and turned and thought of the great ships he had seen at Northport. One day he would sail to America.

9

THE APRIL LIGHT poured in through the large windows which faced across the fifteen-acre lawn. It was a dilute light and it carried little warmth. Kenrick stretched himself under the fine sheets and knuckled the sleep out of his eyes. His mind was dull with whiskey. He put out his hand and took the open bottle of whiskey from the table and drank from it. It burned his guts but brought some clarity to his mind: raw whiskey always cleared his mind in the morning. He looked across the bed at the place occupied by the scullery maid, but she had already gone to the kitchen to wrap the food. He had to draw his thoughts together to remember who had been in the bed. It had been Bridie Farrell. Her father made up part of his evicting team.

'Well, what did Farrell expect when he asked me to give her a job? She was swinging her fat haunches before me and, if she's got, there are plenty to marry her and she'll have land for the bastard.' He drank from the bottle of whiskey and looked at the sky through the light curtains. It was a doubtful sky.

He would soon have to vacate the house and return to the more confined life of the valley. There he had his own two-storeyed house, with its yards and milking-sheds and a small oak wood which protected his house from the hard western wind. He had spent the winter in Lord Lannagh's house.

He took a copy of the *Connaught Telegraph* from the floor and read it again. Frederick Cavendish had written another vicious attack upon him. He hated Cavendish more than any other man in the town, because he was educated in England, well bred and did not fear him. He had called him 'Bastard Dick', 'Dirty Dick', 'Crooked Nose', 'Brandy Belly' and a dozen other names which made Kenrick cringe every time he recalled them. Even the small children, disappearing down alleyways in the town, called him 'Bastard Dick'. He never made a move but Cavendish was on his back, taking in everything with a cool eye and describing what he saw with bitter ink!

'I'm only doing my duty. I am only doing the work of Lord Lannagh,' he would call out to his men after he had read the paper. 'What right has he to take *my* character? I'll even with him. Some day he'll regret that he crossed the path of Dick Kenrick. By God, he'll regret it!' But Kenrick left it at gestures and talk. Cavendish knew the law too well and could carry on his own defence. He would drag things into the open which were known but not mentioned.

Kenrick got out of bed and looked for his leather trousers. They were in a heap on the floor. He dragged them on, and walked over to the windows and looked down at the lawn he had laid out in front of the great house for John Dowling, the previous owner. It stretched out in unbroken green to the lake. Here and there were clumps of chestnut trees, where cattle could take shade in the summer-time. There was no network of small fields here, no constant division of farms until the land had been dried of sustenance. The large lawn with its ha-ha lay just beneath the window. Fourteen years previously, John Dowling had given him directions to improve the land in front of his house.

Kenrick waited until he had returned to London, and in the autumn of 1833 he began the clearances. There had been individual clearances before, but the town had never witnessed anything on this scale before. Everything was done by due process of law. The rents were raised to such a degree that the tenants could not pay them, and then they were served with court orders to remove them from the land. Fortified with these documents, Kenrick could set about his clearing. It took five weeks to clear the land of people. He usually moved in in the morning when people were not awake. He had hauled old women from their beds and personally thrown them out of doors. He had taken his stick to fathers of households and beat them off their land until his name became hated across Mayo. He had had the thatches of houses set on fire and later had sent in the crowbar brigade to beat down the walls of the houses. Each stone had been taken from the houses to the perimeter of the fifteen acres, to form a new seven-foot boundary wall. In late spring of the next year only scars remained, and by summer a green meadow had covered the lacerations. People predicted that healthy grass would never grow on the markings of the field boundaries. 'It will be poisoned land for sure, and no good animal could come off it,' they whispered. But Kenrick, looking down on the large field, knew that the curses and predictions had failed.

The single luxury of cattle grazing on good grass cheered him. Later he shaved, put on his polished boots and heavy coat and made his way down to the farmyard half a mile from the house. There was a flurry when he entered. Already fifteen men were sitting down to a large breakfast of thick bread and boiled eggs. They were filling their stomachs for the long journey ahead of them. Bridie Farrell placed a large plate of bacon in front of him which he immediately set about eating. He ate with rapidity and drank several mugs of tea which brought sweat out on his forehead. He wiped away the sweat with a large handkerchief. He never spoke during the breakfast except to bark some order or other. When he was finished he pulled at his nose, wiped his mouth with his hand and looked down the table at the men who were silently eating their breakfast.

'Eat all you can. There will be no break until we get to Northport, and that's eleven miles away. Have you everything in order, MacDonnell?'

'Everything ready, sir. I had it ready last night, and we've only to harness the horses this morning.'

'Crowbars, spades and the battering-rams?'

'Everything on the list.'

'When I'm out in the middle of a bog, MacDonnell, it's too late to be sending men back to Castlebar to fetch stuff.'

'It's all ready, sir. I checked the lists.'

'It had better be. What about you, Delaney?' he asked, looking down at the man.

'I have all the military tents and bedding packed. Seven tents you told me to bring, each suited to six men. You said we would have to shelter the police.'

'Yes, I took them into the count. I can smell trouble brewing in the bogs. Well, we'll have the police, and with the law behind us we are sound. I have the ejection papers in my pocket, every one of them. There are three villages to flatten. We leave the best house for the herdsman and his family when they move in.'

'What about the people, sir?' Fox asked.

'What about them? They have failed to pay the rents and out they go, that's the law. There will be space for them in Castlebar workhouse. That's what workhouses were built for. There is plenty of feeding there for them, and if they want they can sail for America.'

Fox knew that he should not have asked the question; Kenrick would have settled for a beast rather than a man any day. What Kenrick thought of cottiers and small farmers was simple: they were lice, they were subhuman and savage and they were destroying the land with their overbreeding.

'If they are not drunk, they are at it in these hovels. They waste the land and they waste themselves. Let them go to America. They tell me that there is space there for them,' he told the gathering about the table to reassure them that what they were doing had some respectable purpose.

Kenrick knew the quality of men that ate in the kitchen. They were outcasts in the town. Several of them had been in the county gaol for assault. One of them had killed a man in a brawl, but no one gave evidence against him. They shared one thing in common: they depended upon Kenrick for their livelihood and were afraid of him.

'This work will take a week, so I hope we are all well provided for with tea, bread, meat and potatoes and the bottles of whiskey,' he said to Bridie Farrell, who had been rushing in and out of the kitchen with boxes of food.

'Everything is as you ordered, sir; enough for nine days if it comes raining, for I'm told it is a wet place.'

'Damn and blast the rain! If we set out to do a thing in seven days, we'll do it. Give a mug of whiskey to each man and we'll be on our way.'

She took the large crockery vessel of whiskey and holding

it under her arm poured it into the mugs. The men drank it with relish. It brought warmth to their stomachs and false courage on an April morning.

Kenrick knew how important the large mugful of whiskey was for the men. It would see them through the town, where people turned their backs on them, when they set off on their missions of destruction. 'Fill them again,' he directed, 'and open another jar. We have a long journey ahead of us.' It was rarely that Kenrick treated them to second helpings of whiskey. Soon many of them were drunk. 'We'll be on our way now, men,' he ordered when they had finished.

There were six carts ready in the cobbled yard, covered with tarpaulin. Ropes ran from shaft to shaft, and Kenrick tugged at them to test them. Then he shouted at the men to mount the carts and move out of the yard. He watched them leave, then he mounted his own horse and rode ahead. He led the cavalcade down the long avenue, past the grazing cattle and out of the great gates. They went in the direction of Castlebar. The people of the town turned their backs on them as they marched around the Mall and past the fever hospital and then up the hill past the county gaol. The men on the carts looked blankly ahead of them.

Kenrick looked at the grey sky. The early promise of sunshine had passed away; rain was gathering beyond the drumlins out over Clew Bay. He watched it approach with a stoical eye as it advanced on a south-westerly wind. Soon it was cascading down upon him and spitting up from the muddy tracks. The horses plodded forward. Now and then, Kenrick watched an urchin start from a ditch, like a snipe from grass, and run across the small fields and over the ditches. News was passing from village to village that Kenrick was moving along the road between Castlebar and Northport.

They ploughed on, drenched to the skin, and would have complained but for their drunken state. It was a tedious journey and dulled the edge for destroying houses. People avoided them as if they were lepers. Only one person stood in their way. She was a demented old woman who made the horses nervous with her sharp voice.

'The curse of hell on you, Kenrick, and all that back you and all you others on the carts! May the curse of a widow not go astray and may you rot in hell.'

Kenrick cut at her with his whip. It glanced off her shoulder. He passed forward. She cursed each cart as it passed by. The men feared the curses heaped upon them by the widow woman. It made them irresolute. 'Off with you, you mad woman!' they roared back at her.

'I might be mad but I'm not damned and I'm not bent on the devil's work,' she called after them. 'You are the whelps of Satan, the whelps of Satan.'

Finally they reached the crest of the long winding hill. Below them in the rain lay Northport, sheltered amongst small hills and mature trees.

Sergeant White was far from hospitable when Kenrick arrived at the barracks with a demand note for fifteen policemen to accompany him into the Carraighrua district. Kenrick showed the sergeant the villages he intended to level on a large map.

'We are here to administer the peace and not to stir up trouble. The wretched people out at Carraighrua only require to be left alone. Why should you level their holdings?'

'Because they cannot pay their rents and because I have the eviction papers here,' he replied, angrily brandishing a fistful of documents. 'I am upholding the law. I work by the law and, by God, if you don't give me support I'll report you to your superior officers in Dublin. You have to see the law is carried out.'

'Whose law?' Sergeant White asked caustically.

'The law of the land. The law of England,' Kenrick roared at him.

'The landlords' law. It's a law without any shred of decency!' Sergeant White told him.

'Don't talk to me about decency. There was nothing decent about the flaying Colonel Spiker got from the Whiteboys. He was nearly killed, and I don't see any arrests. Decency, my backside! I have the law on my side and I want protection.'

Sergeant White had made his protest and there was little he could do but order his men to accompany Kenrick out to Carraighrua.

'That's better, Sergeant. That's better,' he said as Sergeant White gave his orders.

Kenrick made his way over to the hotel and ordered a glass of whiskey while he waited for the police to assemble. He sat

86

by the fire and removed his greatcoat. Outside the police barracks the men stood about the carts in small groups, smoking their pipes and feeling the hostility of the people who gathered to look at them. They drummed up inconsequential talk among themselves to pass the time.

Eventually the policemen came through the archway. Two were mounted on horses. They took up their positions in front of the carts. Kenrick watched them getting wet from inside Durcan's Hotel. Fox entered.

'Have a drink,' Kenrick invited. 'Let the rain fall on the forces of the Crown for a while. Keep them waiting.'

In the barracks Sergeant White looked at his men standing in the rain and suppressed his anger. Later he saw Kenrick, his face raw with drink, salute the police in mockery and mount his horse. He gave a roar, and his men mounted the carts; and the cavalcade, led by the police, moved out of the town.

'That man is an official executioner,' Sergeant White said to himself. 'He will fill every workhouse in Mayo with people and he will leave others to die on the roads, and there is nothing anybody can do.'

The cavalcade moved on. Soon the hills fell away behind them, and before lay a vast expanse of bog and heather. At the centre of this brown and famished landscape lay the village of Carraighrua.

As the sun began to set, Kenrick picked out a small dip beside a stream for the camp-site. The men broke some dry whin-bushes and built them into a fire while others set about erecting the tents. The police stood apart in a sullen black group, showing no wish to be associated with Kenrick's men. Many of them felt that they were used both by landlords and by their agents to enforce the harsh demands of the law. That was part of the reason why they were hated in the towns and feared in the countryside.

Kenrick was in a dark mood. He had expected to make better distance, but the rain and the delay in Northport had prevented him moving further into the wilderness. The villagers of Carraighrua probably already knew that he was on his way, and they would take precautions. Poverty generated cuteness and cunning.

'Put up the policemen's tents,' he directed two of his men. 'And over a bit from your own.'

'Why don't they pitch their own tents? Haven't they got hands and plenty of food in their stomachs?' Fallon snarled at him.

'Enough lip from you, Fallon, or I'll have you hanged. I can still lay my hands on witnesses,' he said in an ominous voice. 'Do what I say and don't question my orders.'

Fallon, who had a hot temper, was not awed into submission. 'They have grand notions of their importance, strutting up and down the town in fancy helmets,' he continued.

'Enough out of you, Fallon. Get on with the work or I'll break your jaw with my fist.'

Fallon shook out the canvas tents on the ground and set up the poles beneath them. 'Black well-fed bastards,' he muttered to himself. 'The Queen's men they are, castrated Irishmen every one of them.'

'Keep your mind to yourself, Fallon,' Jennings told him. 'We will have enough trouble without you stirring up any more.'

'Black well-fed bastards,' he muttered again. 'They look down on us and think we're dirt. Look how their tents are pitched away from ours.'

The police lit their own fire and brewed their own tea. They ate bread and meat which Kenrick had provided for them, slowly and with regularity, relishing each morsel. At ten o'clock they entered their tents, smoked for a while and talked, then turned in for the night.

Kenrick slept alone beneath one of the carts on a bed of hay. Canvas sheets kept out the wind and rain. He had a final gulp of whiskey from the bottle he always kept beside him and then fell asleep. He had the ability to forget everything, even his surroundings, and he always slept deeply and soundly. The others at some distance from him had hung lanterns in their tents. They smoked and played cards, cursing at each other and drinking whiskey. Much later they lay back, feet towards the centre poles, and fell asleep. Their actions did not go unnoticed.

Tim Joyce had watched the file of carts and horsemen make their way across the bog, from behind a small hill. His father Liam had set him to observe them as soon as he discovered they were in the area. Tim had a good idea who was leading them across the bog: it was Kenrick of the crooked nose. He also knew that the men behind the carts were policemen from Northport. He had seen them in the town when he went there with his father on market days. He was a boy of eleven. His eyes were deep-set and dark. There had never been a time when he could remember having a satisfied stomach, except perhaps when they dug the early potatoes or trapped a rabbit.

When he reported back to his father, Liam Joyce gathered the villagers into his kitchen.

'This is the end of the village. In three days' time there will be no house or gable standing here,' he announced.

'Could we not pay the rent?' somebody asked. 'You said you had money to pay the rent.'

'That would hold off the day of reckoning for six months and that would see us to winter. We would be starving then. No, we hold the money. Besides, Kenrick is not interested in our money, he is only intersted in the land. Sheep are more important than anybody gathered in this kitchen.'

'It's a sad day when it comes to that,' Owen Joyce said.

'Listen, Owen, it's always a sad day here and a miserable one,' Liam told him, laughing. 'And you won't end up in the workhouse. America is calling.'

'If it is, I can't hear it,' he replied.

'Well, it is towards the west, and our best chances lie there. So we have to face Kenrick the tyrant and take what he gives us and say nothing.'

'I've been brought up in Carraighrua and lived here all my life, Liam. All my seventy years have been spent here and all before me are buried not far from here. I'm too old to pick up my roots, I'm like the bent bush, settled,' Nell told him.

'I've no cure for that, Nell. I know we have a better chance away from here. Don't listen to the talk of your hearts, for they tell you to despair. I know some of you have never been beyond Carraighrua, and that Northport is like a foreign land, but I and other men have journeyed further afield. There are paths on the sea in the same way as there are paths and roads in Ireland. We will take the greatest and widest path, and that is to America. We will take the path west. It will be a long journey but it must be made.' He spoke his words in Irish, with strength and softness, his mind running easily. His mind was supple in this language, and he could express himself easily and well.

No one dissented. He knew that fear filled their minds and they would have to put their trust in him. He knew they would. He had laid his plans of escape thoroughly over the years. At least some of them would soon be on their way to America.

'There will be a moon tonight, so do not use lanterns until you are beyond the Eagle's Nest. At the first light let every man and woman be back in the valley. You have heard of the plays in the big towns – well, tomorrow every one of you will be acting in a play, and your lives will depend upon it.'

They set out their work by the light of the moon. They brought the donkeys and the horse from the fields and put salley baskets on their backs. They took the bales of wool they had hidden in the outhouses and, having secured them to the animals, set out from the village. They made their way along a stony path for about a mile, then they began to ascend the mountain, drawing the animals forward up the steep incline. They called softly to each other in the darkness, though they knew the path almost by instinct. Halfway up the mountain the soggy land levelled off at the lip of a corrie lake. They brought the donkeys through its shallow waters in order to leave no marks behind them on their way to the large cave. There they packed the wool, whispering to themselves, fearing that one of Kenrick's men might be hidden in the rough heather. Five times they had to make the journey to the cave, bringing first the wool, then the potatoes and oats and then the pigs, one to each basket. The heavier ones were drawn awkwardly forward by the boys. The whole village worked through the night.

Light came too early. Perhaps it was just as well, Liam Joyce thought to himself. He watched the countryside come to life: the hills turning purple; the browns of the bogs taking on their separate colours. The endless landscape stretched away to the east, good only for turf or the cropping of sheep. Kenrick of the crooked nose would come out of that endless land.

There was a knot of fear in his stomach. It had been growing all morning. He could not betray his fear, even to his wife, who had a mind almost as strong as his own. By ten o'clock the villagers were working back in the fields, setting the early potatoes. They worked silently, listening for the sound of

90

horses on the rough path. Only the villagers would have known that there were few potatoes in the bags and that the pigs which snouted the earth were old and thin.

They heard the cavalcade on the road. First Kenrick appeared above the valley. He gazed at the people working in the field for a moment, then he signalled his men forward. He had caught the people off their guard, and they would have little time to organise themselves. It was a perfect situation: he would have his work finished here in six hours and he would be able to move forward to the next village by afternoon, with the walls levelled and the animals secured against the rents.

'Round up the people and clear them out, every man, woman and child of them.'

'What about the sick?' someone asked. 'Will we fire them out also?'

'Never mind the sick. That's one of their old tricks. Half the village falls ill when we approach. Out with every one of them and set the thatches on fire. They cannot return to burned-out houses.'

They were well practised in destroying villages, and moved forward, formidable and menacing. To the villagers who watched them from the fields they were a frightening sight. They had never been confronted with such an ordered menace before.

'Who is the spokesman for the village?' Kenrick roared from his horse when he was amongst the houses. Nobody answered. He roared out again.

Liam Joyce emerged from his house. 'Sorry, good sir, but we don't know the English tongue good. I am the only single soul that knows the words, sir, for no stranger comes to this lonely place very often.'

'And do you know who I am?'

'The great man from Castlebar, sir, come to collect the rents. Sure, sir, if you could only give us the half a year we would scrape the money together. You shouldn't have made the long journey, sir, or bothered yourself with the likes of us.'

'Are you an idiot?'

'A what?'

'A fool!'

'Oh, indeed no, sir. My mother was a bit of a fool, and I

91

suppose that's why her brother was a whole one, walking the hills at night chanting holy hymns. But, sir, we'll have the money for you come the next gale day. I swear by the very saints of Ireland and the first and great one, St Patrick, that we will scrape the money together.'

Kenrick was entertained by the antics of Liam Joyce. They were fools by nature and fools from inbreeding, he thought. 'There will be no more rents. The day for rents is over. The village is to come down. Every stone wall will be flattened.'

'You are putting the village to death, sir?'

'Yes.'

Liam Joyce let out a screech when he heard the sentence passed on the village. He rushed through the small street crying out: 'They have come to destroy the village! The great man from Castlebar has come to destroy our village!' He cried out in Irish to the people. They set up a wild lamentation.

'Oh, good sir,' Liam Joyce begged. 'Don't burn our homes! Sure, we'll not have a roof over our heads. Who wants us? We'll starve, surely starve, if you throw us out with only the stars for a roof.'

'Get the people out of the houses,' Kenrick shouted.

'They would prefer to be burned with them, great sir. Sure, they have nowhere to go! Don't pitch them out into the loneliness of the day and the darkness of the night!'

Liam Joyce did not anticipate what happened next. Kenrick raised his whip and brought it down on his back. It cut through his shirt and lacerated his skin. For a moment he almost forgot himself and cursed this ugly brute who looked down on him from the horse. If he had possessed a pistol, he would have blown his face asunder at close range.

'Oh, sir. Don't do that again,' he pleaded, but Kenrick raised the whip and brought it down once more on his shoulders. When he fled through the village, Kenrick followed him. He beat him as he would beat one of his animals. Kenrick always began an eviction by frightening the people.

His men began to move on the houses. They dragged out the old and the infirm and threw them to the ground. Then they threw out the few sticks of furniture which people possessed. The women rushed into their houses to save their few chattels but they were barred from entering by the police.

'Oh, no! Not the house I was born and reared in! Spare it,

sir, spare it. Sure, there is no call to take the little from us?'
one of the women called in Irish, clinging to Kenrick's boot.
He kicked her to the ground and moved about the houses,
whipping people away from the doors and whipping them in
front of him down the small village street. It took very little
time. When the men were finished, they set the thatch alight.
The fire rushed quickly up the roofs, and soon flames and smoke
reached up into the sky. The roofs fell in on the rooms, sending up a fanfare of flames to mark the end of habitation there.

What they had often spoken about in the small thatched
houses had happened. It had happened quickly and without
mercy. Gathered together silently in small huddles they
watched the burning village, which marked the end of their
life in that place.

When the flames died down, the houses were left to
smoulder. Kenrick let the people gather their possessions and
carry them to the edge of the village. In the meantime the
men rounded up the animals and impounded them in a small
field.

Then the final phase of destruction began. Huge tripods of
timbers were set up at the gable ends of the houses. A large
beam of timber was set in a sling suspended from the top of
the tripod. Then six men set the beam in motion. It picked up
a slow destructive rhythm. They beat the beam against the
gable end, and it took only eight strokes to bring it tumbling
down. This exercise was carried on until each house was a
heap of mud and rubble. When the work was finished Kenrick
called Liam Joyce to him. He was smarting under his wounds
and shocked by the sight of the village.

'Move off now. The village is finished. The workhouse is
open to you. Go where you will, but if anybody returns here
they will be shot on sight.' He drew a pistol from his belt and
discharged it into the air.

Liam Joyce gathered his people about him on the small road.
They were carrying with them their small possessions. They
looked back at the village, now a mass of stone and mud, as
they left in a ragged line. Already the crowbar brigade were
preparing to move on to the next village. Liam Joyce knew
that they were fortunate: the village had been destroyed in
late spring.

10

THEY DID NOT MOVE from Carraighrua. They built scalps at the base of the mountain, holes two feet deep lined with rushes and heather and roofed with some of the charred rafters they had stolen from their village. They cut scraws from the bog and placed them invertedly on the rafters. They would now wait until Kenrick had left the area.

Liam Joyce had many decisions to make. They could no longer remain in the area. They could move to Northport or further still to the county town, Castlebar, or they could go to America. If they moved to the town, they would have to seek shelter in the workhouse. In April there would be plenty of room for them. Later on, if famine struck, they might have to remain outside the walls and starve. The partial famine of 1845 had filled the workhouses with people who had discharged themselves when winter was over, choosing to become beggars rather than stay in the confined conditions. They found it impossible to subject themselves to workhouse discipline or the division between the male and female wards.

Liam Joyce put his thoughts to the village: 'We have to divide ourselves into those who will go to America and those who must enter the workhouse. We have not enough money to buy passage for everyone even when we sell what we have hidden in the mountains.'

'We cannot split the families,' they argued. 'We would rather die together than split up.'

'I'm tired of all this talk of dying! The day you start talking of dying is the day you will begin to die. Had Kenrick left us alone, we had some chance of holding out, but now there is no chance whatsoever. I have read to you from the papers what will happen in the towns. The towns are traps, even in summer, for it is then that the fever comes.'

'We cannot survive outside Carraighrua,' they complained.

'We will survive because we have to,' he told them. He spoke to them with apparent confidence, but he had little confidence in his heart. He knew he would have to move the people quickly away from the wide expanse of moor.

'We will wait for another year,' they had argued. 'We will remain another year and there may be an upturn in things.'

'We cannot remain another month, never mind another year,' he insisted. 'If the famine becomes general, there will be panic. It will be like the river in spate when it takes away part of the bog.'

'We seem to be cornered like animals in the pound. There is no way out and we are afraid to make the long journey – some of the older people have not been ten miles from home!'

'If you talk like that, then everything has failed already.'

'Well, then, you let us know your plan,' they demanded.

He looked at the group of men, women and children sitting on the rocks about him. 'I will tell you my plans and they may perhaps tear your hearts. We have passage for six to America. Perhaps we will have passage for ten when we sell what we have hidden in the mountains. The rest will have to remain here.' He looked at their faces. They were like one united family. Severance was beyond their belief.

'Who will remain?' his first cousin asked.

'I have thought of that. Two adults will remain and eight children. In that way we can survive a year on meal. Only the strongest children will remain, four boys and four girls. Oonah and I have decided to remain on to take care of them for the year.'

Even the men were visibly shaken by his words. They had lived together in the village and they did not understand any other way of life. They objected to his decision. They would rather die than split up the village. The women began to wail and turned to Liam's wife, Oonah, and put their arms about her. But she had a firm mind, and he had discussed his decision with her. He knew that she was carrying a child and he was imposing a rigorous burden on her, but she could carry the difficulties of the village better than the other women.

'Could we not go to England?'

'England will be as bad as Ireland, for the ports will be thick with Irish and there is no work there and no new land to till. We go across the seas west or we stay here to rot like the rest of them. Which will it be?'

'We will leave it in your hands,' they said, knowing that there was no choice.

Liam Joyce had walked about the huge wall at Castlebar workhouse. It was like a bridewell. He knew he would have to spend six months separated from his wife, six months confined to three acres of ground, shuffling about the male yard and eating meals of porridge and milk. Once he entered the workhouse he could not lie with his wife, and his child would be born among the women. There would be no joy or talk or coupling. 'The decision is made, then, and there is no going back now,' he told them.

Kenrick returned home by the edge of Clew Bay, well satisfied with his work. He would put Gore in charge of the area. He could build himself a fine house and marry the milkmaid he had been humping for a year. Gore was almost as brutal as himself and he would survive in the harsh landscape.

Something about the Carraighrua eviction troubled Kenrick, but his pride dismissed it, leaving only a nagging sense that Liam Joyce had deceived him in some way or other. There had been something about the village that he could not account for: it should have supported more pigs and poultry, and there had been little evidence of oats in the houses although he knew that many of the fields had been under oats the year previously. Where had it disappeared to? They had not made any effort to pay the village rent, and the land-hungry Irish always did. He could have marched across the countryside to the village again to check these matters, but his men were mutinous and the constabulary hostile.

As soon as Kenrick was clear of the locality Liam Joyce set out to sell the rest of the animals. They brought them together with the wool to the fair at Northport, and Liam Joyce stood beside the bales until he was satisfied with the price. The money realised the price of two fares to America. He put it in his leather wallet about his neck, so that it hung from leather thongs on his chest. The pigs realised the price of another two tickets later.

When the animals and wool had been sold he left his wife in the square and made his way to the quays. He passed a continuous traffic of carts carrying grain to the great warehouses for export. The grain had been sent to pay the rents to Kenrick and his kind, and it was now on its way out of the country while an inferior type was imported. Somebody was making money out of the poverty and famine.

He gazed at the forest of ships at the quays, anchored to the granite bollards, their sails furled, their complicated network of ropes and ladders bare.

He recognised one of the carters sitting on a granite bollard, smoking his pipe. He walked over to him, introduced himself in Irish and told him of the recent happenings.

'Oh, I heard that Kenrick destroyed your village last week. He will make a green desert out of the place if somebody doesn't put a ball in his heart.'

'They levelled everything and threw the old out in the ditches.'

'He'll have a bad end. They say that he has orders to turn the whole countryside into a sheep-run. Well, you can see the price wool is fetching and what they are doing with grain. Good grain going out and bad grain coming in. A queer system – but, sure, I have to work with it. How are you making do?'

'Living from hand to mouth with a bit we have stored.'

'Well, that won't last long. I saw a whole village knocking on the gates of the workhouse last week. They will surely catch the fever if it is going.' The carter smoked his pipe in a thoughtful manner. The tide was filling in slowly behind him, the seagulls whirling about the masts of the ships. 'I'm half a countryman myself. My father came to town thirty years ago. Nothing remains of his village today. Is there any way that I can help you, for it is help you need, no doubt?'

'Do you know much about the ships and their captains?' Liam asked.

'Yes and no. I know some of the sailors out of the town.'

'Well, then, could you recommend a good ship and a good captain, for we wish to emigrate. There is nothing left for us here.'

97

'You need a pile of money to emigrate, and even then you shouldn't pay it until you are sure of a berth. I've seen people swindled here, but it is nothing to the swindling over in Liverpool – I could tell you stories which would wring tears from a stone!'

Joyce let the carter talk on. He had lots of stories to tell, but he knew little about the ships or their captains. However, he did tell him that Tadgh Lyons who drank at O'Connor's pub would give him all the information he needed.

'And mention my name. Tell him I sent you. And don't forget to buy him a few glasses of rum. He's sullen when he's not drunk.'

Liam Joyce made his way to O'Connor's and, having introduced himself to Tadgh Lyons, placed a bottle of rum on the table before him.

'You are mighty generous with your money, sir,' Tadgh Lyons said wryly.

'Well, I want generous information. People from our village are going to America, and I want to know who is the best captain and which is the best ship.'

'Well, you bought me rum and you are a direct man, and I will tell you what you want to know. You should go to the Barrett side of the town. You would do far better there if you could get John Burke to take you on – he is Michael Barrett's right-hand man.'

'I'll pay the passage money immediately. I'll go to Barrett's house with the money.'

'Nobody goes to the Barrett house but the captains and the poet.'

'The poet?'

'Yes, Gill, the hedge-school master and the drinker. Barrett has a great time for the poets – he is related to Rioccard Barrett, the poet buried in Erris.'

Liam Joyce was stirred to intense interest. 'Tell me more about Rioccard Barrett and his relationship with Michael Barrett,' he said, his senses quickening.

'They say that Michael Barrett sings in Irish when he is drunk and that he would give a ship to have some of the manuscripts. You know Rioccard Barrett's second wife burned them all when he died.'

'So there is nothing by the great poet's hand?'

'No, nothing – and, you know, Rioccard Barrett was ten times a better poet than Raftery.'

'I know that,' said Liam Joyce, suppressing his excitement. He went to the counter and bought another bottle of rum for Tadgh Lyons. He poured himself a large glass and pushed the bottle towards Tadgh. Then he held up his glass. 'We'll drink a toast to Rioccard Barrett of Erris,' he said.

'To a rebel and a poet,' the other agreed. 'He was almost hanged, you know, for marching with Humbert.'

'But he survived and wrote great poetry.'

'Indeed he did, and I'll give you a bar of one of his songs!

'There're many ways of collecting pieces
And stacking treasures in heaps of gold
And devil a penny you can take with you
When you lie under the tombstone cold.
If you ruled kingdoms and marshalled soldiers,
A king, a duke or a grand signor,
There's ne'er a penny you could take with you
So lift your glasses and drink some more.'

Liam Joyce joined with him in the song. He was now drunk, and also excited, for events had taken an unexpected turn.

Of all the chance meetings he had had in his life the one with Tadgh Lyons was perhaps the most fortunate. He knew he could now secure safe passage to America for the whole village if he held his head. The town whirled about him and sounds were garbled in his ears as he made his way towards the square. A wild excitement which had been suppressed by misfortune, bad times and sullen earth was burning in his head. Energy was rampant within him.

He called to his wife Oonah as he approached her, waiting in the shelter of a wall. She wrapped her coloured shawl about her with the delicate fingers which he had always admired.

'You are drunk and you are crying,' she said. 'Have you taken leave of your senses, man? You cannot afford to spend money on drink! How much did you spend?'

'The price of two bottles of rum.'

'That is a terrible waste, Liam!'

'It was the best money I ever spent. And I'll spend more, Oonah, for you are coming with me to a respectable house and

I'll buy you a fancy drink, for you well deserve it. I'll drive a plough through the land of America yet! Come with me.'

He took her by the hand and led her through the fair. When they were sitting in comfort and she had a warm drink of whiskey in her hand he told her what had happened.

'I don't believe it,' she said. 'The packet could not be that important.'

'But it *is*, Oonah. It *is*, I tell you. Lucky Kenrick did not burn it with all the rest of the things. I'm drunk, I know, but forgive me. I'll sober on the way home. Tell no one as to what we are after and pray to the Virgin for me and pray hard.'

That night, by rush-light, they opened his leather wallet and took out the manuscript, faded by time and fragile along the edges. He cut the rough binding of thread and took out a single page, keeping it separately. It was early in the morning when he fell asleep. The excitement and the drink had been too much for him.

11

LORD LANNAGH'S HOUSE stood over the tranquil waters of Lough Lannagh, three miles removed from Castlebar. The house was approached by a long avenue through fifteen acres of lawn. This wide expanse of lawn, broken only by careful clumps of beech, ran down to the lake with its many islands.

Lord Lannagh, when he visited his house each summer, spent many days on his lake, moving across the silken water oblivious of time. He frequently drew in the oars and let the boat drift, aware only of the controlled beauty of the water. He spent days upon the lake in total isolation, coming ashore in the late evening and making his way up through the summer mist. He described this land as Paradise. Facing south and on the slope of a hill he built a walled garden and glasshouses where he planted exotic flowers and shrubs. It was a strange place, almost Mediterranean in its appearance, isolated from the poverty and the despair of the countryside. He loved the house and the grounds, and he relaxed here far from the pressures of London society.

He was a dreamer. He saw the estate as a mystical place and he banished from his mind the fact that outside the walls lay a bleak and overpopulated landscape. He visited the place in summer when the countryside was in bloom and he was not aware of the harsh reality of winter, when the snows fell, the cold froze the bone and the peasants huddled over the turf fires, day and night, to keep themselves warm.

He paid periodic visits to the workhouse and the school while in the area. The workhouse was cleaned up for the occasion and fresh rush pallets placed in the front dormitories, and the children in the schools were clean and well dressed. He had little wish to be interrupted during these visits. His solicitor showed him the accounts; he did not enquire how the money for the rents was gathered and only infrequently met his land agent, Kenrick, who gathered them and attended to the animals on the estate. Kenrick was in charge of the house in his absence and it was Kenrick who prepared it for his arrival.

In the presence of Lord Lannagh, Kenrick was subservient, coming only when he was called and staying far away from the house during the summer months when he remained at his own house in the valley of Cullen. Here he attended to his land and gathered the rents for other absentee landlords. Lord Lannagh was quite unaware of all the facts concerning Kenrick and would have been shocked by the truth: he did not know that housed on his own estate were the instruments used to evict a poor tenantry and batter their houses into mounds of clay and stone; nor did he know that Kenrick was employed by several other absentee landlords to put into practice the great clearances.

On a summer day in May of 1846 when his carriage drew up in front of the house he was aware only of the evening light upon the lake, the tranquillity of the vast lawn and the heavy cattle grazing on the dewy grass.

'And a hundred thousand welcomes to the good lord,' Hackett the major-domo intoned as he opened the carriage door. 'It's grand to see you so well and a great disappointment to us that the great lady herself could not travel with you.'

It was dusk now, and the lights burned in the hallway and in the great rooms on the first floor. He raised his eyes to the second storey. Hackett had lit the lights in his library.

'And all your books are unpacked, sir, and on the great table. I didn't dust them, for fear I might do damage, for I know how you treasure them.'

'Good. And how is Mrs Rance?' Lannagh asked.

'Down in the kitchen preparing hot food. She's fidgeting all day, and I had to put her at her ease.'

'Tell her that I will have food much later in the library

but now I will walk to the lake and enjoy the cool evening air.'

'Declare, my Lord, would you dampen the soles of your shoes on the heavy dew? The summer cold is a hard cold to shake off!'

Lannagh felt that Hackett played too hard at being a court jester or an Irish fool. His phrases were too colourful, too free to be honest, but he did his work efficiently and Lord Lannagh did not enquire further.

Walking down the gentle slope towards the lake, he felt the dew on the softened grass and breathed the scent of evening. Cattle munched grass slothfully, their bodies heavy and sleek with prime meat. He reached the edge of the lake and startled a bird in the reeds. It broke the surface of the lake and rose into the still evening air. The lake was soon tranquil again. The tawny reeds hid the small mysteries of bird life. Four swans moved out from the shore as he approached the pier where his boat was moored, and he watched them move across the lake, elegant and without fuss. Undoing the rope, he stepped into the boat and punted it out across the shallow water through the reeds, looking back towards the house. It was darkly outlined against the sky, and lights glowed in the large windows.

His body was relaxed as he rowed out between the twin islands. The peace of the place was settling into his mind. Ireland never failed to refresh his spirits. Year after year he returned to this sacred spot, a small part of his possessions, and forgot that London ever existed. The stars gathered strength in a clear sky, and the moon was deep and mature to the south of the house. It was with reluctance that he made his way towards the shore, and it was dark when the boat crunched on the sand close to the pier. He secured it and walked slowly through the night to the house. Only the sound of his feet swishing through the wet grass broke the silence.

He looked forward to his months in Ireland with pleasure. He would have time to catch up with his reading and study how his exotic plants had flourished during his absence.

The subservient Hackett came immediately to the library when Lord Lannagh settled into his chair. He removed his wet shoes and took them away. He returned and helped Lord Lannagh on with a pair he had warmed for him in the kitchen.

'I am well fit to put on my own shoes, Hackett,' Lannagh told him.

'Ah, sure, the lord deserves every comfort. Hasn't he come a long way in one day and it is my pleasure to welcome him home.'

'You can leave me now, Hackett, and send Mrs Rance. I will have to make some arrangements for a dinner party. It is expected of me, I presume.'

'It is greatly looked forward to and a great occasion for the gentry around the place, and you can give them all the news of parliamentary affairs and tell them about our glorious little queen, queen not only of England but also of the green island of Ireland.'

'Send Mrs Rance, now,' Lannagh reminded him sharply. He had to be careful of Hackett and preferred to keep him at a respectable distance.

When Hackett entered the kitchen his expression had changed. It was domineering. This was the expression which the staff knew and feared during the months when Lord Lannagh was not here and Hackett strutted about the house like the owner.

'He wishes to speak to you, Rance,' he said, 'and if you breathe a word of any irregularities in this house, then it will come the worse for you and that crippled husband of yours in the gate lodge. Do you hear?'

'Yes, Mr Hackett, I hear.'

Mrs Rance arrived with the tray of food and placed it on the large table.

'It is good to see you, Mrs Rance,' Lord Lannagh said.

'And good to see you, my Lord. You carried the fine weather with you from England.'

'Have you kept well during the winter?'

'Yes, sir.'

'And your husband?'

'He is poorly.'

'Well, do not remain too long at the house if you have to attend to him. Tell one of the other servants to attend to my needs if necessary.'

'That will be no bother. You are very good to us with the bad times that are in it.'

104

She was very nervous. She wished she had the courage to tell Lord Lannagh that Kenrick had defiled his house with the scullery and the milk maids, that he brought them to the great room where the lord slept and debauched them there. She wished to tell him that Hackett stole wine from his cellar and the rare meats from his table and that his wife was fat. She feared Kenrick more than she feared Hackett and she thought of her husband crippled in the gate lodge. The times were bad, and if she were turned out of the little house there was no place she could go. There was a tight grip of fear on everybody in the house.

'Have you the list for the guests for the annual dinner party?' Lannagh asked her.

'Here in my pocket, my Lord.' She drew it out.

'I am sure the Dillon sisters are high on the list!' He laughed.

'Sure, my Lord, wouldn't they die if they were not invited? Don't they spend the year thinking about it?'

'And I'm sure I will hear that tedious story concerning the King again.'

'Sure, we have heard that story a hundred times!'

'And don't forget to invite Paddy Corbett, the jockey. I love the lies he tells me about the horses. Is he keeping well?'

'He still trains horses, my Lord.'

'And all his horses are winners.'

'Well, according to him they are.'

They went down the list of twenty. When that was settled on Mrs Rance withdrew.

Lord Lannaugh felt hungry and ate the food which had been prepared for him, before settling into the luxury he enjoyed most. He took one of the books which he had forwarded to the house and delicately sliced its uncut pages. Then he felt the texture of the cover and the spine, caressing the volume with the palm of his hand, and with sensuous delight began to read.

The huge library, filled with bound volumes of books, was the place in which he found most comfort. In this world he would indulge his passion for reading, and his singular weaknesses of inactivity and his indecision would pass without comment. He enjoyed the pleasures of the mind more than the pleasures of society and was only drawn into politics by family

105

obligation. But he knew that he would not be invited by any prime minister to join his cabinet and preferred a comfortable and obscure position.

He did not feel the hours pass. When he looked at the clock which ticked softly on the marble mantelpiece it was half-past two in the morning. He reluctantly left the book aside, extinguished the candles and made his way to the large bedroom. As he lay on the fresh sheets and the comfortable mattress, he thought of the bright summer days which lay ahead. Two weeks previously Kenrick had lain in the same bed with a scullery maid.

Soon after Lord Lannagh's arrival Mrs Rance paid a visit to Eileen Horkan, who lived some miles from the gate lodge and at the head of the valley. It was a gentle summer's day. The leaves had now thickened on the hedgerows, and the trees were green and fresh. From the sidecar on which she sat she could look at the potatoes beginning to show firmly in the small fields. Men were carefully moulding them with soil. Here and there were small fields of grain. They would ripen late and would help to pay the heavy rents which Kenrick collected for the absentee landlords.

The countryside was dotted with small cabins, carelessly thrown up by the peasants. They lived frugally and were sustained by the potato. During the last fifteen years she had noticed how numerous the cabins had become, as men divided their small-holdings up amongst their children. She was lucky to have her position at the great house. Despite her fear of Kenrick and her hatred of Hackett she knew that she was fortunate and that during the hunger, which frequently occurred when there was partial failure of the potato, she would be sustained by Lord Lannagh.

She had been working at the great house for fourteen years. It had been bought by Lord Lannagh, four years after she had commenced work there, when John Dowling had sold it in order to pay gambling debts in London. As long ago as that she had watched Kenrick, under the instructions of Dowling, clear the tenants from the lands between the house and the lake and run the smallholdings into a gentle extensive lawn, having battered down their cabins and thrown them on to the road. Lord Lannagh was not aware when he made his way across the lawn that it had once sustained fifteen families. With the arrival of Lord Lannagh, Kenrick's activities on the estates became less notorious. He became land agent for many other absentee landlords until he was now the most feared and hated man in Mayo. It was said that he was wealthy, but if he were, then he concealed his wealth, living a raw and primitive life in his two-storeyed house in the valley of Cullen. Mrs Rance knew that he had great ambitions for himself. One night, when he was raw with drink and sitting before Lord Lannagh's fire, she had heard him boast to Hackett: 'I'll own Lord Lannagh's house and lands some day, and if it is not his lands, then it will be some other bankrupt's. Don't think Kenrick is without money, Hackett. I've worked hard for what I've got and I'll work harder. My time is coming – they may hate and fear Kenrick, but some day I'll ride to the church in a coach and four with silk seats under my backside. They'll take notice! They take notice when you have money – money buys the power and the position.' He was very drunk, and his tongue was loose. Mrs Rance had listened for a while at the door then moved away, afraid that Hackett might discover her.

She approached Eileen Horkan's cottage. It was long and well thatched, and the walls glowed with a thick patina of whitewash. Apple-trees grew in the front garden, and behind the house were the byres in which the hay and the oats were stored for the winter. Eileen supervised the farm and employed a man and his wife to run it for her. She had not laboured in the fields like other women, and her body and beauty were not broken by worry or hardship.

'I have not had time to visit since December,' she told Eileen when they sat down in her sitting-room. The deal shelves carried the books given to her many years ago by Father Coady and since then many she had purchased herself. A fire of turf and timber blazed on the hearth.

The two women talked about trivial things for some time, but Eileen instinctively knew that Mrs Rance was disturbed about something or other. Her fingers were nervous on her lap, and she seemed to be gripped by fear. Eileen passed her a cup of tea to calm her nerves, but her fingers began to tremble and the cup and saucer rattled so that the tea slopped on to the saucer. She seemed unable to control her hands, and suddenly the cup fell on to her dress, the tea quickly forming a long brown stain on the material.

'Mrs Rance! What is wrong?' Eileen leaned forward and took her hand.

'Everything, Eileen,' Mrs Rance sobbed. 'I cannot sleep at night and I do not know where to turn or who to talk to. We are all gripped by fear at the great house – Kenrick and Hackett have turned it into a bawdy house, if you'll forgive me the expression, but it is the only word which can describe it. . . .'

'Should you not talk to Lord Lannagh about it?' Eileen asked sympathetically.

'If I did, Kenrick would have us out on the road. And I must think of my husband. Times are bad, Eileen. I hate to see his Lordship robbed and his house desecrated.'

'Hackett was always a thief,' Eileen told her.

'I would not mind if he just stole the food – but he treats himself to his Lordship's cellar. I've seen the accounts and I know. Not only does he drink Lord Lannagh's whiskey, but now he also drinks the claret. The lord has no idea what is happening and he never checks the accounts. Hackett and Kenrick have fattened their own cattle on the land and sold them before Lord Lannagh arrived. Hackett must have money hidden in the bank – last year he sold five of the lord's bullocks.'

'And the lord never questions him about these things?' Eileen was puzzled.

'Ah, you don't know Lord Lannagh! He is a dreamer. He spends more time in that garden of his and the glasshouses looking at strange flowers and shrubs than he does at surveying his estate. And at night-time he spends his time reading in the great library. There are more books there than would fill this house and they have gold lettering on them. They come in boxes from London. When he is not out on the lake, he is in the garden, and if he is not in the garden he is reading the books. There is many a morning I went in to rake the fire, to find him still reading and him not knowing the time and it staring at him from the clock on the mantelpiece. He is no match for Hackett, who runs about with "*An musha*, my Lord, isn't it a great day entirely?" and "*Musha*, I hope my Lord had a comfortable repose last night?"'

'And you think that you should inform Lord Lannagh on all that is happening?'

'I am not an informer and I don't mind the petty pilfering of Hackett, but Kenrick defiles the house and the estate. He has gone above himself. He has three women in the locality with child. In April before the lord came he took over the house and slept in the lord's bed, and he had that strap Bridie Farrell up there with him. It won't be long before she's showing a bulge! It took me a week to air the place and get the smell of cow dung and drink out of the room. Himself and Hackett had rare nights at the lord's table with the best of meat and drinking the best of wine. I had to serve the two of them and listen to their abuse. Hackett is afraid of Kenrick. He has the power over him as he has over all the men whom he has drafted into that brigade of his. They sleep in the farm lofts down at the horse stables during a whole month and eat in the kitchens there.'

Eileen Horkan listened to everything Mrs Rance told her and let her get it off her mind. She detested Kenrick herself, and was aware of the fact that he had boasted in Castlebar that he would throw her out on to the road. He had also promised that he would clear the Costellos out of the valley they had inhabited for five generations. He could do this since he now possessed the deeds to the land, having purchased them with the money he had accumulated as agent to Lord Lannagh and the other absentee landlords. More and more over the last two years she had heard talk of the clearances. The land rents no longer yielded enough. Sheep and cattle were now more prized commodities, easily grazed on large tracts of land and little trouble. The peasants, on the other hand, were dangerous. Many of them had sworn they would kill Kenrick, and on one occasion a man had tried to shoot him.

Eileen Horkan was silent for some time. She was uncertain as to the advice she should give. 'It would be dangerous on your part to inform Lord Lannagh on all that is happening. Hackett would flatly deny it, and I do not think that Lord Lannagh would understand the intrigue which goes on. If the information is given to him, it must come from a higher source. Let things rest as they are for the moment. If necessary, I will write a letter to the *Connaught Telegraph*. There is no love lost between Frederick Cavendish and Kenrick.'

'I would not wish to have Lord Lannagh disturbed during his visit,' said Mrs Rance doubtfully.

'And why not? Is he not party to all that is happening? Has he not a share of the blame? He rests on the shoulders of others. Their small pennies help to keep him in luxury.'

'If another were in his place, Eileen, we would be all worse off. You do not know him as I do. I have received much kindness from him and I have no wish to harm him. It is Kenrick and Hackett I detest. They live well off him. Kenrick boasts that he will own the estate some day. He keeps his equipment in one of the barns in the farmyard. No, I will not have Lord Lannagh disturbed – leave him with his books and his garden for the moment. Now that I have spoken with you I do not feel as angry as I did.'

'Well, then, let us talk about his library instead.'

'You would never leave his library, Eileen, if you saw it! I know nothing about books, but there must be thousands in the large glass cases! Even Hackett treats the room with respect.'

'Thousands, you say?' Eileen wondered how many of the books she herself had read in the cheap editions Father Coady had given her. She could never afford the luxury of an expensive book and she was envious of the wealth which permitted a man to indulge his taste in them. 'I would dearly love to visit the library.'

'Sure, I would invite you to the house but for Hackett. He hates you.'

'I know,' Eileen said, shrugging it off.

'The rest bow to Hackett because they depend on him. You do not depend upon either of them, either himself or Kenrick, and they loathe the way you pass through the countryside on your white horse.'

'Dispossession has made us a subservient race. Will we ever raise our heads in pride again?' Eileen asked fiercely.

'We would if we owned something and did not lie in fear at night of being thrown out on the side of the road. It is a terrible worry to live under, Eileen. You have the comfort of books and the right to your land. Kenrick can never lay a hand on you.'

'He will try indirectly. Never you fear. I think that some day we will face each other on some issue and that one of us will be broken. But look – don't worry about Hackett. I will write to the papers about him when the time comes. For the moment we will let the lord have an easy summer.'

110

'You would enjoy his company, Eileen,' Mrs Rance told her as she gathered her things and looked around the room. 'He lives for his books and his garden. I don't think he knows that the words "poverty" or "hunger" exist.'

Eileen drove Mrs Rance back to the gatehouse of the estate. Through the semi-circular row of iron railings she could see the lake and the many islands and surmounting the great open lawn the great house. She dreamed of the huge cases of leather-bound books. It would be her wish to caress and read them.

12

AT SIXTEEN Eileen Horkan was already a beautiful woman, her hair as black as a raven's feather with the sheen of blue steel. Her skin was fine and had the purity of porcelain. At eighteen her breasts were full and pushed against her bodice. Neighbours said that she walked with a grace which bordered on arrogance. Kenrick, who always had an eye for a good horse and a fine woman, knew that there was a rich dash of blood in her which could not be accounted for. Every line in her body from her ankle to the slender column of her neck was correct.

The Horkans had been freeholders for two generations, and Kenrick could not touch her. They farmed thirty acres of fertile land, a considerable farm in comparison with the others about them, but her relations were not so fortunate. They were haunted by the presence of Kenrick, who could throw them on to the side of the road at a drunken whim.

Eileen Horkan had also been fortunate in her education. From the age of twelve she had visited the old priest Father Coady, tidying his house and bringing him food. He sat by his fire and moved only with great difficulty, but he had clear eyes and his mind was as bright as silver. On the table beside him stood his beloved books, as he called them, and he never ceased to read. He told her that he was never lonely with a book and that he had entertained the best minds who ever lived in his small house.

By the time she was thirteen Eileen knew the names of all the books in the house, for he sent her to fetch them from boxes and drawers and deal shelves and place them on the table before him. By the time she was fourteen she had read the best English novelists and many of Shakespeare's plays. As Father Coady grew weaker and his eyes began to fail he asked her to read for him, and it was then that her education truly began. Night after night, by tallow-light, she read for him from his favourite authors.

'You are my eyes now, Eileen,' he told her. 'You are my eyes, and what will I do without you, for all the others are ignorant and don't understand? We drink the deep wine here and they drink the brackish water.'

His obsession with books passed quickly to her. The very touch of a book and the enjoyment it would give brought pleasure to her. During these years she read the Greek and Latin authors to him in translation, the poetry of Dante and Chaucer, the English poets and essayists and the great political thinkers.

He insisted that she should learn Latin, and when she finally did master the language she read the original texts to him.

'If only I could teach you Greek, Eileen, if only I could teach you Greek! But we have not time – I feel the flame failing within me. Greek is the great language. It is the language of the men who first made us think, who first drew the mind away from superstition. It is the language of Aristotle, Plato and a man called Socrates, who had an ugly face. Oh, Socrates was the father of them all. He was so fair-minded that before his death he insisted that Asclepius received a cock which he owed him. . . . Listen to the final lines describing his death: "Such, then, was the end, Echecrates, of our friend; concerning whom I may truly say that of all the men of his time whom I have known, he was the wisest, most just and the best."'

Having recited this, his favourite passage, he would weep quietly. Then when he had wiped away the tears he would tell her: 'I would have given my whole library to have spoken to him, to have spent a day on the dry soil of Greece asking him questions. I suppose he is in heaven like Virgil and all the other good pagans.'

He died when she was eighteen. It was a peaceful death. His small bird-like head almost lost in the white pillows, with the beaken bloodless tip of his nose all that was visible when she entered the room.

'Come here, *allanagh,*' he said. She drew up a chair to the bedside.

'The candle is guttering inside me, love,' he began. 'I can feel death coming. It is like the hemlock of Socrates. Now, I don't mind leaving the world, but I do worry about the books – some barbarian will get his hands on them and not knowing their worth will consign them to the fire like the Mohammedans who burned the library in Alexandria. I wish you to have them. You can pass on the Greek books to Father Jennings, for he is as odd as myself, but one promise you must make. Destroy that book by Ovid, the *Ars Amatoria.* Oh, he was a scamp, a right scamp!'

'I will take care of all your books, Father, and I will always remember the great visions you opened up for me.'

'Yes, we shared great visions during the bleak winters, and the neighbours thinking we were mad. Sure, they are all blind and should be left in ignorance! But promise me that you will get rid of that Ovid fellow. He was a right scamp.'

'I will, Father.'

'Now read to me *The Death of Socrates.* That is my favourite piece.'

She opened the book and began the first familiar lines: 'Were you, yourself, Phaedo, in the prison with Socrates on the day when he drank the poison?. . . .'

He died while she was reading. She was not certain when, but when she closed the book she noticed that he was dead. It was a quiet death, as tranquil as a tide coming in, or silver light filling a morning sky. She closed his eyes and knitted his fingers over his skeletal frame. Then she wept and hoped that his spirit had not died with his body.

After his funeral she brought the books to her house. Her cousin, Seamus Costello, built shelves for her, and on them she placed in order the books from the house of Father Coady. She realised that life for her would never be the same again. Father Coady had given her the possession of too much knowledge. Her mind was no longer parochial. Unwittingly he had enlarged her sensuality.

She settled into the care of the farm. As she walked through the fields lines from Virgil's *Bucolics* would come to her and again, most forcibly, when she tended the flowers in her garden, or watched the apples ripen and the leaves fall at the end of autumn. For her a golden world was imposed upon the peasant world through which her father had moved. Each night, when the work of the farm was finished, she lit the lamp in her room and beside the small globe of light placed her book. She read the books hungry for their beauty and knowledge. She loved the texture of the pages, the shape of the words. The most intense hours of her life were spent beside the globe of light cast by the lantern.

Her father, from whom she received part of her refined mind, held her learning in awe. He was an Irish scholar who knew by heart many of the great poems of the language; a man, too, who knew the happy and sad songs of his race. But his mind was bitter as he watched the language fail and the early promise of repeat of the Act of Union founder. He was locked within the culture of his own language. He had not read Voltaire or Rousseau, or the works of Tom Paine and Adam Smith. One morning, mowing a meadow, he died. When she discovered him, his clothes were wet with dew.

The Dillon sisters, Emma and Caroline, were absolutely convinced of their noble ancestry. A spurious ancestral line, with an uncertain link in the centre, traced their blood back to Henry VIII. As they grew older and uglier and poorer in their house on Fairy Hill, their minds receded into an imagined past which favoured them in all respects.

As their fortunes failed over the years, the servants had been dismissed and they were now served by an old major-domo who shifted rheumatically about the house uncertain of his orders, but hoping, like the Dillon sisters, that one day their true position would be recognised and that for his service to the house for seventy years he would be made a Knight of the Garter. He addressed the Dillon sisters as Lady Emma and Lady Caroline.

The outside world noticed what they had failed to notice: the house was falling into disrepair, the roof leaked, the gardens were wild and a general air of decay hung over their meagre estate.

Each year, in springtime, they waited, feigning indifference, for Lord Lannagh's invitation to be delivered to their door.

The old major-domo carried it on a silver salver into the dining-room. He bowed with difficulty from the hips and said: 'Me ladies, the servant of Lord Lannagh attends a reply to an invitation to supper at Lord Lannagh's domain.'

'Pray tell him to wait,' Emma Dillon said in her imagined Regency voice. Eileen Horkan visited them frequently and read to them from Regency novels of the most banal quality, which they enjoyed greatly.

Taking the invitation from its envelope she read it carefully and passed it to her sister, who had been plain in her youth.

'It's a personal note, Emma,' Caroline remarked.

'The Dillons always receive personal notes. I'm quite sure the other invitations are totally verbal.'

'Quite a fine hand,' Caroline continued.

'An impeccable hand,' insisted Emma. 'Quite faultless, quite faultless.' The invitation was passed back to her, and she read it again. 'I presume, Caroline dear, that on that date we have no other engagements?'

'I don't think so, sister.'

'Then the servant of Lord Lannagh may be informed that the Dillon sisters of Fairy Hill will be quite delighted to attend the supper given by Lord Lannagh, as they are not otherwise engaged upon that day.'

The major-domo returned to the main door and tried to repeat what Caroline Dillon had said.

'Does that mean they are going?' the puzzled servant asked.

'Yes.'

'Good!' He mounted his horse and hurried away.

There was considerable excitement at the invitation.

'I think the occasion demands that we open a bottle of wine, Caroline.'

'Two bottles of wine, sister!'

'Two, then,' agreed Emma with a show of reluctance. She rang a bell, and the major-domo shuffled into the room. 'Darby, could you fetch us two bottles of excellent wine from the cellar? The occasion demands a slight libation.'

'Very well, my ladies.'

He made his way down to the cellar – a journey which he made frequently each week. Emma and Caroline Dillon found many occasions for sending Darby to the cellar to fetch wine.

The death columns in *The Times* and royal births and birthdays caused delight and sadness at Fairy Hill. These required libations. The birth of a royal child was cause to celebrate for a week.

Darby arrived back with two bottles of bad potent wine. It was decanted formally, and the two ladies were helped to glasses.

'To her Majesty the Queen,' Emma toasted.

'To the royal consort Albert!' Caroline rejoined. This was followed by toasts to the royal children and all the Queen's relations. By the time Darby made his second trip to the cellar they considered themselves personally involved with the royal family.

'Victoria is quite a great disappointment to me, Caroline.'

'You are disappointed by the Queen?' Caroline was shocked.

'Emphatically yes! She has not as yet invited us to the palace – this would never have happened in the old days.'

'She is perhaps too young. She may not have heard of us,' suggested Caroline doubtfully.

'Not heard of us?'

'Yes, things get waylaid in the palace. I am sure that is why she never replied to our letters.'

'Do you think so?'

'Certainly, sister. News has not reached her concerning the Dillons of Fairy Hill.'

'Then, we must wait a little longer and I shall write again,' said Emma with decisiveness.

'Yes. That would be the reasonable thing to do. We must not give the impression that we are exigent.'

'An *excellent* word!'

'We did have our day at the court.' Caroline sighed loudly and helped herself from the decanter. 'I am sure that we would find it all quite strange now. The fashions have quite changed – *quite* changed, I'm told. The court is not quite as spontaneous as when the Georges were on the throne.'

'They were halcyon days.'

'An excellent word, *halcyon.*'

'No, *halcyon.*'

'An excellent word,' repeated Caroline.

The present became very uncertain for the rest of the day until finally they swayed upstairs to bed, anticipating the

117

delights of Lord Lannagh's table and the rich wine from his cellar.

Eileen Horkan was invited to come with them to the house. It was not an invitation she would normally accept, but the two ladies were getting frail and she felt that they needed someone to bring them home and put them to bed after the supper. It was accepted that they would get drunk in the most quaint fashion and that their imaginations would be totally liberated at the dinner-table.

She arrived at Fairy Hill in the afternoon. As always the two sisters had not made up their minds what to wear. They had a line of antiquated dresses laid out on the bed, and each one had been tried out in front of the mirror and found wanting.

'Eileen, I wish to choose something which will emphasise the royalty of my bearing,' Emma Dillon told her. 'I was caught unaware by the invitation and had not time to order a new dress from Dublin. I am reluctantly obliged to use one of my former royal gowns. Which shall it be?'

Eileen picked up the least musty dress from the bed and examined it for moth holes. 'This will suit you, Emma.'

'Will it enhance my carriage?' the old lady asked anxiously.

'It will.'

'I believe I wore this dress last year. Will Lord Lannagh notice, I wonder?'

'I'm sure he would be displeased if you did not wear it.'

'Then, that's settled. I think that now the correct choice has been made we must celebrate the occasion. I'll send Darby to the cellar.'

'No cellar today, Emma,' Eileen said sternly.

'Just a *little* glass,' Emma begged. 'In the old days on royal occasions we had a drink prior to our departure to the palace. Is that not so, Caroline?'

'That is so, Emma.'

'Very well, then, just a little drink.'

While Darby decanted a bottle of wine, the two sisters put on their dresses, which Eileen then stitched into place with black thread.

'Oh, dearie, dresses do shrink over the years!' Emma Dillon remarked when she examined herself in the mirror. 'I do wish

118

that the invitation had not arrived so unexpectedly. We could have ordered new gowns from Dublin.'

Eileen left the sisters to put on their make-up. It was theatrical in style, the cheeks too highly flushed, the necks, foreheads and chins deadly pale.

'Make-up carefully applied certainly does make one younger,' Caroline told her sister.

'I think the candelabra-light will enhance our complexions.'

'Such is my view, too, sister.'

They drank the bottle of wine, and Darby was sent to the cellar to fetch another. Reluctantly Eileen did not try to stop them.

'I think we may now call the carriage, Darby,' ordered Caroline. 'Young Staunton will have the special privilege of driving us to the house of Lord Lannagh.'

'The carriage already attends you at the door, ladies.'

'Then, we shall have one more drink as always has been our custom.'

They finished the second bottle of wine, and Eileen escorted them to the carriage, the only decent object they still possessed.

'To the great house, young Staunton,' they called out when they were seated in the carriage. The horse started forward, the wheels creaked into motion and they commenced their splendid journey. Immediately Emma Dillon began with her familiar line.

'What an evening it was, Eileen! I can still see the large antechamber with the glittering candelabra. The King himself honoured us with a visit. My father, Colonel Brian Dillon, was with me on the occasion. You know he had distinguished himself in several battles. I knew London quite well. Indeed, I knew the very best people in my time.'

It took her half an hour to describe the events which led to the arrival of a gouty king and another half-hour to describe the ten seconds it took to bow and have some words with him.

'"What a charming daughter you have, Colonel Dillon. Bless me if she is not the prettiest lass in London town!"'

As a result of these few words she had never got married. No suitor in Mayo was good enough for her.

They drove up to the main entrance. Eileen helped the Dillon sisters up the shallow steps and watched them pass through the lighted hall and into the drawing-room, which

119

seemed full of movement and talk. She looked at the hallway with the magnificent paintings on the wall, the oak panelling, the plastered ceilings and the broad staircase which led up to the second storey. At the top of the stairway was a stained-glass window which seemed to depict a hunting scene. It was a world which she had often visited in her imagination.

She was about to move away from the entrance when she heard the voice of Hackett behind her. It was a gruff voice carrying insult.

'Away from that door! We don't want the likes of you here. Go back to the dung of your farm or I'll take a stick to you. You are assuming great airs, but we'll have none of it here!'

She had rarely spoken to Hackett. Both he and his wife drove to Mass each Sunday in one of the lord's traps. He had an arrogant face filled now with anger. When Lord Lannagh was in London he felt that he was master of the house.

'Mr Hackett,' she began, 'I was invited to accompany the Dillon sisters to this house and I intend to wait in the kitchen until they are finished their meal. I will not have a mongrel bark at me at his master's door. You may lord it over others, but you will not lord it over me!' She stood erect while she spoke. She dealt with Hackett in the only way he understood.

'Get around to the kitchen where you belong! This is no place for Irish Kates.'

She turned away, walked down the steps and went around to the vaulted kitchen where they were preparing the meals. It was filled with activity. Mrs Rance was in charge of the servants who were laying out the food on large silver trays ready to be carried to the dining-room. She noticed the variety of meats and wondered how they could be consumed. It offended her when she thought of the poverty outside the walls and the small patches of potatoes upon which the life of a family depended for a year.

'Can I help you, Mrs Rance?' she asked, feeling awkward standing there while the servants bustled about the place.

'No, you sit down there and don't add to the confusion. My head is always moidered with these big dinners. I've been preparing this for a fortnight for a worthless crowd of rakes and their women – I don't know why he has them in at all. Some of them will tramp the meat into the carpet. They are low company to my way of thinking.'

Eileen Horkan sat down.

'Look, Eileen,' said Mrs Rance quickly, 'go up to the library and examine the books – I don't think any of them will want to go to the library tonight. I'm sure some of them would hold a book upside down if you gave it to them!'

'If somebody found me, I would die of shame. . . .'

'What shame would you die of? Aren't you better educated than the whole lot of them put together outside the lord himself? They say he was at the University of Cambridge.' She turned to one of the maids. 'Here, Brigid. Bring Eileen up the back stairs to the library.'

Eileen Horkan followed Brigid Carney up the stairs and entered the great library where three lamps burned, casting their light on the books. The sight of the books bound in leather and tooled with gold lettering on the spines quietened her fears. Brigid Carney closed the door behind her with a whispered warning.

'There are one or two books there with *awful* pages in them, women with bare backsides and less! They should be burned. They would give Hackett evil thoughts for a week. They must have been drawn by the devil and printed in hell!'

Eileen Horkan was left alone with the books. She opened one of the leaded cases and glanced at the titles. She was amazed at how many of them she had read in the cheap copies which Father Coady had given her. She took out one book and began to leaf through it. Then she examined another and was soon absorbed by the beauty about her.

She did not hear him enter the room. Brigid must have forgotten to close the door. He must have been looking at her for some time before she became aware of his presence. She turned about quickly, gasped and let the book fall from her hand.

'I'm sorry, my Lord – I have no right to be here,' she blurted out. Her face was covered with confusion, but there was no way she could rush from the room.

'You are interested in books?' Lord Lannagh asked in a resonant voice.

'Well, yes. I read books,' she replied, trying to regain her composure.

'And have you read any of these books?' he asked.

'Yes. I have read most of the essayists and all the poets.'

'Then, you have a library?'

'I possess books, but I do not possess a library. I was given them by a friend of mine.'

He moved forward and lifted the book she had let fall on the floor. He looked at the spine. 'This is in Latin! Surely you do not read Latin?'

'I'm afraid I do. You see, an old priest I knew taught me to read it. He said it would help me to look beyond the horizon.'

Lord Lannagh controlled his surprise. He had not expected to discover a young woman in his library who could read Latin.

'I am sorry I invaded the privacy of your house,' she said and explained how she had come to the library.

Her host smiled. 'I have just escaped from Emma Dillon. Each year she tells me that story concerning her meeting with the King – and each year it is added to. I'm afraid imagination has taken the place of reality. . . .'

'It protects her,' Eileen told him. Now she felt more composed, she had time to observe Lord Lannagh. He was tall, with an intelligent rather than a handsome face, and his bearing was confident, as she would expect. He must be a man of about fifty, she thought. She had seen the local squires and squireens close at hand, and with few exceptions they had bloated and patchy faces from too much raw drink. This man was lithe of body and had clear skin.

'You are quite at liberty to stay in the library,' he said gently. 'In fact, you are at liberty to come and go as you wish and borrow whatever book pleases you. Books are to be shared rather than locked in glass cases. There is none here other than myself who reads. If I were to flee from my debtors, I would take refuge here. This is the last place they would seek me.' He controlled his feelings during this speech. The beauty of the woman standing before him had stirred something within him. She had breeding in her face: the skin was fine and clear, not caulked and blotchy like the women chattering in the dining-room beneath. The simple dress she wore stressed the lines of her figure. Set against the rows of leather-bound books and lit by the mellow light and with a lace collar emphasising the slender column of her neck, Eileen Horkan made an impression on him which he was not to forget. They talked for a further half-hour about the books which were about them until, reluctantly, he left the room. He had no wish to return to the dining-room, but decorum directed that he should. He left his unexpected guest in the library, surrounded by the books he cared for more than his horses.

Lord Lannagh's absence had been barely noticed. He looked down the table at figures which might have come from one of Hogarth's drawings. They retained the manners of the eighteenth century: the squireens savaged their food and talked between gulps, washing down their meat with his wine, taking little time to savour its quality. They would as easily have enjoyed the rough peasant wine of France as the fine wine he had let rest in his cellar for six years.

Their conversation was, as always, about horses. He enjoyed their knowledge of the field, the daring with which they took stone walls and fences. They lived only for the sport of horse racing; their stables were kept better than their houses, and their houses were better attended than their wives. Their present topic was the stallion, Pecker, who had sired several spring foals. Some declared that they had the qualities of jumpers, others thought that they would be better in flat races. Paddy Corbett declared that they were good for nothing.

'They will neither run nor jump, I wager. He was never a good stallion. Big and awkward, and that is carried through to the foals.'

But the conversation and noise seemed far away to Lord Lannagh. He wished at that moment that he could dismiss them from his table and send them back to their filthy houses and badly maintained estates. He was thinking of the woman examining the books in his library and the clean glow of light about her and the silence. He recalled the lines of her face as she examined the pages of the books. Her fingers were long and fine. He had seen such features in French émigrée women, the daughters of those who had fled to London during the Revolution. It was with surprise that he recalled she was Irish.

He had an aversion for the Irish. It was something with which he had never come to terms and which he had never examined too closely. He found their religious practices bordering on superstition. Most of the Mayo peasants were illiterate and unwashed. They belonged to an inferior and disordered race; to shake their hands was to feel that one was soiled.

Despite this aversion, his mind returned to Eileen Horkan in his library.

'Wine, sir?' a voice beside him broke in on his thoughts. He watched as Hackett dashed the wine in his glass. With his arrogant gesture he destroyed the quality of the liquor which had rested so long in the vaults. It was almost a studied insult.

'I have told you to pour the wine gently, Hackett! It is not raw whiskey! It has to be treated well. I taught you how to leave the sediment in the base of the bottle.'

'A thousand pardons, sir. I'm apt to forget things. A thousand pardons.' Hackett fell into the apologetic subservient attitude which Lord Lannagh detested. He was taken by surprise by the snappish voice of his master. He should have remembered that he treated his wine with respect.

Hackett was continually testing his position in small ways, testing how far he could be intimate with Lord Lannagh, and Lannagh sometimes doubted his honesty in running the affairs of the house. 'You have to be delicate with wine, Hackett. Take the glass away and bring me a carafe that is properly decanted. It is the one luxury I enjoy. Never pour wine directly from a bottle.'

There was a slight hush from those sitting at the table as they listened to the firm voice. It confirmed something which they easily forgot because of Lord Lannagh's tolerance: he had a dash of royal blood in his veins.

Hackett was distinctly uncomfortable. Rarely had the lord openly checked him. 'Excuse me, sir. A thousand pardons. I'll fetch another bottle and decant it right away.'

'I've changed my mind. It is too late to open a bottle of wine. I will have my brandy instead.'

Hackett hastened from the room. In the corridor he cursed the English lord who had humiliated him before the guests. He drank the glass of wine and rushed to get a bottle of brandy. He would have to be careful with Lord Lannagh and conceal his anger from him. Times were bad, and the great wall about the grounds protected both him and his wife from the poverty of the countryside. If he were dismissed from his position, he had no place to go and no one to turn to but Kenrick. They had both enjoyed winter nights in the great house at the master's table drinking his wine and brandy.

'If I recall correctly,' Emma Dillon said, 'the King, whom I met on my trip to London with my father, also insisted that his wine should be decanted.'

'I am sure he did, Miss Dillon. In fact, I would say that he had a special bottle decanted in preparation for the event.'

'I am not certain. It was a long time ago. But we certainly had decanted wine. It was yellow.'

'Are you sure it wasn't decanted horse piss, Miss Dillon?' Paddy Corbett, the jockey, asked in a drunken voice. Paddy Corbett, small and thin, had won the Galway Plate and was a county celebrity. At forty he was a horse-trainer. The company fell silent. They were horrified at the rough language. They looked down at him at the end of the table. He had overstepped the bounds of propriety.

'Excuse me, my Lord,' he said. 'I apologise for the bad language. I'll take my leave.'

'Did I miss something?' asked Caroline Dillon, who was partially deaf and wholly drunk.

'No, Miss Dillon,' Lord Lannagh said. 'Just an equine remark. Pray keep your seat, Paddy. We all make slips of the tongue.'

Conversation returned to normal but was more subdued. Paddy Corbett did not realise then that his remark would make him famous all over Connaught.

Lord Lannagh laughed inwardly. The remark, which was more than honest, tempered his anger at Hackett. His mind returned again to the woman in his library. He felt a desire to be with her. Strange that a woman brought up in such a harsh landscape and among such filth and poverty should be so accomplished. He could recall the fresh scent from her clothes and body, a scent which he would not find in the drawing-rooms of London and certainly not among the twenty guests gathered at his table. There was an even delight flooding through his body.

He had considered selling his estates in Mayo, for the voyage across the Irish Sea each year was uncomfortable and the landscape did not appeal to him. Once he crossed the Shannon it seemed to become immediately impoverished; the skies were filled with deeper greys; the people were more numerous, ill-housed, ill-clad and hungry. During his stay in Ireland his house and circumstances were controlled by an English way

125

of life. Now that strange world outside the walls had begun to intrude itself in the person of Eileen Horkan.

Eileen remained in the enchanted world of the library. She had time to observe the rows of books muted by leather bindings and, above the library, the deep frieze of white figures set in a background of blue. The same motifs were carried on to the ornate ceiling. Here was the presence of antiquity. Two tall windows looked on to the lake. She stood at one of the windows and looked at the night sky and the position of the stars. Somewhere in the darkness a lantern flickered as a figure moved down the gravel path. The moon, sharp and clear, stood above the lake and invested the islands in mystery.

The beauty of the place and the night flooded her mind and body. It satisfied something within her which was foreign to her background. She moved slowly past the lines of books, running her fingers across the luxury of leather, thinking of Father Coady and his untidy volumes, poorly bound, which nevertheless contained all his classical and European knowledge. She was aware, too, of the carpet beneath her feet and the long polished table with English newspapers spread out upon it.

There was a knock upon the door. She thought for a moment that it might be Lord Lannagh, but Mrs Rance pushed upon the door and quietly stole in.

'We better leave now,' she said. 'You always wished to see the books at the great house – now you have seen them. If the lord himself found you here, I don't know what excuse I would give him, at all at all. He loves this room and spends his nights here reading.' There was anxiety in her voice as she spoke.

'I have met the lord,' Eileen said.

'Oh, God, protect us!' Mrs Rance was horrified. 'I'll surely be dismissed for behaving above my station! I should *never* have brought you here. . . .'

'He told me to borrow whatever book I wish,' Eileen said with a smile.

'And he was not angry?'

'Oh, no! He was charming. He was interested in all that I said.'

'Oh – then, look out, Eileen Horkan, for maybe his intentions are dark! You can never trust a lord. He might have set his eye on you.'

'I'm sure he didn't notice me at all. We spoke only of books.'

'There is more to a lord's life than books. Very well. If the lord gave you a free run of the library, stay where you are. Hackett is in a fury in the kitchen, so I'd better return. The lord made some remark to him about the wine, and I know he will take it out on us.'

Eileen remained on in the library. She took down a volume of the works of Samuel Johnson, printed in Oxford. She sat in the great chair beside the fire and began to read the letter to Mr James Elphinston written in 1750. She had never had the opportunity to read his letters before. They were gentle and easy and very smooth in comparison with his story *Rasselas, Prince of Abyssinia.* The quality of the paper in each page, the firmness of the print made the letters easy to read. She did not notice the time pass.

Suddenly the door was opened with a rough shove and Hackett appeared with a silver tray carrying a bottle of brandy and a glass. His eyes bulged with surprise when he saw Eileen Horkan sitting in the lord's armchair reading a book. It was an unbelievable sight – it made no sense. His anger, suppressed for the last two hours, broke. The bottle and the glass rattled on the silver tray.

'Get out of here, you Horkan bitch! Get out, before I throttle you! I will not be accountable for my actions. You damn upstart, coming up here and setting yourself down as lady of the house!' He banged down the tray on the table and pointed to the library door. 'Out, or I'll leave the mark of my boot on your peasant backside! You have gone above yourself this time with your airs and your graces.' His face began to twitch in anger, and his words became garbled. He would have brought his clenched hand down on her face, but something in her eyes prevented him from doing so. He had made one fatal mistake during the evening and he had no wish to make another. She looked down at the page and continued to read. Fury bottled up within him again and he began to scream.

'What are you doing? By what right are you here? You have no right to be here! Who invited you to this room? Is the great lord going to horse you?'

'She is my invited guest, Hackett,' Lord Lannagh spoke

from behind him. 'I invited her to sit in my library and read whatever book she wishes. Now, attend to the guests. See that the Misses Dillon are accompanied home by one of the servant girls. Have my coach in readiness to take Miss Eileen Horkan home at her convenience. I think you owe an apology to her.'

Hackett was dumbfounded. In one short evening his power in the house seemed to be failing. He had made two serious mistakes, one brought on by the other. Now he had to apologise to somebody he detested. He dragged the apology from his tongue. When he finished he was dismissed and reeled down the corridor in confusion.

Eileen had not lost her composure during the whole event. She still held the book in her hand. Lord Lannagh sat in the deep armchair opposite her and said, simply: 'Read for me.'

She began letter twenty-four. '"I am still confined in Skie. We were unskilled travellers and imagined that the sea was an open road, which we could pass at pleasure. . . ."'

He knit his fingers, rested his chin upon them and listened. She read in a clear voice, her head inclined towards the open book, the fine column of neck showing above the edging of lace. She was not aware that he was observing her.

When she finished the letter she looked at him.

'That was delightful,' he said. 'You admire Johnson?'

'I had not read his letters before. They have a simple charm which his other works do not possess.'

'Then, you shall have all the volumes of his work.' He went to the shelves, took down the eight books and placed them on the table.

'No, I could not take them – they are too fine and, besides, they would leave an awkward gap on your shelves.' She was uncomfortable.

'If there are no awkward gaps on shelves, it means that books are for decoration and not to be read. You received joy from the letters. I wish you would see my library in Kent. I possess some of the actual letters written by Johnson.'

'I have never seen an original letter,' she told him.

'Well, you shall. When I return to England I will have one sent to you.' He resumed his seat and looked again at her. 'Now, tell me about your life. Tell me how you came to possess all your literary knowledge.'

She felt at ease with this man. Nobody had ever listened to

her before. She told him in detail how Father Coady had taught her about books and how she had come to read Latin with facility, and neither of them noticed time slipping away.

It was three o'clock in the morning when Eileen finally left the house. Hackett had been called upon to wrap the books and carry them to the carriage. His manners were controlled and subservient. When he announced that the carriage was ready, Lord Lannagh accompanied her down the great carpeted staircase to the main hall. The lights still burned in the chandeliers.

Leading her to the door of the carriage, Lord Lannagh held her arm while she entered. Then, expressing the hope to see her again, he closed the door. The carriage moved away into the darkness, but as it passed out through the gates she looked back. He was standing at the great door and the lights still glowed in the library.

13

MYLES SPENT TWO DAYS IN CASHEL, enjoying the comfort of a warm bed, simple food and good wine. The men of the village explained to him the geography of Mayo on the great map which they spread out on a deal table while at regular intervals the women came and left the house where Ned Kenny lay. On the second day, just before he was due to leave for Northport, Myles asked to visit the wounded man.

'You will not like what you are going to see,' the woman watching told him before they entered.

Myles looked at the mass of living wounds on Ned Kenny's back. It was without a patch of safe white skin.

'His mind will never be stable again,' said the woman harshly. 'It was rough justice – too rough.'

'We got our revenge.'

'We did, but not enough!' The woman turned away in disgust. 'He is still alive, the man who gave orders for the whipping. The boys made a mistake.'

Brian Burke and Myles made their way out through the valley as the first light poured down through the narrow defile. Looking eastwards Myles could see a vast expanse of bogland and beyond that Croagh Patrick, its flanks running down to the sea. Blue smoke drifted from the surface of the bog. He thought for a moment that the undergrowth might be on fire, .

but then he noticed the small cabins, low and squat, with smoke issuing through the doors. As they approached, Myles had a chance to see the inhabitants, hungry and frightened. In some cases people did not even live in cabins but in holes dug in ditches. No section of the land was left untilled: the potatoes had been planted in lazy beds, wide and black, and small stalks were appearing.

Brian Burke said nothing as they walked along. Sometimes the children came down to the roadside to look at them and call out greetings in Irish, but mostly they stayed at a distance, their eyes filled with fear. The people were famished and poorly dressed, their bodies dirty, the old women haggard from child-bearing. They drew kelp up from the sea in square osier baskets slung on their backs. They had the appearance of beasts of burden, their backs and heads bent towards the land as they moved forward.

'These are the people you expect to take up arms against the landlord and the land agent,' Brian Burke said. 'They have been beaten into the earth. They live like animals. No revolution would set its seeds here.

'This is your noble Irish race! There are too many poor, and they have no heart for an insurrection. They have barely the heart to live. All day they sit around their turf fires eating potatoes and drinking milk if they are fortunate enough to possess a cow. Potatoes in the morning and potatoes at midday and potatoes in the evening, and if they waken at night more potatoes.' Brian Burke's words were charged with fatalism. He, too, was visiting a strange impoverished country. His own village was not yet part of the general destitution.

'They cannot be left to die!' Myles said angrily.

'They have two ways out of their condition. One is that they die and are buried in a ditch. The second is that they take the sailing ship out of Northport and go to America. Only the fortunate make their way across the sea.' He pointed to the wide bay to the north. A sailing ship was moving slowly through the innumerable islands. They could see men clambering up the rigging, small and animated.

'That is one of Michael Barrett's ships. The passengers are lucky; it is well manned. Other ships are no more than coffins: every voyage is at the mercy of chance, and the berths are

131

overcrowded. They are not fit to go to sea, but the profits are high.'

They passed along the rough road to Northport. The land became more fertile. Myles Prendergast looked at the landscape with a judicial eye. If there were to be a revolution, it would have a better chance in Galway with its merchants, and he would tell John Burke so when he met him. For the time being he would continue his journey noting the number of troops in the barracks and the best positions to assault if there was a rising.

Their journey took them by the quays and warehouses of Northport. By now Myles was tired after the journey over the rough road and he sat on one of the bollards on the quay while Brian Burke attended to some business. It was a busy place: men with horse-carts ferried goods between the ships and the warehouses, and Myles began to observe the sequence of things about him. The port was divided into two distinct sections; he was in the Protestant section, which was dominated by the merchants. They stood at the doors of the warehouses or at the foot of the gangplanks counting the bags of meal carried from the holds of the ships. They had firm faces and held themselves aloof from the workers. Well dressed, like the French middle class, they seemed only concerned with their goods.

At the gangplank of one of the ships a large group of emigrants were ready to embark for America. They were obviously well-to-do people from the condition of their dress. A merchant checked their tickets and when he was satisfied with them directed them on board. Before they mounted the gangplank there was the tearful departure as they said good-bye to their friends. The sea lanes to America must be marked with bitter tears, Myles thought to himself. He was angry in his heart. The people left their country with a degree of subservience that he had not witnessed in France. They could see nothing wrong with a political system which deprived them of a right to their own land in their own country. He could understand the anger of the old men in Paris.

The ship which would take the emigrants to America, even to Myles's eyes, looked unseaworthy. It lay sluggishly in the water. Patches of raw wood were exposed along the side, and the sails were sloppily secured to the yards. Further down the quay he noticed the granaries. They had large wooden doors which opened outwards, and eight soldiers standing guard beside them. Myles calculated that there would be eight more inside and perhaps ten lodging somewhere in the town. These granaries must be important to the government, and in his mind he began to plan an assault on the place. It was a mental exercise which helped to pass the time.

His line of thought was broken by the arrival of Brian Burke.

'Have you observed everything?'

'It is exactly as you described.'

'And you have seen the emigrants and the ship they are to sail in?'

'Yes.'

'They bring in the corn from America in the ships and store it. When the price is right they sell it on the markets. At the end of the harvest they export the barley, oats and butter to England.'

'And you accept this?'

'I accept what I cannot change. Of what use are oats and flour to the people we passed today? Some of them would not know how to bake bread even if they were given flour, so great is their dependence on the potato.'

'It is an evil system!'

'I know, Myles, but it is so deep and widespread that nothing can cure it. Each year it gets worse. Come with me and I will bring you across the bridge – you will find it friendly there, and there is less chance of being observed by a spy. You may have sharp eyes, but the eyes of the Castle in Dublin are everywhere. They see this harbour as threatened by invasion from the west and they have paid men everywhere.'

Michael Barrett's town stood to the north of the harbour. It had a clear ordered look about it. The engineers had told him that he could not build on the slob lands, but he had set down deep foundations for the quay and the warehouses, and they had not subsided during the years. The old Protestant part, on the southern edge of the harbour, was connected by a bridge, but there was little communication between the two sides. Michael Barrett, in an act of defiance, had built a Catholic church on the summit of a hill so that the spire was never out of view of the Protestant community. It was a spire out of proportion to the small church beside it.

'They may never worship at our altar and they may despise us,' he had told John Burke, 'but they will have to look at that spire every morning they get up!'

The merchants had launched objections to the huge steeple. They stated that in time of war it could be used to direct enemy ships into the bay and that the allegiance of Michael Barrett was doubtful. But the steeple had advanced until it was finally finished, and it stood above the town as a monument to his stubborn quality. The merchants had been more correct in their suspicions than they realised: in the event of an invasion Michael Barrett would have set up lanterns.

When Michael Barrett built his section of the town it became obvious to the government that they would have to build a police barracks there. However, each night the masonry was levelled to the ground, and they only succeeded in building it with a troop of soldiers standing guard night and day. The police never felt comfortable in the Barrett section of the town, and kept a close eye on every ship which sailed into the harbour. It was known that many wanted men had escaped in these ships and that any foreign spy would be welcomed here.

Both sides of the town had flourished over the years: tall ships stood at anchor beside the quays or in the harbour. In the early forties a new source of wealth was added to the town as the stream of emigration began to grow greater and men sought to leave the stricken land. Northport now became the gateway to America.

Michael Barrett, like the other shipowners, was not slow to benefit from this. He set his prices high for those who were not of his blood or breed. He had turned men away from his office who tried to haggle over the price of a fare to America or who had not sufficient money to buy passage, but he never overcrowded his ships. Unscrupulous captains laughed at his caution.

'What would fifty more mean on board a ship? They can be packed in! It means more money.'

'No! We sail with the legal number and we sail well provisioned or not at all,' he insisted. 'I will not have people die at sea. I will not have the sea lane to America littered with corpses.'

134

When he spoke of men dying at sea and sea burials his whole body shook. Only John Burke, sitting on the granite bollard, knew the reason for this agitation.

Michael Barrett was proud of the mark he had left on the town: he had transformed a small huddle of mud cabins into buildings of proportion and order; his warehouses stretched along the harbour front, solid and firm, rising like his own house, three storeys from the cobblestoned street. He had built them for many reasons and he knew that it would be his monument and far more enduring than a cold inscription on a family vault. Burke had laughed at Michael Barrett when he told him of his plans, yet house by house, warehouse by warehouse, he had watched the buildings rise up until they were completed. All the timbers which went into the making of the houses and warehouses had once been ships. John Burke smiled when he recalled Barrett's plan to beat the British timber tax. He had sailed to Canada where he met the ship-builder, Charles Wood, who designed a ship of solid timber – five times thicker than ordinary ships – and John Burke had sailed it back across the Atlantic. When he reached Northport it was taken asunder, piece by piece, and the timber used for building.

A Customs official had watched with dismay on the quayside as carpenters dismantled the ship. Five times John Burke had made the dangerous voyage across the Atlantic in five ships designed for the same purpose. The voyages paid for the buildings of Northport, because three of the ships were sold to timber merchants.

When the Barrett section of the town had been built the two men had sailed again to Canada and commissioned Charles Wood to build two new ships at Anse du Port. They had stayed with him while he built the models and watched while the large models were taken down to a hut by the waterside and set on a trestle table. Outside, the blocks were laid and, gradually, the keels, the backbones of the ships, rose on them. The ships were made from tamarack, a durable wood, light and fast on the water. The shipwrights had scarfed the beams together with huge pegs of timber and iron, and dovetailed the keels until they were indestructible. Charles Wood believed in iron: even when it swelled and corroded it held a beam of

135

timber together. Later, when the ships were launched into the river to ride at anchor until the decks were built and the main masts put in place, the two men knew for certain that they had come to the best shipbuilder of all.

On their first journey from Quebec they carried hides and timber to Liverpool. It was a lucrative trade, and within a year the ships had almost paid for themselves. Even the red bricks which they carried as ballast on their way to Canada were sold for building houses. Michael Barrett was a shrewd speculator, and all his ships were registered in Liverpool. He read the papers avidly, kept a large map of the world in front of him and benefited from the political unrest in Europe. There was always a need to be serviced, whether it was for gunpowder, guns or wool, and Michael Barrett had no political allegiance where his ships were involved.

John Burke had often argued politics with Michael Barrett at the great house. 'You keep your mind to yourself, Michael Barrett. One never knows which side you are on.'

'And it will stay like that. We have made dubious voyages no doubt when we were a little younger, but as you grow older and wealth becomes respectable you have to keep your mind to yourself. Be seen to put a wager on all the horses. In that way you are certain of a winner.'

'It's not my way of doing things,' John Burke said. 'I know what I am and I know what I want, and the gun will get it.'

'Very doubtful, very doubtful,' and Michael Barrett left it at that. But John Burke knew that it had not always been so doubtful in Michael Barrett's mind.

Myles found John Burke counting bales of cow hides. 'I hate the smell of hide, no matter how well cured it is,' he remarked. 'I tell Michael Barrett it filthies the hold of a ship, but he maintains there is good money in it. I prefer to carry grain and wool and people – but come in and we will talk.'

He left one of his relations to count the hides and led the way to Michael Barrett's office. It was a panelled room, with ledgers and maps and a view on to the sea. A portrait of Michael Barrett stood above the mantelpiece.

'The old man in middle age,' John Burke explained. 'He should have been painted in his rough captain's clothes, but he chose to be painted as a Member of Parliament. Politics and the sea, the sea and politics.'

He took a bottle of rum from one of the cabinets and poured out two glasses. 'To your health,' he said by way of toast. 'You will need it.'

They sat down, and John Burke asked directly: 'Have you come to a decision?'

'Yes. As we came along Clew Bay and I watched the ship sailing to America I realised how close it is by sea. I have also observed the granaries guarded by soldiers and obviously stocked with provisions – and I have seen the state of the countryside. No revolution will come out of the boglands; it must be prepared in America.'

'Good. Then, we are in agreement.' John Burke smiled for the first time. 'In three weeks' time I will sail. You will be brought secretly on board. In the meantime you have three weeks in which to travel through Mayo – it will only strengthen your resolution that something must be done. I have to make a run to Liverpool, and when I return I will sail directly to America. It is a long voyage and an important one. There is a new handgun invented in America which is deadly at close range, called a revolver. It carries five charges – five chances instead of one. The organisation in New York has told me about it. It would change things in our favour. Remember what I told you? We will never again go to battle with pikes!'

'You are up to your neck in revolution,' Myles said, chuckling.

'I am, and so are you.' John Burke was deadly serious. 'Spiker, I am told, is a dangerous man, and we should have killed him. Remember, if he lives, we are pitted against a viper. He will take savage reprisals for what we have done to him.' He was silent for a moment, then he said in a more level tone: 'For the time being you must find your own way to Castlebar. The best man to travel with is Gill the poet – nobody takes any notice of him, and the spies see him as no threat to anybody. Go to Molly Ward in Castlebar. She will give you lodgings.'

Myles would have taken his leave at that moment, but there was the sound of feet on the wooden stairs outside. Instantly he jumped to his feet and faced the door, putting his hand in his pocket.

'Relax, Myles Prendergast, no agent or soldier enters this office, and if they did they would not leave.'

A young woman threw the door open and glared at John Burke. Myles started in surprise: it was the girl he had seen while he had hidden at the O'Hares'. She carried a small riding-whip in her hand. She walked directly to the large brown desk and brought the whip down on the surface.

'You sail to America in three weeks' time?' she demanded furiously.

'It is not settled yet. We depend on the weather.' Burke was calm; he had obviously coped with her before in this mood.

'But you have the voyage planned?'

'Yes.'

'And you never told me! You never told me!' she repeated accusingly. 'You promised that you would tell me.'

'I cannot take you to America without your father's permission,' he persisted.

'I am not a child, John Burke! If I can take a ship from London, I can sail in one to America. You have put it off for too long. My father is growing old and he still does not let me enter the business. When he is dead I will have to take charge of the ships.'

'The seas to America are treacherous.'

'Not with you as captain.'

'You must have his permission.' John Burke was emphatic.

'I have my own permission! He fobbed me off. He told me I should travel to the Viceregal Ball in Dublin. He even suggested I should be seeking a husband!' She was outraged by the thought. 'Well, I sail in the next ship to America. I am tired of the land.'

Myles Prendergast watched her, appreciating her beauty. Her luxuriant red hair fell on her shoulders. Her figure, emphasised by her riding-dress, was elegant and strong, and her whole body was vibrant with energy. Her face was flushed in anger, but the shine remained delicate like Sèvres porcelain.

'Ease your anger, Gráinne. Ease your anger,' John Burke said uncomfortably. 'Your father is an old man. He needs your care.'

'He is strong and clear of mind. He plays upon my emotions. He will not let me have a free life of my own. You know how much I wish to sail to America; I have *always* longed to go there. It is a new place and has a new way of life. I feel I am land-locked at the moment.' Anger was giving way to frustration; Myles watched the flushed face regain its composure. 'I cannot endure the land any longer. I ride my horse all day long through the woods and along the shore until he is worn out. I am going mad.'

'You are ill-mannered,' John Burke retorted. 'Your father wasted his money sending you to that finishing school in England. You charge in here like one of the fishwomen and make demands on me which I cannot fulfil.'

'You can speak to him,' she insisted. 'He listens to you. I demand to go to America! I have my rights, and you have broken your promise to me.' She banged her riding-whip on the table, and her eyes flared in anger.

'Control yourself!' John Burke said angrily. 'We have company.'

Gráinne turned towards the man who sat in her father's chair, looking at her coldly, intently.

'May I introduce you?' John Burke said sarcastically. 'This is Myles Prendergast from France. He is here to do some business.'

'Then what is he doing in my father's chair? It is an insolent gesture that a stranger should walk in here and behave as if he had gained possession of the place! He is no gentleman – a gentleman rises when a lady enters the room.'

'I have seen no lady enter the room. I have seen a wild woman in anger. You did not give him a chance to rise!' John Burke roared at her.

Myles Prendergast stood up. He was tall and wide-shouldered. He looked at Gráinne with hard cold eyes which frightened her for a moment. She regained her self-possession.

'I shall excuse myself,' he said in Irish.

'He is French and he speaks Irish! How do you explain that, John Burke? He may be one of those American revolutionaries that are smuggled into the country in my father's ships.'

'Hold your tongue, girl. You speak rash words and you make accusations which could lead you into trouble.'

'What trouble?'

Myles Prendergast observed their angers. Both of them had lost control, and he feared that John Burke might disclose

139

more than he should. He turned to Gráinne Barrett and spoke firmly in Irish.

'I am the son of an Irish émigré. I am visiting Ireland for my father who has often spoken of this area. After the rebellion he left in one of your father's ships. That is why I am here.'

'With a gun in your pocket?' Gráinne said directly, her eyes burning with anger. 'I saw you put your hand in your coat pocket when I entered the room. I am sure you carry a weapon and I am sure you would have used it.'

'I would.'

'Then, you are here on political business, *everybody* is here on political business,' she said dismissively. 'The spies and the police and the soldiers who guard the granaries are here on political business. None of them will solve our problems.'

'You have no interest in problems?' he asked mildly.

'I have no interest in problems I cannot solve,' she said, moving to the window and pointing to the ships. 'The ships and the sea I can understand. There is no politics on the sea, and the sea is a republic.'

'Have you seen the hunger? Have you watched the emigration?' he pressed, irritated by her irresponsibility.

'I have. But I cannot answer these problems.'

'Someone has to.'

'And do you think that *you*, newly arrived from France, are going to solve problems which have been created over seven hundred years? You should talk to my father some time, or to Frederick Cavendish. They will tell you that the country is finished.'

'They are old men,' he said.

'Men who did more for this country in their time than all the French émigrés put together.'

'We have our means of helping. We have not forgotten this land and the sorrow it has endured.' He was surprised to find himself on the defensive.

'You are dreamers. You are like Gill the poet – but at least he *knows* he is a dreamer.'

'Revolutions come out of dreams. It happened in France.'

'It will not happen here. I do not belong to the politics of Ireland because I know that politics is futile.'

'Then, we differ in our attitude.'

'Yes.'

They had fought each other to a stalemate. They looked at each other hotly.

'I am sure everything has been said,' John Burke remarked to clear the silence.

'Yes,' said Gráinne abruptly; and grabbing the horsewhip she left the room, shouting over her shoulder: 'I am not finished with you, John Burke.'

Myles Prendergast moved to the window and looked down on the quay. He watched her hurry across to her horse and mount it. She looked up at the window and then turned her back.

'She is wild,' John Burke said behind him, 'and the man to tame her has not yet been born.'

Myles returned to his seat, trying to banish the red-headed girl from his mind.

'Before we leave for America I wish to have information concerning the military strength of the fortifications.' John Burke fiddled with his pen. 'Could you bring it to this office, or get word to somebody you trust in Castlebar?' He was firm and businesslike.

'I will,' Myles said, getting up to go to the door.

'You will find Gill in one of the public houses. He is as much part of what we are as the hunger and the military presence and the spies and Gráinne Barrett!'

They shook hands, and Myles Prendergast walked down the stairs and out on to the quays, looking up the road in the direction taken by Gráinne Barrett.

By now she was riding along the long sea-strand, crying at her anger and the bitter turn of her tongue. She had insulted Myles Prendergast. He must think that she was a hard bitter young woman. He must hate her like all young men hated her for her strong character. The wind was in her hair, and the horse kicked up the sea-suds about her.

14

'ONE THOUSAND POUNDS IN RATES!' Kenrick roared. 'Do you think I'm minting gold sovereigns or something? You have the gall to knock on the door of this house with such demands? Go down to the shopkeepers in the Main Street and make your demands on them. You're getting no thousand pounds here.' A net of purple veins broke out in his face. He beat out the logic of his situation on to the table with a loaded bullwhip.

'They pay the best they can. It is the absentee landlords who are in arrears,' protested Edward Silken.

'We are all in arrears, every single one of us. I have to see that the lords receive their rents in England. That is my job. You can take up the question with them.'

'But, as their representative, you can surely administer their funds?'

'I've put up with enough from you for one day. I have work to do. Take it up with the landlords in London.'

'They *will* have to be contacted. The workhouse is heavily in debt!'

'Well, contact them, and don't come here with your demands for money.'

'They are obliged to pay by law,' Edward Silken reminded him hesitantly. At the mention of the word 'law' Kenrick took his whip and crashed it down on the table.

'Law? *I'm* the law in these parts – so don't get any fancy

notions into your head about putting the law on me! We need more hard law to keep down the Whiteboys. You heard what they did to Colonel Spiker?'

'Yes.'

'They tore the back off him with whips and *they* are the ones I'm supposed to feed with a thousand pounds! They and their kind.'

'Only the poor flock to the workhouse and they are desperate. They belong to no organisation.'

'What would you know about them, a fancy boy from England and paid well for dealing out gruel to paupers? Get out of my sight or I'll set the dogs on you!'

With that the interview had finished, and the master of the workhouse made his way out of the house. He mounted his horse and left the valley. The paupers who crowded into the workhouse were caused by Kenrick's clearances – it was he, more than anybody else, who flattened the villages. Silken had seen Kenrick at work with his crowbar brigade backed up by the constabulary and the soldiers; he was the most frightening figure he had ever encountered in his life. Very few in the town of Castlebar would stand up to him, and when he made his way down the main street, followed by his bully boys, children fled down the archways and men stepped aside.

When the workhouse opened it seemed to Edward Silken it could serve a charitable need. It would be a refuge for paupers. He objected to the separation of families who arrived at the workhouse door, but this was their last refuge and they could at least be fed. But in the past few years the number of paupers in the towns had been swelling. In Castlebar they were sleeping in archways and even under the flat tombstones in the graveyard. If Kenrick continued his work, then there would be a flood of paupers banging on the gates of the workhouse. If the potato crop failed completely, then no one could cope with the disaster which would follow.

A heavy despair was growing in his mind. His energies were weakened by brooding. He had neglected his duties about the workhouse and now spent hours looking into the fire. He wondered if he should return to London and find a post there in some government office filling ledgers with neat figures. It did not matter what the figures represented – he was well connected in London.

His thoughts as he rode were disturbed by a small urchin pulling at his riding-boots. He looked down. She was like a small woman with large staring eyes. Her face was pinched, and she had a shawl wrapped round her.

'Would the gentleman please have a penny?' she asked. 'If the gentleman has a penny, I'll pray to God for him this very night. Upon my soul I will.'

He searched through his pockets, found some small change and handed her the money. Clasping it in her small hand, she thanked him. Then she ran across the road into one of the dark hovels.

The inhabitants led a twilight existence which he would never, never understand. He belonged to another world, a world of ordered houses and ordered lives where the women washed their bodies, had gentle breeding and sat down to warm meals. He would not bring a woman to Castlebar. She would not understand the ways of the people, the town with its twisting streets and secretive lanes, its confusion of language and its filth.

The Giant, as he was called by the inmates, had been listening for the sound of the master's horse's hoofs, and inserted a large key in the lock of the workhouse gate and turned it. Edward Silken entered and dismounted.

'Where is Jimmy the Sailor?' he asked.

'With Mr Cavendish, sir. He is filling him with drink up in your rooms.'

'Has a fire been started?'

'It has, sir. Jimmy the Sailor forgets nothing. It is as hot as the heart of hell!'

'Good.'

Frederick Cavendish looked into the large fire which Jimmy the Sailor had brought to life with a hand bellows.

'Begod, Mr Cavendish, but you would want heat to heal your bones in this place. Heat's a great thing. I don't know why I ever came back from Africa.'

'What part of Africa would you have settled in, Jimmy?'

'As far away from the Sahara Desert as I could get.'

'There is only one river through the Sahara Desert, Jimmy,

and that takes you to the port of Jazabelle,' Frederick Cavendish told him.

'Don't talk to me about Jazabelle. I was often there and saw women with nothing on at all. They would give queer thoughts to any man.'

Cavendish invented a new port in a new country whenever he encountered Jimmy, and without fail Jimmy could always describe it in detail, especially if it were in Africa and peopled with women who had nothing on. He had drifted into the workhouse in 1843 and by 1846 he was an indispensable part of the place. He had the gait of a sailor and he always wore his captain's cap to the side, but Edward Silken could never determine if he had been a sailor or not. His conversation was filled with nautical idiom, but Frederick Cavendish maintained that he never sailed in a ship and that he was an ingratiating imposter. But, like a wise fool in a tragedy, he always brought comic relief during black moments.

'There is wine in the cabinet, sir. All the way from Spain, a great country altogether; I was there several times, but I never picked up any of the language.'

'Bad for my gout, Jimmy. Bad for my gout.'

'Have the pleasure now, sir, and endure the pain at your leisure,' he told him, fetching the bottle.

Frederick Cavendish eased himself on the chair. The pain which tore at his toes and leg during the morning had now eased. He had been told by the doctor that his gout was due to intemperance and idleness. The medical books told him that he should avoid night studies and intense thinking. Both he could not avoid. It was an ailment with which he would have to live.

He was chuckling over some recent news he had received: an old general called Leconate had fired on the King of France as he was returning from his drive in the forest of Fontainebleau.

'He should have taken better aim,' he remarked to his wine-glass. 'At least they haven't forgotten that the Republic was hard fought for.' It eased his gout.

What really worried him was that he had discovered the fact that famine was already beginning. He had examined some of the potato crop in the locality, and some of the seed potatoes were beginning to rot. If the blight which had already

145

attacked the potato crop in mainland Britain was carried to Ireland, and if it were virulent, then peasants, weakened by previous famines, would perish in thousands. The gombeen men would now have a stranglehold on the cottiers. To buy seed potatoes they would have to borrow money from them at twenty per cent. Cavendish detested these men. He had once written that the gombeen men should be refused the Eucharist; particularly Kenrick, who lived in a great house at the edge of the town.

His life was ending, and a fatal famine was gathering about him. He felt it in his spirit. The workhouse could not carry the number of paupers who would seek refuge there.

Edward Silken entered the room. 'Good evening, Frederick,' he said. 'I see that Jimmy the Sailor has administered your poison to you.'

'So he has, and we had another discussion on an Africa that exists in our imaginations.'

Edward Silken took off his coat and placed it on a table. He filled out a measure of wine and sat opposite Frederick Cavendish. His face was ashen and tired.

'Well,' said Cavendish, 'you bearded the lion in his den. Did you receive any satisfaction from him?'

'No. The man lacks all breeding.'

'The worst type of Irishman ever created. A sullen ox perfectly bred to serve his English master. You will find one in every barony between Castlebar and Dublin. "Yes, my Lord," and "No, my Lord," and "At my Lord's pleasure". The absentee landlords depend on him, the very keystone of their temple. And about him you will find his bully-boys and his minions.'

Edward Silken looked at the fire for some moments. He reflected on all that had passed between him and Kenrick up at the big house.

'I was almost sick in his presence. I could see the purple veins stand out on his large nose. He was repulsive.'

'That is why I christened him "Old Blue Nose",' commented Cavendish. 'I have not vented half my anger on him yet. I think I will have to wheel out the heavy type and find some more suitable adjectives for him. The pen is mightier than the bullwhip.'

'There is no way you can tame or temper that monster,' Edward Silken said bitterly.

'Well, I'm not going to let this town live in perpetual fear of a hired servant because he rants and roars and bangs his loaded whip against counters in public houses. There is no servant woman at Lord Lannagh's house but that he has not taken his pleasure with. It's well known, and I might as well print it.'

'I wish I possessed your courage. I felt less than brave today as I made my way up the avenue. I sometimes think I am not suitable to this position – I should never have left London.'

Frederick Cavendish did not wish to answer the doubt. The workhouse bell sounded dolefully outside as if it had been cast from dull metal. The paupers would now be making their ways across the male and female quadrangles for their gruel and milk eaten from pewter bowls. They were as listless as the bell whose sound presided over all their movements, destroying thought and freedom of action. Edward Silken knew how many of them were sitting down for their thin meals, and soon he would not be able to accommodate any more.

'Where will it end?' he asked.

'You are seeing only the beginning of things. Ten years ago I described exactly what would happen. I spent two weeks in gaol for my troubles. Yet everything I forecast has already come true. The blight which has hit England will hit this country. If the potato fails totally, the people fail totally. There will not be enough food to go round, and the corn and the animals will continue to be exported from the country. With the starvation will come the fever. I wish I could take a brighter view.' He paused. 'The rate-collectors will have to be more diligent in collecting arrears. After all, the workhouses were established to take those who were dispossessed of their land. If Kenrick clears out villages, then his masters will have to face the debts he creates.'

Frederick Cavendish took another glass of wine, noticing that Edward Silken, too, was beginning to drink heavily. His sharp eye had counted the number of empty bottles in the cabinet when Jimmy the Sailor had opened the door. When Edward Silken had arrived in Castlebar he had been a fresh young man moved by the noblest motives. Since then he had grown old with worry and soured by the hostile landscape that had the bitterness of gall.

147

'Would you ever return to London?' he asked Frederick Cavendish.

'No. I am too old to move now. I am settled in my ways, and at seventy-eight I do not think I have many more years to live. No, I would not change my circumstances.' He checked his gold watch and stirred from his seat. 'It is time for me to remove myself. The day has been passed in a soft armchair. I have other calls to make on my way home.'

Silken accompanied him to the large iron gate. Jimmy the Sailor was waiting for them. He carried a large collection of keys on a key ring secured to his belt. When he walked they rattled against one another and gave him a sense of importance.

'And I shall give to thee the keys of the workhouse of Castlebar,' Frederick Cavendish told him as he watched him ceremoniously unlock the great gate.

'Good night, my Lord. Good night, my Lord,' Jimmy said as he closed the gate behind the broad figure of Frederick Cavendish. 'There is a moon to light your way. It reminds me of nights in Africa and the naked women singing and them wearing nothing.'

'How many in the building tonight, Jimmy?'

'Four hundred and three, but three of them will be dead tomorrow morning and that will give you an even four hundred, so we'll save on bread. The last bird-song they ever heard was today. We live in bad times surely, sir.'

Frederick Cavendish had a strange admiration for the monkey-like figure, in the constable's coat and the sea captain's cap, knowing that he would survive come what may. He was not so sure of Edward Silken, who had left him at the main door.

'Keep the rigging in order and the flags flying, Jimmy, and don't trail your anchor,' Frederick Cavendish told him.

'Like myself, my Lord, you have a great knowledge of the sea,' he grinned.

'And of Africa, too.'

'Ah, and of Africa, too.'

Frederick Cavendish made his way towards the town.

Jimmy the Sailor knocked upon Edward Silken's door at ten o'clock. He carried a lantern with him. They made their way along the main corridor in silence, the swinging lantern casting moving shadows on the wall. Jimmy the Sailor knew everybody in the workhouse by name, he knew where they came from and what had happened to them; for such details his memory was faultless. He was not interested in the dark events which caused all the hardship; to him the workhouse was an independent world of its own, a country whose inhabitants were increasing each year. He was aware, too, of the strain on the food resources kept in the large locked bins in the storehouse. Some instinct told him that his survival depended on such knowledge.

Opening the door which led to one of the men's dormitories, Edward Silken felt nausea. He could never grow accustomed to the smell of stale urine, the filth and the sweat which seemed to have impregnated the plaster on the walls, no matter how often they limed the walls and changed the rush bedding: a cobbled drain ran between the raised platforms on which were placed the timber boxes where the men slept. Jimmy the Sailor held up the lantern and peered into each bed. He listened for a moment at one and said, 'He's all right, sir,' and then passed on.

Sometimes a gaunt figure would spring up when they shone the light over the bed, an empty stare in his eyes, then sink back again on to the rushes. There were fifty in each dormitory. The air was heavy, and the staleness was almost as offensive as potato rot. In the third dormitory Jimmy the Sailor stopped at a bed and listened again.

'He's gone, sir. He was one of the ones I had in mind. I knew that he would never make it. It was written all over him when he was taking exercise in the yard today. He's been failing for a fortnight. He's from beyond the mountains, evicted three months ago by Kenrick. The cold and damp got into his lungs. He has no one left but his daughter in America. I'll enter his name in the book tomorrow. Don't worry, sir – I'll have him out of here in half an hour and coffined.'

Edward Silken could never understand how Jimmy the Sailor managed to remove the corpses from the wards at night-time. Jimmy had set up his own system, and Silken did not examine it too closely. He knew that the next day the body would be coffined and on its way by handcart to the cemetery. There were always six coffins in readiness at the storehouse, plain oblong boxes without cross or ornament. Each day a doleful procession made its way through the town following the handcart to the plot set aside for them in the cemetery just above the lake.

When they had finished the inspection, Jimmy the Sailor wished the master a good night and disappeared back into the mystery of the workhouse. Edward Silken wondered if this little man, compounded of jester and villain, ever slept. He entered his room and sank into the large chair before the fire. Pouring himself some wine from the bottle on the table beside him, he began to drink. It helped him to forget.

Jimmy the Sailor quickly made his way to the dormitory where the corpse lay under a thin blanket. He began to search the body and soon discovered what he was looking for. He opened the small purse, suspended from about the neck on leather thongs, and poured out the contents on to the palm of his hand. He gasped in surprise: it contained a sovereign among the small pieces of money – it was a rare chance to find a sovereign on a workhouse corpse. He had found only five since he arrived at the workhouse, and that was a long time ago. Next he searched the pockets and discovered a lump of tobacco and a small knife. He would sell the knife, but had good use for the tobacco.

He took his lantern and made his way to another dormitory. There he found the Giant sleeping in a double space in one of the corners. The Giant understood simple orders and preferred to be told what to do at each moment of the day, otherwise he became irritable and moody. The other inmates of the workhouse were afraid of his mad fits, which had occurred less and less frequently since Jimmy the Sailor took charge of him.

Jimmy the Sailor shook him from his deep sleep. He snorted awake and asked: 'Is it morning? Is it morning?'

'No, Timmy, but we have work to do. Look what I brought you!' He held up the lump of tobacco. 'Enough smoking for a whole week and all for yourself. You know how you like to smoke, Timmy.'

'I love to smoke. I don't know what I would do without you, Jimmy the Sailor. You always put the bit of tobacco my way. What have we to do?'

'Put a man in a coffin. Another soul flew away to heaven tonight. I saw him leaving his body about an hour ago.'

'Was he bright?'

'As bright as the moon and the stars on a good frosty night. The soul was the brightest I have ever seen leaving the workhouse. We had better coffin the body or it will return to haunt us.'

'How is it that *I* never see the souls departing? I was often there when they died, right beside you!'

'I don't know. I don't know. You weren't there at the right time, and maybe it was never dark enough. There is surely some reason for it. Some night you will see one and that will be the night.'

'Did it have wings?'

'Yes, great silver wings. He found them a bit difficult to use at first, seeing that they are not natural to him, but after faltering for a while he managed them fairly well. He perched on the roof for a while and then he was away like the cuckoo at the end of summer.'

'I would have given a quarter of tobacco to see a soul in flight! It must be like the picture you showed me in the book.'

'Just like the picture, all coloured silver with gold in the tips of the feathers.'

'Well, we better get the body over to the outhouse or he will come to haunt me.'

'Yes, we'll do that.'

By now any hardness in the Giant's mind was softened by the visions which Jimmy the Sailor had drawn for him – he had noticed that, for some reason or other, his mind always went quiet when he saw coloured religious pictures. They brought tranquillity to his mind. Jimmy the Sailor had a whole set of them which he often showed the Giant, explaining exactly who the saints were and inventing stories about them as he found necessary.

The Giant drew on his trousers and put on his boots, which Jimmy the Sailor then laced up for him. They then went along the corridors until they came to the dormitory. Carefully the Giant took the corpse from the bed and put it across his shoulder. It was already stiffening and would not bend for him. He held it firmly by the buttocks so that it would not slide on to the floor.

'It's no weight at all,' he said mournfully. 'No weight at all.

There was no meat on him. They seem to get lighter every day.'

'There is hunger outside the walls, Timmy, and from those who straggled in lately and told me of the bad times there will be more hunger.'

'Does that mean I'll have to go without my dinner?'

'No, Timmy. While I'm around you'll never go without your dinner.'

'You promise me that?'

'I promise.'

The Giant followed Jimmy the Sailor as quietly as he could, the corpse slung across his shoulder at an ungainly angle. They made their way across the quadrangle to the outhouse where the coffins were stored. Jimmy took one of his innumerable keys and opened the door. A smell of fresh unpainted timber wafted out at them, and the light of the lantern fell on six coffins slanting against the wall.

'Have we one to fit him?' the Giant asked.

'Let me see now. Try him in this one.' He placed the body against the coffin. It was too short. They tried another coffin. This time it was the correct length. The Giant laid the body on the ground, set the coffin on two trestles and laid the body gently into it.

'He had a sad life, sadder in the end than in the beginning, for he often told me about it. I hope he's happy with the angels.'

'But I thought you said that you saw him flying up to heaven from the roof,' the Giant said querulously.

'And so I did. So I did. But heaven is a long way off, and it might take him a while to make the journey, so if he is not there tonight he'll be there tomorrow night.'

'I see.'

They looked at the corpse for a while, its face pale and tranquil. The Giant took the arms and forced them into a crossed position.

'They always look better with their arms crossed, like Lazarus in the picture you showed me. *He* was laid out properly.'

'Yes, there was nobody ever laid out as well as Lazarus with his white robes and all.'

'Will we, too, rise again, Jimmy?'

'So the promise goes. So the promise goes.'

'Will you be there when I rise, Jimmy?'

'I'll be there bright and early, bright and early.'

15

MYLES PRENDERGAST walked into the heart of the town, his mind
filled with thoughts of the woman he had encountered and the
final moment when their eyes met before she rode up the quay
and out of his vision. As he walked he recalled all that had
happened since he took the coach from Paris to Bordeaux. He
had set out with no clear ideas in his mind except that he was
returning to some mystical island on the western coast of Europe. Now that he was walking on the soil of Ireland, France
seemed a long way away. He had seen the poverty and the
hunger; he had watched men and women embark for America;
he had joined an organisation which seemed to have cells in
Europe and America; and he had met a woman who would haunt
his vision like no other woman haunted it.

He had no difficulty in finding the pub in which Gill was
drinking. Everybody seemed to know who Gill was. When he
entered the pub he did not make direct contact; as always he
sat with his back to the wall and observed the people around
him. He knew that the tall spare man who raucously called
for whiskey was Gill. He was drunk and careless in his talk
and threw back the glass of whiskey while he called for another
one, pushing men aside as he tried to get near the counter.

'Silence,' he roared in the crowded bar. 'I'm Gill the poet and
I'll give you one of my songs.'

Nobody took any notice of him.

153

'Will you shut up!' he called again.

'Shut up yourself, Gill!' somebody called back to him. 'Let us drink in peace. We have more to do than listen to your raucous voice.'

'You have no respect for your betters,' he roared.

He made his way back to his seat. As he did he lunged forward and fell across a table, knocking over some of the glasses. A hand reached out and pushed him off on to the floor. He rolled over and tried to rise. A man passing out to the latrine kicked him on the backside, and Gill shot forward on his face. It was then that Myles Prendergast moved. He walked over to where Gill lay on the floor, bent down and helped him to his feet. His eyes were dazed.

'I'll sing a song for a glass of whiskey,' Gill mumbled drunkenly.

'No, there is no need for you to sing a song. I'll buy you a drink anyway.'

As Gill drank the whiskey the man who had kicked him returned. He had a rough heavy face without feeling.

'Do you want me to soften the other cheek of your arse, Gill?' he asked. The crowd began to laugh. He caught up Gill's glass of whiskey and poured it over his face.

'Lick it off the floor, Gill!' he taunted.

What happened next came as a surprise. Myles Prendergast hit the man on the chin with a clenched fist. It was a hard fast blow. It cracked a bone in the man's jaw and he slumped on to the floor.

'That's my brother you hit!' a man said, rushing up to Myles Prendergast. He was given no further time to protest. Myles hit him on the side of the head with deadly accuracy, and he fell beside his brother. Myles took out a small pistol from his pocket and pointed it at their dazed faces.

'One more word from either of you and I'll blow out whatever brains you have. Now, run and keep running until you reach home.'

They dragged themselves off the floor and moved to the door. 'We'll get you, Gill, when you are alone, and we will make it up to you,' they shouted through the door.

Myles Prendergast took Gill by the elbow and brought him to a quiet corner. Men watched in silence, and moved away from him when he sat down.

'You are a gentleman, I can see,' Gill told him. 'As for the rest, they are only pig-dirt. They take advantage of me in drink.'

'*I* will buy you more drink. But hold your tongue; I wish to talk to you.'

'I'll keep my peace.'

Myles ordered a small bottle of whiskey and placed it in front of Gill.

'Now, what do you want from me?'

'I wish to travel with you to Castlebar.'

'Why with me?'

'Because I do not want to attract attention to myself and I do not know Castlebar.'

'Well, I'm your man. One of the carters will take us. We can lie in the back of the cart and look up at the sky.'

'When will you be able to travel?'

'When I have finished the whiskey.'

'Very well,' Myles agreed. 'Now, tell me about your poetry.'

'Once upon a time I wrote not only good poetry but I wrote great poetry. They know it will be remembered. But the gift left me – poetry is a fickle mistress – and when it passed I began to drink. I once enjoyed the patronage of Michael Barrett, but that, too, passed. Now I live amongst bogmen and drink their swill. But I have seen better days. I am a spoiled priest. They all know that: it is no secret. I went to the seminary in Paris and then I took up with a low woman. I could have been happy in Paris, for I knew some of the language. I could have looked at the happenings of Europe from a chair on a pavement or a seat in the park. I once saw Napoleon ride past on a white charger. It was soon after the time he came from Russia. He was a worried man. I hated him. He led young men out to die. Well, I'd prefer to die of drink, something which I am doing now.'

Myles was interested in the ennui which seemed to pervade the mind of Gill. But he did not permit himself the luxury of having pity on him. Perhaps Gill's answers to his own questions were the best solutions which could be found.

'I outlived Napoleon,' he bragged. 'With all his splendour he had no regency over death. He was a tyrant and caused the death of many young men. An upstart from Corsica.'

Gill talked endlessly and recited some of his poems. Myles

Prendergast enjoyed some of them. Many of them were pure doggerel.

'Do you know Gráinne Barrett?' Myles asked.

'I wrote a poem for her once. Oh, she is the beautiful lady but she is one of the Barretts and, like them all, wild and awkward. Her mother died under strange circumstances. But she is one of us. They sent her to a fine school in England to give her the English polish, but she would prefer to climb a mast with the men. She has all the beauty of her race. That is why I wrote a poem for her. I wouldn't do it for Michael Barrett. He is stubborn. I tried to make amends, but he would have none of it. I was kicked out of the house by a scullion and fed with slops the last time I visited the house. That's no way to treat a poet. Look at my boots! The toes are sticking out – it's cold when you have no proper boots. But I'll get even with Michael Barrett. Some day the gift will return, and I'll write a satire on him. He wasn't always Michael Barrett the merchant and the half-English gentleman he is today.'

Eventually they left the public house and made their way to the outskirts of the town where they waited at the side of the road until a cart came up the hill loaded up with hay.

'Will you give us a lift to Castlebar, McTigue?' Gill shouted as the carter approached.

'Lie on the top of the hay but don't fall off,' he directed, waving them aboard.

They climbed on to the cart, and Gill stretched out on the luxuriant hay looking up at the sky. 'Now, if soldier boys come by riding two by two, sir, you bury yourself in the hay and let me do the talking.'

'Very well.' Myles burrowed down.

Gill was half-asleep from drink when they heard the sound of horses' hoofs. He shook himself awake and looked up from the comfortable bed he had made for himself.

'Declare that you should say there is a man with me, McTigue, or we could be in trouble! You know they are out searching, and I can see from here that one of them is a constable from Northport. Leave the talking to me.'

He began to sing as the horsemen approached and stopped the carter.

'Do you carry any cargo other than hay?' the constable asked.

'Only the poet Gill, only the poet Gill,' replied McTigue.

Gill cried drunkenly from the top of the cart: 'I was writing a poem in praise of the great Queen Victoria and I have been rudely interrupted by her minions!'

'Enough lip from you, Gill,' the constable shouted up at him. 'You should not be on the open road. Hold to the town of Northport where you can be identified. There is a search on for the Whiteboys who flogged Colonel Spiker.'

'Oh, I'll keep to the town of Northport. Declare if I won't return to Northport on the very morrow.'

'On your way and less lip from you, Gill, in the presence of policemen. I cannot always give you a fool's pardon.'

With that remark the soldier and the constable passed down the road towards Northport.

'A fool's pardon, a fool's pardon, that's the way they treat quality. I hope a few Whiteboys waylay them and skin the arse off them – then they can call out for two fool's pardons.'

Myles Prendergast lay deep in the hay until the danger had passed, and then sat up. 'That was sharp thinking, Gill,' Myles congratulated him.

'Always play the jester when in danger,' Gill told him.

'Take the constable's advice and return to Northport as quickly as you can,' warned Myles. 'These are dangerous times, and I suspect that the soldiers are everywhere.'

'Tomorrow early I'll be on my way back. I smell danger when it is on the wind. I was in the barracks for questioning before, and it's no comfortable thing to be behind bars and not a drop of drink in the house. Two days they held me on some trumped-up charge because I wrote a ballad about the local judge. I disclaimed all knowledge of it and said that it was written by an inferior poet. So I'll keep out of danger's way.'

The cart made its way into the centre of Castlebar. It was market day, and the great square was filled with bustle and activity. Myles and Gill slipped down from the hay and moved easily through the dense mass of people.

'I'll show you Molly Ward's pub,' Gill told him, 'but I may not enter. I have been barred. I insulted the soldiery there one day and nearly created a war. I am *persona non grata*. But it is a great town for drink, and there are other shebeens that will welcome Gill's company and custom. Your best approach

157

is through the back entrance. You will come in from the stable-yard and you won't be noticed.'

'Thanks, Gill, and here is some money – but don't remain in Castlebar. You could be picked up. If you mention me to anyone, I will break every bone in that body of yours. You understand?'

'I declare I never set eyes on you before,' said Gill, backing away.

'Be out of this town tomorrow or you might be getting a visit from the Whiteboys.'

'I wipe the dust of Castlebar from the soles of my feet early tomorrow morning.'

'Good.' Myles handed over some money and made his way down the archway and into the stable-yard.

The pub smelt of hard tobacco and stale drink. The lighting was dim and shabby and opaque with tobacco smoke. Molly Ward stood behind the bar, at some distance from him, engaged in conversation with a group of soldiers. She had a heavy body, and the skin formed in folds under her eyes in her rough face. She wore a coarse apron on which she dried her hands after she had carried black measures of drink to the soldiers. She observed the stranger, looking at him for a moment and then turning away. Later she made her way down behind the long counter to where he stood.

'What's your wish?' she asked.

'A whiskey.'

'Good. Are you a stranger to town? I haven't seen you before. We don't get a lot of strangers – it's better for them to keep to the hotels.' Her voice was tuneless and deep, and she looked with suspicion on him.

'I was directed here.'

'You were, were you? From where?'

'Paris,' he said quietly.

She looked at him for a moment. Her suspicion grew deeper. 'I know of nobody in Paris.' She was becoming restless. The soldiers were calling for more drink. 'I'll hear more about this when I have time. You come at a bad day when the soldiers are spending their pay. Sit in the corner there, and I'll talk to you later.'

She returned to the soldiers and joined in their conversation. Later she joined in their singing, but when they tired of it and

158

returned to their normal conversation she came over to Myles.

'Who mentioned my name in Paris?'

'Your brother Hugh.'

'I am a single lady who runs a public house. I have no brother in Paris.'

'He is dead now. He died some years ago, but he is survived by a wife and two sons.'

'How do you know these things?'

'I have come from Paris,' Myles said evenly. 'I was told that this was a safe house.'

'My brother Hugh, he was sprightly on his feet?' Her eyes gleamed.

'No, Molly. Hugh walked with a limp. He was wounded in his flight from Ballinamuck.'

'Then, you are well welcome to this house. Go now and walk through the town – keep to the populated places and return here at nightfall. I'll be ridding the place of the soldiers then.'

Myles spent four hours walking about the town, noting the people and the buildings. He went as far as the workhouse and looked at the imposing walls and the high gables that rose above them. People had gathered at the great gates and were waiting to be admitted. They chattered in Irish, and he pretended that he did not understand them, but from their talk he gathered that they had been dispossessed by Kenrick the landlord's agent. Some of their relations had gone to America and would pay the passage money for them when they had put their savings together. Many of them had walked a great distance and had not eaten for a whole day, and he saw that many wore no shoes and their feet were bleeding.

Molly Ward was well known through the town for her foul tongue. She could swear in both Irish and English, and only soldiers and the lower classes frequented her bar. Her outward vulgarity, however, belied the fact that Molly Ward was a highly intelligent woman. The respectable women of the town might pass to the other side of the street when she approached – she was known as a Soldier's Judy – and even in church they made it their business not to sit close to her, but, like Jimmy the Sailor, she played many parts and knew more of what was happening in the town than the constabulary.

Her brother had followed General Humbert to Ballinamuck, and after the defeat he had hidden in bogland for two days

159

waiting while the redcoats raked the area with musket-fire. Then he had dragged himself home to the tavern, moving at night through the rough places and the mountains until he reached Castlebar. He had remained hidden in the attic for a year before escaping through Northport to France. Only Frederick Cavendish knew how much she hated the soldiers who drank in her bar.

It was late when she got rid of the British soldiers. They had spent their pay in the bar and now, penniless, they made their way up the main street in the direction of the barracks, singing a revolutionary song.

'They are neither English nor Irish,' Molly told him in a whisper, 'but royal fodder marked to march into battle at the behest of the Queen.'

She had observed one particular fiddler during the day. He now lay stretched on a line of barrels snoring heavily, his chest bare and greasy. He held the bow in his hand, and his legs were wrapped around the fiddle. She shook him.

'On your way! I'm not running a kip,' she told him roughly.

'Leave me lie here for the night, Molly. I'll be in right order in the morning and I will slip away. If you put me out now, I'll have to sleep in a doorway or in a hay-shed,' he whined.

'Out!' she ordered and opened the door. The fiddler staggered on to the pavement, swearing and cursing.

She turned to Myles. 'You may come and join me now in the little snug I keep for special friends.'

He followed her through a door and found himself in a small room with a fire and a hatch leading to the bar.

'I suppose you think that I am a rough woman, cursing with the soldiers and throwing a poor fiddler on to the road? Well, that fiddler is one of the lesser spies, and his ears have been cocked all day listening for information. The police pay him for any news he can pick up. Usually it is fabricated, but a loose word can mean a lot to a man like that. So keep your eyes open.'

Myles Prendergast had the feeling that one half of the country was spying on the other half.

'Sit down, and I shall bring you something to eat,' Molly said more gently. 'It will be rough and ready, but it will take the edge off your hunger, for I'm sure you have gone the day without a taste in your mouth.'

Before he could object she left the small snug and went down

160

a corridor to a kitchen. After some time she appeared with a plate of potatoes and bacon.

'Eat that, and I'll clean up the place as is my custom. And then there is much you can tell me.'

She left the snug and set about cleaning the filthy bar-room, while Myles Prendergast set about the plate of food which had been put in front of him.

Frederick Cavendish pulled his heavy coat about him against the raw night, making his way past the mud cabins. There were few candles burning in the windows. Some children were still playing out of doors, thin and sickly. An epidemic might carry them away quickly.

'Enjoy your laughter while you can,' he mused. 'And dance and sing and enjoy your street games. The morrow is uncertain for us all.'

This was once a street of tradesmen. Now their tools had been sold and they were destitute, for there was little work in the town. They now killed the hunger pangs by remaining on in bed until midday.

The whole town had the smell of decay about it. The shop windows were opaque with street dust, and the paint on the doors was chipped. The linen industry was dead. Flax lay rotten in the pits, and looms were gathering dust in the attics. The town had begun to fail at the same time that the country about it began to fail. The dispossessed who feared the workhouse were bedding down in side-streets and archways. The population of the town had risen rapidly in the last two years, and only the shebeens were doing good business: all night they remained open at the end of alleyways. Men and women fell into a drunken stupor which deadened them to reality and destroyed their minds with raw alcohol. Some time back Frederick Cavendish had welcomed Father Matthew to Castlebar to preach temperance to them, and there had been a general reformation, but now men and women were in the pit again. They killed their fears and their hungers in drink. He could hear their rough songs as he made his way through Linenhall Street. He had reached the main street when a woman emerged from one of the archways carrying a ragged bundle in her arms. She held it up towards him. In the light from a tavern window he could see that the child had a scabbed mouth and its lips were chapped and raw.

'Would you have a penny for the baby, sir? We haven't eaten the whole day. Not a sup to wet our mouths. For Christ's sake and His mother's sake, have a charity,' she pleaded. He fished through his pockets and produced a shilling which he pressed into her hand.

'The blessings of heaven on you, sir. No man today offered me a brown copper. Sure, sir, I'd give you a night's comfort for two shillings. I'm only twenty and a clean woman and not touched but by a dead husband! A night's comfort, sir, for two shillings!' He was shaken at her offer. He looked at her face, which was young and haggard. Her voice told him that she was a country woman, the first time he had seen one offering herself as a prostitute in the streets of Castlebar. He searched in his pocket for more money and offered it to her. She took it.

'I'll follow you, sir, if you lead the way. I'll stay at a distance so as not to shame you, for I see that you are a respectable man.'

'No. Keep the money and feed yourself. Tomorrow go down to the workhouse and ask for refuge there.'

'Oh, sir, they would take the baby from me,' she told him, drawing back in fear.

'Who told you that?' he asked.

'It's the rumour, sir. It's the rumour!'

'I have just come from the workhouse. Go and seek refuge there while you can. What is your name?'

'Nora Flaherty,' she said.

'Well, go to the workhouse and I will see what can be done for you. Are you long in this town?'

'Four days, sir, and with little to eat. I was at my wits' end until you came. I nearly sold myself to a soldier.'

'Well, go to the workhouse. I will look after you there.'

'Are you sure, sir?'

'I am. Say that Frederick Cavendish sent you.'

He walked away from the young woman reflectively and went on through the archway to Molly Ward's tavern. He knocked at the side-window three times, and after a minute she opened a door. The old man made his way in from the darkness; he had no wish to return to his lonely house and the pains which his gout brought on.

162

Myles, who had finished his meal, listened to the conversation. He was aware that Molly Ward was indirectly giving him information concerning the visitor.

'We have a visitor, Frederick,' Molly announced, 'a young man filled with talk and wonder.'

'Good. Conversation helps me to forget my pain and my old age.'

Molly opened the door into the snug, and Frederick Cavendish limped into the candlelight. His face was thoughtful, and his eyes suspicious. Heavy jowls hung over his collar.

'Port as always?' Molly Ward asked.

'Port as always,' he repeated, staring at Prendergast.

'This is Myles Prendergast,' Molly told him when she had placed an opened bottle before him.

'I cannot endure silence,' he said to Myles, and filled up his glass. 'In my old age it knocks against my head. Where are you from?'

'Paris.'

'A beautiful city.'

'You know it?'

'I was there a long time ago. Has it lost its taste for revolution?'

'There is always talk of revolution. All Europe talks of revolution at present.'

They were searching out each other's mind. Frederick Cavendish drank his first glass of port directly. 'At my age I cannot live without drink,' he said. 'It kills the pain of gout and feeds it. But this bottle will kill it for the moment.' Then 'What brings you here?' he asked Myles abruptly.

'I was sent by the Circle in Paris.' Myles had decided on frankness.

'What circle?'

'Men who still owe allegiance to the country. They are old men now. They are émigrés.'

'And what do you think of the country? Do you think it is fit for revolution?'

'No, but perhaps for rebellion.' He chose his words carefully.

'There is a subtle difference. Rebellion is a failure before it begins. This is a land for failures.'

'It seems the only choice. I have walked the county and I have

163

observed many things. I do not think the people will rise out.'

'What do you mean by *people*? You have seen the hunger? The people who are hungry do not think. They have no noble ideas or ideals. When your belly is empty, then you think only of food and not of rebellion.' He was feeling for Myles's responses.

'It should not be so.'

'But it is so; and where is there a voice who will speak for a mute people?' Frederick Cavendish asked.

'You speak for them.'

'I do, but I am a Canute who tries to stop the approaching tide. No words of mine have any effect any more.' His voice was deep and cynical.

'Then better to stand and fight than die of starvation.'

'I agree, I agree. But you tell that to the mass of illiterate people who live on the roods and half-acres. They cannot read. They have not your view of history and they do not know that the French Revolution has happened and that Napoleon has come and gone. The peasantry would be wiped out by a trained army. They are less prepared physically or mentally than they were forty or fifty years ago!'

'Then what can they hope for?'

'They can hope to stay alive and beyond that hope for an extraordinary change in their bad fortunes.'

'You despair, then, of ever doing anything?' It was Myles's turn to question.

'For the moment I despair, and of course I may only have the moment. I have lived to see Europe thrown into a turmoil which has changed all things. Eventually the changes may come here but they will come through legislation and education. And the unfortunate thing is that the education must take place through the English. A civilisation is dying out in the bogs at this moment as the Irish language, complex and old, is dying. The children will learn English and ape after the English ways. That will be the final colonisation. You will ask how an English gentleman knows so much about the Irish language. I have picked up the phrases and I have the literature translated for me.'

It was a long statement and it turned Myles Prendergast's mind away from the thoughts of revolution and the memory of the hungry landscape he had just passed through.

'And I'll shock you further,' Cavendish continued, 'by saying that I saw a young woman prostituting herself in Castlebar this very hour. She was a young countrywoman. The hunger had got to her, and she had her child with her. You see, small incidents like that show you that dowellings are coming loose. But you make up your own mind. Talk to me about Paris. We do not often have visitors from that city.'

They forgot about the starving hordes who populated the bad lands and the bogs while Myles Prendergast told Frederick Cavendish the latest news from Paris.

'The Revolution was tempered and made moderate on the day Louis-Philippe met Lafayette at the Hôtel de Ville and stood on the balcony of the building with him wrapped in the tricolour. The crowd went wild. The monster was tamed on that day. Louis-Philippe likes the throne and will sit on it. Wouldn't you, if you had been a teacher in Switzerland? France is prosperous at present. You can say that your revolution succeeded and that it failed. The merchants are in charge now, and you can expect no direct help from France. Paris is not the city you knew as a young man.'

Frederick Cavendish looked at the man intently. His eyes grew suspicious. 'What do you know of my activities as a young man?' he asked sharply.

Myles Prendergast realised that he had made a slip. He should not have mentioned anything, but he decided to tell him the information he had received from the Circle in Paris.

Frederick Cavendish was disturbed. 'It was all a long time ago. We were caught up in the revolutionary fever. The fever has now died. The old men in Paris follow foolish dreams. I do not wish to have any mention made of it.'

Molly Ward looked at him. Now she knew for the first time that Frederick Cavendish had a strange political past which he did not wish to revisit. She broke the silence.

'You may stay here while you are in Castlebar,' she said to Myles. 'I will prepare a room for you at the back of the house. It will give you a chance to escape through the gardens if the place is searched. We will hold to the story that you are a buyer from England. And keep your mind to yourself – but I am delighted that you brought news of my brother: I will sleep easy tonight knowing that he found peaceful rest in the great city of Paris.'

'To local news, Molly,' Cavendish interrupted. 'How is Spiker?'

'He got his own medicine. He's lying up in the barracks half-dead. They did a bad job, whoever did it, for they say he will live.'

'The Whiteboys, then, are to blame?' he said, drawing her out.

'They are, I'm sure,' she said sarcastically. 'Do you think a crowd of cattle rustlers would have the courage to flay the back off a colonel? They would wet their drawers! But I'd say that Jeremiah Egan the patriot knew that it was going to happen, for the very night it happened he was in here. If they bring him into the barracks for questioning, he'll say he was drinking with the soldiers and his lieutenant Sean McHale as well, but there was plenty of water in his whiskey. Why, he must have drunk a quart of water that night! He was running in and out all evening. He has very weak kidneys – brought on, I would say, by fear.' She began to laugh at the thought of him. 'In and out, in and out, he was going, drinking water and getting rid of it. "You'll flood the town," I told him. "You'll flood the town! Your piss, McHale, is the only thing you'll spill for Ireland!" He knows well that I haven't much regard for him.' She sipped at her glass and then, remembering it all again, spluttered into her port. 'Such are the ones who will save Ireland!' she said. 'The soldiers say that they flayed off his backside and that he sleeps on his stomach. And not one of them has a *thrainin* of sympathy for him, for they say he had it coming to him ever since the day that he ordered the whipping of Ned Kenny! It was an awful scene. Soldiers dirtied their trousers as they do with fear in battle.'

Frederick Cavendish had written a leader in the *Connaught Telegraph* when Ned Kenny was flogged, and was more than a little interested in the flaying of Spiker. It had been a skilful operation. No one had yet been brought to the police barracks for questioning, and there had been no rumours in the town.

'And where's Spiker now?' he asked, looking at Myles, who turned away.

'He is in the infirmary lingering. He roars in his sleep and calls out orders. In saner moments he says that he will have his revenge.' Molly had a precise order in the way in which she expressed herself. She was passing on information which

166

Frederick Cavendish did not possess. He looked at her face. The lines of tiredness about her mouth were broken only by her humour. Her eyes were always sharp, and there was little which she failed to notice. 'There are restless feelings among the men. You can feel it in the air. Many of them hope that Spiker will die and some feel that he should have been killed the night the sentry discovered him.'

'He certainly suffered for England,' Frederick Cavendish said wryly.

'The boys would have deserted, but where would they go? They have signed up for the duration and they feel that the famine is about to strike. Better be up in the barracks than out in a scut of a shelter. They have their own reasons for staying on.'

'There will be revenge taken on whoever did it. Mark my words.'

'That's if they ever did find out; for, Frederick, you know as well as I do that these were no unpractised fools. Maybe we have the making of the revolution yet. I pray that this time we'll get it right, for we only got it half-right the last time.'

'I don't think so, Molly. People were hungry, not starving, during the French Revolution, and it was not the hungry who set the fuse but the middle class. The middle class are firmly Castle Catholics here. We are bound to England, and I don't think we can ever free ourselves.'

'You have lost heart, Frederick Cavendish,' Myles said suddenly.

'I haven't lost heart. I'm using my head. When I see, as I did this evening, a young countrywoman offering herself as a prostitute on the pavements of Castlebar I know things are getting bad.'

'There is no money to be made by prostitution in Castlebar. She should go to London!'

'You have no heart, Molly!'

'I have. We all sell what we have when things are bad. The rich can sell their silver, but that young woman has nothing to sell.'

It was a rough statement, and Frederick Cavendish had to agree that it was true. Nobody had a better grasp of reality than Molly Ward. Certainly the politicians at Westminster had no complete view of what was happening and only would have one when some disaster struck. Of what use were political views in the vortex of a famine?

'I can only see famine. I cannot see a rebellion, not in present conditions,' he said finally.

'We have become too serious, Frederick Cavendish. Sing that song of yours for me, for I love it dearly.'

'What song is that, Molly?'

'It's the song by the man Wallace.'

'"Scenes That Are Brightest", from *Maritana*?'

'The very one. The very one.'

'I'm getting a bit old for that, Molly.'

'Leave be the excuses! Leave be the excuses!' she told him.

'Very well, then.'

He sang the song very softly. His voice, even in old age, was very firm; and in singing it he felt that it drew away some of the bitterness and hopelessness that resided in their hearts.

It was a strange scene; darkness would soon descend upon them all. This was a small ephemeral candle. Molly had her eyes closed. Her mind was in some marble hall, her body beautiful, her face young. She conducted his voice with all of her ten fingers and hummed a little. Then the short dream ended. She opened her eyes.

'Well, I have a public house to be running, Mr Cavendish. It might not be the greatest public house there is, but it trades under the name of a hotel. If I stay here any longer listening to them immoral English songs, I'll be damned. But it's lovely talking to you, sir, and even abusing you sometimes. You have a lovely cultivated voice. I always noticed that Protestants have fine cultivated voices.'

'And is not your own cultivated?' he asked.

'No, Frederick. It is musical and sad. Musical and sad' – and with that she left the room and went off to finish cleaning the bar.

Frederick Cavendish poured himself another drink. The gout was becoming active in his foot. Weariness and dejection of spirit would soon set in if he stayed much longer. He looked at Myles sitting opposite him, with his bright eyes and his fine face.

'You are an excellent young man caught by the fire of revolution and rebellion – but this is not the time for rebellion,' he said in a deep voice.

168

'Perhaps not, but one is drawn into action. The intellect is not the only voice.'

'The heart can be foolish.'

'The intellect is sluggish,' Myles replied.

'I cannot counsel you, young man. We must take our own directions. If I can help you in any way, contact me. And beware – Spiker is alive. You have a dangerous enemy on your hands.'

'I will remember.'

'I must go – these are the black hours, which I hate, when one is alone and there is no human activity. Give my goodnight to Molly Ward. I shall let myself out.'

He drew himself up from the chair and wrapped his cloak about his shoulders. As he went out of the side-door and moved up the alleyway, he passed a soldier vomiting against a wall. Soon he was on the main street. It was dark, not unlike the darkness now settling on his mind.

After Frederick Cavendish had gone Molly Ward returned to the snug. She carried an old bottle of wine with her which was covered in dust.

'He is a very imposing figure,' Myles Prendergast said.

'There is no end to his charity and his courage. He is old now, but you should have seen him in middle age. He was lion-like. He is welcome here at all hours of the night, for he cannot sleep and I often feel that his mind is troubled.' She uncorked the bottle of wine. 'It has been in stock for a long time, and I hope it tastes sweet, for you are welcome to this house. It is not often a man from Paris comes into this house with news such as you carry.'

She poured out the wine for him, and he sipped it. It was firm and mature.

'But you say my brother is dead? Tell me about it. Does he rest in a peaceful place and did he find peace in life?'

'Yes, it is in a walled cemetery. There are trees growing there. It once belonged to religious sisters, but they fled the country at the outbreak of the Revolution.'

'Ah, that sort of a revolution would not do in this country at all! We would have no truck with Danton and Robespierre and those other atheists. But never mind the atheists. Is the grave well tended?'

169

'The old revolutionaries from Ireland tend it – the cemetery is quite close to the River Seine. His name is carved over the grave.'

'On a stone slab?'

'Yes.'

'Then, it will endure. It will always remind people of my brother. What is inscribed upon it?'

'It states the year of his death and the fact that he took part in the '98 rebellion.'

'He would have been seventy-five if he had lived. He was a handsome man. He dragged himself here after Ballinamuck. Two days he lay in a bog while the redcoats raked it with musket-fire. I often carried food to him in the attic at night and changed the bandages on his wounds. Sure, I'm all that is left of my family. They are all dead.' She began to weep quietly. He left her to her thoughts for some minutes.

'And now tell me of the woman he married,' she said, recovering. 'Was she quality?'

'She was a lady.'

'You mean she was royal?'

'Yes, yes – I suppose so. She was from a great house and she possessed some money. He met her one day in the forest of Saint-Cloud with a friend. They were introduced and they got married a year later. He became a wine merchant and he bought a house on the bank of the great river.'

'And so my brother married royalty, you might say!'

'You could say that, Molly.' He smiled gently.

'Well, we were royal ourselves in our day. The Ward family, before the penal laws, ruled their own kingdom. And they had two children?'

'Yes, two boys, Georges and Jacques.'

'Repeat that again,' she commanded.

'Georges and Jacques.'

'I would never manage to pronounce words like that, but when you get back to Paris (as get back you will) tell them that their aunt was asking for them. And when you are describing the place say I own a hotel and I keep important people.'

'I will.'

It took him several hours to answer all her questions. He told her how many rooms were in her brother's house, he

170

described the street where he had set up his business, he described his wife and he worked out a rough family-tree for her.

Finally, she stood up. 'I am tired now, and if you follow me I'll show you to your room. You will be safe here and you will find that the window of the room leads on to a shed which leads directly to the yard if you wish to escape.'

They made their way up narrow stairs. When they reached the room she turned to him and said: 'You have brought great happiness to my old heart. I'll be thinking of that great house in Paris all night. But before you enter the room will you repeat the names of my nephews again?'

'Georges and Jacques,' he said patiently.

She tried to repeat the names after him, but gave up. 'No, I could never get my tongue around strange names like that. Good night.'

'Good night, Molly.'

He entered the small room and placed the lighted candle on a stand. He turned to close the door, and as he did so he could hear the old woman trying to pronounce the two French names. She moved out of earshot, and there was silence in the house.

16

As Liam Joyce descended the hill he looked at the houses and warehouses built by Michael Barrett beyond the river. The tide was low as he passed across the bridge to the Barrett quarter of the town, the scent of seaweed heavy on the air. The harbour wall below the tidal line was black with barnacles. There was little activity on the quayside except for a few men repairing a large sail stretched out on the ground. He looked up at the green hills which surrounded the town and out towards the sea. Northport was a safe place. It was protected from the gales, from hunger and from the landlord and his agents. He could be happy here; with a few acres to till he would never be hungry again and he wouldn't have to lie in bed wondering how he would put the heavy rent money together. He wondered if he would have the same luxury of feeling in America.

He dismounted from his horse and led it to a water-trough, where some children were playing.

'And where are you from, stranger?' they asked.

'I'm from beyond the Reek.'

'That's the holy mountain where Patrick fasted and prayed.'

'Yes. Did you ever climb it?'

'No, but our fathers and mothers did. They were all cut from the stones. They climbed it in their bare feet. Did you ever climb it in your bare feet?'

'I did.'

'Then, you are as daft as the others!'

'Now, where would a man get a drink here and a bit of entertainment?'

'You can get a drink in any of the shebeens, but if you want a song or a recitation, then you better go to Widow Hopkin's, for Gill the poet is there. He was out dancing in the square last night, dancing and singing and shouting abuse at everyone.' They pointed in the direction of Widow Hopkin's shebeen. 'And don't rise him, sir – he's easily risen. He might even take a knife to you or write a poem about you. Everybody puts up with him because he is a poet and a friend of Lord Barrett.'

Liam made his way down a miserable lane cut by an open drain. It was a narrow place where the sun rarely entered and where the squalid lived. There was cow dung heaped in front of one of the doors, and the air between the houses was fetid. He entered the Widow Hopkin's shebeen. It was a place of half-light, and the stench of the street was equally strong here. Men were sitting about an open fire drinking poteen. Some of them were chewing pigs' crubeen. The poet Gill was noticeable among them all because of his height: he had a narrow body and a narrow head, and his face was sharp.

'Are you staying long?' Widow Hopkin asked him directly.

'Not long,' he replied.

'How did you find this place?'

'The children told me where it was.'

'There are plenty of other places you could have gone to, in the better part of the town.'

'I know, but I chose here. There is no law against it.'

'I'm sure you are here on business?'

'Yes. Emigration business.'

'All the emigration business is done in Michael Barrett's office. The merchants have offices in the far side of the town and they sail regularly.'

'They do; in half-rotten ships and with rough captains. But I've heard Michael Barrett is reliable.'

'You seem to know a lot.'

'I ask a lot. There is no law against that.'

'There are laws and laws. What's your name? You might be a spy. We have ways of dealing with spies here.'

'I'm Joyce.'

173

'What Joyce?'

'Joyce from beyond the Reek. My village was destroyed by Kenrick of the Crooked Nose last week.'

'Kenrick of the Crooked Nose?' Gill repeated, having just woken from his slumbers.

'The very one.'

'How did you come here?'

'On a horse.'

'Well, how is it you still *have* a horse?' Gill asked.

'It's a village horse. We hid our possessions in the hills the night before Kenrick arrived. I'm not one to sit on my backside around a fire and do nothing. I'm here on business and I'm damn well not going to say aught else. Can I have a drink?' His voice was rough.

'We have to be careful,' the Widow Hopkin told him sullenly.

'I'll buy a drink for Gill the poet if he gives us a song,' Liam said in a more friendly tone.

'Would you now?' said Gill. 'Do you think I could be bought by a glass of poteen?'

'I do.'

'I should crack your jaw for that remark,' Gill told him. 'But I'll take the drink instead and maybe sing a bar of my poems.'

'I've often sung the same song myself,' Liam Joyce told him after the poet had finished.

'What did you think of it?'

'The first two verses will last for ever. The other verses won't. They have ornament without feeling.'

'You are insulting me!'

'I'm not. People only sing the first two verses. They know themselves that the others are no damn good.'

'He's insulting you, Gill. Snout him!' the crowd urged. They rose in an angry mood, interested in some small excitement.

'Leave him be,' Gill told them. 'At least he is honest. He is the only one who ever said that to my face, and it's what you all believe, you bastards!'

'Buy Gill another drink,' Gill said to Liam Joyce. 'He's the last of the Irish poets and a miserable one. After Gill, poetry will be dead. You insult me, Joyce, but the others insult me behind my back and I make a fool of myself.'

'Give the poet some whiskey, for poteen will rot his guts,' Liam Joyce directed.

Gill took the whiskey-glass in his hand and drank it directly. 'Now I'll sing one of my other songs,' he said. He sang one of his songs, but his memory was gapped and he composed bad lines as he went along. There was froth on his mouth, and his eyes were glazed. Liam Joyce bought him more whiskey.

'You are a gentleman. The rest of these lugs buy me poteen and laugh when I soil my trousers and goad me to dance in the square. I, who once dined at Barrett House and talked Latin, eat pig-swill and sup with pigs. Now, sir, for you seem to have some breeding, sing for *me* an old gentle song.'

'I'll sing a song by Rioccard Barrett,' Liam said.

'Do, Liam Joyce, and I'll join in, for I know them all.'

Liam began to sing 'My Cause of Sorrow' slowly and gently.

Gill listened intently to the words, his head bowed. 'Sweet as a bird, sweet as a bird,' he commented quietly, raising his hands to clap at the end of the third verse which brought the song to an end. Then Liam Joyce began to sing a verse he had never heard before, and suddenly Gill became alert, his mind clear, all the darkness pushed aside. He was ready to say something, but Liam Joyce indicated with his eyes that he should remain silent. When he finished Gill had tears in his eyes.

'You have the missing verses! I knew they were somewhere. I was told it in Belmullet. Barrett often put extra verses to his poems at wakes, like myself, but he never wrote them down. The new verses put the proper finish to the song and bind it together!'

'There was another verse still, but it is half-finished and Barrett struck it out in the manuscript.'

Gill's eyes became sharp, and Liam Joyce knew that his last statement had interested him. 'Barrett never left anything in his hand!' the poet insisted. 'His second wife burned everything he ever wrote when he died. I have it from the neighbours who saw her take out the trunk and burn the contents.'

'Be that as it may, I have a Barrett manuscript. It was a dunaire of poems belonging to Barrett. He put his own name to the bottom of every page.'

'That means there are other poems?'

'Yes. Some you know already, but several are unknown. They have been forgotten. There are thirty in all.'

'In his own hand, you say?'

'That's what I said.'

Gill now lost interest in his surroundings. He would have given a lot of money to possess the poems. But, then, Michael Barrett of Barrett House – he would be more than eager to know that they existed, and would probably give Liam Joyce a small fortune for them. He wondered if Liam Joyce knew how important they were.

'Could I see you outside the door for a minute, Liam Joyce?' Gill asked in a friendly voice.

'I'll wait until I have finished my drink, then I'll go and talk with you.'

'This is of great importance.'

'It can wait.'

'I want to make you an offer.'

'Make it here.'

'This is a big offer.'

'I'll see you when I've finished my whiskey.'

Gill was as nervous as a cat as he waited for Liam Joyce to finish his drink. He wondered how he had come into the possession of the manuscript. Perhaps it was a forgery.

'I'm ready for you now,' Liam Joyce said, and they left the stench of the shebeen. Gill caught him by the arm and hurried him down the narrow street and out on to the square where they could be alone.

'I'll buy the manuscript from you,' he said directly. 'Ten pounds.'

'Where could *you* get ten pounds? I have never heard of a poet with money.'

'I don't believe you have it at all. It was just a chance that you knew the last verses.'

Liam Joyce put his hand inside his coat and drew out the leather wallet. He opened it and showed Gill the poem he had just sung. 'And look carefully at the bottom.'

'Let me think, let me think,' Gill said excitedly. Liam Joyce looked at the lines in his face. They were sensitive and troubled like his fingers.

'We'll take a chance on it,' Gill said eventually. 'I'll go with you to the Barrett house. He might listen to me. It would be a shame if the manuscript were to disappear. But wait until I clean myself. I haven't washed in a week, and the house is a palace,' he said humbly. 'I'll have to borrow a pair of trousers

176

and a shirt from a widow who lost her husband a month ago and I'll have to shave. There's a week's growth of hair on my face.'

He staggered across the square and disappeared down one of the small narrow streets. Later he reappeared, his face shaven and cut, wearing a stiff pair of trousers and a white shirt.

'I hope they were not taken from a corpse,' Liam Joyce told him.

'No. He wore his third-worst pair at the wake. She is a sensible woman. I feel cleansed of soul with new clothes on. Poetry is a lonely and peculiar gift, good or bad, and one must have pity for poets. She has. She wanted me into the bed with her, but I told her that I had come by a manuscript of Rioccard Barrett and such pleasures must wait. So I will have to pay a price for the clothes!'

He mounted the horse behind Liam Joyce, and they made their way out of the old part of the town followed by the children who skipped along beside them. Soon they were on the sea-road which led to the house. When they turned into the great avenue Liam Joyce was impressed by the order of the trees above him, forming an arch which was high and spacious. When they broke from the avenue he saw the noble house on a platform of lawn and, below, cattle grazing on rich parkland. He looked at the façade of the house: wing was balanced with wing, and the windows held their proportions. Smoke rose from solid chimneys. Gill was a fool, he thought. No man would permit himself to be banished from such a fine house. As he got closer he was overawed by its magnificence, and his courage weakened. He felt shabby in his long coat and worsted trousers.

'We better approach from the back. If I knocked at the front door, I would surely be thrown out. Anyway, it is only the gentry in carriages who approach the broad doors. We'll make our way to the kitchen.'

They took a side-path, entered a cobblestoned yard through an arch and dismounted. It was an enclosed place, where the horses were stabled and the fuel stored. The windswept valley and the broad bogs where Liam Joyce lived seemed far away. This was a place which one would not wish to leave. The contentment of order was about him.

177

'I don't know what sort of reception I can expect,' Gill told him nervously. 'They may have forgotten my misdemeanours.'

He knocked at the door and bowed his head. A servant maid appeared at the door. 'Off with you!' she said directly. 'We have orders not to feed you. We were told we could feed every beggar in the country except for Gill the poet. You made an amadaun of yourself on your last visit.'

'I'm not a dog,' he told her. 'Tell the Master I have news of great importance for him.'

'No news of yours, Gill, could be of any interest to the Master. You are exaggerating as you always do. Soft words or important ones won't get you anywhere, so be off!'

Emboldened, Liam Joyce stepped forward and took the wallet from his pocket.

'Tell your master that I am in possession of important documents which might be of great interest to him. They deal directly with one of his family. I think it may be of great concern to him.'

'What document?' she asked, impressed by his appearance.

'A document which is only of concern to both of us.'

'Are you acquainted with him?'

'No.'

'Wait for a moment,' she said and closed the door. They waited for a quarter of an hour. Then a manservant appeared.

'Come with me, sir,' he said. 'You stay in the kitchen, Gill. If you wish to have some food, you can. Do not enter the main house.'

'I was not always treated as a beggar here, sir,' Gill said acidly, recognising the man who had once kicked him on the backside and told him that he was a writer of doggerel verse.

'You are now,' the manservant said impersonally.

'The glories of the house are gone,' Gill said, entering the kitchen. 'Bodachs run the sculleries of the great.' The sentence was expressed in Irish and was harsh and cutting.

Liam Joyce entered the large vaulted kitchen with its wide tables and large ovens. The smell of rich food filled his lungs, and he realised that he had not eaten during the day. His stomach turned. He felt that he was going to vomit the raw poteen he had taken in Northport. He tightened his muscles to keep it in. They passed along an arched corridor, their footseps sounding on the flags, and made their way up to the first storey. A wide staircase with shallow steps took them up to the second. Liam Joyce tried to observe as much as he possibly could in order to give his wife, Oonah, every detail later. She would ask him about the curtain hangings, the colours of the walls, the great pictures, the shining furniture and the huge fragmented lamps which hung from the ceilings. He followed as the footman led along a well-lit corridor, stopping in front of a wide panelled door. He knocked twice. A loud voice called from within.

'You may enter now, sir,' the footman directed. 'Michael Barrett is ready to see you.'

Dress them in velvet and they will become Englishmen, Liam Joyce thought. He stepped into a bright spacious room. The ceiling was ornamented with cherubs and a strange figure, half beast, half man, who held a set of pipes in his hand; the air smelt of snuff and rich wine. Framed by one of the windows and with his heavy back towards him stood the figure of an old man. He had grey hair, and his hands were knotted behind his back. He looked down across the trees towards the sea.

Michael Barrett turned slowly about and looked at the man standing inside the door. He looked at the lines in his face, his eyes, and the manner in which he presented himself. It was clear that he was a peasant farmer from the clothes he wore. They were neat and tidy, but the large coat was too small for him. Probably the only greatcoat in the village, Michael Barrett thought. No wonder *Punch* finds the Irish peasant so easy to caricature. He was impressed, however, by the stature of the man who stood before him: his eyes were not subservient, though he was certain that the man was hungry.

'I believe you have important documents for me,' he said directly to the man. He spoke in Irish, knowing the man would be uncomfortable talking English. He resolved to test his mettle.

'Yes, sir. I think they are of some importance to you. I do not carry them all with me. I came directly to Northport where somebody told me of your interest.'

'And on the way you befriended Gill, in some shebeen or other. Was he preaching revolution?'

'No, sir. He was reciting poetry.'

'Well, if he's not preaching revolution he's reciting bad

poetry, and he is always drinking and rotting his guts out on poteen.' Barrett spoke with disgust.

'He is a poet, sir. He is a rake of a man, but he will be remembered by the poor.'

Michael Barrett moved closer to Liam Joyce and examined him more closely. 'You look to me like a respectable fellow,' he said.

'I would have come better prepared, but I came on horse-back.'

'So you *have* a horse?'

'Yes. We possessed a horse in the village. But now there's no village – Kenrick destroyed it: there is not a stone upon a stone.'

'Kenrick the leveller?'

'Yes. He intends to make a sheep ranch behind Croagh Patrick. Three or four other villages have been levelled. I do not know what has become of the people. They have probably taken the road to the workhouse.'

'All roads lead to the workhouse. Why did you not make your way there like the others?'

'I have more respect for myself. I made small provision for my village, and we are not yet starving. And if the whole population of the county makes its way to the workhouse and the great towns there will be no food for them there, either.'

'How do you know all these things?'

'I read the papers. I watch what is happening.'

'Then, you have read that the blight has hit England?'

'I have read the report on the potato failure in Kent. I know, too, that the English labourer eats potatoes as we do. I know that it has attacked the eastern coast.'

Michael Barrett was impressed by the man's grasp of what was happening in the outside world: he was not as vulnerable or as confused as the others. He admired the strength of the man's voice and the pride of his stance. Joyce was not cowed by his parliamentary voice. He decided to test him further.

'Eventually you will join the others. The peasants always give in. You let them knock your village to the ground without offering any token of resistance. No wonder the English papers think that you are slaves, that you rut and overpopulate and that you are too feckless to think of tomorrow.'

The muscles in Liam Joyce's face tightened, and a fury

180

began to burn in his eyes. He controlled his anger. 'You never had an empty belly,' he replied accusingly. 'You never starved through June and July and huddled together with your family in winter to keep warm. When you are hungry and ill-clothed you cannot withstand the might of Kenrick backed by the strength of the police.' He pointed to the weal on his face. 'This is the mark of Kenrick. He also left his signature on my back. I have come to the wrong house. I heard that some Irish blood ran through your veins, but you are a Sassenach bone and sinew and I will not stand here and allow you, in a warm room and with a belly filled with wine and food, to hurl insults at me. I have endured enough. The gun is the only answer for you and the lot of them. I would as easily shoot you now if I had a gun and take the consequences in the court of Castlebar with its packed jury and the gallows outside the gaol. Good day, Michael Barrett. I am not a peasant and I do not rut.'

Liam turned to leave. Tears started in his eyes. He had overreached himself and he wondered where his confidence and his wild words had come from. He should have armed the village and put the money in guns rather than in tickets to America. Even a pike at close quarters in a narrow pass could wreak havoc on horse and rider.

'Just a moment, Mr Joyce,' a sharp voice came from behind him. 'Nobody turns his back on me in my house.'

'Well, I do, sir, and damn you and yours. May your children's children come twisted and strange from the womb.'

Liam Joyce placed his hand on the ivory knob of the door in order to let himself out. Michael Barrett spoke to him in a quieter voice.

'I'm sorry, Mr Joyce, if I pushed you too hard. Your village must be proud of you. Not many would have said the things which you have said. Courage is not a virtue found amongst people who work the soil. We need more anger in this country, and that might shake the British government and vipers like Kenrick who use the courts and the police for their advantage. Sit down.' He indicated a large leather armchair beside the fire.

'I have never sat on such a chair before,' Joyce said, sitting down. 'We do not have much furniture in our houses.'

'I know only too well what you have in your houses. Do you drink wine?'

'No, sir, I have never tasted wine.'

'Then, I'd better get you a whiskey.' He filled a large glass from a square decanter. Liam Joyce accepted the glass, feeling the luxury of fine crystal in his hand.

'To your good health and your courage, Liam Joyce,' Michael Barrett said. 'And now down to business. You tell me that you have a valuable document for me. Let me say that I cannot think of any document you might possess which could be of interest to me.'

'Could I recite some poetry for you, sir?'

'Yes, as long as it is not one of Gill's poems. I am tired to death of them. There are only three that are of any value or will last.'

'No, I will recite one by Rioccard Barrett.'

'Yes. Do that. If you can sing I would be better pleased.'

'Then, I will sing it.'

Michael Barrett eased himself into his large leather chair. He gazed into the fire and relaxed. It was strange how listening to the poems could do this to him. The old sea captain, Roderick Byrne, had brought him up on Irish poetry and song, so he knew good Irish poetry when he heard it and he knew the history of poetry as far back as the seventh century. He had sat at a court of poetry once, while the few remaining poets of Mayo had tested their poetry against each other. Rioccard Barrett was supposed to have attended the court that particular night but had got drunk on his way from Erris.

He listened to Liam Joyce singing 'My Cause of Sorrow'. He knew the verses very well. They were as dark red as the port he was drinking. When Liam Joyce began the fifth verse he started – this was the great missing verse which put finish to the poem. He did not interrupt.

When Liam Joyce had finished Michael Barrett said: 'That is the missing verse. Sing it again for me.' His mind was excited by the pleasure. Liam Joyce sang it again, knowing he had trapped Michael Barrett in the silken net of words.

'Where did you discover it?' he asked.

'Where I discovered the other nineteen lost Barrett poems – in the dunaire which I possess.'

'I do not believe you. None of his manuscripts survives. I sent a man down to Erris in search of them. I even offered a large amount of money for anyone who could discover them.'

'I was not aware of your interest in them until I met some-body in Northport who told me. I will sing you another Barrett poem. You know the first verse and the air.'

'Please do.'

Again Michael Barrett listened intently to the poem, fearing he might lose a phrase. 'It's a Barrett poem for certain. It has all his cadence and images. It will last for ever. It will be here when this house has fallen to the ground.'

'I believe that you are correct.'

'How much do you want for your manuscript? Name the price,' he said excitedly. 'It will be amongst my most treasured possessions.'

'I come with a price, sir. It is a heavy price.'

Michael Barrett looked at this peasant who was bargaining with him for a manuscript on cheap paper that nobody else had any interest in. He was playing his cards well, dangling a bait before him which he could not resist. He should have controlled his emotions.

'What is your price?'

'The free transport of my village in one of your ships to America.'

'How many people?'

'Twenty-five.'

'It is not worth it. My ships are filled with emigrants. They know I sail safe ships. They pay top prices to me. Every ship of mine which leaves Northport during the next three months has every berth allotted.'

'I know that. I made it my business to enquire. I am asking a high price, but I am offering you something priceless.'

'It is only a poem on paper.'

'It is the heart-blood of your race I'm offering you, Michael Barrett – something more important than the stones of this house.'

'You are taking advantage of me.'

'Kenrick took advantage of *me*. *You* take advantage of the emigrants.'

'It is too much you ask. I never permitted anyone to travel free in my ships.'

'I am not asking to travel free. I am offering you something to buy passage.'

'You can travel in November.'

'No, I cannot wait. By November many of my people will have died. I know what will happen if the potatoes fail. The government depots do not carry enough food to feed all the people. We hate the Indian corn. Have you ground it? It is as hard as iron.'

'I will not permit a whole village to sail from Northport free in my ship.'

'Then, I will destroy the manuscript page by page, beginning now. All a poor man can do with a manuscript is wipe his backside with it!' Liam took the wallet from his pocket and held up the manuscript page.

'He has his name to it!' Michael Barrett cried excitedly.

'I know. Now, if you look very carefully you will see me tear it right down the centre.' He held the page in front of Michael Barrett and slowly began to rip it in half.

'No,' Michael Barrett shouted. 'Stop! I'll give you what you wish. I will give you what you wish.'

'Then, the first page of the manuscript is yours,' and Liam handed the old man the torn sheet.

Barrett took it with a small tremble in his hands and studied it carefully. He remained motionless as he read it. He felt a strange fulfilment in his life. 'I will fit you in. But it will be uncomfortable,' he warned.

'Life is uncomfortable. We will go under any conditions as long as it is before the end of the summer.'

'You deserve to survive,' Michael Barrett told him. 'You found my single weakness and you bargained well. When may I have the manuscript?'

'I will deliver the manuscript to you when the last person in the village is on board the ship to America.' There was a pause as Barrett weighed up Joyce.

'Do you know where America is or how large it is?'

'I have no idea. To me it is just a free country! I follow its history in the newspapers.'

'Let me show you.'

They walked across the room to the large table. Michael Barrett took a map from a cylinder and stretched it out carefully in front of him. He placed two statuettes of horses on the edges to keep it flat. He pointed to a large landmass in a sea which had been washed in blue. 'This is New York. Everybody starts up in New York. But you should not rest in New York:

there are too many Irish there. Move away from it as quickly as you can. Keep driving westwards. Move out towards the central states. There you will find land ready for development.'

'Why do you tell me these things, sir?' Liam Joyce asked.

'If I were young, I would take my chances in America. I would bring my ships there. I would start life anew. It is a young raw place and you have an equal chance in that great land. Here we have problems which we cannot solve. I think you will be lucky, Liam Joyce; you are the only one who ever attempted to take a village out of this hell. I hope luck goes with you.'

Liam Joyce began to weep. Heavy sobs shook his back and his shoulders, and he could not look into the eyes of Michael Barrett. He had been carrying such dark troubles within him for as long as he could remember, and now suddenly there was a bright light piercing the darkness – all because a chance conversation led him to a former Member of the House of Commons who loved Irish poetry. He would cry now, but never again, not even when the ship sailed out past Clare Island and Ireland disappeared for ever beneath the horizon. Given a chance, he would never be poor again.

'Don't weep, Liam Joyce,' Michael Barrett said kindly. 'You made a good bargain. You were born lucky. Before next winter a million people could lie dead in this country.'

'It's the anguish that has been inside me.'

'Sit now and tell me about yourself.' Michael Barrett felt paternal towards this peasant who had made such a great impression upon him. 'It is an evening for conversation. Tell me about yourself and sing more of the Barrett songs for me.'

Liam Joyce sat until early morning with the owner of Barrett House and the ship which would bring his village to America. He told him how he had learned English from an uncle who was a hedge-school teacher and a fiddler. He had also taught him the value of writing and of figures, so he could measure land and write letters. He told him of the manner in which he had outwitted Kenrick and how he had played the village idiot before the police and the crowbar brigade. But he did not tell Michael Barrett that he already had money set aside for the voyage to America which would have bought passage for five people to New York.

Late in the night, after he had sung several of Rioccard

Barrett's poems, Michael Barrett asked him how he had acquired the manuscript.

'It's a strange story,' he began. 'My uncle, the hedge-school teacher and fiddler, had the habit of travelling around the country. He found himself in Erris one night at a wake in the company of Rioccard Barrett. Rioccard Barrett sang his songs, and my uncle played for him. That night or early next morning they decided to hold a contest. My uncle put up his fiddle, and Barrett put up the manuscript.'

'What was the contest?'

'Barrett said that he could piss higher than my uncle. They went to the back of the whitewashed house, and by lantern-light the contest was held. My uncle won, and that is why the manuscript survived.'

Michael Barrett looked incredulously at him. 'Is it true?'

'Upon my word.'

Michael Barrett began to laugh until tears ran down his eyes.

It was very late when Liam Joyce left the room. Gill was waiting for him in the kitchen.

'Did you meet Michael Barrett?'

'Yes. Come with me, Gill, and I will buy you a bottle of whiskey.' They left the house and, mounting the horse, returned to Northport. His luck, and the luck of the village, was beginning to change. Liam Joyce thought of the long journey to America.

17

EILEEN HORKAN moved through the flowers, tending the garden as she did each morning. Their colours and their arrangement about the garden brought a great sense of joy. She had been late rising, having slept uneasily the previous night. She had enjoyed the company of the English lord and his bright conversation, and now felt she had betrayed her allegiance to her own roots.

Her father, who had a wide understanding of Irish literature and the hidden streams of Irish history, had given her pride in her lineage. Despite the thirty acres he farmed, he had always felt a dispossessed man. 'We have been pushed back across the base of the mountains and into the swamps and the bogs. We have been made poor and ignorant. Laws have been put on the statute-books to keep us ignorant and out of any office. Remember, the British seek to destroy us. They might not wipe us off the earth, but they can destroy the language and the memory we had of ourselves. Never forget that you are equal to and better than those in the great houses. Most of them are descended from Cromwell's Roundheads, a dark, morose brood.'

Her reading had tempered his vision of things in her mind. Yet, instinctively, she felt she had betrayed his memory by remaining on at the great house. She recalled, too, what Father Coady had often remarked to her in their conversations beside the fire at the presbytery. He had a revolutionary view of things and he rarely referred to the Celtic world of her father. For him the Celts were a feckless race destroyed by the order and power of Rome. 'They ran into battle with bare backsides, roaring. As if that was any protection against Caesar's legions! Beware of the Celtic strain. It is full of longing and nostalgia for a past which never existed. I would have some respect for them if they had worn leather trousers,' he told her, and then chuckled to himself in delight.

'Now, the revolution which has changed France and is sweeping through Europe is a different matter. There are many French ideas in the air. They are like winged seeds and they can even take root in the bogs. The British did not build Maynooth for the spread of Popish teaching. They built it to keep out revolutionary thoughts from abroad. They want to turn us priests into parsons. I'd swear to God they would expect us to take the Oath of Allegiance.'

Walking through the flower garden in front of the long low cottage she recalled the small figure of Father Coady, sitting at his fire, wrapped in a blanket and preaching revolution. 'We could be put in gaol for treason,' she had often told him as they laughed together.

She was about to return to the house when she heard the sound of a horse and saw Hackett drawing up at the gate, carrying a parcel. He dismounted and entered the garden. She looked at the expression on his face; he was in control of his emotions.

'Good day, Miss Horkan,' he said formally. 'Lord Lannagh directed me to bring you this parcel and letter.'

He handed her the parcel and the letter. She knew from its weight that it contained books.

'Shall I wait for a reply?' he asked.

'You may,' she told him coolly. She went indoors and opened the parcel. It contained five volumes of the writings of the eighteenth-century essayists, in red leather covers. She opened the letter quickly. It simply stated that the lord wished her to have the present books to add to those of Johnson. He felt that they complemented each other. At the end of the letter he expressed the wish that she might visit his house again. It was a formal letter, with no liberties taken. She sat down, took her pen and thought out her reply. She hesitated for some minutes. Should she break their relationship or keep it on a formal level? When she read her reply through she discovered she had expressed more sentiment than she had intended. The second draft simply stated that she would visit him at some later time. She sealed the letter with wax, a precaution against the prying eyes of Hackett.

'You may carry this to your master,' she told him and handed him the letter. 'I am sure you continue to enjoy the fine wines of France,' she added, eyes glinting. He recoiled.

'Ah, sure, not a drop of wine ever passes my lips these days, Miss Horkan. Where would a man like me find money to indulge in the luxury of the rich?' His voice had the whinging tone of a menial, but he knew why she had made the cutting remark. It signalled that he should hold his tongue about her association with the lord. If the friendship grew between them, then a word from this woman whom he detested could have him dismissed from his position. He would have to tread carefully. He would have to take counsel from Kenrick.

'I do not see the signs of hunger and hardship upon either you or your wife. Rich meat keeps hunger at bay.'

'Sure, what rich meat ever crosses my lips? The few hens we have lay out. I have gone to bed hungry betimes.'

'How unfortunate. You should ask the lord for a rise in your salary.'

'I wouldn't bother the great man. We have enough to keep skin and bones together.'

'Well, I can see your skin, Hackett, but I cannot see your bones, and they are even less visible in your wife.' She had been aware of his cruelty to the servants and others before he had insulted her in the library and now she wished to protect herself against his venomous gossip and get her revenge.

'My wife is naturally plump. Sure, she has only to look at food and she goes out. But I better be off now, for the lord seems anxious for a reply. I'll say good day to you.'

She watched him depart quickly down the road and went indoors to read the letter again. Despite all the arguments she had raised in her mind in the garden she felt at heart she wished to see this man again. His figure, seated in the great chair and listening to her voice, returned as she put down the letter, and her feelings to him were warm.

When Hackett was out of earshot he cursed her for the

insults she had piled on him. Her education gave her an edge over him. She knew that he had stolen wine from the cellar and taken meat from the larders. He would have to tread carefully with her.

Late that night Hackett made his way back down the valley. His mind was troubled. He moved as quickly as he could in the darkness, urging his horse forward. The sinister hedgerows were full of danger; at any moment he expected to be set upon by hungry peasants who would tear his clothes apart in search of money. He entered Kenrick's cobblestoned yard. He felt secure surrounded by the few outhouses and the two-storeyed house. A dog barked in a kennel, then another within the house, and the door was thrown open. In the half-light of a lantern he could see the figure of Kenrick, a pistol in his hand.

'Who's there this hour of the night?' he called. 'Come forward out of the darkness until I see your face.'

'It's only me, Kenrick,' Hackett told him.

'A queer time to come visiting and everybody in bed.'

'I had to come in the night so nobody could see me. Now that the bastard of a lord is back I have never time for a rest and I can't escape from the house.'

'Come in.'

Hackett followed Kenrick into the great kitchen. Portions of cured bacon hung from the brown rafters. A long wooden chest which contained bags of flour ran from under the open stairs to the end wall. The heavy dresser was lined with plates bearing blue pictures. They were of rough and bulky china, not fine like the plates at the great house. Kenrick's heavy boots were drying by the open fire, and Hackett could smell the unwashed sweat from Kenrick's feet.

'What brings you out at this time of night?' Kenrick asked when he sat in his great wooden armchair.

'It's advice I need, Kenrick. My mind is troubled with several mistakes I made at the great house.'

'It's not your nature to make mistakes, Hackett,' Kenrick told him as he lit his pipe with a coal from the fire.

'I know it's not, but wait until you hear what happened.' Kenrick listened as Hackett told him in anxious sentences how Lord Lannagh had insulted him in front of his guests, how he had departed in anger from the dining-room to discover

190

Eileen Horkan in the library. 'I lost my temper entirely. I even said that she was there to be horsed, that she was the lord's tally-woman.'

'And is she?'

'Not at the moment. But I know human nature, and he has taken a great shine to her. You know that he never touches any of the women – I offered to procure him a woman once and he nearly dismissed me – I think he has lost his head over this one.'

'So he hasn't humped her?'

'No. She has only been to the house once.'

'Then, beware, Hackett. He's not your raw buck or your squireen. And, remember, he has the power. A word from him and you could be on the road. You have taken advantage of your position.' Kenrick seemed to be unfriendly, and Hackett looked anxiously at him. He was smoking his pipe and looking down at the dying embers of the fire.

'I treat you like a lord when the bastard Lannagh is in London.' Hackett's voice was threatening. 'I'm not to blame he's taken to her.'

'Stop whinging like a cur!' Kenrick snapped. 'Don't you know that I want that woman out on the road? She makes me feel that I'm a planter, that I have no rights to the money from the valley or the labour her relatives give me each year in the spring and autumn.'

'Then, is there no way to get at her?' Hackett asked.

Kenrick reflected for some time. The lines on his forehead were tight in thought. 'There is, but it's not a thing I could do directly, for I have sworn my own vengeance on her. Next winter I'll have her relatives on the way to the county home. I want the village and the fields for sheep. There will be money in cattle and sheep during the next few years. Come spring, and there will not be a wall in the upper valley.'

'That will make her whinge. That will make her whinge,' Hackett chucked venomously.

'Yes! I'll set her relations on the ways of the world. I'll knock the pride out of them – and out of her cousin Seamus. A day will come when the rents squeeze them too hard and they will have to take to the road. They can go crying to her, and there is naught she can do for them, for she has no redress before the law and the law will always be on Kenrick's side.'

191

'That will take the heat out of them,' Hackett crowed.

'I'll make them knock on my door yet. They will beg for food. But keep your eyes open and bring me all the information you can gather. We'll brand her whore yet. The day will be ours.'

'That I will. My eye will be in all corners.'

'Good. Now, go. I'm a busy man.'

Kenrick did not offer Hackett a drink; when the conversation ended he showed him to his horse. Hackett mounted and made his way out of the valley.

18

John Burke and Michael Barrett always held a consultation before a ship sailed. Barrett made the final decisions as to when they would weigh anchor and what they would carry on their return voyage.

John Burke was worried. On the last occasion he had sailed to America he had returned with guns and ammunition which they had safely landed at his village and which were now secure in the mountains. The crew were bound to secrecy by oath. Yet there was always the danger that in drink they might reveal the secret cargo they carried. British agents were everywhere. He could be transported to Australia if the guns and ammunition were discovered.

He made his way up the broad stairs and knocked on the door of the map room. Michael Barrett told him to enter. He was sitting before his large desk. Gráinne Barrett stood at the window looking towards the sea. When she saw him she rushed to him and threw her arms about him in a spontaneous gesture that he loved. 'I am going to America with you, John! Father has decided to let me go at last.'

John Burke smelt the clear skin of her body, felt the opulent red hair against his cheek. The child he had once brought across the bay in a small rowing-boat had become a beautiful woman. 'It is a long time since I brought you out to Clare

Island in my small boat,' he said. 'Do you think you are fit for this journey? It can be rough on the great sea, and the conditions on board as rough as the sea itself.'

'I am willing to face any gale and do a man's work on deck if necessary,' she told him.

'My sea queen will not have to work!'

'She is not sailing as a sea queen,' Michael Barrett told him sharply, 'she is sailing as a crew member. She will keep the watches like all the others, she will eat the common food, she will climb aloft if necessary. She will have a private cabin to herself, but that is all I ask.' His voice was firm and unemotional. If she wished to have experience of the sea, then she would have it as a common deck-hand, bearing the rigours of the watch and the hard toil. 'Some day she will sail her own ship. She is not fit to be a sea captain until she has suffered what every sailor suffers who has sailed before the mast. So it was with me fifty-five years ago when I sailed under my father.'

There was no further discussion on the matter, and Michael Barrett called them to gather round about the maps which were set out in front of him on the great table. John Burke no longer needed to study them: he knew every line and figure on them. However, Michael Barrett loved the ritual, feeling perhaps that he had an active part in the voyage. 'If the wind is fair, the journey should take thirty-five days. You normally take two hundred passengers. There will be some additional ones on this journey. Make provision for them. I have heard accounts of captains sailing without proper provisions. These are hard times, and the journey is difficult enough; there is no need to make it more difficult still. On your return journey carry only corn. It is cheap and it will help people over the winter.'

'Why the additional number of people?'

'A whole village is sailing to America.'

'How can a whole village pay its passage money?'

'That is something I am not willing to discuss.' Barrett's voice was gruff, the answer final.

They sat and talked until it was time to leave for the port and provision the ship. 'I am going with you, John Burke,' Gráinne told him. 'Do not refuse me. You always said that the most important part of a journey is the beginning, in provisioning the ship and testing every rope and spar. I wish to take part in that work.'

'Very well,' he told her as they went down the stairs.

'I will be with you in a second,' she said, and went into a small room off the main hall. When she emerged she was dressed in men's rough clothes with a woollen cap concealing her hair.

'I don't know whether to laugh or cry,' John Burke said, looking at her in surprise. 'You are setting yourself a hard task.'

'It is my own choice.'

All that day she filled casks with fresh water. Then she beat the plugs into place in order to secure them. Her body ached, and the soft palms of her hands became raw. Towards evening her hands bled, and she cauterised them in salt water.

John Burke examined her palms at the end of the day. 'Why didn't you tell me your hands were bleeding?' he asked her.

'Because I am stubborn, John Burke, and because my father thinks I am not fit for man's work. I have the determination to keep working.' The palms of her hands were swelling. They were losing their fine sensation.

'Tomorrow you rest,' he told her.

'Tomorrow I will be here at the break of day to take further orders.'

That night she slept deeply, her body exhausted by work. She rose wearily the next morning with stiff limbs. She bound her hands with bandages and, having had something to eat, set off for the quays before the others were stirring. Today her work was more difficult. She had to carry the pork to the salting-barrels, half-sides of meat in rough bags. The fat stuck to her neck and matted her hair. In the evening she reeked of the meat. The crew members complained.

'It's not work for a woman, John Burke. Not even a skivvy in a town house would be asked to do what she has to do.'

'If I want advice, I'll ask for it. She is not a woman, she is a crew member.' He left it at that.

But his heart hurt every time he watched Gráinne Barrett enter and leave the warehouse. He admired her endurance. Soon all the people of Northport knew what was happening.

195

Nobody came to watch, but they spoke that night in the public house of this woman who worked like a common sailor.

'It's strange,' one of the crew said. 'She does common crewman's work and yet she remains a lady.'

'There is quality in her blood. She will take command of the ships yet. She is not a soft city woman.' It was a general comment upon which they all agreed. She did not meet her father up at the house for the whole three days' work on the dock. Then, on the day when they were due to sail, he came to her room as she packed.

'You have made a rough choice,' he said softly.

'You made it for me a long time ago,' she told him.

'You can still remain at home. You are under no obligation to sail to America.'

'I have made the choice and I will not change.'

'Then, my blessings go with you,' he said, his eyes watering.

'Thank you,' she replied almost coldly. She made her way out of the room and down to the stables, carrying with her a leather bag with her requirements. She mounted her horse and set out to join the ship. Michael Barrett watched his daughter disappear down the avenue and he began to weep. He wept for many reasons.

Liam Joyce and his village had spent the night on the quays in a close huddled mass. It had taken them two days to travel from the base of the mountain to the seaport. They had travelled together, giving each other mutual comfort. The first night they had slept in the sand dunes on the rough marram grass. The tang of the sea in their nostrils was strange to them; it was a warm night, and they did not suffer any discomfort. They carried with them all their possessions in sacks. Their money rested in leather purses hung about their necks.

As dawn broke, Liam Joyce looked towards the sea where the ship rode at anchor, fine of line, motionless. Three tall masts carried the furled sails. The rigging was a mass of ropes and net. This was the timber ship which would carry his village to America, a long way off. He could not comprehend the distance of three thousand miles; he could only imagine a ship sailing westwards, night and day, for a month and then for a week. Then the coast of the new world would stretch out in front of them. He would never return to Ireland again. He was taking his leave for the last time. In his sack he carried part of his hearthstone. Somewhere in America and at some future day he would set it beneath another fire.

Crowds were gathering along the quay. Many of them were well dressed. They sat by their large trunks, full fed and confident. Would he ever get away from the feeling that both he and his people were poor, that they were despised? A strong resolve grew in him as he surveyed the large warehouses of red sandstone, the merchants with their satisfied look, that he would tear his hands with work to make something out of his life: he would never want again; he would never pay rent; he would never take off his cap in obeisance to any man.

A horseman rode towards him. He dismounted and came in his direction.

'Are you Liam Joyce?' he asked.

'Yes.'

'Then, you have a parcel for Michael Barrett.'

'Yes.'

'Well, then, I'll take it and be away.'

'You will take it when the last of my people are on board the ship,' he replied directly.

'You do not trust me.' The man was sullen.

'I do not trust anybody. I have no reason to trust anybody. Two months ago Kenrick levelled my village. We have been living in makeshift shelters ever since.'

'You bring your aged with you. Is that wise? The sea is a treacherous place.'

'If they are to die, then they would prefer to die on their way to America, with the sea as grave, rather than starve in this cursed land for the want of a potato skin.' Liam spoke roughly because he lacked confidence in himself, overawed by the magnitude of his undertaking. He felt that everybody was hostile to him and that at the last minute something would go wrong with his plan. His eyes had the alertness of a frightened animal.

John Burke came down to the quay and looked at the passengers. He was curious as to how the Joyce family had managed to persuade Michael Barrett to give them passage to America.

'Have you paid the passage?' he asked Liam Joyce.

197

'No. My passage and the passage of my village are in this parcel. It is for Michael Barrett himself, and I will deliver it to him when my people are on board,' he said, taking a shabby parcel from inside his coat.

'You have put me out. I had not planned on taking you. You will be the last to be taken on board, and I'll see where I can fit you in.'

Liam Joyce held his anger. He must remain silent. He must get on board. He could give phrase to his anger when the wind caught the sails and Ireland slipped down behind the horizon.

The horseman stood like a sentry by them. Liam was alert to everything that was happening, trying to impose sequence on the movement about him. He looked at the people of his village. They had asked him to make the final decision, and he had made it; the care of the village was in his hands.

'Take courage,' he whispered to his wife. 'Tonight we will be on the great sea. It is dangerous and new. There is no going back now. Take your final look at the land. We will not return to it again.' He looked at his children clinging to her red skirt, the only clothing of any value she possessed. In America they would never know hunger again. They would never cry in the night for food which he could not give them.

The older people said nothing. They had never journeyed outside their village before. Everything was new to them. They thought of their ancestors buried in Murrisk Abbey for two hundred years; they had wished to be buried beside them. Now in old age they had to embark upon a journey across the sea.

Gradually the passengers were brought out to the great ship. The crew called out to them as if they were unworthy creatures. Finally only Liam Joyce and his village stood beside the granite steps. He watched the boat come across the water from the ship: it was time for the village to embark. Many began to cry as they stepped off the granite steps into the boat. Liam Joyce waited until all his people were on board when the boat returned for the final time and, having satisfied himself that everything was correct, he handed the parcel over to the horseman. He stepped on board the boat, and a crewman pushed off from the pier. Liam watched it recede, begin to tighten about itself and become part of something larger. He looked towards the ship: the decks were crowded with people.

198

He looked at the sailors rowing the boat, and it suddenly struck him that one of them was a woman. She wore rough clothes, and beneath her cap was thick red hair. Their eyes met for a moment.

Myles Prendergast retained his small room behind Molly Ward's public house. It suited his purpose. In the event of making an escape he could slip through the window on to the roof which slanted towards the yard and during the day he could conveniently enter the room from the alleyway. He had spent two years at a military school close to Paris where he had learned precision of thought.

He moved quietly through Castlebar, keeping as inconspicuous as possible. He studied the position of the military barracks situated over the town. There was no possible way of taking it with a small force. Colonel Spiker had stiffened the discipline amongst the soldiers, and even Molly Ward could see that they had very little accurate information on what was happening in the officers' rooms. Extra soldiers had been drafted in from Dublin. They were accurate marksmen and lived in a separate building.

He discovered that the weakness of the military system lay in the smaller towns, which were relatively unprotected: the constabulary were backed by only a small force of soldiers. A military force would have to be created which could move rapidly across the country, disappear into the hovels and the alleyways and re-emerge when needed. They must never take on the enemy in open combat. This singular fact was the basis of the report he wrote each evening as he sat at his table. He stated that he could not work out the offensive in detail until he had surveyed the military defence of each town and village but he pointed out that the best effects could be obtained in the villages. The military presence there would be driven back to Castlebar, and the great houses of the landlords would be defenceless.

Myles visited Frederick Cavendish at home when he had finished his report, and found the old man wrapped in a blanket and his feet soaking in a tub of hot water.

'It is brilliant,' said Cavendish, after he had heard Myles out. 'But it is on paper, and you are like all military-minded men. You think that if you set facts and figures down on paper, then all action will later follow these plans. Military action is not a proposition by Euclid; battles have been won on the off chance. If old Blücher had not come up at the right time, Wellington would not have beaten Napoleon at Waterloo. And, if my memory serves me right, Blücher was drunk on vodka and found it difficult to stay in the saddle. Napoleon had his attack on Russia well planned but he happened to forget that Russia had generals January and February fighting on its side. I do not think that war is a military game – it often depends on chance.'

'But we must draw up some type of plan,' Myles protested.

'Of course you must. You say that Ireland must be rid of the tyranny of the British. Do you think that the noble Irish are fit to govern themselves? Those who take up arms always assume that God is on their side and that they are noble and well intentioned. Well, let me tell you, young man – they, too, can become corrupt. Nature never changes, and the Irish nature is as bad if not worse than the English nature. Let me tell you that your plan is brilliant on paper, but find me this army who will take to the fields and disappear into the backstreets of the towns – the British would have them flushed out in a week! And where are the mountains and woods in which they can take refuge? The scale is too small.'

'You dismiss this plan too lightly,' Myles said angrily.

'I dismiss it because I am old and because I know human nature and I am sceptical about new dawns and new republics.'

'Well, would you have people lie down and die?' Myles asked.

'No, I certainly would not.'

'Well, better die in trying to fill their bellies and better their conditions than live like animals in bogholes, and on the sides of mountains.'

'The future is with you, young man. The past haunts me.'

They drank some port and spoke of more pleasant things, but Myles was still frustrated and angry when he left Cavendish.

One of the carters who made the daily journey between North-port and Castlebar brought news to Myles that John Burke had arrived back from Liverpool and would soon set out for America. Myles immediately set off for the port, carrying his plans neatly set out on sheets of paper in his greatcoat.

John Burke was waiting for him in the office when he

arrived. All day he had supervised the rationing of the ship and now he was almost ready to sail. 'Have you made out the report and the plans?' he asked directly.

'Yes.' Myles unbuttoned his coat and laid his report on the table. 'But on the way to America I can enlarge upon my ideas and set them out at greater length.'

'The cell in New York have asked for these plans – they are professionals, which is why I need you there. They will wish to know how their money is spent.'

'Do you really expect help from America?' Myles asked him.

'Where else will help come from? They are our own people. France will not give us aid, and Spain is a useless kingdom.' John Burke went to the window and looked towards the sea. The last passengers were going on board. 'I have set a small cabin aside for you and arranged for some clothes. We could be in New York in forty days. It will be a new experience for you.'

'I have always wished to visit the home of freedom,' Myles said wryly.

They were just about to leave when they heard someone coming up the stairs. Gráinne Barrett entered the room.

'I think you should meet our new crew member!' John Burke laughed.

'You try to humiliate me, John Burke!' Gráinne was embarrassed. 'You did not tell me that this Frenchman was here.'

'Not only here, but he is travelling with us.'

'No, he is not!' she said hotly, flinging him a glance.

John Burke moved quickly towards her and grasped her by the shoulders. 'Listen, and listen well,' he told her. 'I am tired of your angers. You are a crew member: you live like one, you eat like one and you will keep your silence!'

'If my father knew that you were carrying revolutionaries on board his ship, he would have you whipped.' Gráinne stood defiant.

'You arrogant bitch! You know *nothing* of the dark side of the Barrett history. You know nothing of what happened on the sea. Nothing.' He shook her body as if it were a limp puppet, and her anger subsided: John Burke had never treated her in that manner before.

'I'm sorry,' she said in a small voice. 'Forgive me.'

201

'There is no forgiveness – I don't forgive. You are a common sailor. Now, prepare to take us on board.'

Gráinne left the room shaken and humiliated, and walked down the stairs, across the quay to the boat. What was the dark side of her father's history? she wondered.

'I am sorry all that occurred,' John Burke told him, 'but perhaps it is just as well it happened as it did. There is no reason now for high intrigue. She knows that you are on board the ship, and I assure you she will keep her lips sealed. Now, let us be off.'

They left the building and made their way down the steps and into the small boat. Gráinne Barrett, still shaken by the roughness of John Burke, waited quietly for them. Casting off, she grasped the oars expertly and bent her body forward to draw them slowly away from the quay. John Burke looked sullenly into the water. Myles caught her eye for a moment then he turned away. She looked fragile, as if John Burke had momentarily broken some confidence within her, but she rowed them expertly towards the ship, then climbed quickly aboard and disappeared.

19

It was the first week of June. The summer was warm, and the soft clouds which moved across the sky carried little rain. The potato stalks were strong and healthy. Men said that the crop would be abundant: the land was not cursed after all. Hopes were raised in all quarters. Hedgerows and woods were luxuriant with leaf and flower.

Eileen Horkan had often thought of Lord Lannagh since their first encounter in the library. Her answer to his invitation had been evasive, and there had been no more communication between them. She did not wish to have her life disturbed by this man: she had enjoyed a tranquil even life with her books and the supervision of the farm. She also wrote letters to the *Nation* under an assumed name and took a serious, but detached, interest in politics, valuing the time she spent in her room reading and writing. A visit to Lord Lannagh's house so soon after their first encounter would have been both imprudent and common, she felt. Nevertheless, her attitude towards him was ambivalent: her background dictated that she should detest him and, though he wasn't the owner of vast tracts of land like other landlords, he possessed lands which carried high rents. The very books he had sent her could have been purchased by the rents paid by peasants who had spent long hours in the fields attending to their crops or fattening pigs in their kitchens and lying down with them at night-time in single-roomed cottages. Her father had told her that the nobility should be destroyed in the same way as the French monarchy was destroyed.

'Get rid of them once and for all and start afresh like the French did. If they could guillotine a monarch whose blood-line stretched back a thousand years, why not Cromwell's henchmen?' Her father's hatred for the aristocracy was in her blood. She had watched her cousin, Seamus Costello, grow old in a mere three years, trying to pay Kenrick the heavy rents he imposed upon the upper part of the valley.

Then there was another section of her mind which was sympathetic towards the great house and all it stood for. It was noble and organised; life there was filled with the joy of living. The lawn which stretched down to the lake might have once been the land of fifteen families but, looking at the even sweep of pasture, the disposition of the trees, the cattle grazing there, one forgot these things. Mrs Rance had told her of the walled garden behind the house with its glasshouses and rare plants and flowers. Why should all this be destroyed? It did stand for something noble, and for a mind that was refined. And, she asked herself, should all the books be burned when the revolution came? She would have rushed to defend them from the fire. Lord Lannagh himself was a man of gracious manners. In a landscape where such people did not exist Eileen Horkan found herself attracted to him. He lived in a remote world of courtesy and habits to which she had only gained entry through her reading, and sometimes she felt that she did not belong to any culture but to a world of the imagination without trouble or the terrible legacy of history.

Prudence, however, cautioned her to be careful. She knew that she had a mortal enemy in Hackett. She was certain that he had carried news of her visit to the house and the library to Kenrick.

Eileen Horkan saddled her horse, a quiet animal with trusting eyes, white except for a dab of black on its forehead, and decided to ride up into the forest. Here on a platform of rock she could look down on the lake with its islands and, on the far side on a gentle incline, the house of Lord Lannagh. She often came here in summer-time where she could sit undisturbed by the presence of people or the brooding melancholy of the small fields and the drab cabins.

204

She made her way along the great wall of Lord Lannagh's estate, then turned right at the entrance to the forest and rode carefully along the forest path, soft with withered leaves which had fallen over the years. The sunlight was dappled through the branches, and there was no wind. Only the soft sound of the horse's hoofs echoed among the trees. Water trickled over the rocks from puffy moss, and the stream-beds which ran across the path were dry. The forest was full of mystery for her as she moved through the shafts and columns of light entering through the canopy of leaves, and her mind was filled with thoughts of summer. After an hour she reached the open platform of rock. She dismounted and tied the reins to a branch, sitting down on the platform to look down on the lake. She could make out all the islands clearly with their growths of shrubs and trees, forming cool fan-shaped masses. To the east lay Castlebar vague in the summer haze. As her eyes travelled across the lake to the house, she saw the walled garden with its glasshouses and she wished that this perfect moment could have lasted for ever. There was no tension or tug of feeling within her: the earth was sweet and fruitful, and there was birdsong in the forest. She lay back on the warm heather and looked up at the sky above her, clear and blue, and she imagined that the skies of Greece and Rome had such clarity and that the earth and stone there carried the same warmth. The wood was filled with light narcotic scents that seemed to drug her mind, and her body brightened with sensuality, which she had never explored. Only on a warm day on a platform of rock above could she admit to such feelings; they were like foreign voices in her blood.

In the middle distance, on the slope of the mountain, she could just make out a horseman making his way up the steep incline. The air was hazed with heat below her, and his image was uncertain, but as he moved upward he became more defined and she recognised the figure of Lord Lannagh. Periodically he stopped his horse and broke a twig from a tree which he examined carefully, smelt and then placed in a leather satchel on the flank of the horse. She hoped he would veer away across the slope of the mountain, but he continued to move towards her and she sat, transfixed by his progress, until it was too late to mount her horse and rush away. He had noticed her by now and was moving quickly up through the thicket, his eyes intent upon her. He waved to her, and instinctively she waved towards him and smiled, and then he was on the platform of rock beside her.

'I hope I have not disturbed your reverie!' he said directly.

'My mind was totally blank,' she assured him.

'I cannot imagine that! I am sure it was full of the poetry of the day. May I dismount?'

'Certainly,' she said with a smile.

With a quick movement he descended from his horse and tied the reins to a small shrub. He was dressed in light riding-clothes which emphasised the lean lines of his body.

'I *am* sorry I disturbed you,' he said, moving towards her. 'Strange that we should meet in such a delightful place on such a day.' He sat down beside her on the dry rock and looked down on the landscape, ordered and calm.

'I thought you kept to your estate,' she said.

'Oh, no. I often find my way up here – it settles my mind. Besides, I have an interest in botany. Perhaps some day in a crevice I may find a new flower and give my name to it. It would be gratifying to be remembered as the discoverer of a new flower.'

'Are you really worried about immortality and what men shall think of you?' she asked laughingly.

'Not really, but I would like to discover a new species of flower. I have made out a map of this forest and this mountain and entered on it the positions of each species of flower – they grow at different levels – and, in fact, I have written a paper on the subject.'

'Not very interesting,' she remarked.

'But it is.' He looked at her in surprise. 'I find it very interesting. I would gladly spend my life cultivating rare flowers.'

'And neglect your friends and your estates?'

'I think so,' he said innocently.

'I believe you would,' she said.

She looked at his fingers. He had plucked some heather and was opening the small flowers with great care. They were long aristocratic fingers which had never touched harsh objects. The skin was white, the nails carefully pared, the cuticles clean. She had never met a man with such fine hands. While

206

his eyes were intent on the heather, she observed his face closely. It took eight generations of breeding to create such lines. There was a scent from his body and his clothes.

Why *should* I hate this man? she thought, and she did not care at that moment what the history of religious beliefs dictated to her. It was a warm summer day, and there was sensuality in the air.

'I tried to grow this heather in one of my glasshouses, but it did not thrive there. It is a small tough plant and belongs on the high mountains.'

He let the heather fall from his hand and looked at her. Their eyes were locked together for a moment, then they both turned away and looked down on the landscape filled with summer light.

'Do you often visit this place?' he asked.

'Only in summer when the paths are dry. I discovered it a long time ago when I was young.'

'I discovered it during my first summer here. When I return to London I often think of this ledge of rock and the view beneath. It haunts me— However, I talk too much.' He turned to her abruptly, almost shyly. 'Would you care to join me in a glass of wine? You will find that it is light and delicate.'

She nodded her assent, and he walked to the horse and took a basket from the back of the saddle, to which it had been strapped. He placed the slender wicker basket between them and opened it, taking out a bottle of white wine and two glasses.

'Let us begin with some white wine,' he announced. 'I think that you will find it suitable to the day.'

The wine sparkled as he poured it into the glasses. She did not find the elegance strange; it was suited to the summer day.

'To the flowers of the forest,' she toasted. 'And let us hope that hidden in these woods is a singular one which will carry your name.'

'I know that there is something beneath some tree or in a crevice in a rock waiting to be discovered and named.'

The wine was light on her palate. She had read that Europe was divided into two civilisations: the Roman civilisation drank wine; the Nordic civilisation drank beer. She recalled Roman lines which celebrated wine.

'What thoughts are passing through your mind?' he asked.

207

'I was recalling the Virgilian phrases in which he talks of wine,' she replied, flushing.

'Recite some for me,' he said eagerly.

'You would think that I was trying to impress you with a little learning.'

'Well, impress me, then.'

She recalled some lines from Virgil and recited them.

'There is always that great sadness in his lines,' he said when she finished. 'He caught some melancholia of the civilised mind. Did you know that there was a Celtic strain in him?'

'No!' she answered in surprise.

'There is good evidence for it.' He smiled at her.

'Do *you* possess the melancholia of the civilised mind?' she asked pointedly.

He looked at her intently for a moment, and there was a certain sadness in his eyes. 'Yes,' he told her directly and looked away.

He was silent for some time, opening and closing his fingers elegantly about the glass, and staring at the blue haze. 'I presume that is why I gather rare flowers and books and why I do not take any great interest in politics. Everything passes so rapidly, delight and pain and the flowers that have just a season. We only belong here for a season.'

'So nothing is important, then?' she asked.

'The moment is important.'

'This moment?'

'Yes. The moment between event and event: an hour spent on a ledge of land; a moment that has not been planned.' He looked towards her. The beauty of her body and the richness of her mind stirred him with desire for her. He wanted to place his glass aside and make love to her, filling out the moment with total and physical delight, but she would not cry with pleasure beneath him and the moment would have been soured. He turned from her beauty and looked at the dry rock.

Eileen studied his profile. This was not the spore of one of Cromwell's Roundheads, she thought. He was rare like one of the flowers he grew in the glasshouses within the walled garden. At that moment, if he had put his arms about her, she knew she would not have protested. She was momentarily startled by this thought, then brushed it from her mind.

'You did not accept my invitation,' he said directly.

'But I did not refuse it,' she answered, looking down.

'It was a delicate refusal. Have I given offence to you?' he asked.

'No. You have not given me offence, but I thought it would be rather immediate after my first visit to the house.'

'You are always welcome,' he said warmly. 'Feel free to enter the library at any time and borrow my books.'

'You are very generous.'

'No, I am not. Very few people talk to me of books.'

Time passed. They spoke of many things on the ledge of rock. Eileen looked down at the lake and noticed that noon had passed into evening. 'I must hasten home,' she told him. 'I have to attend to my work about the farm.'

'Shall I see you again?' he asked.

'Perhaps,' she said. 'I think I would like to see the exotic flowers you have so carefully grown in your glasshouses.'

He helped her on to her horse, and she felt his firm fingers on her arm. She said good day to him and moved down along the forest path.

As he had promised, Lord Lannagh sent her another parcel of books the following day; it was a firm bond between them. Eileen duly returned the books, and within a week Hackett carried another parcel to the house. He was less forward in his behaviour this time, for he possessed the low cunning of a peasant who knew when his position was threatened. When the time came, he would be quick to point out that Eileen Horkan was a tally-woman but meanwhile he feared her independence and her influence with his master.

She read the books avidly. The texture of the pages told her that they were expensive editions, and as she touched the leather covers she was moved by a sexuality which surprised her. Much as she tried to push the thoughts of this man to the back of her mind, his features and his gait returned to her. In a world on the verge of starvation and death, he was elegant of body, his bearing free from the heavy miseries which now beset the country.

The effects of the hunger were brought home to her by Seamus Costello, who lived in the valley below her.

'We are already behind with the rent,' he told her. 'Kenrick insists that we pay immediately or we will be out on the road.' She gave him most of the money she had on hand.

'Do not give it all to Kenrick,' she advised him. 'Buy food and sustain yourself.'

'And what shall we do, Eileen, when the money runs out? I cannot repay you.'

'When the money runs out, come to me again. I will find some way of raising money even if I have to go to the bank. The bad times will not always continue.'

'I hope that we shall live to see brighter days,' he said grimly as he slipped away. She sat by the fire and looked into the dying embers. She had made a rash promise.

Lord Lannagh, for his part, had been brought up to regard the Irish as an inferior race. The Roman legions had never planted their standards in this soil, and they lacked the order which had shaped the British mind. The country had been planted and replanted, and the Irish driven into the thin boggy lands where they had clawed sustenance from the earth and survived. He always felt that they were unwashed; it was a deep prejudice which he could not root out. His agent could have provided him with Irish women, but he felt that contact with them would have soiled him.

He was haunted by thoughts of Eileen Horkan. Every time he went to his library and tried to read, his mind returned to this woman.

He walked in his gardens, drafting an invitation letter. The woods smelt rich with honeysuckle, and the cushion of moss underfoot was soft and springy. Outside, he had seen hungry people walking along the roads as he returned from Galway in his coach. They were talking in the city of famine and of the inability of the British government to deal with it. Yet within the walls, surrounded by the culture of rare plants and in the luxurious atmosphere of his library, he could shut himself away from the starving people.

His letter finally dispatched, Lord Lannagh waited anxiously for the reply. When it came and he read the contents, to his surprise she had agreed to see him again. Hackett had noted the expression on his face. I have never known him to take any interest in a woman since he first visited Mayo. This

210

Horkan woman has a power over him, he thought. He kept his feelings and his anxieties to himself – he could not even trust his wife, who was a gossip. He must alert Kenrick to what was going on; it might be to his advantage to know what was happening. 'There is no fool like an old fool,' he repeated to himself when he went down to his quarters. He would have to take stock of his position. Outside the wall there was hunger, and Hackett was partial to rare wine and good food.

The night before her meeting with Lord Lannagh, Eileen retired early to her room and with slow sensuality bathed her flesh until it was soft and perfumed. She examined the perfection of her body by candlelight: her breasts, cupped in her hands, were firm, the nipples erect between her fingers. The slow movement of cloth on her hips and inner thighs gave her a warm pleasure which seemed hostile to the narrow room in which she lived. Did Father Coady realise what sensualities he had started within her when he taught her how to read the Latin classics? By the fire she combed her long dark hair, untangling the strands until they were free and fine, letting them fall down her back. She slept that night between linen sheets, aromatic with herbs she had brought from the garden, and her dreams were ordered and tranquil. She had blocked out images of famine, of the poisoned fields, of the air heavy with rot.

Wednesday was a bright day. The sun was mellow like a ripe fruit, and a light wind played on the lake as she approached the great house. She passed a group of starving men on their way to the Board of Works drainage scheme. Their faces were faint and grey. 'The Englishman's whore,' somebody called after her as she passed them on her white horse. It was a sharp intrusion: already the gossips were talking about her. Hackett must be poisoning their minds against her. He was an evil man, jealous of his position. The word 'whore' rankled in her mind and soured the pleasant thoughts which the day had engendered.

Hackett was waiting for her when she arrived at the great house. 'You are welcome, Miss Horkan,' he said with studied formality.

'Hackett, I want words with you,' Eileen began. 'If you do not hold your tongue and do your master's bidding, you will be joining the stream of people making their way to the

211

workhouse and you will not be fattening yourself on stolen meat.'

He cringed and mumbled excuses with native humility.

'I don't wish to hear any of your excuses. You blacken my name, Hackett, and you will be dismissed!'

He was shaken by the violence of her words. He was in a position of weakness: she could disclose information about him which could destroy him. 'I'll get even with that Horkan bitch,' he muttered to himself as he led her horse away to the stables. 'I'll get even with the whore.' The words gave him some satisfaction.

She made her way to the library. Lord Lannagh was waiting for her at the door.

'You are very welcome,' he said directly and with formality. 'Thank you for accepting my invitation.'

'Thank you for offering it to me,' she answered. She had not exaggerated his appearance in her mind: he was tall, with greying hair, the features fine, the movement aristocratic. He offered her a glass of port and directed her to an armchair opposite him. She sipped from the glass: the port had a velvet quality appropriate to the library, with its leather armchairs and the mahogany table.

'May I be permitted to smoke my cigar?' Lannagh asked. 'It is one of the pleasures I enjoy in the library.'

She nodded.

'Tell me again of your interest in books,' he said, having lit his cigar.

'It is a scandalous story,' she said.

'I like the breath of scandal!'

She told him again of her education and of how Father Coady had called her to burn his volumes of Ovid. 'I did, of course, but only after I had read them. My good priest said that to read Latin poetry is to visit the Elysian fields.'

'And have you visited them?'

'I have. I have seen beyond the Alps. I have been to Rome.'

He was surprised at the firmness with which she expressed herself. 'You were lucky. I wish I had known such a man.'

'Oh, he was a small insignificant man, with a small head and a face like old parchment. The world was full of tears for him.'

'And is it for you?'

'At present, yes.'

'I know. I, too, have watched the hungry make their way along the roads. These are sad times, full indeed of the tears of things.' He did not wish to continue this line of conversation and brought it back to books. He led her to the great table, and opened a huge volume for her; it carried brightly coloured pages of birds against delicate tranquil backgrounds.

'These were done by Audubon. They give me endless pleasure – sometimes, when the days are wet and the skies grey, I look at them.'

'They belong in an enchanted world,' she agreed, falling under the spell. 'They have a dreamlike quality.'

Later, as they walked in his garden, he explained to her the origin of many of the plants. The time spent in his company passed rapidly, and she could not say at what precise point she had fallen in love with him: it might have been in the gardens, or among the woods, or as they made their way up from the lake, or when they sat down to an evening meal under the soft candelabra lights. It was very late when she left the great house, and during the next weeks she returned more and more frequently.

One night she remained until morning. He had sent his great carriage for her, and all evening she had been preparing for her visit. Her body was washed and smelt of lavender, her black hair fell finely on her shoulders as she walked about her room in quiet excitement. She was pleased with the blue velvet dress which gathered about her waist and fell elegantly from her hips. It was soft to her touch and had not been worn before.

There was a sense of pleasure in her body which she had not experienced before. She had not been asked to be born into this landscape and she banished the idea that people were hungry and dispossessed. The gathering disaster was not of her making.

She examined herself in the mirror while she waited for the coach.Then she heard the wheels grate on the road as it turned and, gathering her dress about her and certain that everything was secure, she left the house.

As the great carriage made its way along the road she looked up at the distant sky and the mountains. The colours were

213

delicate, and she knew that the good summer weather would continue.

In the great house the lights were already burning in the windows. There was a late summer haze on the great lawn which led to the lake.

'We shall have dinner in the dining-room,' Lord Lannagh told her as he took her arm and led her across the great hall to the dining-room where the two candelabra sparkled with fractured light. Their dinners had not been as formal before.

He had set out one of his rare orchids on the table, and the great fireplace was filled with garden flowers. The heat of the summer night was gentle in the room and almost tangible. Through the great windows they could see the moon on the lake.

The meal, which consisted of five courses, was light, and their conversation dealt chiefly with books. He spoke, too, of a trip he had made to Italy as a young man.

Eileen drank the white wine slowly as she listened to his conversation. She could not take her eyes from his face: particularly the sad Virgilian eyes which seemed remote. 'You are sad tonight, Edward,' she told him.

'No. I am very happy, very tranquil. This is one of the wonderful moments we have between sad events. I am totally happy. And you? Do you like my summer tales?'

'Of course, I love your summer tales! You recount your journeys very well. You have had all the great experiences of life.'

'No, that is not true. That is not true. But before we go to the library – I wish to give you something. I would like you to remember the occasion with a little gift.'

He went to a wide sideboard, took an ornate box which he had placed there before her arrival and handed it to her. 'And here is the key,' he said, taking it from his pocket.

'Should I open it?' she asked.

'Yes, please do.'

She opened the box slowly. It was a knee desk with silver inkwells set in mahogany and a leather leaf on which one could write.

'It is beautiful, beautiful,' she said as she looked at the exquisite craftsmanship.

'And, by the way,' Lannagh said casually, 'you may be interested in its previous owner.'

214

She examined the inscription on a silver plaque. It read 'George Noel Byron'.

'No! I do not deserve this. It is priceless.' She was suddenly alarmed.

'You do. You have brought me delightful days. Having met the lord himself in Italy, I am sure it would be his wish that you should have it.'

Her fingers ran along the edges of the small writing-cabinet. Her mind was exhilarated by the contact.

'Now it is time to retire to the library,' he told her. 'I will have the writing-desk sent to you if you wish.'

'No, I shall take it with me into the library. I will not let it out of my sight.'

'I shall carry it for you.' He took the small writing-desk, and she followed him to the library. Wine and port had been set out on the large table. He poured some wine and carried it to her, but she left it aside and continued to examine the ornate writing-desk. She observed a small keyhole close to the base that she had not seen before.

'I have discovered another compartment!' she said excitedly. She placed the key in the keyhole, turned it and pulled out a small shallow tray. It contained three letters. The name 'Countess Guiccioli' was written on the back of each letter. She flicked through them and examined the signature at the bottom of each letter.

'They are Lord Byron's letters,' she said.

'I know,' he said, smiling at her. 'I would have let you discover them later.'

She left the letters and rushed towards him, throwing her arms about him and placing her head on his shoulder.

'Oh, why should all this happen to me? And why should it happen now? Why should it happen now?'

He took her head in his hands and looked at her. 'You deserve all the gifts I can give you. Why did this not happen to me when I was young?'

'But you are young. Yes, you are' – and instinctively she kissed him. He took her face in his hands again and looked at her. Then he kissed her slowly on the eyes and on the mouth and ran his fingers through her hair. Passion began to surge in her body, without logic and without control.

'I have desired you more than anything or anybody I have

215

ever seen before,' Lannagh said in a low voice. 'I have wept here thinking of you. Thinking of the delight of touching and caressing your body.'

She opened her dress quietly and let it fall to the floor. 'I am pagan and naked before you and I love you,' she said.

'How beautiful you are, and how your eyes shine.'

'And you, too, have beauty.'

'Will you come with me?'

'Yes.'

He opened the false library door which led to his room. He closed it firmly and looked at the white beauty of the woman who stood before him. 'Night after night I thought of you,' he told her.

'Then love me quietly – for this is a moment between the sad events.'

'A moment between the sad events.'

Many years later, when she was asked who the father of her child was and how he had seduced her, she would not answer. She could not describe how they had lain between soft sheets on a summer's night, and made love slowly and with few words. She would not tell anyone that her being had been filled with sensual delight and that she had cried out as ultimate pleasure filled her body.

All that summer night they did not sleep: they knew, instinctively, they would never enjoy such happiness again. Forces were gathering about them over which they had no control; they had enjoyed the moment between the sad events.

216

20

THE SUN WAS MOVING DOWN behind Clare Island when they were ready to weigh anchor. The ship moved out through the innumerable islands with minimum sail, but beyond, in the broad bay, there was a light swell upon the sea. For many this was their first introduction to the sickening unsteady movement of a ship.

The passengers crowded the decks to catch their last view of Ireland. They could see the towering hump of Clare Island to the south and to the north a continuous line of rugged mountains. As they passed Clare Island there was only a small glow of light to the west. The island was dark and without dimension, but they could make out small points of light on its flanks: it was their last memory of Ireland. To the west and in the darkness lay a vast expanse of ocean and a promised land; to the east the land they had abandoned, a pestilence growing in the soil.

Gráinne Barrett climbed aloft with the other sailors when they passed beyond the island. The movement of the ship and the incline of the mast and spars over the waves caused her no fear. She had often climbed aloft before, and her body moved to the rhythm of the ship and the sea. They unknotted the ropes and unfurled the sails, which flapped for a moment and then, catching the wind, stiffened. The ship became alive; the masts and the sails strained under the pressure of the wind, and the riggings sang. Below Gráinne the prow of the ship moved across the waves, cutting their crests into fine spray and foam. Under such conditions their journey would be safe, but she knew that in mid-Atlantic they would run into storms. Here she would test herself against the uncertainties of the sea, the element into which she was born and the element in which she must spend the rest of her life.

Above her the dark night was crusted with the comfort of stars, cold and sharp. The firmness of the North Star was the pathfinder across the limitless seas: John Burke had taught her the names of the stars in Irish and how to chart her position by them. Below her on the deck a lantern swung to the rhythm of the sea, casting a faint light on part of the deck and the rope coils. Some people still lingered on the deck, but others had moved down to their narrow berths. She moved in along the spar with the others and descended the ratlines. It would be an uneventful night: the first nights at sea were always uneventful.

Below deck, in cramped quarters and in darkness, Liam Joyce began to settle his people for the night. They were in a narrow place, on the lowest deck of the ship and partly under the water-line, right up forward where the timbers curved in towards the prow. It smelt of tar and sea-water, and the air was stale. The small cabin rose and sank as the ship moved over the waves, and already their stomachs were unsettled; many wished to rush on deck and vomit over the ship's railings. Their heads were reeling as if they were drunk. They were not only confused by the forward pitching of the ship but also by its rolling sideways movements.

In the darkness Liam Joyce began to arrange people for the night. The old were placed in the lowest bunks, the younger children crowded in twos and threes in the middle bunks and the adults in the highest. Liam Joyce chose to sleep on the floor with his wife.

'If you feel sick, vomit into the bucket,' he told them. 'Call out, and I will bring it to you. Do not vomit into the bunk.'

Already he had carried the bucket to two old people, a man and his wife, who had no children. The stench of their vomit filled the cabin. He opened the door, hoping that some air from the passageway might enter the cabin. Outside in the passageway there were latrines. He had had to explain to the people how to use them in direct words. 'The ship is not a field; you won't find bushes growing on the decks.'

Finally Liam Joyce found time to rest, lying on the hard deck-floor beside his wife Oonah. In bunks about him lay the whole village, their minds and bodies confused. The journey would take almost seven weeks, but he did not mind the hardship to which he would be subjected. His life had always been one of hardship and fear, and he would endure sickness and the elements patiently in order to reach America. It beckoned like a light.

He could not afford the luxury of thinking of all that had happened in the last weeks. Kenrick had forced him into a final decision, and now, despite the small area of the cabin and the confined space in which they would live, he felt happy. There was no nostalgia in his mind for the levelled village and the acres, half-bog and sour, that they had abandoned. He would take his chances on the high seas and in a new land.

John Burke took a pen and entered the events of the first day in the log. It was a dry factual account of his departure, his position, the number of passengers on board, the wind direction and the progress of the voyage. The lantern hanging from the beam in his cabin moved gently to the movement of the ship. It would not always swing so gently, he thought. But worse than the storms that might suddenly blow up from the south, driving the ship northwards and tearing at the sails, was the possibility of fever on board the ship. He had known ships where it had raged during a whole voyage; the sea route to America was marked with the bones of the dead. He worried, too, about Gráinne Barrett. Could he trust her on the high spars in a storm when the winds tore at the riggings, when the timbers cracked under the strain?

He poured out a glass of rum and reflected on the days which lay ahead. He must keep the ship scoured: fever was generated in filth; the ship would have to be fumigated every third day. He would nail the regulations to the mast and keep the passengers active. He tested his gun; he might need it.

Before he slept he made a final check of the ship. He walked slowly along the deck, checking ropes and knots instinctively, looking aloft at the sails carrying an easy wind and listening to the tell-tale sound from boom and spar. He could detect in the darkness any sound of faulty rigging. Below deck the passengers would be trying to sleep. He knew that many of them would already be sick and that within two days the ship would reek of vomit and excrement. He *must* keep the ship scoured. He was obsessed by the thought that fever might seed in filth. The holds would need air. Then there was the danger of fire. He knew that at that moment somebody below deck was smoking a pipe. Carelessness could turn the ship into a furnace.

He reached the prow of the ship where he found Gráinne Barrett, leaning against the mast, keeping watch. She was wrapped in a large woollen cape against the wind which came off the sea.

'Well, what do you think of your first day at sea as a common sailor?' he asked.

'Raw,' she stated bluntly.

'I watched you climb aloft. You had me worried. I do not think your father intended you to go aloft.'

'I will do what the common crewman does. I will not be made an exception of. When I sail my own ship I want to know what it is like to wash a deck, sew a canvas, haul a rope and climb the shrouds in a storm.' Her voice was hard with determination, but he knew from the sound of her voice that her body was cold. Even the wind from the summer seas was cold at night.

'Here, drink from this,' he said and passed her a flask of rum. She took it from him.

'I suppose if I'm a common sailor I might as well drink like one,' she said and took a drink from the flask. It was strong and warm in her mouth.

'Keep it during the watch,' John Burke said. 'Take the wheel later and get used to handling a ship under canvas. You can feel the whole ship through the wheel when you get to know it. The life of the ship is in the wheel.'

'Yes. I shall do that. How long will the voyage take?'

'One never knows. The winds are fair now and in our favour, but if we run into storms we could be driven northwards, and if a mast snaps, then we will limp into New York a fortnight late – you cannot say what the sea will do. Good night now, and keep an eye out for other ships. The chances are that you will not see one, but at the same time one never knows.'

She caught sight of his figure, wide shoulders, hooped with age, under one of the lanterns for a moment, then he disappeared into the darkness. He had been on the seas fifty years, sailing for the first time as a cabin-boy under her grandfather. He knew the seas as others knew the land and had an instinct for all that might happen.

Leaning against the mast she looked forward into the darkness of the night. The rum had warmed her blood. Sometimes the wind carried the fine spray on to her face, but she felt secure in the solitude. The sea was in her blood, they told her, and she could feel now that she was part of it. She recalled her education in England and Sister Geneviève, the last of a generation who had moved down the roads of France in horse-drawn carriages and attended the court at Versailles. She had learned the life of refinements in the convent and now she was learning the nature of the sea. There would always be the tension in her blood between the great house overlooking Clew Bay and the three-masted ships which sailed the oceans of the world. The sea was her master, and she must return to it again and again to renew her knowledge of herself.

The hours passed. She was caught up in the rhythm of the masts and sails and the heaving sea beneath her. When the bell rang for the change of watch she suddenly felt tired – it had been a long time since she had slept – and she returned to her small cabin and took off her heavy cape and her men's clothing. She slipped in between the luxury of white sheets and fell asleep.

When Liam Joyce woke next morning he thought for a moment he was at home, then he realised that he was on his way to America. He shook his wife awake.

'Did you sleep well, Oonah?' he asked.

'No, all night my head turned. I feel sick. Will I ever sleep on the journey?'

'You will. In a week's time you will not notice the movement of the ship,' he told her.

'It plunges like a wild horse. Up and down, up and down it goes. Twice I had to carry the bucket to people.'

'Well, I'd better get rid of it into the sea,' he said.

'It's not a man's job.'

'It is for the moment. When I have worked out the order of

221

things somebody else will do it, but for the moment we must try to eat. It is important that everyone should have food. We have enough rations for six days, then I will have to buy provisions.'

A grey light entered the cabin from the gangway. Bodies were beginning to stir in the bunks and children to cry. The air in their cabin was fetid. He took the bucket of vomit and carried it up the rough stairs and on to the deck. It was a slate-grey morning, and about him was the immensity of the sea, flat and empty. He was suddenly conscious of some of the passengers looking at the bucket of vomit in his hand. He rushed to the side of the ship and threw the green slime overboard. Then he took a rope from the deck and, tying it around the handle, cast the bucket into the sea to wash away the filth.

'What are you doing with that rope?' a sailor asked him brusquely in Irish.

'Scouring the bucket,' he said.

'If you want a rope, you buy it. Do not use ship's tackle. We run an orderly ship here. And get over to the barrels if you want the day's ration of water.'

'Can we not have water when we need it?'

'No, water is served each day, a half-gallon per person. If you are not there when it is served, then you have to wait.'

Joyce looked along the decks. People were queueing by the casks of water and he joined them. Then he remembered that the bucket which had recently carried the sour vomit would not contain enough water for the whole village, so he rushed down the gangway into the cabin.

'Are we in sight of America? Are we in sight of America?' an old man from the village called, when he saw him rush into the cabin.

'No, America is far away,' he told him patiently.

'We should never have started on such a long journey in a timber boat,' the old man told him. 'It will surely be the death of us all. I should have stayed at home. My head is reeling all night and my stomach won't hold food.' Liam Joyce knew that he would have to listen to many such complaints during the long journey.

'They are sharing out the water,' he told them. 'Gather every

222

utensil you can and follow me to collect your ration. Food we can do without, but not water.'

'And what of the sea?' another old man said. 'Are we not surrounded by water?'

'You cannot drink salt water, old man. It only aggravates the thirst.'

Some of the young men and girls followed him up the gangway and queued with their basins and buckets for the water pumped from the casks. As he stood waiting Liam Joyce looked at the other pasengers. They were of the farming and merchant class he had seen in Castlebar and they could pay for their passage to America. It was strange for them, having spent a night of discomfort in a narrow berth, to stand in a queue while a sailor pumped water for them from a barrel, but for Liam Joyce standing in a queue held little humiliation. He had lined up with others to receive a plate of gruel during the famine and he had stood at the Board of Works office to wait for a job and he had stood in the market-place with his spade while some middleman examined him as if he were an animal. Now that they were all sailing towards a new world together the difference of rank would diminish. By the time they reached America it would have disappeared altogether.

As he took the water down to the cabin he looked at the regulations nailed to the mast. Beneath them were his ration entitlements. He studied them carefully. The people of the village could easily survive on the one pound of flour and the five pounds of oatmeal allowed each week. They would have no use for the two ounces of tea; he would collect it and sell it to the better-class passengers.

The best shilling he had ever invested was in giving a drink to an old crewman living not far from his own village, who had explained to him how to survive on a long journey. They would have to stay on deck and breathe the fresh air and keep active, staying in the stale air of the cabin as little as possible, and wash it out every day.

During the day the people from his village made their way reluctantly on deck. The sight of the immense sea frightened them. 'May the Son of God and His mother protect us from this lake of water,' one of the old women said. 'The boat is too small for such a power of water! There will be an end to us before the setting of the sun.' Others were mute at the size of

223

the ship, the full sails, the complex rigging and ratlines. They watched the crew members climb nimbly aloft and called out prayers for their protection. Liam's wife noticed how shabbily dressed they were compared to the other passengers.

'We are out of place here,' she told him. 'There is nothing but grand people from home here, people who lived in fine houses with good furniture. I preferred the village.'

'And the hunger and the famine that's coming – would you have preferred that? The children will be given an equal chance, and I want no more talk of grand people.' He was angry at the humiliation she was suffering. Would a day ever dawn when he would feel that he was more than a poor man? Then he remembered with pride the manner in which he had carried his village this far: the worst was over. But he must keep his mind clear and his eye alert. He must anticipate danger and questions. What should he do if a storm blew up? The sea was now running high and the ship running evenly, but he knew that a storm, such as the ones that often blew up the valley, would be another matter.

'If the ship holes,' his mother told him, 'then we are all done for. Better a grave in soil than a watery bed, and better to be buried among my own.' Come what may, none of them would be buried beside the mouldering monastery close to the sea; they would die in a new land, the earth above them would be foreign.

They lay or sat on the deck with the others during the day, eating the oatmeal mixed with water. It was rough food for the wealthier passengers, but for Liam Joyce and the others it was tasty and substantial. They ate it with their hands, sharing out the water in a tin mug. It grew cold as evening came, and the passengers deserted the decks and went below. Liam Joyce lit the lantern he had bought for three shillings, and looked more closely at the cabin. It was indeed a cramped space, but with some lantern-light it looked more certain and comfortable. The young women settled the old people and the children for the night, then sat on the bags of luggage and sang songs in Irish or talked away quietly. The fear of the great ship was gradually leaving them.

At midnight Liam Joyce crept on deck alone. The air filled his lungs and sharpened his senses. He could hear the sound of the dark sea about him. His movements were careful and

224

measured. He had not ventured this far before. Suddenly a voice spoke beside him. It was the voice of the young woman.

'Do you find the sea and the ship strange?' she asked him in Irish.

'By the souls of the Saints! It is strange, and I feel uncertain – it is strange, too, when I see a young woman climb the rope ladders!'

'Oh, I have to learn my trade. I was born to the sea, and its nature is in me. I find the land as strange as you find the sea.'

'Then, you are not a town person like many on board the ship. They have the English tongue, and it is sweet and easy for them to talk in the language of the towns. They make the speaker of Irish and the Irish ways seem odd and backward.'

'And are you odd and backward?' she asked directly.

'In my village and on the mountain and bound to others of my habits I feel dignity. But in this wide sea and with these people from the towns in fine clothes I do not feel at all at home. I feel awkward.'

'When the storm blows and the sea gets round, then you will see the grandeur disappear.'

'I fear the sea and I fear the storms. When a storm blows across the land I know how to deal with it, but on the sea I do not know how to cope,' he told her.

'You will know when the storm is approaching. Secure everything and every person with ropes. Let nothing break loose. Where are you placed?'

'At the front of the ship where the large timbers come together. We toss through the sea all night, galloping up and galloping down. It's like being in the saddle of a wild horse!'

Gráinne Barrett found this man interesting. When she spoke Irish as she did now a certain part of her nature came alive. It was native and Celtic and had an understanding of this man and his village. It came from the idiom and life of the language. Had she spoken English with him, their relationship would have been strained and faulty. They sat down on a bale of coiled rope. The wind was light, and Gráinne Barrett could tell that there was no danger of a rope snapping or a spar breaking free.

'As you boarded the boat at the pier, you handed a small

bundle to a man. He seemed very eager to gain possession of it,' she said. It was an indirect question.

'That bundle bought me passage in this ship,' he told her.

'It must have contained a wealth of sovereigns.'

'No, a wealth of words.'

'I never thought words could be so valuable,' she laughed.

'Oh, these words were valuable indeed to Michael Barrett on the hill and in the large house among the woods. I gave him a dunaire containing several poems by Rioccard Barrett the Belmullet poet.'

She suppressed her excitement. Rioccard Barrett was a magical name, the only poet of the Barrett name, and she knew of her father's great interest in him.

'But his wife burned his poems after his death,' she said.

'And the best thing she ever did as far as I'm concerned, for they said that the poems only exist in the mouths of the people and there only in part. But my grandfather won them from the poet in a contest outside a shebeen close to Cross graveyard where he is now buried.'

'And what type of contest was it?' she asked.

'A pissing contest! Oh, it was the strangest contest ever held in Mayo!' – and he told her about it. Her voice exploded in laughter, and she laughed until tears flowed down her cheeks.

'I don't believe it,' she said when she had gained control of herself.

'It is true, as sure as I am sitting here.'

'And you told this to my father?' she said, and suddenly realised that she had revealed her identity.

'Your father?'

'Yes, my father,' she said quietly, angry with herself for letting it out.

Liam Joyce was overawed when he realised that he was in the presence of a woman whose beauty and temperament were celebrated in Mayo. She had been compared with her ancestor the sea queen Grace O'Malley. Yet when she talked to him in Irish, so native was her accent that she concealed her English upbringing.

'Had I known who you were, I would not have been so forward,' he told her, embarrassment flooding his voice.

'And you would not have told me the story.'

226

'No. And what is a fine lady dressed in sailor's clothes for?' he asked, plucking up courage again.

'Learning the true skill of sailing. It was my wish to sail as a common crew member. Now, tell me your story from the beginning,' she directed, turning the conversation again.

He told her the story of his village situated behind the sacred mountain, of Kenrick and of the impending famine, of his journey to Northport and his meeting with the drunken poet Patrick Gill in a shebeen. She listened intently, admiring the courage of this man and the sharpness of his mind.

'And what do you expect to find in America?'

'I do not know. They say it is a golden land. But I do know there is no hunger there and I will work my hands to the bone to stay alive. I have brought the village this far, and it remains for me to ensure that they survive. Another year of famine and we would have starved to death. I would prefer to die in an attempt to reach America than to die in a ditch. No agent will ever leave the remains of a lash on my face or back again.'

The humour had now left his voice, and there was muted fury and anger there in its place. They talked freely during the watch, and he recited several of Rioccard Barrett's poems for her, ones which she had never heard before. She could understand why her father had purchased the dunaire.

'If I can help you in any way during the voyage, let me know, for I, too, love the poems.'

'Fortune has smiled on me tonight, lady, for I felt a stranger on board this ship, a man ill-dressed and out of place.'

'We will speak again, but – please do not reveal my identity. I would have too many of the town people crowding about me and they would not understand why I dress like this or climb the rigging.'

'I do not think I will have much truck with them.'

The bell sounded for the change of watch. They parted, and he made his way back to the crowded and ill-smelling cabin where the villagers slept fitfully.

Myles Prendergast found his cabin confined and narrow. He was quick to realise that if he did not engage his mind and body in rigorous activity he would find the voyage tedious. He visited John Burke in his cabin and asked him if he possessed any books.

227

'Books? I have no time to read books, and the only three I possess are on navigation.'

'Then, I will take them and a chart to study, too.'

'But why?'

'To keep my mind occupied in a narrow space, John Burke! I would like paper to write on.'

'Take all you need,' John Burke waved his hand.

'I will make out very detailed notes and maps – it will help to pass the hours and when we meet the organisation I will be well prepared,' Myles told him.

He returned to his small cabin and drew up a plan for each hour of his day, almost monastic in its precision, but as he pored over the chart he could not concentrate. He kept thinking of Gráinne Barrett, dressed as a common sailor and sharing the work of the men. Each of their meetings had some fatal flaw. Eventually he returned to the navigational book and opened the first few pages where the positions of the stars were set out clearly. He did not know their names or their places in the sky, so he set out to memorise the first set of positions. It was a rigid logical exercise which gave him pleasure. All his life he had been a city man and he had rarely examined the masses of stars in the sky. Now, cluster by cluster, he committed them to memory. Then, to test his accuracy, he set out the chief constellations on a sheet of paper and compared them with the original star-maps. He was satisfied that his memory was sharp.

Each day he exercised on the large main deck like the rest of the passengers. He joined the queues for water and bread and ate slowly, drawing pleasure from the simple food. Whenever the opportunity arose he joined in conversation with people and asked them many questions about their past history, the reasons they left Ireland and their expectations on reaching America. Many carried bitterness and hate with them across the Atlantic: if aid would come from any source it would come from America, he thought.

He had seen Gráinne Barrett on a few occasions, busy about the ship. She kept away from the areas where the passengers exercised, and their eyes had met only three or four times. He knew that she was still stung by the humiliation she had endured before him in her father's office.

A week out to sea he decided to test his memory. He had

become familiar with the star positions on the pages of the nautical manual, and he wished to see if he could identify the stars from the deck of the ship, choosing a night when the sky was clear and crisp. He brought the manual with him and set it down on a bale of rope beneath a lantern. Then he went forward to where it was dark and looked up at the sky. He was filled with wonder at the brightness of the stars and he did not notice the figure approach him.

'I thought that all land-lovers would be in their bunks by now,' Gráinne Barrett remarked.

He shook himself from his reverie and looked at her, dressed in a heavy man's coat, barely discernible in the darkness. 'And so they should, but I have set myself the task of learning the positions of the stars.'

'From a manual?'

'Yes.'

'John Burke taught me the names of the stars in Irish when I was a child – I'll test you if you like. Point out the North Star to me.'

He found the North Star, and from that he moved to the more common clusters. But soon he was confused.

'For you these stars are mathematical exercises in books; for me they pulsate with life. You will never learn how to love them as I do. Your attitude is cold and disrespectful.'

He felt that she was mocking him. Their third encounter seemed already growing sour. 'I agree with you,' he said humbly. 'I have no proper knowledge of the stars and no feeling for the sea.'

'Then, what do you feel for? Plots and intrigue with John Burke?' she asked.

'A certain justice,' he told her. 'I have come to Ireland from France. I was brought up on revolutionary ideals as a child and young man, but during my days in Ireland I have seen more injustice and inequality than I have seen in Europe.'

'And you will change all that?'

'No, I will not change it. I am a realist and I see things as they are. That is my training.'

'What training?'

'You have been trained to the sea, and I have been trained in a French military academy. I deal with men in the field.'

229

'You deal with a dangerous man when you deal with John Burke.'

'I know.'

They looked at the stars again for some time. There was a small healing in their relationship. One could not afford to quarrel on the sea.

'I recall your phrase "the republic of the sea",' Myles said. 'I have not heard that before.'

'My father often spoke of it when I was a child. He belongs in this republic.'

'You love your father?'

'I respect him. He has had a strange life. He detests living in the great house – it makes him angry and introspective.' She turned away.

'Do you know much of his early life?' Myles persisted.

'No.'

'It is interesting,' he remarked lightly.

'How should you know?' she said quickly.

'We keep files in Paris. I have seen some of them.'

Her mind was sharpened with interest. Perhaps he could explain John Burke's angry remark to her in the office. 'What, then, did John Burke mean when he said that my father had a dark history?'

'I do not know.' Myles was evasive.

'Well, what *do* you know?' she asked.

'It is privileged information, and I must leave it at that.' He picked up his manual. 'It is time for me to retire. I shall study my stars again and perhaps you will examine me when I am better informed.'

'I shall,' she said.

He wished her good night and returned to his narrow cabin.

She reflected on their meeting. She had not quarrelled with him as she did during their previous encounters. Unlike her he had total control over his words and his emotions and would not readily grow angry. She found him mysterious, this stranger who had been taken into the confidence of John Burke. He carried information concerning her father which would be of interest to her. Her mind was troubled by his words, and she had no key to the mystery.

21

JOHN BURKE wrote up his log and plotted his position on the large map on the table each evening. He permitted his crew to drink rum but kept a close eye on them: he had known crew members to fall from rigging under the influence of drink, their bodies broken on the spars and the decks below or falling directly into the sea and drowning.

'It has been too smooth,' he told Gráinne Barrett one night as they studied the map.

'It may be smooth all the way.'

'No, there is a storm seeding somewhere to the south. Mark my words!'

Life on board the ship had so far been normal. The stench of bodies rose from the holds each morning, but he was familiar with such things. The people were fed at regular intervals, and the water in the casks was abundant. Many people had been seasick, and as the days passed the old were growing wasted, their faces thin. Even the stronger passengers were becoming listless. An old man stood at the prow of the ship each day hoping to catch a view of America. The strain was showing, too, on Gráinne Barrett's face. There were tight lines on her forehead and under her eyes. Yet each day she did her duties and kept the watch with others.

Four weeks out the storm blew up from the south. John Burke read the warning signs in the sky. The wind force

231

increased. The heavy sails and masts began to strain. Dark clouds moved into the sky, and distance was foreshortened. Rain came on the wind, making the rigging wet and dangerous. This was the beginning.

John Burke put on his heavy woollen coat and buttoned it to his neck. He went to the top deck and stood beside the wheel chest-high and rimmed with bronze. From this position he could survey the three-masted ship with all its tackle and sail. Unexpectedly the wind increased, and the masts began to strain as the ship raced forward. If the wind was too strong for the crowded sails, it would wreck the masts and bring sails and spars down upon the deck.

John Burke ordered his men aloft, watching them clamber up the shrouds agile as monkeys. As they mounted the rigging they looked small and insignificant against the black clouds driving up from the south. They moved out along the foot-ropes beneath the spars, then slowly furled the mainsails and secured them. As the ropes slackened and the sails were drawn up he could feel strain lessening on the ship.

But the wind continued to increase. He ordered further sail to be taken in. The waves now began to come forward in large masses breaking over the bow. The broken deluge rushed down the deck and out the scuppers. Life-lines were set between the masts, and men secured themselves to them.

John Burke had to balance canvas against the wind. They must move steadily towards the edge of the storm. He could not risk the main course and the topsail. He looked down into the storm, judging the force of the wind. Its central fury was not yet upon them. He bellowed out orders against the roar of the sea.

Then his heart missed a beat: on the highest spar stood Gráinne Barrett securing a sail. He had ordered her aloft in the confusion. He watched in fear. The storm caught her body and attempted to prise her from her insecure perch. The masts bent under the pressure, the winds cried out on the rigging and the waves grew greater. He continued to gaze at the frail figure on the spar rope.

For Gráinne Barrett climbing aloft in a storm was a new experience. The wind whipped at her body as she mounted, and when she moved out along the spar rope the force of the storm was open and direct. She tasted fear in her mouth, like fine dust. A loose rope-end lashed across her hand and drew blood. It sharpened her to the danger about her.

'God Almighty, Gráinne Barrett, what are you doing up so high? If your father knew that John Burke ordered you on to the spars, there would be blue murder!' one of the crew members roared in her ear.

'It's rough,' she told him.

'This is only the beginning. Move rapidly and then we'll get below.'

The ship began to sway. At one moment the deck was below her and at another moment the spar was far out over the sea and the waves were baying at her like hunting dogs. She began to be afraid at the many movements about her. Her foot slipped. Quickly she drew it back on the rope and gripped the spar tightly.

'Do not look down,' the crewman said. 'Keep your eye on the business in hand.'

They were finally spread out across the spar. The sail was hauled up, and they secured it firmly. Her woollen cap was blown away, and her red hair now blew freely behind her. With the work finished they made their way back to the mainmast and clambered down on to the deck. She secured herself with a life-line. There was little time to breathe a sigh of relief. Every object on board must now be roped securely and the passengers battened down against the storm.

With the sails close-hauled across the wind and the canvas lightened, the ship sailed towards the north-west in an attempt to outrun the storm.

John Burke was relieved when Gráinne Barrett reached the deck. He called her to the wheel, his face red with anger. 'You young fool! Who ordered you aloft?' he bellowed.

'You did,' she answered.

'I did not,' he insisted.

'You called upon us all to climb aloft and trim the sails. That included me.'

'I have no time to argue with you. Secure yourself in your cabin. It will be a rough night. I will not make it to the edge of the storm.'

'No, I stay on deck. I came to learn the craft of sailing. The craft is best learned in a storm.' With that she was gone. She moved down the deck and secured herself with a life-line.

'A wild Barrett like the rest of them,' he roared after her. 'Wild as horses. Never can be tamed even when they send them to finishing schools in England.'

'This is my finishing school,' she shouted back.

He was relieved now that she was secured by a life-line and away from the mast. But John Burke had underestimated the power of the storm. The wind continued to harden, tearing itself on the riggings like a demon who wished to shred the sails and tear the ship asunder. And the waves now became huge masses of water, swelling up in the greyness and throwing themselves over the deck, washing backwards towards the stern. John Burke feared that he might lose steering power and that the ship would turn broadside; if this happened, it could capsize. So with old experience he moved cautiously forward across the waves, always edging northwards. It was growing dark. He was still carrying too much canvas: he would have to order the men aloft again. He called out his orders to them. Against a wind of fifty miles an hour, the crew members mounted the shrouds and made their way out along the spars.

For Gráinne Barrett the next half-hour was the most frightening in her life. She was no longer aware of her height above the deck but of the horrible force of the wind beating upon her body. The sails were wild and heavy as they pulled them upwards and secured them. At any moment she could have been swept into the growing darkness. Finally they secured the canvas, and the ship was relieved of the heavy pressure of the storm. She made her way down the rigging with the others, reliving the dangers that she had just been through, and when she reached the deck she vomited.

'That woman will be the death of me. She will surely kill herself – and me – before the voyage is over,' John Burke told his cousin standing next to him.

'We surely have a wild Barrett with us, John Burke,' his cousin replied. 'But the sea is in her veins, and no harm will come of her. She will captain the ships yet, and men will talk of her courage.'

'That is fine talk for the taverns when the voyage is over – it's unsettling when a captain has to live through it! I should have her put in irons!'

All night the storm raged, cracking some of the spars under the strain. All night the crew worked on deck cutting them loose. But the masts held firm; the ship rode the storm solidly and well, and by morning they were out of danger. John Burke looked at the ship from the wheel. One sail had been torn loose and flapped, ungainly in the wind. Many of the ropes were frayed, and some of the casks of water had been lost. He wondered what injuries had been inflicted on the passengers. Even above the cry of the wind he had heard them crying below deck, in confusion and darkness, fearing that the great timbers might smash and that they would be drowned. Unsecured trunks and boxes rolled around, as deadly as sharp weapons. For the old it would be the most terrible experience in their lives.

At the approach of the storm Liam Joyce had taken Gráinne Barrett's advice. With the ropes he had purchased from a sailor he lashed the trunks to the bunks. Then he lashed the old to their small berths. But when the full force of the storm was on them he knew that even these precautions were not enough.

Later, as an old man in America, he could only recall the pitching of the ship in the darkness; the screech of the children in the confused world of the small cabin and the groaning of the old as they vomited and soiled themselves in fear. It was the longest night he had ever spent. It was during the storm that his wife lost the child she was carrying. In the morning he would wrap the foetus in sacking and quietly consign it to the sea. His wife would never conceive again. None of his children was to be born in freedom. And he always finished his story by lifting his left hand. It carried only four fingers. The small finger had been sliced off by the sharp edge of a trunk which had broken loose. It was only after the storm that he realised he was injured.

The ship had outridden the storm. The damage could be repaired during the coming days. John Burke was exhausted. He had been on deck for sixteen hours, his mind alert to all that was happening. Now it went slack. As he went below he thought of Gráinne Barrett. He knocked on her cabin door and entered. She was sitting in an armchair. He looked at her forehead. It had been torn by the cutting edge of a frayed rope. The mark would always remain below the hair-line. Her hands were wrapped in bandages. He undid them and looked at bleeding palms.

'You are the first of women,' he said. 'I am proud of you. I

235

am sorry that your forehead is marked. Leave your palms exposed, they will heal more quickly. Sleep well now.' There were tears of pride in her eyes.

He turned from her and went to his cabin. Before he slept he thought of the young girl with the red hair, whom he had taken fishing on Clew Bay many years ago, and of the young woman he had carried to England to be educated. And finally he thought of her on the spar ropes amongst the men, the sea and the gales testing their powers against her. She had proved that the sea was in her blood and, as his cousin had said, no harm would come to her. With that final thought he fell into a deep sleep.

For Myles Prendergast the storm was a frightening experience. His small cabin was thrown into confusion, and he had secured the chair and table at which he worked. He blew out the lantern-light but, lying on his bunk, he remained awake, his stomach heaving as the great ship faced into the great waves which bore down upon it. He retched several times on the floor, and became nauseated by his own vomit. When he emerged from the cabin next morning he was grey and weak, and he drew the sea air into his lungs with relish. He listened to crew members talk of the storm and the events of the night.

'She tore her hands on the rope,' one man said.

'And her forehead; a loose rope almost took out her eye. And she was aloft during the worst of it. A rare woman. Not even John Burke with all his experience had ever witnessed anything like it before.'

'Well, she didn't lick it off the rocks, and no man can say that she is not an equal to them.'

Myles went directly to Gráinne's cabin and knocked on the door.

'Who is there?' she asked.

'Myles Prendergast,' he called.

'Do you know the positions of the stars?' she asked tauntingly from the cabin.

'No. I came to enquire after your health.'

'Come in,' she directed him.

She was sitting on a chair and washing her hands. He looked at the rope burns across the palms and the laceration across the forehead.

236

'I don't want pity or praise,' she said directly.

'You endangered your life.'

'On every sea journey you endanger your life. I would prefer to be on the spar during a storm than at the Viceregal Ball in Dublin!'

'You must rest,' he told her, looking at her drawn face.

'I'll rest when we reach New York. In the meantime I am a sailor doing a sailor's work.' She spoke without pride, factually. She took her hands from the basin in which she had steeped them and, taking a towel, she sponged the sensitive palms.

'Does it hurt?' he asked.

'Of course it hurts! It hurts like hell! And, by the way, *have* you learned to name all the stars?' Her eyes were watering with the pain.

'I think so.'

She looked at him. He was grey and gaunt and looked vulnerable. The storm had taken its effect on him.

'Were you ill?' she asked more gently.

'Yes. I was violently ill.'

She smiled, and then she became serious as she examined her torn palms. 'Could you tell me what you know of my father? I think I have earned some right to know.'

He thought for a moment and considered his position. She *had* earned the right to know and perhaps the information was necessary to her.

'Your father was in France during the Revolution,' he began. 'He was with Frederick Cavendish during its most bloody moments. Later, he broke the blockade in the North Sea and carried arms and uniforms to the revolutionaries.'

'*With Frederick Cavendish?*' she cried out in amazement.

'Yes.'

'So he has blood on his hands!'

'No. He actually carried some of the émigrés into exile – he did a deal with the revolutionaries. Of course he was well rewarded for his services. The émigrés paid a high price for their lives, and the revolutionaries had to pay for their uniforms and ammunition.'

'So he made money out of the Revolution?' Gráinne was somehow satisfied.

'Yes – but he did save lives.'

'And Frederick Cavendish?'

237

'He stayed with the Republic. There is blood on his hands, but he was a young man in a fresh cause. That is basically what is in our records, and you have earned such information.'

'But it does not explain the mystery John Burke mentioned.'

'No.'

He stayed with her a little longer. Then he left her cabin and returned to the deck. The wind was fresh, and it carried them forward at a steady pace.

22

THE WINDS HELD FAIR during the rest of the voyage, and the days became increasingly tedious for the passengers. They moved about the upper deck aimlessly. At night-time a fiddler played music and some of them danced. The water from the casks turned brackish and the salted pork from the barrels made them thirsty, and life below deck and the tossing seas was taking its toll on the passengers. Many of them had lost weight, their features were grey, their gait listless. Six people had died on the voyage. They had been coffined and consigned to the sea.

Liam Joyce's hand healed. The loss of a finger was a small thing; he had paid a higher price with the loss of his unborn child. Since then his wife Oonah had been ailing. Gráinne Barrett brought her bowls of broth and nursed her. The woman told Gráinne of her pride in her husband who had brought them across the large ocean. 'Had we remained, it was death for us. We would have died of the hunger, and none would remain to bury us.'

Liam Joyce got talking to members of the crew who knew the streets of New York to find out what it was like. He could hardly believe that any town could carry a population of over four hundred thousand people. He heard that men were murdered in the streets; that the port itself was full of thieves and charlatans who would rob any unsuspecting immigrants.

And he was told to avoid the Old Brewery where the sailors took their pleasure. But above all he learned that he was to move quickly away from the port area. Here confused immigrants, uncertain what to do, remained in the garrets and the damp basements until their money ran out. If he sought work, he should seek it in the shipbuilding trade along the East River. 'Move up into the city,' they insisted. 'Take any work you can until you have learned the ways of the place. The further you move away the better.'

It was practical advice and bought cheaply. He knew that it was not a golden city now; the struggle he had carried on all during his life must now be continued there, but at least he would be his own master. He would work until every limb ached and until he had money to move inland and buy a farm. They said that beyond New York the lands stretched onwards for a thousand miles unbroken by any mountain.

During the last night of the voyage he sat with Gráinne Barrett on a rope coil. The claw mark of rope was healing on her forehead. Her face was brown from wind and sun, and her hands were hard. She had learned much from Liam Joyce concerning the trials the peasants endured and realised for the first time that the great house, Northport and the ships were only part of a greater world where most people endured great hardships.

'Tomorrow we should sight America,' she told him. 'Are you relieved?'

'I suppose I should be. I have succeeded beyond my wildest dreams already. Many of the passengers think that it is a land of plenty and that there will be a welcoming hand for them, but I know I must move towards the edge of the city to find work. I have enough money to survive for six days perhaps.'

'You always use the word "survive".'

'Had you lived as I have lived, it would be the only word you could have used. But there will be a time when I can sit down and read books and educate my children. All I need is a few acres of land, food, a house and a bed at night.'

'You ask for little.'

'For me it is a great deal.'

'Recite for me again the songs of Rioccard Barrett,' she asked. They were a bond between them. Quietly he sang the songs. They were tender and bitter and humorous.

240

'I shall not see you again, Liam Joyce,' she said when he had finished.

'Never say such things. Our paths may cross again or perhaps the paths of our children may cross. No one can look into the future.'

With these words they parted, each preparing for the sight of land on the morrow.

Next morning, after forty-seven days at sea, they sighted the shore of America. It began as a small sliver of grey on the horizon, slowly becoming firm and certain. The immigrants cheered, and those below deck rushed up the gangways to take a look.

'We almost hit New York on the nose,' John Burke said proudly. 'A half-day's journey south and we will reach it.' For four hours they sailed south, passing small fishing smacks close to the shore. The people were amazed that the fishermen were human and ordinary like themselves. Several three-masters, under full sail, moved east towards Europe carrying Indian corn for a starving continent.

They approached the great port. Several ships lay anchored in the harbour and more than fifty were berthed by the wharf itself. On the sea-front they could see the constant activity of dockers unloading the holds. A strange circular building, called Castle Garden, floated like a buoy close to a promenade, with trees growing beyond it. Running down to the centre of the city was a wide street known as Broadway. The passengers were amazed at the innumerable buildings, which seemed to stretch for ever along the waterfront.

They were all equal now in their doubts and fears as to what lay ahead of them: tired and confused, they counted for little. A doctor came on board and examined the passengers rapidly, finding no evidence of fever. With him were two Customs officials. The ship was pronounced healthy and permitted to dock.

Gráinne Barrett watched the gangplank being lowered. Slowly, like cattle, the people began to descend the wooden walkway to the New World, forming a confused group on the dock as they landed.

She watched as Liam Joyce gathered some dust from the road in his hand and let it trickle slowly through his fingers. He looked up at her, waved his hand and smiled. About him

241

his village was gathered. He would survive, she thought, as he made his way up through Broadway, followed by the young and the old, carrying the poems of Rioccard Barrett in his mind.

To Gráinne, New York was a vast and thriving place; it had the vigour of London about it. Everywhere she went there were people busy about the affairs of the day. Everywhere she walked ships were at anchor along the quaysides. From the shipyards along the East River, whalers, clippers and packets were launched. 'It's a young city,' John Burke told her, 'and like all growing things it is pushing outwards and not certain where it is going; but mark my words – you can make a fortune here or you can fail. It gives no comfort to the weak and the old.'

The city was as active as an antheap. She became familiar with Broadway, lined on either side with brownstone buildings, five storeys high. But in the streets off this thoroughfare she found only thick muddy passages, with cart-drivers cursing each other as they dragged forward their horses, and pigs and hungry dogs roaming around freely. But despite the muddy streets and the heaps of rubbish all the goods of the world seemed on display in the shop windows.

While she was discovering the city John Burke and Myles had another task in hand. They made their way to the Old Brewery with two of the crew: if there were English agents on the quayside, they would hardly follow them into the sinful entrails of the city, worse than any European port for its dosshouses and prostitution. Drunken women, with careless hair and filthy clothes, invited them to enter their quarters, and they were also approached by menacing figures from alleyways, who slunk back into the shadows when they produced pistols. The Irish Bar was crowded with people, the air stale with smoke and spit and the heat of unwashed bodies. The owner recognised John Burke and directed him into a back room. He set drink before them and sent a servant boy to get Jim Willis the gunsmith.

Jim Willis arrived some time later, still wearing his leather apron, stained with oil. He was a small man, with a small head and oval-shaped glasses with thick lenses on his nose. He was nervous and uncertain of himself.

242

'Well,' John Burke asked, 'did you manufacture them your-self? I presume that our men here were in contact with you.'

'Yes. But it was a difficult task. They had to be tested. Testing is noticed, and I had to make several journeys into the countryside to make sure that they were correct. It all cost money.'

'Do they work?'

'Yes, at close range they are accurate. But I cannot give you a guarantee beyond a range of thirty yards.'

'That is sufficient.'

From an oily parcel Willis unwrapped a pistol with a rotat-ing cylinder. They had not seen anything like this before.

'Look,' he said excitedly. 'Each time a chamber discharges it brings another into place. You have five shots instead of one.' He pulled the trigger, and they watched the empty chambers revolve into place.

'And good at thirty yards?'

'Yes,' Willis said confidently.

'How many can we purchase?'

'Fifty, but there are none like them in New York, and that makes them expensive.'

While they talked, Myles weighed the weapon in his hand. It was balanced and well tooled by the gunsmith. He watched in fascination as the chambers fell into place with a precise click. He knew that this could give the organisation a firm advantage: it would have a withering effect upon an unsuspect-ing enemy.

John Burke took some gold from his belt and counted out thirty sovereigns. 'There's a sovereign for every yard. I will pay the rest of the money when I have tested three of them. Bring them to the house of James Shanahan.'

'You have an excellent weapon, but you must never let it be known that I made it. The patent belongs to Samuel Colt. My gun is better than his, but I cannot stamp my name on it.' Willis collected his money from the table. There was gun oil in the ruts of his face and under his nails. He left them and disappeared back into the Old Brewery.

Later, on board ship, Myles and John Burke examined the gun more closely. Once primed, a man had five chances instead of one: for close-range fighting it would serve their purpose well.

'We will have to test them, Myles, to see if they live up to his promise. Do you think you understand it well enough to maintain it if anything goes wrong?' John Burke asked.

'Yes, but we need ten extra cylinders,' Myles warned. 'They could crack from the explosions.'

'It is a neat weapon surely – much better than the single-barrel guns.'

'The day of the single-barrel pistol is over for ever. This is the weapon of the future,' Myles said grimly.

Early next morning they went on deck. There was a slight mist giving the ships a dream-like quality, and they could barely see Staten Island rising out of the river.

'Throw an empty barrel into the river,' Myles ordered. John Burke lifted a barrel above his head and sent it in an arc out over the tranquil water where it landed twenty feet from the ship. Then John Burke aimed at the floating barrel and pulled the trigger. The ball tore the water beside it. Myles Prendergast could not see what had happened because of the puff of smoke.

'Did I hit it?' Burke asked.

'No, you were a bit ahead of it.'

He moved down the deck and shot again at the floating barrel. This time there was no mistake. He scored directly. He emptied the whole cylinder into the barrel until it was shattered. It was a strange experience for him to have such power in his hand. Once he became accustomed to the recoil he knew that he could handle the weapon expertly. With a brace of revolvers in his belt he could fire ten shots in succession.

'In close fighting it is the perfect weapon,' Myles assured him.

'Is it worth the money, Myles?'

'It is worth double the money and it is easily concealed in a ship.'

'If Michael Barrett knew that we were using his ships for smuggling guns, he would have us in irons,' John Burke remarked.

'Michael Barrett has had his day; he is an old man now. He knows little of what is happening. If we fight, then there are many here in this city ready to join us. We must be ready for the day.'

'I don't know, Myles – it's a big thing to ask starving people to rise out.'

'Well, they either rise out or die. Another famine is a sentence of death for them. Better fight and take the consequences than die in a ditch. If only we could organise the towns!'

The mist was still on the river and about the ships in grey scarf-like wisps, and the sounds of horses' hoofs and men's voices were musical and without edge as they were carried on the air. No wind stirred the ships at their moorings, and the ropes and furled sails were damp with dew. A spectral ship in the middle distance moved out of port with slack sails, uncertain in the gloom.

In the east, the sun was beginning to rise. Soon it would burn the mist about the raw harbour. They had felt its protection. A British agent on the quay might have heard the shots but he would not be able to locate them. Suddenly a barrel turned over, and they quickly spun round. Gráinne Barrett was looking at them: they had walked the whole length of the deck and failed to notice her. There was a flash of anger in Myles's eyes. He rushed up the steps and stood beside her.

'You have been listening to our talk,' he said belligerently.

'Of course I have been listening to your talk *and* watching you shoot! If I were a British spy, news of you would be already on the way to England.'

'You know too much about us. You are dangerous.'

'And you, too, are dangerous. You have given me enough information to hang you.' She stopped short. 'I live in a man's world here and I have shared the same hardships and dangers as the men; I have washed the decks and cleaned out the emigrants' filth. I, too, may have my feelings about revolution, but we ought to be running food into the country, not guns! No Barrett ever went whispering to the constables. And if you think I am dangerous – well, then, I am.' She took out a loaded pistol from her coat pocket. 'I have only one shot. You come near me, Myles, to do me an injury and I will lodge this in your guts.' They looked at her in surprise. John Burke was shaken by the conversation.

Later that morning John Burke knocked on her cabin door. She invited him to enter. 'Would you have shot me?' he asked.

'Yes. Why blame me for loose talk? I came on deck when I heard the pistol shots. You should have been more careful.'

'I spoke roughly to you. The fault lies with me.'

'I know that if I were a threat to you, you would kill me.'

'No, Gráinne. I would never do that. I have known you since you were a child.' His tone was conciliatory.

'That was a long time ago. The world is a different place now.'

'Many men's lives would be at risk if you disclosed the information you overheard,' he pleaded.

'And do you trust your own, who get drunk and talk openly in taverns, more than me? *They* are the dangerous ones. How many people know that you are buying these new pistols?'

'Eight.'

'That is six too many. People talk, and there could be a loose link in the chain. And can a woman not love a cause as well as a man and perhaps better?'

John Burke looked at her with a new respect. He was dealing with a woman with more courage than many men he had known. She was no longer the girl who had sailed in his boat and soon she would be mistress of the ships.

'How many years have you been running guns?' she asked imperiously.

'Three.'

'Then, you have an organisation.'

'Yes. It extends as far as Galway.'

'Does Myles Prendergast belong to this organisation?'

'Yes.'

'If my father knew this, he would order you off his ships.'

'He is an old man now.'

'And are you not an old man, too, John?' she said sarcastically.

'I have a young heart. The cause is still bright in my mind. I love the land of Mayo. I'd die for it.'

She looked at the timbered floor for a moment, reflecting. Then, looking at him and considering her position, she said: 'I wish to be sworn into the organisation. None of the crew must know, John Burke.'

He was taken aback, but he agreed. 'I will have you sworn in at a secret meeting today. You will meet men who hold high rank in the army and in the government.'

'Do you trust Myles Prendergast?' Gráinne asked carelessly.

'Yes. I have already tested him and he is cool and thinks

clearly, and he is intelligent. The organisation needs minds like that. We are not Whiteboys who crop cattle's tails.'

'Then, you have hope for this movement.'

'Once you are in,' he said grimly, 'there is no leaving it.'

'I know.'

'It is a thing I am reluctant to do, for you may be called upon at some future date to serve our cause. Some day you may marry an English gentleman – and what then?'

'I have no intention of marrying an English gentleman. And if I am called upon it must only be in an extreme case.'

'Very well. I will arrange it.' John Burke left the cabin wondering if he had done the correct thing. He stood at the ship's rail and looked at the men carrying bags of grain up the gangplank and pouring it into the holds.

The quayside was wide awake now and filled with the noise of horses and heavy carts. He reflected upon many things as he looked down upon all this human activity. Perhaps he was too old after all for rebellions and revolutions; perhaps a younger man should take charge of the course of history, maybe he would stand a better chance of success. He should stand down from it all, he thought.

The next morning Myles, John Burke and Gráinne Barrett left the ship. They took her to a great house on the edge of the expanding city. When they entered the main doorway she was surprised by the presence of men dressed in uniform. They were led to a central room where, about a circular table, sat five men of high military rank. 'We will swear you in at this table,' John Burke told her.

In the presence of the seven men she took the oath of the organisation. 'Now you are one of us,' John Burke said, 'and party to our secrets.'

Myles Prendergast opened a wide holder and produced several carefully drawn maps, which he secured to one of the panelled walls.

'I have examined the reasons leading to the failure of the last rebellion: it was ill-planned and spontaneous – in other words, the troops had only raw courage and no military experience. If we are to rebel and have a chance of succeeding, then it is obvious we must have cells of men in each town and careful links between them. They must be so well organised

247

that if one cell fails another takes its place, and we must watch for spies. Now, most important, we need arms that are modern and we need to feel that we have strong backing in America. Further, we desperately need a newspaper. I do not know if it should be printed in New York or in Ireland, but we do need a newspaper to express our ideas. Right – I will explain in detail how I would set about a local insurrection in Mayo.'

With precision and detail he spoke for an hour. Then he was questioned by the military men. He answered most of their questions to their satisfaction.

'When can you expect a rising out of the people?' one man asked as a final question.

'I cannot guarantee that there will be a rising, but we *can* prepare the ground for one – you never know when a spark will set the fuse on fire. When it does, then we expect immediate help from America.' Myles sat down, and the discussion continued.

Gráinne sat at the table and listened to their talk of arms and strategy. She had never heard men talk of freedom in that fashion before, and the power of England looked puny in comparison to the great power of this new country. 'They are all immigrants,' John Burke told her later as they made their way back to the ship by carriage. 'They are men of rank in the American army. With them behind us we are not talking of useless street-battles. Even if the fight does not take place now it will take place later. Freedom will come from America.'

They remained two more weeks in New York, during which time Myles and John Burke purchased fifty additional revolving pistols with plenty of ammunition. They sailed from New York with a cargo of grain, intended to stave off hunger; they had no idea they were returning to a country already in the merciless grip of famine.

23

IN THE ADVENT of a total famine, half the valley would die. It was a a bleak place. The stream which had gouged it out had brought with it rich deposits from the mountains during the many million years of existence, but the fields bordering the stream belonged to Kenrick, the land agent. The flanks of the valley had a rough peaty surface and had been cast into lazy beds where potatoes could grow. It was land which had been wrenched from heather and whin, and it would quickly return to mountain grazing if neglected.

The land agent's house and his barns had slate roofs. The tenants spent the best days working his lands – part of the price they had to pay for living in the valley. They were bound to Kenrick by fear and debt: he could throw them off their small-holdings if they incurred his displeasure. Each year some of them took the emigration routes while the rest worked on in the fields to pay the heavy interest they owed to Kenrick.

Kenrick had married a woman half his age; like all his deals she was a bargain: her father gained five acres on a thirty-year lease by it. Her beauty had marked her out from other women, but in eight years of marriage she had produced no children for him.

'Kenrick is infertile like a jennet,' one of the Costellos had remarked in Northport. 'There is a curse on his seed. None of his breed will work the land, and the ravens will fly in and out his windows.'

Kenrick had picked up the pox from the soldiers' prostitutes. He knew that he was blighted like the potato tubers: there was a rot in his testicles.

'The Costellos will regret the day he spoke out against me,' he had bellowed out in a shebeen in Castlebar. 'For I will see to it that they wear out their backs in work and have nothing to show for it. Give me a fertile woman and I'll prove if my seed is dead!'

But the thought that he would be without progeny tortured him as he looked down on the valley from the mountain gap. He carried the curse for ten years. They said that there was no curse deeper or blacker than the curse of a widow woman, and a widow woman had placed her curse upon him. However hard he tried to banish the picture from his mind, he was haunted by the curses she threw at him in Irish from the side of the road: 'May your seed be fallow! May you die from fever and none near you, and may you rot in hell from the beginning to whatever end eternity has!' He had brought the whip down on her back and thrown her on to the few possessions she owned. It was a long time ago, but part of the curse had already come true. It poisoned his mind, and when he drank whiskey to forget it a fury moved across his mind. In his fury he often beat his wife. She feared his drunken bouts and would listen for the sound of the horse's hoofs on the cobbled yard. Dry fear would grip her throat, and she knew that he would beat her. He would drag her from the bed by the hair and take his whip to her. Time and time again he brought it down on her back as savagely as he could. He took delight in her screams.

'Who is the most powerful man in Mayo?' he roared.

'Kenrick, Kenrick,' she would cry.

'And why?'

'Because he owns all of us and everything!'

'Yes, I own you all!' His savagery was well known throughout the valley.

Those at the lower end of the valley were subservient to him; they did his bidding. But the Costellos, who inhabited the upper end, detested him and had a pride he could not break. A blight would suit Kenrick well. He would bring them to their knees. But as he looked down at the valley in the July

250

of 1846 everything looked fair. The sun shone down on the flanks of the mountains, and he could see the luxuriant stalks of the potatoes. It would be a good year for his corn. The men had tilled the mountains to their limits.

Kenrick knew that he was despised both by the British and by the Irish. He was an in-between man, isolated from his own and never on a certain footing with the people of the town, and so he sought the company of the soldiers. He controlled the valley itself, but immediately beyond stood the substantial farm belonging to Eileen Horkan whom the land sustained in comfort. He had watched her, mounted on her white horse, ride through the valley and up the mountainside. There was an independence in the manner in which she held the reins, in the manner in which she sat upright in the saddle.

'If she hadn't thirty acres of land to her back, it's on her back in my bed she'd be,' he told the labourers as they watched her ride by.

'She has learning, Kenrick,' one of them said, 'and is fair with the pen. It is said that she can write in Latin, the old tongue of the Romans, which is used at the Mass.'

'That's a queer mouthful from a spalpeen,' Kenrick told him. 'Her cousin has a taste for revolutions and killing landlords – the Latin won't be much use to him at the end of a rope! Some day he'll make a mistake, and she'll be an easy cailin to talk to.'

They had watched her pass and made comments to suit Kenrick's temperament. One had always to soften Kenrick's humours by agreeing with him.

But Eileen Horkan was aware that Kenrick's eyes were upon her on that July day as she rode through the valley. She knew his nature too well.

Seamus Costello visited her at night when the valley was dark. She gave him food and, sometimes, money to pay the rents. He looked older than his years.

'He continues to put up the rents – he is trying to wring us dry! In the lower end of the valley they are secure. He is going to have his vengeance on us.'

'It will not always be like this,' she told him. 'A day will come when you will own the land. You must hold on,' she argued passionately.

251

'It is too far away, and I cannot see the day. In the meantime we must be silent and die. I want to take a gun to Kenrick. I do not have to spend the rest of my life working fourteen hours a day keeping Kenrick in whiskey. There is an end to patience.'

'Keep your tongue and your counsels to yourself. There are spies everywhere.'

'This valley is a prison! *You* live in comfort, *you* sleep in a feather bed and you eat meat. You have never gone without. Tonight I will sleep on rush. Smoke from wet peat will burn out my eyes. I will rise early and have a meal of cold potatoes, and then I will work on the land. It is no life for any man with pride. My mind is on fire with hate and I haven't God's charity to quench it.'

'There will be blood spilt, Seamus Costello, and I fear what may happen.'

'They brought it upon themselves. Kenrick has brought whatever is coming to him upon himself.'

When Seamus Costello left, Eileen Horkan did not immediately retire. Her mind turned to the talk of rebellion. It was in the air like spores, lodging in young men's minds. They no longer listened to the pacifism of Daniel O'Connell. They were tired of the monster rallies. There was a drift towards rebellion.

The famine struck in August. It came suddenly, the work of a single night, as the old people said many years later. The luxury of the July potato bloom had been deceptive. Travellers through Connaught had commented on its promise. Then a poisonous dew had fallen, the leaves had turned black; the stems quickly corrupted, and with them went the potato tuber itself.

Men had tasted the dew – the July dew had always been honey on the tongue, but the strange dew which now fell was acrid like vinegar. Some, in explanation, said that the soil was poisoned; others looked towards the sky and said that the blight was carried on the wind. Many said that the curse of God was on the land. During former famines, many fields had escaped, leaving the countryside a patchwork of greens and blacks. But this blight was virulent and set no limits to the damage it caused. In the *Connaught Telegraph* office in Castlebar, reports from all over Mayo confirmed Frederick

Cavendish's fears. The blight would bring famine. There was no way in which sufficient relief could be rushed to people to prevent them starving. For years they had waged a war of words against the lack of preparation by the government in London. Their *laissez-faire* policies, aimed at the merchants in the great cities and the bankers in great houses, had little relevance to an overpopulated country where the soil was thin and where men worked thin land. The very base of existence was withering. The rains were poisonous: they discoloured the clothes with black stains which ran like ink.

All morning Frederick Cavendish had sat in his office compiling the centre page of his paper, writing in a neat copperplate hand. Once his thoughts were set in motion he wrote swiftly. Joseph Foy, his office boy, came to the office each half-hour and carried the sheets of paper down to the typesetters.

'Have my horse saddled, Joseph,' Cavendish told him when he had finished writing. 'I wish to see for myself what damage the blight has caused.'

'We will surely all starve to death, sir, after a week – that's what I hear them say. There was plenty of talk at the market yesterday as men tried to get rid of new potatoes. I saw potatoes turn black in the bag, and they smelt like the guts in Shambles Lane.' Joseph Foy brought him all the news of the town. Frederick Cavendish sometimes compiled his reflections into a humorous paragraph and inserted it in the paper.

Joseph returned to the office half an hour later. 'The horse is ready, sir, but do you think that you are fit to mount it?' he asked.

'Are you referring to my size, Joe?'

'I meant no offence, sir. Sure, I have only your best interests at heart! Take care of Mr Cavendish, my mother warns me, for he keeps bread on our table.'

'I appreciate the interest your mother and yourself take in me, but I'm still fit to ride a horse,' he said drily.

But as he lumbered down the stairs and into the yard he wondered if perhaps Joe Foy's mother was right after all. He felt short of breath and heavy. Too much claret, he thought to himself. He would have to reform his habits; he knew that he never would.

'I'll hold your leg, sir, and if you want I'll get a box and help you up,' Joe Foy told him as he slowly lifted the old man's leg into the stirrup, pushing him upwards on to the saddle with his shoulder.

'Don't try to dismount, sir, until you get back,' Joe shouted after him as he made his way out under the archway to the street.

He rode slowly through the town. The weather was warm and thick like soup, unusual weather for August which could only generate disease and fever. The soldiers were much in evidence about the town. Ever since Colonel Spiker had been whipped to an inch of his life, the discipline at the barracks had hardened, and it was known that Colonel Spiker, slowly recovering from his lacerations, was planning his revenge. The Castle thought that he was the best officer to quell the insurrection they feared.

There were few country people in the streets. The shop-keepers stood at their doors looking up and down the streets in anticipation of some activity. Cavendish made his way over the bridge and along Linenhall Street. Even at this hour of the day he could hear them singing in the shebeens: the visit of Father Matthew, the temperance priest, the year previously had made no noticeable change. Men still scalded their guts with raw poteen and lay drunk on the sidewalks.

He passed the large walls of the workhouse and out of the town towards the brooding brown hills, the famished land where the dispossessed cottiers lived. They had no land of their own, and the half-acre or rood which they rented was held at a high rate from an agent, who in turn rented the land from an absentee landlord. The rot was heavy on the air. The small patches about the thatched hovels were black; the green stalks had turned to slime. The land was mute and without complaint. That was the strange thing about the Irish peasant: he remained mute in the dire circumstances in which he found himself. They have been beaten down too long. They will never rise up against the oppressor. The movements of history have not been in their favour, Frederick Cavendish thought to himself. There is a fatality about the Irish that I never found in France. There is no yeast in the blood.

He watched people grub the earth with their hands for potatoes. Some were still wholesome but they would not survive the winter pits. These people were the most wretched of all in Mayo, living at the base and on the flanks of mountains. Before the famines, they had been a healthy-looking people; now they were gaunt and hollow, particularly the women who had been pregnant during the hungry years and who gave birth with regularity. They looked much older than the men. Their eyes had sunk deep into their sockets, and they had the bright glow of hunger about them. People jabbered at him and pointed to the fields. Frederick Cavendish spoke only a few words of Irish, but he understood the words for hunger and death, repeated many times. There was no fire or anger in their voices. They seemed resigned to the curse which hung over the land.

Finally he came upon a man who spoke English fluently. He was a man of fifty-five, dressed in rough clothes, his feet bare. 'It came in a night, sir. We went to bed with the stalks and the leaves green, and next morning there was the stink of death about the land. It reminded me of the wars in Spain and the stink of death on the battlefields after the warm sun.'

'Have you no oats to keep you from hunger?' Cavendish asked.

'The oats we have go to the agent to pay the rent or to the gombeen man to pay for last year's loans. The pig goes in the same way. This is the end of us, sir. Better if I died in Spain. If I had a gun, sir, and I was in my prime like the time we fought with Wellington against Napoleon, I'd march on the agent's house and shoot him and then I'd march to the quays where the grain lies in hills in the warehouses and wrest the grain from the hoarders.' There was anger and pride in his voice.

'And what of the others?'

'What did they ever see? They say it is the curse of the Lord for their sins. I tell them that the kings of England have committed sins and the Lord did not visit harsh punishment upon them. But they will not listen; they will sit and die rather than raise a hand against the agent. And, sir, it is only starting. There is still heat in the days. What will we do in a month's time when the final potato has rotted and we are starving? Eat grass, is it? Give me a gun, sir, and I'll die standing up rather than lie down and starve.'

'And what of the Board of Works?' Cavendish was grasping at straws, already knowing the answers.

255

'The Board of Works will soon have to carry the whole countryside. We will be building roads into bog holes and making walls across mountains. I served the King and the Queen well and I end my days at the base of a mountain, hungry.'

Frederick Cavendish rode further into the mountains, the same sight greeting his eyes everywhere he went. He knew now that there was no hope for the people: a famine of great immensity was beginning. It was beginning among the hills and at the base of mountains. What winter would bring was beyond anything he could imagine. Each week would be a further step towards ultimate starvation.

It was sunset when he turned towards Castlebar. His mind was weary, and he felt the weight of his years about him. All passion had been spent. Now he could only sit and write articles which would draw the attention of London to the plight of the starving peasantry. Had he been young like Myles Prendergast, he might have entered the revolutionary councils – he had sat with revolutionaries before. Perhaps Myles was taking the correct path. Did England ever listen to a logical voice?

As always on his return from the country he made his way towards Molly Ward's. He slipped in the back entrance and knocked three times against the small hatch. It slid open, and his bottle of claret with a fine glass beside it was placed on the ledge. He could hear the loud voices of the soldiers in the main bar, singing army songs.

'I heard you were out riding by yourself,' Molly Ward told him when she entered the small room. 'Joe Foy was down with the news. He's worse than a newspaper. You are too old to be making long journeys into the country. What did you see?'

'What you will all soon see, Molly: hunger. Make no mistake about it; the crops really have failed this time. I travelled deep into the mountains. The people will soon have eaten everything there is to eat. Let us hope that the winter is mild.' There was little joy in his voice.

'You are too old to be worrying about others.'

'I know.'

'And you are too old to be riding out the country on that horse of yours.'

'I know.'

'And you are too old to be drinking a bottle of claret every night.'

'I will not answer no to that. It helps me to forget.'

'And so there will be no *Maritana* tonight?'

'No, Molly, no *Maritana* tonight.'

She left him to his bottle of claret. It warmed his stomach. A brooding melancholy settled over his mind. He recalled the French woman who had shared his bed during the bloody days of the Revolution. She must be old now, he thought. He tried to remember her name – it was Françoise, but he could not recall her surname. He could recall with ease, however, the contours of her body and the smell of the scent which she wore, although it was a long time ago. His child was French and carried her name; he couldn't remember what he looked like.

24

EILEEN HORKAN had become Lord Lannagh's mistress: they were correct when they called her 'the Englishman's whore' as they made their way past her cottage to the workhouse. She knew now, too, that life stirred within her. It was ironic that it should have happened when the potato failed, when the nation entered its agony.

Love had been too easy. Her flesh had been filled with joy, her mornings with delight. She lived only for her hours with the English gentleman and she forgot Seamus Costello and the people of his village. Her mind was blinded by passion so strong that any other voice was soon quietened. She would take delight with this man; later she might suffer for her sins, but while sin was sweet she would enjoy it. She would be chaste and patriotic on the morrow but not while delight beckoned: she did not realise that her passions could be so violent or the hunger of her flesh so consuming, and she could not hate this man who made love to her with such tenderness and affection. He had wakened hungers within her that had lain dormant during the years.

In her delight she forgot that men and women now began to starve. They had been hungry enough during the early forties, but now there was no food at all to eat. The base of existence had withered. Her sensual hunger for Lord Lannagh brought her to his house, and each morning she made her way home thinking only of the moments when they would meet again. On one occasion she had driven her horse through a mass of hungry people who had lifted their hands to her in anguish. Their plight did not stir any feeling in her, but during more rational moments when sensuality had died she did question her wild passion. Had she abandoned herself too freely with this man? He was part of the cause of the starvation which now spread deeper into the valleys and the villages.

As the sensuality began to lessen and her passion, satiated with delight, slowly settled, she became aware of the tragedy about her. She began to read again and to go for long walks to try to restore some balance to her life.

She took the path which led to the river, bordering on her farm, and found that the flow of even water tempered her mind. It was lined with osiers which the peasants cut and shaped into baskets, and ran through fertile fields for about three miles until it descended from a ledge and formed a waterfall. She decided to pass the rest of the day walking across the moorlands above the fall. It was a difficult ascent, but once she reached the edge of the waterfall the flat land stretched as far as the eye could see. She continued by a sheep-track across the wide expanse of moor, skirting black pools of water and wet patches until, after an hour, she came to a road which cut across the bog. It had been built by the Board of Works and led to a morass, ending on the edge of a black pool. It was one of the many futile undertakings by the Board in order to give employment when field labour was finished in June.

Far in the bog Eileen saw the lone figure of a woman carrying a basket of turf on her back. She was stooped under the heavy weight and once or twice she stumbled as she made her way from the bank of turf to the roadside.

'The blessings of God be upon your work,' Eileen called out in Irish as she approached.

'And the same blessings be upon you,' the woman replied wearily. Eileen looked at the ashen face. It carried the marks of exhaustion and hunger.

'You have worked long hours?' Eileen asked.

'Since the whitening of the sky.'

'Then, it is time for you to eat,' she said.

'I must work until there is red in the evening sky.'

She knew that the woman was hungry from her drawn face. She could have been young or old; it was difficult to tell the effects of age from those of hardship and hunger.

'How long is it since you have eaten?' Eileen asked.

'Two days, good lady,' she said directly and without self-pity.

'And your husband? Has he eaten?'

'He is dead these two years.'

'And your children?'

'It is two days since a taste of food passed their mouths. But I will earn four pence for my day's work, and that will buy some meal or bread for them.'

'And where are your children now?'

'At home in the cabin. They sleep all day and night, so as not to feel the pang of hunger. I should take them to the workhouse – they say there is gruel there and beds, and what more could one want? – except I have the fear of being divided from them. They say they divide the children from their mothers in the workhouse, and I would not have my children divided from me.'

She spoke in a strong voice indicating that she would rather die than go to the workhouse. She had a pride within her which, despite hunger, gave her a false energy to continue to work beyond the edge of exhaustion.

'How will you get by in the winter?'

'I don't know. I never think beyond tomorrow. The potatoes are rotting in the fields and the smell is everywhere, except in the bog here. The patch I had myself is rotten. I have turned over every spadeful of earth in search of a healthy potato, but they are soft and rotten like corpses. They say that we are cursed for our sins.'

'What sins have you ever committed?' Eileen was angry now.

'Only ones that would earn me money to feed my children. Only ones that would feed my children,' the other said, choking back her bitterness.

Eileen remembered the literature she had read on the dignity of man. The phrases of Voltaire, Rousseau and Thomas Paine were so simple and strong. In their time they had brought down the French monarchy and the rotten system built around it, in a fever of revolutionary thoughts. They gave men a cause to fight for; yet they had not taken a firm root in Ireland. They had not inflamed the imagination.

Eileen had brought some food with her, and she now took the parcel from her pocket and undid it. The woman looked at the buttered bread and the meat lying on the cloth napkin and could not disguise the flash of hunger in her eyes as she finally admitted to herself that she was exhausted. Yet she did not move towards the proffered food.

'Eat it,' Eileen told her. 'It is for you.'

'And will the lady not go hungry?' she asked.

'No. I had some eggs this morning and I have done no hard work.'

'Thank you kindly, good lady, and may the blessings of God be upon you and the cloak of His mother about you.'

She ate part of the food slowly, turning it about in her mouth, drawing taste and satisfaction from it. Eileen did not interrupt her as she ate the bread, looking instead across the desolate brown moor, dotted with stacks of turf. It was lonely as far as the eye could see, except for the insignificant movement of one or two people in the distance. She thought of the thousands of people spread across the wide landscape of Mayo who were in a similar position, gradually succumbing to the hunger. Their hearts and minds were crowded with fear of the land agent and the gombeen man. Why such men could ever be admitted to the Eucharist was something she could never explain to herself. She knew that she and the child she was carrying could survive the famine, but that this woman beside her would die.

The woman ate only part of the food. When she had finished she wrapped the remaining bread and meat in a cloth and put it in the pocket of her rough dress. 'It will see the children through two days,' she said directly. 'They will find the taste of meat strange. When I was a young girl we tasted meat three times a year, but my children have not tasted meat that often. They will have to eat it slowly so as not to vomit up the goodness.'

'And have you no hope of food?' Eileen asked.

'You must be a stranger to this country, good lady. Where is the hope of food? The earth is like a barren woman. No seed takes life in it.' Eileen was acutely aware of the great empty space about them. 'I saw better times, good lady. My father had six acres and a cow. We had milk on the table and butter

261

on our potatoes. But the rents became a burden and another took his farm. The landlord's cattle graze on the ground where our house once stood.'

Eileen took some shillings from her pocket and gave them to her. Tears started to the woman's eyes as she looked at the money; in the silver coins she saw enough money to stave off hunger for two weeks. 'I hope every blessing will follow you,' she said as they took leave of each other.

Eileen's return journey across the wide moor was slow and reflective. The sun was warm on her back and the sky almost empty of cloud. The famine was beginning, and she could no longer enjoy a selfish happiness.

Kate Brady watched Eileen Horkan return across the bog. She had delicate shoulders, her gait was independent and free, yet she had talked to her in Irish and she had felt lucid and free in her company. She watched her until the outline of her figure became black against the sky.

Then she felt weary again. For six hours she had carried the heavy baskets of turf on her back until the rods had franked her back. During her journeys across the spongy moss she had called out in prayer for help. It was natural for her to do so. Then, unexpectedly, her plea for help was answered. She looked at the shillings in her hand for reassurance. They were real. She ran her nail around the image on the coins. The luxury of minted silver made her almost light in the head. In her pocket and pressed to her thigh there was also food for her children.

For Kate Brady the last two years had been dark. She had been dispossessed of her precious single acre because she was a widow woman – it had been divided between two families. She had worked in the fields during the planting season, picking up her wages at the end of the day, eating the raw potatoes when the owner was not looking. She had carried stones in panniers when they built the committee roads until her fingers bled. She had dragged herself forward until her mind was light from exhaustion. On two occasions she had slept with sailors in Northport in order to make a shilling for food. If she had once possessed pride, it had now been taken from her: she was a beast of burden, driven by the hard urgency to survive. But this urgency was now growing thin, and she wondered where she would find food during the winter.

She lifted herself wearily from the stack of turf where she had been warming her body in the sun. She felt drowsy and wished that she could sleep, but knew that she had five miles to walk to the small cabin where her children were waiting for her. The food she had eaten gave her a small strength. She drew herself upright, put the empty basket on her back and made her way home. Fear gripped her mind, and she became suspicious: perhaps the two figures in the distance had seen her receive food. Perhaps they suspected that she had received money. She must keep a firm grip upon herself and not appear too confident.

At the edge of the bog a family had built a rough shelter against a bank. They had sunk posts into the soft ground, and thin rafters of ash formed the roof, covered by scraws cut from the bog. She passed the inhabitants and saw the dark pigment of hunger under their eyes and the way they looked listlessly at the blue smoke drifting up from the fire, their hunted eyes following her. They did not exchange greetings and they did not move their bodies. For a moment she thought of sharing her good fortune with them, then suppressed it, thinking instead of her children waiting for her. She could not feed ten people; she must think of her own. During these hungry times everybody must think of themselves. She passed several such shelters on her way to her cabin and remembered a hundred starving eyes. One could tell when the children were starving: they had thin fleshless limbs and bloated stomachs.

She left the osier basket at the wall of her cabin and went in: it was low, and she had to bend down to enter. When she had a fire the smoke escaped through a hole in the roof. There was another hole in the wall which let in the air and which she blocked with a rag on cold nights. The floor was of beaten clay. In the corner of the cabin her two children lay on dry rushes covered with sacking.

'She has been crying all day with hunger since you left,' the boy told her when she entered. 'Sometimes she cried herself to sleep but most of the time she was awake crying for you. Her face is dirty with tears.'

'Did anyone call?'

'No. It was lonely all day. The people don't call any more. Did you get food?'

'Yes. I got fine food, *allanagh*. You must have been praying for me. Maybe times are getting better. Don't wake your sister yet. We will surprise her, for I'll make the bread into goody and it will be soft in her stomach.' In the half-dark she broke the bread into a wooden bowl and softened it with water. She went over to the small child and knelt down beside her. 'I have goody for you, *allanagh*,' she whispered, but the child did not stir. She tried to shake her gently awake. She felt her forehead. It was cold. The child was dead.

She went outside and wept. The urgency to live was broken within her. Later she tried to explain to her boy what had happened, but he could not understand. He shook his sister but could not waken her.

That evening she dug a grave close to the cabin, wrapped the child in the sacking which had covered her and placed moss on the bottom of the grave. Then she laid the light body of the child on top, pouring the soil back into the grave until it covered her. The sun had turned the mountains purple by the time she had finished her work and gone indoors. She had forgotten that she had a parcel of meat in her pocket.

'I carry your child,' Eileen said directly. They sat on opposite armchairs in the library. Between them a fire blazed. It was mid-October. Here the cold and the darkness of the landscape had been banished. Had it been at another time and in another place she would have been happy.

He did not speak for a moment. He did not look directly at her, continuing to gaze into the heart of the fire. All his life he had wished for an heir to his name and to his lineage; now an Irishwoman would give illegitimate birth to his child. His seed would go amongst the peasants, he thought, not resentfully but with truth. But perhaps it should not go among the peasants. It had been spun from good flesh – Eileen Horkan by any standards was an exceptional woman; she would pass on her great gifts of intellect and heart to the unborn child.

They had been lovers for many months. For both of them it had been a revelation: he had taken joy from this woman's body in a subtle and full way, and she in turn had uttered words in his ears which had opened the gates of deep fulfilment

264

for her, words that had belonged to her culture for a thousand years, raw and fine and dark.

'Are you certain?' he asked softly.

'I am,' she said with certainty.

He looked at her, unable to disguise his pride. 'All my life I wished to have an offspring. I did not wish to go down into death without issue.'

'It will be termed a bastard,' she said directly. 'It will not have your status.'

'No, this child *will* carry privilege.' He was decisive, almost optimistic. 'All these things can be arranged. I will bring you to England. You will have a country house beside a river. Money will be available to you. I only wish that this child could carry my title.'

There was an excitement within him. Some impotency had been broken with the knowledge that he could transmit life to a fruitful woman. Their lives were mixed within her. 'If things were different,' he mused, looking her in the eye.

'Things are what they are.'

'When will the child be born?'

'In summer.'

'A golden time.' He moved towards her and stroked her hair. She took his hand and held it in hers.

'This child will be both Irish and English. It will carry the strains of two races in its blood.'

'It will have a double advantage, then!'

'It will, only now I shall be marked as your tally-woman.' She spoke without any self-pity.

'Tally-woman? Tally-woman?' he repeated, not knowing the meaning of the word.

'It means a kept woman,' she told him directly.

'But you are not a kept woman.'

'When they gossip in the corners they will say that I am.'

'Then, come away with me. You will not have the breath of scandal about you in England. You are my real wife.'

'I cannot leave. Those of the blood of this child are now dying. I will not leave and let them die.'

'I will let you have money to feed them.'

'I would be a whore, demanding money in exchange for love. I wish that there were gentler times, lawns where peacocks roam, a gentle landscape where cattle graze. I wish to be in a place with dignity,' she said longingly.

'But you can be,' he pressed.

'*No!* I must remain with my people. They need me now.' It was final. She had resisted.

'What do you wish?'

'I need money. I need enough money to feed a whole valley.'

'All that I will give you. Now let us talk of other things.' He was deflated, empty, at her refusal.

They talked for a long time. They drank wine slowly and later, as the urgency of love grew in them, they made love. It was neither rough nor rushed– it was love of a thousand delicate touches. Her body wakened to passion, and she forgot her obligations towards the hungry. She cared little if a servant woman entered the room.

'Am I an Englishman's whore?' she repeated to herself, turning the phrase over in her mind, as she returned home through the autumn landscape of rain and cold. Now that she was on her own she felt soiled. She wondered if she were the traditional whore, using her unborn child as a pawn to obtain gold. She searched her mind for an answer. Yet, she told herself, she could have escaped from this landscape and lived a civilised life and instead she had used the unborn child as collateral for the valley. Had it been a less harsh year, she would have carried and given birth to the child without obligation. But the night she had visited the valley with her cousin Seamus Costello had changed all that.

He had knocked upon her door one night. She admitted him, and he followed her to the room where she kept her books. She was surprised at the change which the weeks had brought: his face had lost flesh, and his clothes were loose about him. His eyes had the glazed look of hunger, and his voice was uncertain.

'What has happened to you?' she asked anxiously.

'What is happening to us all – hunger and the want of food. The Englishman must be feeding you well up at the house.' He looked her up and down contemptuously.

'How dare you speak to me like that, Seamus! I have always been generous to you. I have not seen you go without. If I choose to go to the great house, that is my business.'

'There are rumours. . . .' He was disconcerted at her anger.

266

He looked nervously about him. 'I'm starving, Eileen. My head was going in a reel coming up out of the valley. Two days ago I clawed a turnip out of the earth and I haven't tasted food since then. Whatever I have I give to my father and mother. Kenrick has us for sure this time – he says he will starve us out of the valley and he has raised the rents. In December we will be dead, and there is no leaving the place. The pigs and the cattle are sold to buy bad meal at the markets. Now nothing remains but to go to the workhouse, and we would rather die than do that!'

'Seamus, hunger has its rights, and one of its rights is to be angry. I will fetch you some food.' She had forgiven him.

'I can only eat bread, Eileen. I would vomit meat. It is too rich for my stomach.'

She brought him milk and bread. He ate it slowly, his mind bent on the pleasure it was giving him. When he had finished she said: 'I will go with you into the valley.'

They travelled by night into the silent valley. He led her from house to house. Her heart became desolate. People whom she had known from childhood stared up at her from pallets of straw, their faces wasted. These were the men and women in whose houses she had once played, listening to them sing and watching them dance. Now they were without sustenance and had no will to live.

'I cannot believe it, Seamus! I cannot believe it!' she muttered in a shocked whisper.

'I would have come to you sooner, but pride stopped me.'

'You *should* have come much sooner.'

'Kenrick is to blame for it. I could kill him and feel no compunction.'

'Keep these murderous words to yourself.'

Her mind was filled with confusion. She had slept in the bed of an English gentleman, whispered words of love in his ear. She had felt his arms about her and had tasted rare wine and hung meat. Now she was with her own, and the stench of death was in her nostrils. 'God, Seamus, I swear that these people will not starve!' There was hot anger in her voice.

She visited all the houses. Old people who had taken her upon their knees and crooned the old Irish songs to her now called out for food. 'You will have food. You will have food and you will live,' she answered, wondering how to fulfil her promise.

She left the valley knowing that she had to become the instrument of their salvation before it was too late. Seamus came with her and carried two bags of food to the village on the back of an ass. As they ate the food they blessed Eileen Horkan that she had come to their aid during their great hour of need.

That night she sat in front of her own fire, anger growing in her mind. If she could, she would destroy the land agent Kenrick. For the moment, however, she had not the power to do that. She was already using her influence over Lord Lannagh as far as she could.

'These are not the Elysian fields,' she told herself. 'These are the fields which have been blighted. I carry within me a child that is partly Irish and partly English. He is blood to those who suffer.' The most she could do was to use the gold Lord Lannagh had given her to purchase food to keep her people alive. She had bartered herself that others might live through the famine.

25

MICHAEL BARRETT looked out from the window of his map room towards the sea. Each day, using a telescope which he had carried on all his voyages, he scanned the horizon, hoping to catch a glimpse of his ship returning from America. He knew he would never sail the seas again; his daughter would take his place. He felt the texture of the charts, strong and firm. The room itself smelt strongly of leather. His charts, like wine-bottles, each in its leather-covered cylinder, lay in racks about him, the muted voices of mysterious seas.

'The sea never was tranquil, as it is now in my mind,' he told himself. 'The winds were more awkward than fair. It was a cold uncomfortable place. The sea is an inhospitable place.' These days, as he looked down on his maps, he thought only of sunny days and the landfalls of Spain.

He left the maps and went towards the window. The sea was quiet, the islands warm and green beneath the sun. He could see clearly the even wash of the waves on Mulranny strand. There was no sign of the ship yet. It was not overdue, but he thought that with a fair wind it might arrive ahead of time and he longed for the return of his daughter, Gráinne.

He thought of her mother who lay buried in the family tomb in the small clearing in Eisirt wood. He had not visited the walled place in a long time, and his wife was a far memory, part of his life in middle age, not of his old age.

269

He drank more wine. He was beginning to drink too much, but it kept his mind warm. 'I drink my claret, and men are beginning to die out there. The base of life is withering,' he told himself. He was well informed on all that was happening; from the moment the potato began to fail he had had news brought to him of its extent and the havoc it caused. No field had been spared: the green patches had become black, and the black was everywhere. He had lived through other famines, but they had been less severe; this one had the mark of fatality upon it, and he had known that it would come a long time ago. The merchants at the far side of Northport were now selling meal at twenty shillings a hundredweight. They were a plague upon the backs of the people. They had cornered the markets and could now make their profits. 'What now becomes of your remark, Lord John Russell?' he said to himself. '"No Irishman would die of want while an English government could prevent it." The merchants will bleed every penny from the peasantry. The money paid by the Board of Works is a pittance in comparison to the price of food. Soon money will not be able to buy food.'

He was familiar with the merchant class. They followed the English customs, spoke like Englishmen, had their daughters play pianos, and sent them on visits to London, the centre of the Empire. They lived in the towns, kept their own company and looked upon the peasants as vermin. He decided to go and see for himself the ravages that the famine had caused, to visit the grave of Rioccard Barrett and return to his roots.

There was consternation in the servants' quarters when Michael Barrett announced that he was going on a journey to Belmullet and that he wished food to be packed.

'He's going soft in the head! At his age he's not fit to make a journey to the end of the avenue,' Mrs Jennings told the servants.

'He should be roped to a chair!' her son suggested, half-seriously.

'Who will rope an old lion like that to a chair? Is it out of your mind you are? He would have us all out on the side of the road if we even suggested that he stay at home! Oh, I wish Gráinne was here – she is the only one equal to him.'

'Well, I'll tell you, it will be the death of him. He hasn't been on a horse this year. If it should take fright and throw him, there would be queer work, queer work, and those who should be taking care of him are sailing the wild seas. Somebody should at least go with him.'

'He'll have no one. He's awkward. Sure, I feel like running when I see him coming.' Mrs Jennings raised her eyes in despair.

They made indirect suggestions to the old man as he came down the stairs and they walked beside him to the yard continuing to give him advice.

'I need no advice,' he said impatiently, brushing them aside. 'I need no protection. Michael Barrett makes his own decisions, so go away and leave me alone. I am going to Belmullet.'

'But it is miles and miles away,' they told him.

'Away or I will take my stick to you all!'

The servants watched from the windows of the great house as the old man set out on his journey. He had food and drink in his leather bags and a heavy cape on his shoulders. His back was old and massive and globed as if he carried some great weight. His grey head was immobile and looked neither to the left nor to the right.

'It will be the end of him,' they said to one another. 'The road to Belmullet is windswept and cold, and his bones are brittle like chalk. If he falls off the horse, his bones will turn to powder and there will be a queer of trouble for everyone.'

Apart from his immediate reason for making the journey, Michael Barrett knew also that there were deeper ties drawing him north. He wished to have a final look at the Belmullet peninsula where he had been happy as a boy, and he wished to pay his respects to Rioccard Barrett the poet buried at Cross halfway down the peninsula and facing the western sea. He was also saying goodbye to life: the urgency now was to return to places where he had been in his youth, to memories full of sun and the sea.

There was a certain amount of initial excitement as he set out upon his journey. The road and the hills running to the hard and high mountains lifted his heart. But very soon he caught the fetid smell of decay everywhere; the fields were black with rot. Men with wooden spades dug mechanically in the earth, the women bent behind them, hoping that some potatoes might have escaped them. Further on he saw people picking the berries from the bushes and the nuts in the hazel

271

woods. They were voiceless with despair. They were pitiable ragged creatures and did not look human. And it is only the end of October, he thought. What will November and December bring?

He moved onwards, his body awkward on the horse. Sometimes because of the warm sun he felt that he might sleep, but he always shook himself awake. Two hours later he passed through the defile at Mulranny and faced into the open expanse of bog, uneventful as far as the horizon. It was in this brown and flat landscape that he found the first direct effect of the famine. In a ditch at the side of the road he found an old man dying. His body was fleshless, his eyes deep and lustrous and looking madly from black sockets. He looked very old. Starvation had tightened the flesh about his forehead and his teeth.

When he saw Michael Barrett excitement lit his body. He threw his arms about him in wild gestures. But his words made no particular meaning – parts of prayers, old idioms, names of relations. Michael Barrett was surprised at the huge energy within this emaciated man and brought his horse against the ditch and dismounted. The old man, his eyes staring still at the infinity of the bog, continued to chatter. As Michael Barrett approached the old man, the talk stopped and the man fell forward. He was dead. Michael Barrett was to see many times on his journey to Belmullet that people before death were possessed by a strange and fierce energy. He waited by the corpse for half an hour, meditating on the horror of it all, until he was aware of eyes peering at him from a rhododendron patch. He beckoned the people forward.

'I will pay you to bury the corpse,' he told them in Irish.

''Tis not money we want, sir, but food. We cannot eat money, and there is nothing we can buy with it.'

'Very well, then, I'll give you food' – and putting his hand in his leather bag he drew out bread. They took it and ate it ravenously, like hungry dogs, tearing at its soft substance.

'Eat it slowly,' Michael Barrett said. 'It will be to your advantage.'

But they did not heed his advice.

'What was his name?' Michael Barrett asked.

'Pakey Malone. He had no one to take care of him. The old will always be the first to die.'

'Are many dying?'

'In along the bog they have begun to die. It's a wide place, and you would not notice them.' Their voices were factual and cold. 'They say it's a curse for our sins, sir,' they said.

'What sins?'

'All sorts of sins,' they told him.

'If the likes of you are suffering for sins, then there are a lot in the House of Parliament who will scald in hell,' Barrett replied, his old face twisted in bitterness. The word 'hell' meant much to them, but they had never heard the word 'Parliament' before.

He left them with the dead man and slowly mounted his horse again. 'If you give bread to people to bury every corpse you find between here and Belmullet, then it's eight cartloads of bread you would need!' one shouted after him. Even on the edge of death their thoughts took on humour and exaggeration; it was black and macabre.

He stayed that night in the village of Ballycorric. Here in the vastness of the bog there was some cultivated land. Michael Barrett was known here; he sat beside a fire and shared the people's drink with them, receiving a bleak picture of all that was happening. They would not survive the winter, and it was time to get out. Some were making tracks to Dublin. They would be fed in the great cities of Liverpool and Manchester if they could get there. There was no winter living in a bog. A rumour had spread through the locality that food was on its way from the depots in Belmullet, a vague rumour which gained substance as their hunger advanced. Some had decided it would be better to move towards the great towns, where people were rich and lived in luxury and which, they were told, were bulging with food. But always there was the news that somebody was dying of starvation or already dead. The names of the first victims were recorded, but by winter nobody remembered any more.

He slept that night in a rough bed. When he rose in the morning he discovered that somebody had stolen his food. They had not touched his money. He said nothing but departed.

He made his way to Belmullet. By now his mind and his eyes had become accustomed to starving people. The wind coming across the bog was cold; it seemed to penetrate his heavy cloak and chill his bones. He took a flask of brandy from

273

his satchel and drank from it. It warmed him for a time.

Belmullet was not as yet affected by famine. He sat down to a heavy meal in a small hotel and talked to the landlady. Yes, there was talk of famine and death and there were some country people wandering about the town and begging; but she had little more to say – she was a woman who had no general interest in things. She was well protected against hunger.

He made his way out of the town, across the narrow bridge, and headed down the peninsula. It did not stir his imagination to excitement as he thought it might; memories returned only fleetingly. He passed a small village with a tavern, turned to the right and made his way through the sand dunes to Cross cemetery. This was the place where his pilgrimage ended and where the bones of obscure ancestors lay at rest. He looked at the crooked crosses, the mounds with withering grass above them, and he listened to the sound of the eternal sea. Slowly tranquillity entered his soul and his early memories returned to him. He thought of the rakish poet who lay buried at his feet and of the dunaire which had cost him a small fortune. Rioccard Barrett would be remembered for ever whereas his own name would be consigned to oblivion. The verses of the poems came slowly to his mind.

And then he heard somebody recite the poems behind him. He recognised the voice. 'Are you trying to buy your way back into my life, Gill?' Michael Barrett said without looking round. 'You defiled my house and you took advantage of my hospitality. What brought you to Belmullet?'

'Patronage, sir. I felt that I had exhausted the generosity of people in Northport, and they said that there was a noble house here, sir, and food and comfort.'

'And did you find patronage?'

'No, sir. Only hunger and disrespect and poor lodgings in the shebeen beside this graveyard.'

'Well, no one lamented your departure from Northport.'

'I can well imagine that, sir.'

'They eat fish here.'

'Well I know it. My stomach turns when I see a fish, and I nearly choked several times on the sharp bones.'

'More is the pity you didn't choke,' Barrett said angrily.

'I'm sure some would wish it so, sir.' Gill was humble.

274

'You are a reprobate.'

'I've changed my ways, sir.'

'Have you given up the drink?'

'Well, not fully; but I'm not half as bad as I was.'

'You could not change your ways, Gill, if the pledge was handed down to you by Archbishop McHale.'

'Standing here in front of Rioccard Barrett's grave and behind you, sir, I swear to God that I'll never cause you bother again.'

'Come round here until I see you.'

Gill came from behind. His face was grey. He was hungry, and there were tears in his eyes.

'Have you been drinking?'

'To be honest, sir, I have. But what else can I do when there is no food? It's terrible in this bleak place, open and empty, where they have no thoughts for a poet. Take me home or I'll die.'

'Give me one good reason why I should not let you die here. You soiled yourself in my house, you have vomited on my floors, you have come roaring up the avenue drunk when the world was asleep and pounded on the main doors and hurled curses at me.' He looked at Gill as he spoke. He really would die if he left him in Belmullet. Raw living had left its mark on his face and gait.

'Because I am a poet, sir, and I wrote one good poem,' he said with dignity.

It was not the answer Michael Barrett expected. 'You are learning humility, Gill.'

'I have no pride left in me for the hunger. I'm old, and the fire has gone out of me. I'm only ashes.'

'How do you expect me to bring you from Belmullet?'

'I'll walk beside you all the way, starving though I am, and if I falter I'll hold on to the tail of the horse.'

'You are full of answers today, Gill,' Michael Barrett told him. As he looked at the haunted eyes his old affection was returning for the rake. They had much in common.

'When did you last eat?'

'I had a kipper two days ago. I hate kippers, and it made me sick. I never could eat fish.'

'Well, then, eat this,' and he took some food which he had purchased from the hotel from the leather satchel. He admired

275

the fashion in which Gill ate his food. He chewed it slowly and fastidiously and wiped away the particles from his mouth. 'You wouldn't have a drop of drink to wash it down, sir? It's only to wash it down,' he repeated, seeing the look in Barrett's eye.

He handed Gill the bottle of brandy and watched as he took a deep gulp from the bottle before handing it back.

'You still like the drink?' Gill asked.

'It's an old habit, an enemy and a friend.' Barrett put the bottle back in the leather satchel. 'Now help me on to the horse,' he said.

'Sure, you can stand on my back if necessary, sir' – the old wheedling tone coming back as he felt better.

'Stop this humility, Gill! It doesn't suit your nature. Hold my leg and help me up.'

'I'll walk beside you,' Gill told him when Barrett was mounted.

'Get up behind me before you fall dead,' the other told Gill curtly.

The spectral figure of Gill got up behind Michael Barrett, and they made their way towards Belmullet. An hour later Gill asked for a drink.

They reached the gates of the great house two days later. Gill dismounted and set off for Northport. 'If you are ever hungry, call to the house,' Michael Barrett told him.

He watched Gill make his way down the road, then ordered the horse forward. Michael Barrett suddenly felt cold in his body in the shaded avenue. He was heavy with despair as he dismounted and was helped to his room and when he sat before the blazing fire the chill refused to leave his bones.

Michael Barrett's health began to fail. His mind began to lose clear sequences and his strong body was now racked with coughing. The whites of his eyes turned into raw nets. He fell into heavy depressions and wept for the past.

In November he suddenly became old. The round globe of his back and shoulders sank, and his clothes were loose about his body. His firm gait became loose as the flesh melted from his body day by day, and he shuffled from place to place.

Then his mind began to fail: at first he began to forget things, then he would ask where he was and sometimes he had to be directed towards his room. But always the famine sequences returned to haunt him.

'It will be only a wasteland like Raleigh's Munster. There will be no voices. They will perish from the earth, and their bones will bleach the sides of the roads. We are cursed. We are cursed and not from any sin.'

The servants in the kitchen muttered amongst themselves. At least they had him contained in the house and he could be led easily from place to place like a child.

'His mind is ravelling ever since he returned from Belmullet. There must surely be something wrong with him when he brought Gill on the back of his horse from Belmullet – and Gill banished from the house for pissing in his trousers amongst other things!'

'Maybe Gill can still his mind. Poets have strange powers in unusual circumstances, like David and Saul,' one suggested.

'Oh, leave Gill where he is, drinking in Northport! He is boasting and blathering that he is reinstated at the great house and that his gullet will be filled during the hunger. To bring Gill here is to buy trouble,' Mrs Jennings told them.

A long wide corridor divided the first storey of the house. Hour after hour Michael Barrett paced up and down this corridor pausing only to gaze out of the tall windows at each end. His mind found tranquillity in the vistas leading through the woods of Eisirt. His wife, he recalled, was buried in the woods. The winds would now be singing about her. She had always been haunted by the music of the woods, too fragile for this landscape, as fragile as a pink coral shell.

The fragile coral shell reminded him of the sugar island of Mauritius. It was the most beautiful island in the world, paradisial and narcotic. He could not remember the name of the Creole woman with whom he had passed pleasant weeks, close to the beach, while his ship was repaired in the docks at Port Louis. He had limped into port having survived a cyclone. He had sailed on its edge for two days desperately avoiding its dreadful calm eye, for no one had ever been through the eye of a cyclone. But he did not remember the wheeling winds; he recalled only the sound of the waves breaking on the reefs, the sound of the coconut fronds brushing drily against each other. Was it a long time ago; was it yesterday? It seemed only like yesterday.

'Will my daughter never return from the sea?' he cried out. '*She* will be captain of my ships. She has the sea in her blood like Granuaile. The ships are her horses, the seas her green meadows.' Then he would become lucid, and his mind would sharpen. He would go to the map room, take his telescope and look west for the sight of sails.

Once, longing for the sound of Irish, he summoned Gill from a shebeen. Gill sobered up on the way to the house and straightened his wild hair.

'He's not himself, Gill, calling you,' the servants told him. 'He must be out of his mind to summon you. So take care of yourself and behave,' they advised him.

He was ordered into the large room above the main hall. It was a room filled with light. The pictures which hung on the wall had been chosen by Barrett's wife and were of delicate themes; the long bevelled mirrors doubled the light, and a huge fire burned in the marble fireplace. The windows could be opened on to the balcony. Barrett's wife had often sat on this balcony in summer-time, looking east.

Gill had never been in the room before. He felt soiled and he noticed that one of his shoes was cracked, a dirty toe showing through the worn leather. But he had been in rooms such as this a very long time ago. The room renewed a sensuality within him which an embittered landscape had almost destroyed.

'Sit opposite me, Gill,' Michael Barrett ordered. 'I am not well. There is a deep chill in my bones. My mind is uncertain sometimes.'

'All our minds are sometimes uncertain,' Gill told him. He went forward and sat in the chair. He looked at Michael Barrett and was shocked by his appearance. The old man's face was grey, and the blood-vessels in his cheeks had ruptured. His eyes were withdrawn into their sockets, wet and uncertain, and despite the shawl drawn over his shoulders he seemed cold. He began to cough, which cut through his frame. He spat green phlegm into the fire.

'Remind me to give you a good pair of boots before leaving, Gill. I can see your feet through the toecaps. And you have cowdung on the ends of your trousers. Nobody with cowdung on the ends of his trousers was ever permitted to come in here.'

'I came in a hurry, sir,' Gill apologised.

'Well, how do I look, Gill?'

'Right and proper. Right and proper, sir,' Gill lied.

'The long mirrors on the walls don't tell me that,' Barrett said grimly.

'Then, sir, the mirrors are liars, worse liars than sheep-stealers.'

Michael Barrett looked directly at Gill, ravaged by drink and hunger. His eyes were alive and active. 'I am not well, Gill. I am old and I creak and I recall the past and sometimes I weep. Sometimes I mix up things in my mind.'

'Think nothing of it, sir. The world is full of the tears of things. It's the bad weather and that blight which is affecting everything. If the fields get black, sure, the blackness gets inside one's head. It was inside my head when you rescued me from Belmullet and a diet of kippers and barnacles.'

'I'm *dying*, Gill. It's over with me! Pains are beginning to cut my insides. I do not tell these things to the servants. I die from within and I die from without. No sweat-house could cure me.'

Gill felt uncomfortable at the direct honesty of the man. In his sober moments, he feared death, wondering whether a hostile God would condemn him to one of Dante's circles. 'Put such dark thoughts out of your head. Spring will come as it always does, and the heart hoists its sail and you will be right.'

'Are you sober, Gill?' Michael Barrett interrupted.

'I am.'

'Unusual for you. Take some whiskey, then, and sing for me. You will find the decanter on the sideboard.'

'And a drop for yourself?' he asked, making his way to the decanters of whiskey.

'No, Gill. It does me no good.'

Gill looked at the decanters of whiskey set out on a wide sideboard. They were unmarked, so he poured out the one which carried the deepest colour. With his back turned to Michael Barrett he gulped back a glass of whiskey and filled it again before returning to the armchair.

'Well, you fitted plenty into the glass! It's a bucket I should have given you. A gentleman never fills a tumbler to the brim.' Michael Barrett's sharp eyes bored into him.

'Sure, I'm no gentleman, sir.'

'You would sell your soul for a drink of whiskey.'

'I've sold it several times in pubs writing bad verse for fools. But I feel warm when I drink it. I'm warm now and I'll sing for you.'

In the room filled with light, even at the beginning of November, Gill felt some dignity return to him. He looked into the fire for a moment. Then, when he was ready, he began to sing 'Donall Og' with a sad voice which did not belong to him.

'Donall Og, if you cross the ocean
Bear me with you. Do not forget
At market day, I'll bring you presents;
The Greek king's daughter shall grace your bed.'

The voice and the poem had a subtlety which suited the room. The fine images were pared of excess. Gill did not break the sequence of the long poem by drinking whiskey, and for the duration he was transformed into what he might have been, had fortune and stable character been granted him.

Michael Barrett bowed his head in awe. His mind was filled with clear images, fine as silk. 'God, it's a poem shaped in a beautiful way,' he interjected. But Gill did not hear the interjection. He ended with the final words:

'You stole my east, you stole my west,
You stole the past and what lay ahead.
You stole the moon and the golden sun.
You stole me from God.'

There was silence at the end of the song. There was nothing they could say, for they knew that it was excellent. After a minute's reflection Gill drank the whiskey in a vulgar gulp.

'The language will die, Gill, and with it the great songs and the great poems,' Michael Barrett cried out passionately. 'They say in Dublin that it is the language of the barbarian, but they have not lived inside it as we have. Take more whiskey, Gill, and sing another song for me!'

'Well, I will, if you don't mind.' He filled his whiskey-glass. He was not sober but he knew that he could recall any of the five hundred poems in his memory at that moment. He returned to the armchair, reflected for a moment and then began the song 'At Creggan Church'.

They did not notice the light withdrawing from the sky outside the high windows. Much later, and with only light from the great fire, Gill sang 'Christ's Heart'.

When it was finished Michael Barrett said: 'That is enough. Sing no more; it is a suitable ending. I hope that in the afterlife my sins will not come too heavy against me and that I will walk on silk-smooth plains and pastures of satin.'

Gill looked at him and recited the last lines, changing them a little. 'There will be a secure mansion in His heart for all of us, poets and merchants.'

'Go now, Gill, and on your way you will get the servants to give you one of my greatcoats, for what you are wearing is green with age and threadbare at the elbows.'

'And what about the shoes, sir?'

'Tell them to give you a pair of shoes also.'

'Will I see you to bed, sir?' Gill asked.

'No, but come to me when I'm dying and sing for me "Adoramus Te, Christe".'

'I will, sir.'

'It is my final wish.'

'Good night, sir.'

'Good night, Gill.'

Gill stole quietly from the room. The light from the fire lit the old man's body, and the eyes looked directly at the fire, now a glow of bright embers.

The tide is going out on him, Gill thought to himself as he went down the stairs. The chill has got into his body, and he will surely die and with him any dignity I ever had.

He went down to the servants' quarters and demanded a cloak and a pair of shoes.

'And what have you done to earn them?' they asked.

'I sang poems. I made the man's mind quiet.'

'What if he misses his cloak and his boots tomorrow?' they asked.

'He told me to have them and also a bottle of whiskey.'

They gave Gill the cloak, the boots and the bottle of whiskey. He said good night and made his way down the avenue. He was going to throw away the green coat he carried on his arm, but then he decided against it. It could be worth three glasses of whiskey for him in exchange. He made his way into the sea wood and hid the whiskey in the earth, then he set out for the

281

shebeen. Later in the night he did trade the coat for three tumblers of whiskey and he sang for common company. He forgot that during the day he had sung the finest of Irish songs for Michael Barrett.

Up at the great house a servant entered the room where Michael Barrett was now asleep by the fire. She wrapped a blanket about him, threw some logs on the embers and left him to his remote dreams.

26

THE WIND WHEELED DOWN FROM THE NORTH. For three weeks now the winds had been fresh, and the ship moved forward on crowded sail, but as John Burke surveyed the northern sky he knew that out of that quarter he could expect snow, and added to this was the fear of ice-drifts. To sail directly into an ice-floe with crowded canvas could mean disaster for the ship. At night men were posted aloft, wrapped in heavy woollen clothes, to keep a look out. With the moon favouring them they could maintain firm progress.

The snows came on the cold wind, blowing across the ship with a sharp edge so that men had to shovel it from the deck. The great fear now was that it might frost up during the night and become dead weight on the ship, for it fell persistently. Before they went on watch the men crowded together over the stoves cursing the cold weather which had taken them by surprise. At least the cargo in the holds was firm: at that time of the year it would have been dangerous to carry timber. The seas became sullen and the ship ploughed forward relentlessly. The men wished they were in port, hating the severity of the snow and the gales.

Gráinne Barrett had not witnessed such weather before. She looked in awe at the power of the elements about her as they sailed forward through cold mists, locked in a world of their own. John Burke refused to let her climb into the rigging. He gave orders that she should be forcibly prevented if she made any attempt. 'You have done more than enough to prove your ability on the journey out. I am taking no more risks. You can learn more from the deck by studying the sails and the rigging under winter storms.'

She studied the great ship from the decks, observing the movements of the masts, the tension of sails against wind, the order and the positions of ropes. John Burke tested her on the name of each rope, each knot, each correct order given to the men aloft. 'Their lives will depend on the calls you make from the wheel. A foolish judgement on your part could mean death. You must have an accurate judgement and be skilful in decision. So – no more climbing aloft; your education from now on is from behind the wheel.'

He stood beside her while she took charge of the ship. He did not interfere but kept a close eye to the rigging. The wind blowing across the deck was cold, and soon her fingers were numb. She released the wheel a fraction to regain circulation, and it spun out of control, letting the ship veer away from the wind. The sails lost their tension and flapped uselessly. He did not move forward to help her. She fought with the wheel and brought the ship slowly back into the wind, panting with the effort. 'Had the crew been aloft,' he told her, 'half of them would have fallen into the sea.'

'My hands were cold.'

'They are not supposed to be cold,' he said roughly. 'There is more to mastering a ship than climbing the rigging. The ship is controlled from the wheel, and you must never let it out of control.'

Later in the evening he visited her cabin, bringing a bottle of rum with him as was his habit whenever he wished to talk.

'You were disappointed with me today,' Gráinne said miserably.

'No. Today you learned your first lesson in mastering the ship. You only made one mistake.'

'I will make many more mistakes before I can take full control of a ship,' she said humbly.

'You learn by mistakes.' He was firm and conciliatory. 'Each day you will sail the ship for two hours and I will stand beside you. You already understand the ship and its moods and you judge the wind well – I did not take control of a ship until I was thirty-two and by then I had spent fifteen years at sea. Have no fears. I have confidence in you. It is in your blood.'

Soon their conversation turned away from the ship and they talked about the condition of Ireland and what would happen in the future. 'You have seen New York. It can be a rough place, but at least they do not starve there. It is the very centre of the world now; you are watching the birth of a new nation. The old world is spent, like a sow that has farrowed too much.'

'Then should we look to the New World?' she asked eagerly.

'The only reason people will not do so is because they were never there. It is outside their comprehension; they are in a cage which time and history have made. They have not crossed the great seas as we have. If I had my way, I should ship all the landless to America and give them a start there. On the other hand, why *should* they have to leave the country and why *should* they have to leave the land? They have a right to it.'

'And so we are back to revolution again?' she said.

'Oh, I suppose you are always back to revolution,' he replied wearily. 'There must be change of some sort or other, and the British government will not change until they are forced to.'

'And will we ever govern ourselves?'

'Are we fit to govern ourselves? I don't know. I only know that we should be free to take our chances.' He sipped his rum and then said, more gently: 'Show me your hands.' He took them in his and examined the palms. The rope-cuts were healing. 'Your palms will harden to leather, you know. You should have care for them: soap them and keep them soft.'

'I am not preparing for a ball, you know, John Burke!' Gráinne said with a grin. 'When will you accept that I will have to take charge of the ships soon? Treat me as an equal – I think I have proved that I can sail the heaviest seas!'

'And so you can,' he said soothingly. Then he went on, after an awkward pause: 'How fares your relationship with Myles Prendergast? You may have to work with each other one day.'

'He stays in his cabin and reads those books he purchased in New York,' she retorted. 'I think he is more interested in guns and military strategy than he is in people.'

'He sang for us in Bordeaux when we first met.' John Burke chuckled at the memory. 'He even got drunk, and we had to carry him on board.'

285

'I don't believe it!'

'Oh, believe it you must. He has even recited poetry to me in his weaker moments—'

'Then, why has he cold eyes which never rest?' she interrupted.

'Are they cold?' John Burke was surprised.

'To me they are. He has little humility.'

'Then, that makes two of you.'

She began to laugh. 'We will have to make a peace treaty, then.'

'Have you taught him the names of the stars?' he asked slyly.

'Oh, yes,' she replied, caught off balance. 'He has a quick mind.'

'So maybe there *is* a spark of heat in his heart. You should try to discover it if there is.'

'Should I?' Her tone was careless.

'I think you should – there is more to life than sailing ships and preparing for revolutions, and you should not always wear a serious face.'

'We are not all rogues like you!'

'Well, you should be. There is a time to sing and dance and put your arms around a man and feel the heat of his body. I envy youth and I wish I were beginning my life all over again. I would sail the South Seas where the oceans are unexplored and the women soft as the summer breeze and the air is scented. . . .'

'You are a romantic, John Burke!' she accused, laughing at him.

'Devil a bit, am I – except I loved the soft women of the south.'

'And are the northern women cold?'

'No – civilised, and that's the worst curse of all.'

He was about to leave the cabin, when she took his wrist and held him back.

'John, I have been disturbed during the voyage. That time in your office, you suggested that there was a curse on the Barrett money. What did you mean?'

'Only on some of it,' he said uncomfortably.

'Why?'

'Oh, I will tell you one day. I spoke words in anger which I regret.' He seemed anxious to leave.

'Then, you will not tell me?'

'Some day I will, but I cannot do so now,' he said.

'That leaves me unsatisfied!' she persisted.

'I will tell you when the time is ripe. It was something which I vowed to carry to the grave, but when the old man dies I shall tell you. You will be then captain of the ships and, in a way, master of all our destinies. You have earned the right to take control. Now, *you* tell me something – it has been bothering me since the voyage began. You were friendly with that Joyce man on the voyage out. Where did he raise the passage money to pay the way?'

'Will you believe me if I tell you that he sold my father a dunaire by Rioccard Barrett?' she asked gleefully.

John Burke left his tankard on the table and looked at her in amazement. 'No, I don't believe you! Sure, Rioccard Barrett never left a dunaire!'

'Well, listen to this, then,' Gráinne said in triumph, and recited one of the better-known poems, adding the lost verses.

'Well, he deserved free passage, then!' Burke cried. 'He discovered the one weakness in your father. How did he come by the poems?'

'A pissing match, John!'

He spat out the drink in his mouth and began to cough. He hit his chest again and again, and broke into choking spasms. He looked at her, grinning for a moment, and started to laugh again. When he felt easy he looked at her. Her face was serious.

'A pissing match?' he repeated.

'Yes.'

'Tell me the story.' She told the story as she had heard it from Liam Joyce. 'Well, you have put me in good form for the rest of the voyage. That story will go into oral tradition for sure and, if Gill gets his hands on it, into a poem. It's rare, Gráinne. It's rare!'

It was during the return voyage that she learned how to handle the new revolver. She took it apart and put it together again, and learned how to prime the five cylinders and cap them with wax. For short-range firing it was rapid and formidable. As she became accustomed to the recoil she became more accurate. The action of the gun in her hand gave her a strange sense of power.

The news they had received before their departure from New York had been far from reassuring. They knew that the blight which had been widespread when they departed had now become virulent. Apparently all the potato crops had been affected and the basic food stock had been destroyed. The corn they carried in the hold of the ship would do little to offset the general hunger.

They approached the Mayo coast under cover of night. They furled their sails and flashed their lantern-lights. After a long wait four curraghs approached them, the men calling out to each other in Irish. Revolvers and casks of brandy were lowered over the sides into the boats and rowed away into the darkness.

Next morning as the grey dawn grew out of a cold sky they made their way past Clare Island, mist-bound and sodden. The waves were dead and the wind slack and wet as they sailed through the cut into the protected bay of Northport. As they looked shorewards from the deck of the ship they knew something was wrong: the activity about the quays was light, the doors of the warehouses closed.

Gráinne Barrett was the first to reach the quayside. She noticed a crowd of starving people waiting for the boat, as silent as statues. When she climbed up the granite steps they drew themselves towards her, crying. Gráinne Barrett had never looked into the face of starvation before and she felt sick in her stomach. She looked again at the wasted faces and fingers.

'But what of the food depots?' Gráinne asked the man who had come to secure the boat. 'Are they not filled with food?'

'There are no food depots, and the warehouses are guarded by hired men with guns. The food is carried under escort to Castlebar where it fetches high prices.'

'Are there no potatoes?'

'No. They have rotted. The fields have been dug again and again. They leave the villages now and come to the big towns and beg for food.'

'Is there no food in our own warehouse in Northport?' she asked desperately.

'There is, but who is to receive it? Somebody has to make a decision as to who will live and who will die.'

'Well, then, I will open the warehouse myself and give these people grain.'

They had now gathered in an expectant circle, the hard glitter of starvation in their eyes. She looked at them again. They were not human. They were animals, dying silently, the voice of hard protest taken from them. John Burke now joined her, looking at the whimpering figures about him. He, too, was angry and shocked.

'Damn those who rule this country!' he said. 'They have no right to be called human. Are all the people like this?'

'Almost all of them. The hunger is everywhere.' The seaman's voice had a careless tone about it.

'You do not seem disturbed by the news or by these people,' Gráinne Barrett said.

'They come every day – I'm used to them. Some die in the streets and are carried away to an open grave. It's happening everywhere. It's worse in Castlebar, they say. But I have not been there and I do not know. I had a bit of gruel this morning and water to wash it down. I'm not starving, but I'm hungry.'

Myles had slipped quietly ashore with a number of the crew members, wishing to move quickly out of the town. He was appalled by the sight of the listless hungry people, and a cold fury grew within him. When he left the people had been hungry; now they were starving, and he had not witnessed starvation before. Hurrying from the quayside, he suppressed the tears in his eyes, confused and angry at what he had seen.

John Burke sent a boat out to the ship to carry food to the people, giving them some of the rough bread that had been baked aboard. They hardly had the strength to eat it, moving it about in their mouths with difficulty. While Gráinne Barrett looked at them eating the bread a woman fell forward to the ground, the first victim of starvation she was to witness.

'There is nothing more we can do here, Gráinne,' John Burke said bitterly. 'Let us go down to the tavern and find out what has been going on. We won't bring any corn ashore until I have a clear idea of what is going to happen to it. It's not for the merchants at any rate!'

Gráinne was not aware that she was dressed in filthy sailor's clothes and that her body needed washing: the sight of the dead woman had stunned any feelings within her. Together she and John Burke made their way into the side-entrance of the public house. People were now going down to the quayside to see the ship, and they avoided the direct route. Inside, he

289

ordered two glasses of rum and then called one of his relations into the small snug.

'What in hell happened while I was away?' he asked angrily.

'I don't know where to begin, John, but the country is no longer hungry; it is dying. There isn't a bit of food left, and what is left is fetching high prices. The blight came overnight.'

'I thought the depots were filled with food. Didn't the Prime Minister say that no Irishman would die of lack?'

'Only words, John. Only words. You hear so many stories now of people dying that you don't notice them any more. You pass people dead in ditches and count yourself lucky that you are alive. That's the way it is. I never thought that my heart would grow so hard.'

'The warehouses at the far side of town, what of them?'

'The merchant's day has come. He will take the last shilling from the poor. He won't lack food himself. The gombeen men are buying people's belongings cheaply – all people think about now is food.'

At that moment Gill opened the door of the snug and staggered in. 'Well, John Burke, you are welcome home from the land across the sea! What fair zephyrs blew you across Neptune's domain?' he shouted drunkenly.

'Get out of here, Gill, and let me have peace!' John Burke roared back at him.

'Only the dead have peace, my friend. Only the dead have peace, and the drunk have partial peace.' John Burke rose to throw him out. 'Cease, my friend, unhand me! You lay your hands upon a poet.' Gill drew himself up to his full height.

'Stop this *rameis* and talk the Queen's English,' John Burke ordered. 'I come home to a country caught in the grip of starvation and I have to listen to this drivel.'

'My heart is choked,' Gill protested.

'And your gut is rotting with drink,' the other retorted in disgust.

'But my mind is sad, John Burke. I have kept watch for you for many days, for I have come from the great house. I have been with my great friend, Michael Barrett, and I have recited for him. Behold me accoutred in his fine coat. I wear his heavy boots.'

'So you have been forgiven for your vile behaviour?'

'Too late, John. The old man is ill, and I am come to tell

290

Gráinne – I alone know how sick he is. I think the death wish is in his mind.'

'What do you mean?' John Burke was shocked.

'He is dying, for he did a foolish thing. He set out for Belmullet to make a journey back to Cross, and the cold got into his bones. He brought me home on the back of his horse from Belmullet. Otherwise I would have died of starvation.'

'You are certain he is ill?' John Burke asked in a low voice. 'This is not drink talking?'

'No. I'm half-sober now, John. Will you break the news to the young girl? I would weep if I told her.'

John called Gráinne aside. They were engaged in conversation for some minutes, then she came over to Gill.

'Is it true?' she asked.

He nodded his head. She brushed past him out of the room and ran down the street in search of a horse.

Gráinne Barrett's mind and imagination were in turmoil as she rode through the cold weather towards the house. The bitterness of the parting with her father had been forgotten, and the great affection she had for this man who had dominated her life and the life of Northport made her anxious to be with him.

She noticed how black and spectral the woods were on both sides of the road. The leaves had fallen during her absence, and were mouldering in the mysterious empty spaces between the trees.

The servants looked at Gráinne Barrett in awe as she jumped from the horse, ran across the courtyard and up the stairs. Her rich auburn hair was bunched under a cap and she looked like a young sailor just arrived from one of the ships. She had lost the soft flesh in her features, and her complexion was browned by the sun. Her movements were more active and decisive than they had been before she departed.

Mrs Jennings met her at the top of the wide stairs and she noticed how lithe Gráinne's body had become and how her fair skin had hardened on her face. She stared at her for a moment, then she threw her arms about her.

'Gráinne a chroi, but you are strange in your sailor's clothes!' she cried. 'We are delighted that you are home to take charge. Sure, your father is not himself at all and will listen to nobody.'

'What happened?'

'Oh, he took the foolish notion to go down to Belmullet and have a look at the grave of Rioccard Barrett and he caught a cold which never left him. He slept in wet beds on the way. We tried to restrain him, but he was stubborn and would have taken the whip to us.'

'How ill is he?'

'His body is weak, and he forgets where he is. He slips in and out of the past as if it was yesterday and speaks a strange language now and then and talks of people I never heard of.'

Gráinne opened the door of the big bedroom quietly and entered. Her father was lying in his large bed, his head sunk deep in white pillows. She was shocked at his appearance: he looked fragile and very old. She remembered the great figure who once had shouldered up her world; now he was aged beyond recognition. The years he had held at bay had suddenly taken their toll.

'I heard you outside the door, Gráinne,' he said in a weak voice. 'I should have been looking for the arrival of the ship from the window but I'm ill. I did a foolish thing going to Belmullet but I had to go. Something in my heart told me to go. You know who I found there?'

'Who?'

'That rake Gill. He would have starved but for me. I brought him home on my horse. But the other day he came and sang for me, and so I sent him to fetch you. Forgive him, Gráinne.' Tears ran down his parchment-like cheeks. He looked at his daughter, bending over him. He could see the changes the sea had wrought in her appearance. He had been proud at the sight of her dressed for a royal ball in the past, but the sight of her in raw sailor's clothes brought joy to his heart.

'Did you enjoy the voyage?' he asked.

'I could not say that I enjoyed it but I learned more about handling ships than I otherwise would have.'

'Did John Burke treat you well?'

'Yes. He is the best of captains.'

'And the corn? Did you bring home the cargo of grain?'

'Yes. It is out in the bay. We do not know if we should unload it or not – the quay was crowded with starving people. Some of them will die. We thought that if we carried the grain to the warehouses they might have been attacked.'

292

'It *must* be given to those who need it, Gráinne. I will leave that business to you. Again and again I said that the British government should be prepared for this. It has been coming a long time. But there is very little which can be done now. Death is stalking the land, and the merchants are thriving. Those who should die are living in luxury and will make a profit. They always make a profit out of misery. My heart is broken. I have lived to see the race perish.' He became agitated, searching for images to express his anger and his sadness at the turn of events.

'Take it easy, now,' she told him. 'Do not exert yourself by talking too much. I will get you a glass of port. You always loved your port.' She filled a glass and, lifting his head with her hand, held it to his mouth. He sipped a little.

'You smell of the sea,' he told her when he lay back on the pillow. Then a pain shot through his body. He tightened his muscles in the hope of containing it. 'Oh, I hurt, Gráinne! A thousand small knives tear at me.' After the pain passed, he lay in the bed in silence, his fingers nibbling at the sheet edge. She waited beside him until he had fallen asleep, and then she left the room to walk in the woods of Eisirt and bring her thoughts together. After the vast spaces of the sea she wished to walk in the intimate paths between the trees. As she meandered, half-conscious in the dilute November light, images of the past and the present flooded her mind and she remembered how happy she had been during her childhood. But these memories were quickly replaced by the more recent scenes of Northport quay. Her father and the times were placing obligations on her shoulders she felt she might not be capable of bearing.

She walked back slowly to the house, had something to eat and then returned to her father's room. He was awake, and his face showed that the pains which had cut his body were now passed. Light food was brought to him which he tasted and put aside. She told him that she had been to the woods, and he recalled how he, too, had loved them since he first saw them as a boy and how he had planned to set out his house amongst them. 'But that was a long time ago,' he said. 'We must now talk of the future as my father talked about the future to me when he was old. I wish to leave my affairs in order and plan the future with you. Upon you depend the destinies of this house and this family.'

'No, there will be another day for that,' she told him. 'And do not talk of dying.'

'I must talk of dying. It comes to us all. I have had a long life, and in the main it has been happy. It grieves me that the country is now passing through such unhappy times and there is nothing we can do about it – even the British government is powerless.'

'Very well,' she agreed. 'We will talk. But do not tire yourself.'

He sat up in the bed, and she gathered the pillows about his back.

'I have set my thoughts in order, Gráinne, during the last weeks. Sometimes my memory fails; sometimes in fever and pain strange sequences from the past return – it is always so when the body fails – but now I am clear. The fortunes of the family and the responsibilities they bring now pass to you. I have the deeds and the papers in order.' As he spoke she looked at his eyes. They were clear and certain, and she saw that his mind was sharp. What he was saying was his final testament, stamped with the authority of years. Gráinne felt that the fortunes of the family were passing on to her at this moment, and that the differences of age and temperament no longer existed. She was becoming heir to heavy responsibilities.

'One should never commit one's wealth in one single place, be it England or Ireland,' he began, gathering strength. 'It should be spread out so that if it should fail here, then part of it is available elsewhere. And always keep the ships apart – never have them anchored in one harbour and always have one close to Northport in case it is necessary to depart quickly. All my life I have kept a diary of all which happened to me, and often I have had to plan for a quick escape. I have not always been the solemn thoughtful man you remember. The gaps in your childhood, when I was away at sea for six months at a time, will be filled out for you; for there is a part of my life which is known to very few and which is recorded in my diaries. You must promise to read them only when I am dead.'

She was surprised that diaries existed and that they were secreted somewhere in the house. She was surprised also that there was a side to her father's life which she had not suspected. Then she recalled her childhood and remembered her father's long absences during which her mother, isolated in the great

294

house, and in the great woods, had become more and more remote and, as they whispered, mad in a quiet and desperate way.

'Hope lies in America,' he was continuing. 'Keep your vision clearly on all that is happening there. Europe is spent and very uncertain, and nobody knows where all the political agitation will carry it.'

'And what of Ireland?' she asked passionately.

'It is a tragic place, and if I were young again I should leave it.'

'And Eisirt woods?'

'Even Eisirt woods and this house. There are other woods where the air is as pure and mystical, and you must find them. I shall be buried in Eisirt woods, but do not think you will find refuge there. The country will be weakened by the famine, and the next generation will come from famished wombs, and no good breeding comes out of hunger. Move when you see things fail; cut the moorings that bind you to the place and do not let your mind be bothered with memories. Take your wealth to America: another great house can be built there.'

He was tired again and fell into a light sleep. It gave her the opportunity of leaving the room to have a warm bath. She washed herself slowly in a hug tub until her body no longer reeked of the sweat of the sea. When she dressed, she chose a long red gown trimmed with Brussels lace at the collar and the sleeves, which showed the fine contours of her body. She brushed her auburn hair until it was fine and fell freely on to her shoulders.

She returned to her father's room, and his eyes brightened when he saw how beautiful she looked. She carried all the perfections of the Barretts. 'You looked like the mistress of the ships when you visited me last. Now you look like mistress of the house.'

She noticed that his strength had improved in sleep and knew she must arrange to have sleeping draughts dissolved in his wine, for all care would have to be taken to conserve his strength. It was clear to her now that he was dying, and she had to admit to herself that he might not survive the winter.

He directed her attention to a key beside his bed. 'Open my desk and bring me the files I have placed there. You will find that they are in order.'

She rolled back the lid of the great desk and brought him the files neatly bound in ribbons, placing them beside him on the bed. He directed her to open the first file.

'That is the most important one,' he told her. 'It is a summary of all my business interests. The rest of the files contain the legal and banking documents which will help you gain access to them.'

She looked at the neatly written pages. They were all in her father's own hand and clearly legible. She was surprised at the extent of his investments.

'You have heard of the Barrett wealth,' he told her, smiling. 'Well, there it is!' – and with a fine gesture of his frail hand he indicated that it was widely dispersed.

'Most of it is now in America and in the hands of a solicitor. I bought several pieces of land in New York early in the century which are now built upon. I leased them, and there will always be a steady income from it. Listen – never sell land, lease it. Land is the final value for all things. You will find all this information in more detail in the other files.' They were accurate documents, and once she understood the relation of the first folder to the other ones on the bed she had no difficulty in finding what she needed to know.

'You have properties in Spain, too,' she said.

'Oh, yes. On the slopes of the hills which receive the Mediterranean sun. And if you look closely at the map in the Spanish folder you will find the drawing of a small house among the vines. It belongs to you. I have always loved Spain and I kept the land for reasons of sentiment. But, then, you *should* have properties in Europe. You can seek refuge there.'

'You are a wily old fox,' she said fondly, taking his hand in hers.

He was pleased at the remark and smiled up at her. 'Yes, I am. When you read the diaries you will see that I have lived two lives. There is a final file which you must not open until after my death. Do not be surprised at what you shall find there.'

He said no more. She did not question him further on the matter, and while he fell into a shallow sleep again she became more acquainted with the files. She discovered that he possessed properties in London and in Paris. They, too, were leased and the affairs run by a firm of solicitors. He had arranged to have the money paid into several banks under accounts with false names. She had no clear idea how much wealth he possessed, but it was considerable and would continue to grow.

Very late that evening John Burke arrived at the house as was his custom after each journey. Gráinne left him with her father: they had been friends for a long time and they had much to talk about. John Burke had helped to build the Barrett fortune.

She was waiting for him in the library when he came downstairs. His hands were shaking when he entered the room. 'Give me a large glass of whiskey, Gráinne,' he said. 'I have been drinking since you left, trying to take the edge of pain off my heart, but it is no use. What I have seen upstairs has shocked me.'

'He is dying,' she said directly.

'Yes. The flesh has fallen from his limbs. I knew him in his power and his strength – I have seen him take a ship through the storms. He could judge the wind and the weather better than any man I knew. We sailed to America one winter and we sailed into the ports of France in storm conditions when they were blockaded by the British. It is awful, awful.' He repeated the words again and again. 'You have to make the decisions now. I must take the orders from you.' He looked at the woman in red who stood in front of him, elegant and trim. Two days ago she was a common sailor; now she was master of all the ships.

'John Burke, I will never give you orders. I will take counsel from you.'

She sat with him for two hours. She did not tell him the extent of her father's wealth but she did tell him that when the time came she should move to America.

'It is a wise decision. We will always have a ship close at hand if it is necessary to get away. This country is finished. Reports are coming in from all over with the same story. By the end of the winter the land will be black and empty, and nothing can save us now, for no ship will bring in supplies during the winter. But there will always be a ship ready for you if you wish to depart when your father dies.'

'Will you come with me?' she asked.

'No, Gráinne. I have a final battle to wage. I'll not stand by while the merchants grow fat. If we go down, we'll all go down together.'

'And what will I do with the corn on board the ship and in the warehouses? Should I open kitchens on the quays?'

He reflected for a moment. 'You cannot open free kitchens. You will draw the starving from every corner of the county and you will keep them alive for only a short time. It must be kept here in Northport and it must be wisely administered. It is sufficient to keep the town and perhaps some of the villages along the coast through the bad months. But none outside these villages must receive any aid.'

'I cannot make a decision like that!'

'You must.'

'I won't.'

'Then, where will we get food?'

'What about the warehouses at the far side of the town? They are heaped with grain. The granaries hold enough food to stave off hunger for two months. *They* should be opened to the people.' Her voice had grown angry when she thought of the decision he had tried to force upon her.

'And how are we to open the granaries?' he asked.

'You are the military planner. You and your talk of the last great battle: it's for you to decide.'

'Maybe you are right. I will discuss it with the Frenchman. But consider what I told you about distributing the corn: you would be cleaned out of supplies in three weeks, and it would be all to no avail. In a general famine most die and only some have a small chance of living. The people of Northport could have some chance of living.'

'I will think about it – I am sorry I was angry. I have never had to make such decisions before. I never thought that people's lives and deaths would depend on me.'

'It is a decision you will have to take, and you will have to live with the consequences for the rest of your life.'

She went with him to the main door. It was dark and cold outside. He mounted his horse, and she watched him disappear into the darkness before returning to the library.

27

MYLES PRENDERGAST set out for Castlebar from Northport with certain plans forming in his mind. It was important that he should use Castlebar as a base for the next few days.

A sense of fate hung over the grey roofs of the town, and each day brought worsening news. In Molly Ward's pub he had only to sit and listen to the talk of small farmers to know what was happening. There were menacing circles of hunger about the towns, which broadened as the days passed by. Those who could bought passage to America and left without a tear. 'Things will get better – the English Parliament will not let us starve. There is hope yet; the depots are filled with food,' he heard some of them say. But by the beginning of winter men had begun to change their minds. It was evident that the government would not provide people with free food. The laws of trading must not be interfered with. The merchant class who were the backbone of the country could not be destroyed. 'I declare,' said one small farmer, 'that there will be a rebellion. A million people will not let themselves starve.'

'The army is well fed this time. There will be no taking them by surprise.'

'Ah, Napoleon gave them a right start last time!'

'There is no Napoleon in France now, and nobody else who cares for us,' another replied.

'Better to rebel than to starve. We all have a right to land.

Every son of Adam born is entitled to part of the earth. I read it in a book.'

'Tell that to Kenrick and his carters!' the others jeered. 'Even last week they moved out to Glenisland and destroyed another village. I saw men taking the foundations of the houses and building them into walls. Tell Kenrick that we will get him when the revolution comes and he will bring a whip-butt down on the back of your skull. You must go easy with your talk. The Castle has spies everywhere, and you might end in gaol or in a transportation ship.'

'Well, at least it would save me. There will be plenty of company for me in gaol if things continue to go from bad to worse.'

Even the British soldiers from the barracks knew that something was happening. 'Mad Colonel Spiker', as they now called him, had tightened discipline. Dispatches arrived frequently from Dublin, and the ammunition stores had been replenished. The warehouse at the barracks was bulging with food. It was known that several spies were operating about the country. Each morning the crackle of rifle practice could be heard in the town, and once a week the regiments of soldiers were marched through the streets to emphasise the military strength of the army.

But while order was established in the barracks the disorders brought about by hunger were spreading. There was a noticeable show of beggars in the town – men and women who crawled down alleyways or slept in sheds during the night. There was fear of the dreaded fever.

Myles Prendergast recalled the forces which brought about the revolution in Paris. A mass of women from Paris had marched on Versailles and called out for bread, invading the palace, sweeping through the ornate gates and across the acres of cobblestones. Unimpressed by the beauty of the architecture, they had attempted to assassinate the Queen, forced the royal family to leave Versailles and taken them to Paris. Marie-Antoinette was never to return to the Petit Trianon or play as a shepherdess in her rustic village. But there was no monarch in Ireland; there was no palace which could be destroyed. The power was in the towns; the middle class belonged to the British culture, and it gave them cohesion.

Myles decided to test the quality of the young men of

Castlebar. He had read in the local paper that they held meetings frequently and discussed literary and historical matters. A visit to one of their gatherings would give him some indication of their allegiance. If strong cells were to be built in the towns, then they must be built by young men. He arranged with a young man named Eoin Hoban to be invited to one of the meetings.

Before he went, he called Molly aside and showed her a list of those who belonged to the historical society. She studied it carefully.

'Five I would vouch for; they are from good stock,' she told him. 'The other three I am not sure about.'

'If there were a spy, who would it be?'

'Michael Kilcoyne. I would keep an eye on him. They go with every side, but they have the British mentality. His father is half merchant, half gombeen man. He is one of those you learn to despise early. I wouldn't have the likes of him near any talk of revolution. And always remember that you are a buyer from Dublin. Don't reveal yourself to anyone.'

'He's not planted by the Castle?'

'No, but I'm sure he has his contacts with someone there.'

Myles attended the meeting held in the home of Eoin Hoban in Market Square. It was a two-storeyed stone house with a fantail above the main door. A fire burned in the front room, casting light on a heavy sideboard with decanters and a bookcase containing many books. The historical meetings always took place here. The themes were usually safe and the subjects general. Tonight Fergus McNulty, a thin and nervous character, and uncertain of himself, was to read a paper on nationalism.

'Without Napoleon there would be no nationalism in Europe,' he began in a high excited voice, and went on to describe Napoleon's climb to power and how in the end he crowned himself Emperor. 'He had become like those he would destroy. He set his own up as kings and queens all over Europe. Grandeur had returned to France, and nationalism at that moment had begun in Europe.'

'Nationalism was always there. People have a feeling towards one another. It is formed by language and custom,' someone claimed.

'If Napoleon had not moved into Germany, Spain and Russia,

do you think that there would be nationalist feeling there today?' Fergus countered.

'There would. It was always there. It may not have gone under the term "nationalism" but it was always there.'

'No, I cannot agree. Nationalism is a new thing. It is a new word and a new thing. Look at Prussia today! Defeat at Jena almost destroyed it, but it learned from the French tyrant. Today it is the strongest force in Europe.'

'There are others who speak German, and they have not been drawn into this new Prussian nation. Where now is your argument about culture and language?'

'It will happen. It is not a thing that occurs in a single year. Wait and see.'

'How long?'

'You cannot put a time on historical progressions. But it will happen.'

There was tension in the debate. Myles Prendergast was impressed by Fergus McNulty's mind but thought that had he been in France during the French Revolution, he would have eventually died under the guillotine: he was inflexible in his opinions. Myles could not see Prussia developing into a great power.

'You have a language and culture in Ireland,' Myles stated. 'Yet you seem to me to be a downtrodden race and you are starving at the moment. I think you miss something in your analysis of the Prussians. They already had a national spirit; there is no nationalistic spirit in Ireland. You are a subservient race and will continue to remain subservient.' He spoke in a cold voice. There was a hint of irony in his tone.

'We are not subservient!' Eoin Hoban answered hotly.

'I think you are,' he told them.

'We need no British gentleman to tell us this,' Sean O'Donnell said. 'What knowledge have you of the country or our ways? You are a traveller here.'

'Am I not entitled to my opinions? They are either true or false. Prove them false if you can.'

'We will,' Fergus Ryan spoke out. Myles Prendergast had noticed this young man when he entered, because of his physical appearance and because he was uncomfortable in his chair. An anger burned in his eyes. He continued: 'The mass of people are afraid to rise out. Unless a group of young men bind

302

together and take things into their own hands and spark off a revolution, then nothing will happen.'

Myles Prendergast knew that within a week this man's remark would be recorded in some ledger in the Castle at Dublin.

'We should obtain guns and take the course of history into our own hands,' Fergus Ryan said.

'And where are guns to be found?' Michael Kilcoyne asked, speaking for the first time.

'You know as well as I do that guns are being run into this country,' Fergus Ryan said.

'I don't,' Michael Kilcoyne told him.

'They are. Some day they will be used. Never fear, guns are available to anyone who wishes to take up arms.' Michael Kilcoyne had walked him into a trap. Molly Ward was correct: he was the weak link. His pious boiled face had a treacherous look. It registered no emotion. He was the spy in the camp.

At the end of the meeting Myles Prendergast thanked the group for allowing him to be present and left before the others. He was waiting when Michael Kilcoyne left the meeting. He followed him through the dark streets as he made his way to the Mall close to the police barracks. A policeman emerged from behind a tree. They spoke for about half an hour, before parting company.

Two nights later, as Michael Kilcoyne made his way down the archway to his family store, a cold gun-barrel was put to the back of his head. 'Ah!' he called, and jumped like a frightened animal. 'What do you want from me? I don't carry money. The father has the money. I'm a counter boy.'

'Have you a spade?'

'We sell spades.'

'Then, we will go and find a good one, for you are going to dig a hole.'

'What kind of a hole?'

'You'll see.'

Michael Kilcoyne opened the store and, by lantern-light, picked a new spade from a barrel. His hands were trembling, and his boiled face was loose and sweaty.

'Who am I talking to?' he asked.

'Never mind who you are talking to. Now move down to the

303

end of the garden. If you call out, then that will be the last call you will ever make. Understand?'

They moved down the garden path. It was filled with coarse grasses and weeds. When they were a good distance from the store Myles Prendergast said roughly: 'Start digging!'

'I won't. Get one of the counter boys to do it,' Michael Kilcoyne protested. A clenched fist was thrown up into his face. He fell on the ground and cried like a rabbit. 'Now dig,' he was ordered.

He dug with difficulty, unpractised in the work. Soon he was short of breath, and beads of perspiration ran down his face. The hole was knee-deep. The stranger stood behind him and did not show his face.

'Do we have to dig much further?' he asked.

'Keep digging,' the stranger said, brandishing the gun in his face.

'Keep that away from me. It might go off. Guns have been known to go off.'

'It has every intention of going off.'

'You are not going to kill me?' He was panicking.

'That depends on you. Dig deeper.'

Michael Kilcoyne continued to dig. His clothes were sodden with perspiration, his hands and face marked with the black dead clay.

'What depth is it?' the stranger asked after twenty minutes.'

'Four feet.'

'Good.'

'What have you got me digging this for?'

'It's one of two things. It's a hole at present, and it could become a grave.'

Kilcoyne, with his head and shoulders above the level of the earth, looked up in fear. He began to jibber. 'I'm too young to die! I've done nothing,' he whimpered.

'Shut up whinging! You have to answer some questions. I already know the answers, so don't play tricks with me. To begin with, are you an informer?'

'Informer? Informer?' he said. 'What makes you think that?' The barrel of the pistol was pushed into his temple. 'I am. I'm afraid of the constables.'

'How long have you been an informer?'

'Three years. It's me father that's to blame. He sells meat to

304

the barracks. He cannot lose the contract. The money is the making of us.'

'Now tell me exactly what you told the policeman.'

The information he gave Myles Prendergast was direct: he had reported the meeting and those who had attended it. The chief information concerned Fergus Ryan and the suggestion that he knew where guns were stored for an uprising.

'Fergus Ryan is now a marked man,' Myles Prendergast said flatly. 'You have traded his life for money. Now, upon the next question depends your life. Name the other informers in the town.'

Michael Kilcoyne began to gasp for breath. 'It's as much as my life is worth to tell you,' he said.

'At this moment your life is worth nothing. I want names.' He received two names. One would have been sufficient for Myles Prendergast: he could now begin to work through the network. 'You have bought your life with that information. Tomorrow morning you will take the coach out of town. Keep going until you reach America. Eyes will be on you all the way. Get out and run.'

Michael Kilcoyne dragged himself out of the hole and blundered up the garden path. In the archway he vomited from relief. Next morning he went down to the end of the garden again to assure himself that the incident had not been a nightmare. He saw the careless mounds of earth about the hole. He looked down; on the bottom was a coffin-lid bearing his name.

Two days later he left for America. During the next fortnight five more men slipped out of town. It became common knowledge that Michael Kilcoyne had been forced to dig his own grave by the Whiteboys and that his release was secured by informing on the Castle spies in the county.

The next meeting of the historical society buzzed with excitement. It was rumoured that there were foreign agents now operating in the town and they spoke openly of rebellion. When the meeting broke up, Prendergast called Fergus Ryan aside. They walked out into the country together, passing by the edge of the lake. 'Keep your thoughts to yourself,' he told him when they parted. 'Never let excitement rule your judgement: that is the first rule you must learn. Decisions may be taken during the coming months which will involve rebellion. I will tell you nothing more. I will give you all the information you need as I think it necessary. Are you with us?'

'Yes. I am angry with all that is happening. I cannot stand by and watch my own die and food in the warehouses.'

'Make a list of those you trust. I will call you when it is necessary. The times for talking are over. Our actions must be unknown and secret.'

It was now the middle of October. Every day saw a new influx of beggars into Castlebar. They left behind blackened fields and their dead.

Myles Prendergast made his way from Castlebar west through rough countryside. The land was spongy and wet. Here and there, like mange on old cattle, red sandstone showed through. The movement of his horse was dull and inert. He had purchased the horse from a farmer in Market Square who was selling his possessions in the hope of obtaining passage money for America and had stabled it behind Molly Ward's public house.

Riding through the countryside during the past two weeks, he had observed military defences and the locations of the warehouses.

'Whoever starves,' he told Molly Ward, 'it won't be the soldiers and the police. They are well supplied for three months. They are building up their stocks for the winter.'

'The price of allegiance is now the price of a plate of porridge,' Molly said bitterly. 'And there will be no revolt because the people have been starved into submission.'

During the days at the end of October he was appalled at all he witnessed. As long as he lived he could never erase from his mind the faces he had seen, small and wizened and old. Always there would be the memory of dried and fleshless arms. No single face remained in his mind – he could only recall the crowds pleading with spectral fingers and thin hands.

He had asked himself the question: 'Why do they sit and die? Why do they not march on the warehouses or tear down the gates of the barracks? Better to die with dignity than starve to death.'

But as people turned to the wall and died official life continued as usual. The two local papers continued to appear. The

306

military ball was held at the barracks for the squires and their ladies. It was unusually gay, the paper reported, and the military band had exceeded every expectation under its director, Sergeant Ivan Curson.

As Myles passed along the bleak road unprotected by tree or bush he remembered, above all, the old faces of children, with rough sacking about their bodies, their legs attenuated and weak. There was a darkness on the blighted earth and it had entered into his mind. He did not blame a malevolent God for all that had happened; what had happened had come from a long sad history of the country. No general revolution would ripen here, and he wondered if he should return to France. But a sense of anger and pride prevented him from taking a ship from a blighted land. His thoughts were turning now towards a revolt: it might startle the British into taking some measures to prevent total famine. The food resources of the country should be made available to all the people.

On several occasions he had secretly met Fergus Ryan and the others and discussed matters with them. His suggestions were tentative and he had to restrain their impetuosity. He did explain to them that quick anonymous attacks on food stores would be the most efficient way of effecting some change in things.

'We cannot engage them in the open,' he continued to tell them. 'We would be open targets. You work in the night or when it is least expected and then you disappear.'

'And what stations and depots should we attack?' Fergus Ryan asked him.

'I will tell you when the time comes – if it ever comes. I've sat all day in taverns and watched the coming and going of soldiers. I have memorised their movements and I know exactly how many are positioned in the barracks and where the food supplies are. When we move, we move quickly and attack the unprotected points, where there are small complements of soldiers. We *have* to make some gesture.'

He thought of these various plans as he rode to Northport. Not even in the worst day of hunger in France had there been such desperation. The trickle of people towards the towns which had begun in August would soon be a deluge.

Everything is wrong, he thought to himself, but how can I set it right? There is no mark of order or beauty on anything.

He rode into Northport with its narrow sea-streets and hoped that he did not draw attention to himself. Darkness was filling in the streets, and his figure was shadowy. A constable watched him from a doorway and marked his passage down the street.

Myles Prendergast got down from his horse and watered it at a stone trough. He looked up and saw the constable beside him.

'You are a stranger here?' the man began, making a statement and asking a question.

'Not exactly. I am from Castlebar.'

'What would bring you to Northport?'

'I am a journalist. I wish to report on the progress of the famine. I am visiting the whole area.'

'I am sure you have papers to prove that you are a journalist. It is important to carry identification papers during these dangerous times.'

'Yes, I carry identification papers,' Myles said evenly and he drew from his pocket some forged documents stating that he was a journalist from Dublin. The constable, heavy of jowl, examined them slowly, filled with the sense of his own importance.

'Are they in order?' Myles asked in a controlled voice.

'They seem to be,' the constable said, but he gave the impression that he was suspicious.

'Very good,' said Myles as the papers were returned to him. 'And now that you are reassured could you give me *your* opinions of the present condition of the county? It is obvious you are an observant fellow and know everything that is happening.' He took out his jotter and a pencil and poised it above the page. 'Could I have your name, please, to begin with?' he asked.

'I'm making no statement to the paper. I have nothing to say.' The constable was uneasy.

'But you are bound to have something to say,' Myles said, pressing him.

'I've nothing to say. I don't wish to have my name mentioned.' The man moved quickly down the dark street. Myles smiled to himself and put away the notebook. He had already used the same ploy on three other constables; they had all acted in the same way.

John Burke was drinking in the tavern. It was filled with tobacco smoke, and the men were huddled together in groups. They were suspicious when he entered – they did not welcome strangers – but when John Burke rose to greet him the hostility vanished and everyone resumed their talk and their drinking.

'Most of them are related to me,' John Burke said with a smile.

They sat in a small back room, and John Burke ordered drinks. Nothing could be discussed in Ireland, Myles thought, before somebody ordered drinks. A spy could not survive in such circumstances. He would end up drunk and then dead.

He told them about his encounter with the constable.

'That's Heneghan. He's shrewd and misses nothing, but we keep an eye on him.' John Burke was reassuring. 'He's up at the barracks this very moment wondering who you are and entering the account of your presence in the town in some ledger or other.'

John Burke sent one of the men to watch the barracks and then they settled down to serious talk. It was obvious to both of them that their points of view had become closer during the last weeks since their return from America. They had seen the ravages of famine; the spirit of the people was broken.

'There will be no rising up in my time, Myles,' John Burke said. 'I have waited for fifty years to have one decent even fight with the oppressor. Now I see it wiped out.'

'Not yet, John Burke,' the younger man said fiercely. 'You may have your hour of glory. We cannot let the nation sink into oblivion without making some gesture. I have been caught between the wish to return to France and forget this hell-hole and making some stand. Each generation has to make a stand, and I make it here!'

'Then, you have laid out plans?'

'Yes' – and he explained briefly what he had in mind. He took some rough sketches from his pocket and laid them out on the table.

'Gráinne Barrett is now in charge of the great house, the warehouses and the ships,' John Burke said when he had looked at Myles's plans. 'Her father is very ill, and I fear that he may die before the year is out.'

'That's a heavy burden on her shoulders.'

309

'There is a heavy burden on all our shoulders. Must the whole nation go down?'

'No,' Myles said firmly. 'I never felt more caught up in the cause than I did during the last two helpless weeks. Look . . . ,' he said hesitantly, 'should we bring Gráinne in on this now?'

'She wants to be with us – she feels responsible towards the people. She knows that the grain in the Barrett warehouse will be quickly consumed.'

'If anything goes wrong, she must be protected; she could lose everything,' Myles warned.

'She is willing to lose everything.'

'Then, we'll discuss this further tonight. Have you notified everyone?'

'Yes, as soon as I received your message from Castlebar.'

'Good,' said Myles, and left the tavern, making his way down to the quay and the warehouses there.

Later that evening, at a sign from John Burke, some of the men left their seats in the tavern and made their way up the narrow stairs to a low-ceilinged room above. Eight men sat about a table, their shadowy faces lit by one conspiratorial lamp. They were joined by Myles Prendergast and John Burke. Outside the door stood a man with a revolver. He was told by John Burke that if the police tried to come up the stairs he was to use every shot accurately.

Gráinne Barrett was the last to arrive. She was wrapped in a cloak when she entered the room.

'God, Gráinne, are you one of us?' one of the Burkes asked her in amazement.

'Wasn't I always one of you!' she told him, laughing. The men were in obvious awe of this woman.

John Burke stood up. 'I do not have to introduce you to each other; we have all taken the oath. Any person here who mentions what takes place in this room to other than our trusted friends takes a heavy weight of responsibility upon himself. He who would betray us forfeits his life for the betrayal. These are not times for loose talk. I will now introduce you to Myles Prendergast. Some of you know him – he is from Paris, a son of an émigré from Galway.'

'Has he taken the oath?' one of the men asked.

'He has,' John Burke said and sat down.

Myles looked about the table at their eyes. He was looking for the one who would betray them. His father had told him that each uprising had been betrayed before it ever took place, that men were always led into set traps.

'I came to Ireland with the intention of reporting back to Paris on the condition of the country with regard to an insurrection. I have observed conditions in Mayo. I did not go to the north-west where I'm told starvation is extreme, but I have visited all the towns and watched the barracks. Let me tell you that they are well defended: they have been provisioned with weapons and food. There is no chance of overpowering the main barracks even if we wished, for none of the soldiers will join in a rising – you can be certain of that. If you must strike, you must strike at the weakest point. You must be certain of success and you must be certain of escape.'

'And where do you suggest we should attack?' asked one of the men.

'I will mention four likely places, but the place which is most vulnerable is the granaries, the weakest point in the system. The warehouses are piled high with grain; we could cut off the food supply to the military barracks and give them a touch of starvation.'

He let them talk amongst themselves for some minutes. They asked him several questions to test his knowledge of the area, but he had observed it with a military eye and he satisfied most of them.

'And why should a stranger from France wish us to attack any place? You read too much into our meeting here. The purpose of the gathering was to set ideas before us and not to present us with a plan of battle.'

Myles noted the man who asked the question. He did not have a clear view of his face, but something in the voice made him suspicious. He could not give any reason for his doubt and resolved to discover his name. 'I thought perhaps that the condition of the people made it imperative to take some direct moves,' he said with some asperity.

'Would anything be achieved by this uprising except the useless death of men? How many would be engaged in the attack, and can you assure us of any support?'

'I know some men who would take part in an uprising. They

have a stomach for such things. I am not at liberty to name them, and they do not belong to this organisation.'

The exchange between the two men was hostile, and there was silence when Myles finished his speech.

'And when should it take place?' John Burke asked.

'Perhaps the beginning of the year,' Myles suggested.

John Burke reflected for a moment. 'The weather is turning bad. An attack in January would take the soldiers by surprise. The people will be so hungry that they will rush the warehouses once they are opened.'

'You treat the hungry as if they were pawns in some chess game you are playing!' one of the men said, slamming his fist on the table.

'They are pawns already.' John Burke was bitter. 'They became pawns the day the blight struck.'

At this point there was a knock on the door, and the man on watch entered and whispered in John Burke's ear. He stood up abruptly. 'Heneghan has two of his men at the front door. Gráinne, you have a horse. See Myles through the streets and out of the town. The rest stay here.'

Myles and Gráinne Barrett left quickly by the side-entrance. She led him out into the side-street and away from the crowds.

'Can you find your way to Castlebar?' she asked.

'I had planned travelling back to the town tomorrow.' He was uncertain and spoke more coldly than he meant.

'And so you will. It is too harsh to trust yourself to a dirt track at night. . . .' She paused and added almost shyly: 'You may stay at Barrett House.'

They mounted their horses and soon they were free of the town and riding beside one another along the sea-road. It was bitterly cold, and the wind complained in the trees. She pulled her cloak about her to keep warm, aware of the stranger whose face she could not banish from her mind.

The lights of the great house could be seen in the distance for a long time before they reached it.

'Those are the lights of Barrett House,' she told him.

'This house was built by your father?'

'Yes – I can see the lights burning in his room. He is slipping away from all this. He has lost his interest in living.'

'I was sorry to hear of his illness,' Myles said gently. 'I know

312

that a great burden has been placed on your shoulders.'

'I have to carry it. I knew it would come, but the famine and my father's illness have hastened it.'

'Should you have come to the meeting? Was it not ill-advised?'

'No. I must be part of what is happening.' She was resolute.

'Rebels hang.'

'I do not think that a single life is of any importance now. What is important is that as many people as possible survive. *Our* differences are of little significance.'

'I did not think that we ever had differences – just met on the wrong occasions.' Myles's eyes were laughing at her.

'Perhaps,' she commented drily.

After they had stabled their horses Myles followed Gráinne through a corridor under the courtyard and up to the ground level. She left her cloak on a chair and showed him into the library, and some coldness melted inside him when he looked at the leather-bound books and the fire in the deep fireplace. It reminded him of Paris and of better times.

When Sergeant Heneghan made his way up the narrow stairs to the upper storey of the tavern and entered the low-ceilinged room he found eight men playing cards. They were drunk, and several empty bottles stood in the centre of the table.

28

Kate Brady had been cautious with her money. She spent it carefully bit by bit in Castlebar, returning home in the evening with sufficient food to see her through three days. Nobody was aware that she had hidden the rest in the earth close to the small cabin.

Two miles from where she lived a whole village died in October. During better times it would have been a tragic event and she would have lamented their deaths, but now her heart had no feeling for those who perished. She passed through the village on her way to Castlebar because it provided a short cut to the town, but in the evening she took a longer way home, to avoid watching them perish. They had scoured the woods for food and when that failed they boiled nettles. When there were no nettles left they began to eat grass, chewing it like animals, their mouths stained green. They went indoors to die, lying on the floors on a bedding of rushes. Their flesh melted from their limbs. The limbs and hip-bones and ribcages pressed out against the sagging flesh. They did not cry. They looked at her through the doors with glazed eyes. 'A handful of meal, Kate, or a boiled potato is all we need to see us through another day,' they called weakly to her.

She deafened her ears to their calls. She wondered if some curse would descend upon her because her heart had become hard. 'Take the baby with you, Kate,' one woman called to her

314

from a doorway. 'He has drained me of any milk I have. Take him and hold on to him.'

That night she returned by the village and entered the small cabin. The mother had died. The child, no more than a year old and purple with cold, was feeding off a dead nipple. She took him and carried him away from the village. The smell of corrupting flesh filled the air and seemed to cling to her nostrils. Fifteen people had died in two weeks, and the others had lost interest in living. They lay on the floors and let hunger eat the substance of their bodies. They grew skeletal and followed each other quickly to death.

Somebody had the charity to set the cabins on fire. The remaining flesh was consumed; the stench of death cleared from the place. She could now pass through the blackened village without fear. At night she prayed and cried out that their souls might find relief from purgatory and that they would be spared torture of soul. She cried out, too, from her own anguish, hoping that some relief might be brought to her as the snows of November began to fall and the wind cut to the bone, for by now her money had run out and her flesh was falling from her bones. She would have to draw herself out of her despairs and seek work, but the depots for food were far away and they had not been opened, although it was rumoured that they were filled with food.

She set out to look for work on a cold November day. They told her that they were building a road on the outskirts of Balla. It was a ten-mile journey, and the wind was hard and carried sleet, wheeling down from the north-west. She stumbled along the small muddy road in the dark, her boots sucked down with each step, drawing the strength out of her. The threadbare shawl on her shoulders held the cold rain, and soon her body was wet through. She must keep warm, she told herself, she must keep walking.

An hour later the day began to break in grey light. She had not realised she was so hungry. She stopped at a stream and filled her stomach with water in order to kill the hunger pains. 'I have only five miles to go,' she told herself. 'Only five miles to go, and maybe a sup of milk and a bit of bread at the end of it.'

The thought of food and milk kept her mind alert, but exhaustion was setting in and her feet began to stumble. She passed down the wide street of Balla, joining others who were going in search of work, walking silently with the mass until they came to the works.

'Have you your work tickets?' the overseer asked.

'What tickets? What tickets?' they called back.

'You cannot work unless you are issued with tickets! Do you know how many people are applying for work?' he asked them in a harsh voice. They looked at him. He carried a whip and was well fed.

'We need the work. We have no money. Sure, three shillings would see us through a week. The children are starving,' somebody cried.

'The whole country is starving. It is no use going forward unless you have a ticket,' he told them.

Kate Brady pressed stubbornly forward with the others.

'Go back, I tell you,' the overseer shouted. 'You cannot work without tickets.' He raised his whip and brought it down on the group. It had no effect upon the people; they swarmed forward relentlessly, and one man fell with exhaustion. They trampled on his body. The crowd was dense now. The ganger was running forward with them, bringing the whip down on their backs, but hunger and exhaustion had deadened their sense of pain. Now they joined a greater crush. Those who had gone before them were confronted by a line of men carrying axe-handles.

'Do not come further,' they called out. 'No more can be taken on. Move back or you will be in trouble.'

After a moment's pause the crowd pushed forward again and the men charged, bringing the axe-handles down on people's backs and beating wildly at the heads around them. People fell about Kate Brady bleeding from raw gashes. Then she was hit on the side of the face. There was a brittle snap: her jaw was broken. Pain shot through her head, and as she staggered forward she was hit again and she fell down the embankment.

She had no idea how long she lay on the cold ground. When consciousness returned to her, blood was streaming down her face and her vision was strange when she looked upwards, filled with double images which would not remain in focus. She crawled up the bank and looked about. Men passed by her with panniers of rocks for the new road. She struggled towards a stall by the side of the works.

'Could I have a drink of water?' she asked.

'Be off with you,' the stall-owner called to her, 'I sell poteen, not water.'

'Is there anyone who could spare a shilling so I could buy food for my children?' she pleaded, tears in her eyes.

'Off you go, I said!' the stall-owner roared at her.

'But my children are dying at this very moment. They are small and weak. They will die if I do not bring home food.' Her mind was in a whirl, and pain was beating within her forehead.

'There is no food here,' the stall-owner repeated and, coming forward, he caught her by the hair and threw her on to the trampled patch before the tent.

She drew herself up from the mud. 'What will my children do?' she cried. 'I don't worry for myself. It's for my children I worry.'

The men continued to carry their panniers of stones to the head of the road. Hunger made them mute to her pleas.

'I must return to my children. I must return to my children,' she said to herself anxiously. 'I will hoe the earth again. Maybe there is a potato left.'

With her eyes out of focus, and drawing whatever strength was in her body, she made her way through the rain towards Balla. She blundered up the wide street, her mind filled with reeling images. Her body was parched. She must find water. Outside the town she came to a stream. She knelt down and then bent forward to the clear water. Her mind went blank.

She did not die of starvation; she was drowned outside Balla in a small stream. The flowing water washed the blood from her hair. That evening it snowed, and the part of her body lying on the ground was covered in snow. Her head lay in the ink-dark water.

The boy wondered why his mother did not return. Eventually he went in search of her. He got lost in the vast expanse of bog and died of cold next morning. The baby she had rescued from the village died in the cabin.

The Parliament in London was aware that it now had a problem on its hands, and reports appearing in all papers indicated how extensive it was. But in London, with its wide streets and the order of civilised living, it seemed distant and academic. Since 1841 there had been reports each year on famine from Ireland. There had even been reports of death and starvation, but these were quickly forgotten as the House of Commons moved on to other business. But in 1846 the reports were so frequent that it was obvious the problem would be with Parliament all through autumn and winter. They could only await the advent of 1847 and hope that a good crop of potatoes would be returned.

It was also evident that the distress in Ireland could cause a rebellion. If the teeming masses took the law into their own hands, then the military and the administration could not deal with the situation. Certain middle-class rebels were moving away from the ideals of the old and tragic figure of Daniel O'Connell.

In 1846 the capitals of Europe were seething with new revolutionary thought, and these revolutionary seeds were finding their way to Ireland. For many they were like heady wine, and they were willing to sacrifice their lives in the pursuit. The creaking, impossible political systems of the seventeenth and eighteenth centuries could be brought tumbling down. Britain had only to look to America to see what a large part of the earth she had lost to revolutionary ideals.

The empire-builder, Napoleon, had stirred thoughts of nationalism in Italy and Prussia, and the destruction of his great army during the retreat from Moscow had stirred the intellectuals of Russia. The government was determined that the contagion be prevented from reaching Britain and Ireland.

The British spy system was an old and tested one: its agents were not only widespread in Ireland, there was a network of spies all over Europe consisting of sea captains, merchants, travellers and traders. In each principal city of Europe there were organisations which kept the government informed of what was happening there.

Myles Prendergast had been noticed moving towards Bordeaux in early summer: the old revolutionaries who gathered in his father's bookshop were well known and listed in London. It was known that seditious pamphlets were printed at the back of the shop on an old printing press. These pamphlets were regarded as of little importance, and so the shop was not burned, but the chief anxiety was that this group might gain influence with a revolutionary French administration. Another revolutionary government in Paris might send Europe into convulsions again.

Myles had not paid much attention to his fellow-passengers on the journey to Bordeaux and did not suspect that the middle-aged lady who spent her time knitting had been sent to report on his movements. The determined clicking of needles simply became one of the inconveniences he had to suffer on the journey. The British spy she had contacted in Bordeaux had kept a close watch on Myles and, although fear prevented him from venturing into the sea-front taverns and he missed his departure from the city, he knew that Myles was on his way to Ireland and was almost certain that he had boarded a Barrett ship, which meant that he would disembark either in Mayo or in Galway.

This information, along with other titbits, found its way to London in late summer. By the beginning of autumn the news had reached Dublin.

Colonel Spiker's eyes had a mad glitter. For three months he had lain on his stomach while the weals on his back scabbed and healed. He had only to recall the humiliating whipping he had endured at the hands of the Irish peasants to stir fury in his mind. They had desecrated his fine skin, and he resolved to have his revenge upon them.

During the painful recuperation he had had much time to think. He now walked with a limp, and his spine was partially twisted. Some fascination always drew him to the double mirrors he had ordered to be brought to his rooms in which he could see the red weals on his back. He would carry the marks of this humiliation to his grave. 'You are deformed and marked, and you will never ride a horse with elegance,' he would whisper to his reflection. 'The country has left its curse upon you. But you will have revenge. For every stroke on your body a rebel will die.'

A mad logic controlled his mind. He did not immediately send soldiers on useless excursions into the countryside in search of rebels; he sat down and thought out things carefully. The whipping was in revenge for his whipping of the stableman – he could not even recall his name but, having sought the man's drinking companions at the barracks he discovered that he had been a lonely and solitary figure and concluded that the attackers had come from outside.

'Why should they avenge the whipping of a simpleton?' he asked himself. It was a question he could not answer. The man who had been whipped was of no obvious importance to anybody. Even the agents who were sent into the public houses could come up with no certain information.

Finally he decided to invite Kenrick to his rooms – an invitation which was readily accepted. He recognised in him the best of allies. He was in the twilight region between peasant and gentleman, despised by both and not accepted in either culture.

Knowing that Kenrick was a whiskey-drinker, Spiker placed before him a bottle of expensive whiskey when he arrived. The gesture was not lost on the agent: in other houses he would be offered raw inexpensive whiskey. He was also aware that he would have to pay a price for the bottle of whiskey. He knew that he was a hated man in Castlebar and he derived a sense of dark pleasure from the thought, yet he had only to look at Colonel Spiker's glazed eyes to know that this man sitting in front of him was dangerous and to be feared.

He drank the bottle of whiskey rapidly, displaying his peasant origins, and another bottle was placed before him. He pulled off the cork and threw it aside, but this time he sipped it more slowly, enjoying the mature and expensive taste.

'I believe, Kenrick, that your knowledge of what happens in Castlebar is wider than that of any other person living here.' Colonel Spiker was deliberately flattering.

'I may not know what goes on in the higher circles, but I know what people are thinking and I know whatever bit of information it is necessary to know. I have relayed information before to the Castle.'

'Well, then, I think you know what is on my mind. You know as well as everyone in the barracks and the town of the attack made on my person by those vermin.' The Colonel clenched his fists.

'I have known they are vermin for a long time. They are everywhere: in every fold of the hills and on the sides of the mountains you will find them. And they are lazy and suspicious. While they talk to you they are plotting against you. I know them.' Kenrick spoke carefully, testing his ground.

'Then, you have advice for me. I wish to set about and discover those who carved up my back and twisted my spine. Do you know where I would find the perpetrators of this action? Information will be rewarded. I am generous to those who do me service.'

'I listen to what men say. It is the language of the vermin, but it is good to know it. I know more than the planted spies.' Kenrick was not giving direct information. He was enjoying his sense of power, aware of the suppressed anxiety of Colonel Spiker.

'Then, you think that somebody in Castlebar was capable of organising the attack upon me?'

'No. The attackers did not come from Castlebar. They cannot hold their secrets here. There are a few old rebels here, but there is nothing behind their talk. No, the attackers did not come from Castlebar.'

Kenrick drank more whiskey and looked at Colonel Spiker. He did not speak, but was obviously growing impatient, and Kenrick realised he could not trifle with this man. 'Do you know the Burkes?' he asked finally.

'No. How should I know the Burkes?'

'Then, you should make it your business to find out more about them. They are a wild undisciplined lot. They live off the sea and from smuggling, and they crew the ships of Michael Barrett. They have a long lease on their mountainy land and money in the banks. They are rebellious and are not bound to the land.'

'And you suspect them? These could be the people I am after?' Spiker shifted in his chair excitedly and shuddered with sudden pain.

'Perhaps. The stableman you had flogged publicly was related to them.'

'I was not aware of that connection!'

'The connection is there – and the soldier you flogged is not dead. He survived, which is why your life was spared. If he had died, you would now be resting in some military plot or other.'

Spiker knew he had been right to invite Kenrick to his quarters. He could give more information than the whole

321

network of spies in the county put together. His hatred of his kind made him more ready to impart what he knew, and the mature whiskey was giving him a sense of pride in himself. He decided he would be more expansive with this man.

'I believe that you fear an uprising.' Kenrick spoke grandly. 'The whisper about the town is that spies have been drafted in from Dublin. I hope that they are in disguise, because they will be noticed – they should have been planted among the people a long time ago.'

'There is always the fear of a rebellion.' Spiker was noncommittal.

'Well, you can tell your superiors that there will be no rebellion of any great consequence. The best friend the British ever had is the famine. It will leave the people too weak for rebellious talk.'

Colonel Spiker placed a third bottle of whiskey on the table, but it was a mistake on his part: Kenrick became dour.

'You think that I can be bought off with a bottle!' he cried angrily. 'You think you can invite me here and that when you have filled me with drink I'll tell you everything that you want? Well, I'm not one of the peasantry. I am above them, and you with your English manners will not drag me back amongst them again. I'll not be bought with whiskey.' His anger was swelling within him, and he felt abused by this crippled Englishman who sat opposite him. There was a look of disdain on his face. 'I refuse to talk further and I refuse your whiskey.' He swept the bottle of whiskey off the table and it broke on the stone slabs. The fine liquor splashed across the floor, and suddenly he realised the danger he was in.

The door was thrown open and two soldiers appeared. They carried pistols. Kenrick felt the barrels on his shoulders.

'Will we throw him in prison on charges of assault, sir?' one of them asked.

'Not yet,' Colonel Spiker replied. 'You may withdraw. I'll call you when I have made a decision.'

'Assault?' cried Kenrick desperately.

'Yes. These soldiers will give evidence against you. We can add attempted murder if necessary,' Colonel Spiker said in a cold voice. Kenrick was trapped without protection.

'Now, listen very carefully, Kenrick,' Spiker began when

322

the soldiers had withdrawn. 'If you do not give me the information that I need, I will have you thrown in gaol.'

'Not with scum and vermin!' Kenrick howled.

'At this very moment I could throw you in gaol and leave you to rot there,' Colonel Spiker said dispassionately.

Kenrick began to sober quickly, and his native cunning took over once more. 'What information do you want from me?'

'Enough information to justify your walking through that door a free man. I will be the judge of the value of the information.'

For the next hour Kenrick talked and Colonel Spiker listened, breaking the talk with questions and writing down the information. He had discovered that there was a stranger in town called Myles Prendergast, who had been at the meetings organised by the historical society. He believed this man had broken the spy system and that this was the reason why all the Castle plants had fled the town. He also told him that Molly Ward collected information at her pub from the soldiers and that this could be of use to rebels. She knew exactly how many men were in the garrison, how much food was in the storehouse and what preparations had been made to defend the barracks in the event of an attack. Most important, he indicated that the Burkes were smuggling guns from the Continent and America.

'You may go now, Kenrick,' Colonel Spiker announced when the man had finished. 'You have withheld information that could be important to us; as a result many soldiers could have died. And, remember, this makes you a suspect. By your silence you have given evidence that you are in sympathy with the rebels.'

'You have twisted my words. You have twisted my words,' Kenrick said bitterly, suddenly very afraid of the man sitting in front of him.

As he made his way home he cursed Colonel Spiker. He had walked into a trap and had been cornered by the subtle mind of the Englishman.

Colonel Spiker ordered the soldiers to clean up the broken glass on the floor. He was satisfied with the night. Now had he to lay his plans. He knew he must bring the Burkes out into the open and destroy them legally; only then would he have complete revenge.

As he made his way painfully to his bedroom he could not dismiss the feeling that there was something missing in the information he had received, something he did not quite understand. The spies had quit the town, and his network had become faulty, but Kenrick had not disclosed the reason for their departure. He wondered where Myles Prendergast had come from and what he was doing in Castlebar. Somehow it was connected in his mind with the night of the whipping and with French numbers; there was a confused association somewhere he could not fathom. He carried these thoughts with him to his bedroom and mused over them before he fell asleep.

Kenrick was afraid for the fortune he had amassed. That night as he made his way across the mountain path to Glencullen he considered his position with Colonel Spiker. He had made a serious mistake.

Some time later, among the correspondence from Dublin, was a letter which indicated that a French gentleman called Myles Prendergast had left Bordeaux in a Barrett vessel bound for the west of Ireland.

The morning after Kenrick's visit Colonel Spiker finished his breakfast in his quarters. Before he was helped from his bed, his batman had started the fire, and it was warm in the room. The cold had become intolerable to him; it set the torn nerves on his back quivering. The batman cleared the table and then helped Colonel Spiker from his seat. Now the agony began: with slow actions he began to move his arms in circles and then in wider circles until they became limber. Pain stung his face as some nerve or other tore at him, renewing the paths of the lacerations. When his back and arms were supple he walked slowly up and down the floor like a child learning its first steps.

'The soldiers are now ready on the parade-ground,' his sergeant informed him. Spiker stood at his window and watched their drill, demanding a precision which was almost impossible. Each morning he sent a complaint to one of the officers. It made them sharp.

He looked across to the huddled roofs and the narrow streets with their conspiratorial airs, but he knew that no great plot would be hatched there. Beyond the town were the mountains, their upper flanks covered in snow.

'The vermin will quickly perish. They will be flushed out from the folds of the hills. The snow and the wind kill better than the sword, as Napoleon discovered on his way from Moscow.'

As Kenrick had remarked, the famine was doing his work of extermination and the snow would hurry this process: if it did not kill them, then at least it would move them down from the scrawny soil from which they tried to draw life.

'The weather is working on our behalf, Tom,' he told his new batman, who nodded his head in reply. Tom was an illiterate mute and had been chosen specially by Colonel Spiker to attend him. 'They will pay for what they caused me to suffer, Tom. I will not rest. I will not rest.'

Having finished his breakfast, exercised his body and watched the troops perform their drill, he was ready to begin his day's work. He was a man who believed in precision, and the letters neatly arranged on his desk would be attended to before they brought him his lunch. His orders from London were clear: he must at any cost prevent the outbreak of rebellion. He had maintained a constant correspondence with the Castle in Dublin, informing of the guns that had been smuggled into the province from the Continent and America (he used the word 'province' rather than 'county' to impress upon his superiors that an insurrection would be general); now he wrote concerning the French spy whom he believed he had located and had put under surveillance. Moneys would be made available by return to him to deal with the situation.

Later, he called the local constables to the barracks, directing them to make out the names of all those whom they might suspect of rebellious sympathies, and he ordered them to set up a new spy ring since the old one had been infiltrated by foreign agents.

'It is difficult to start again,' one of the constables said. 'The whole town is aware that they were threatened with death. One of them was forced to dig his own grave.'

Spiker next turned his attention to spy rings in the smaller towns and villages. He summoned the police officers from the

325

small stations to his quarters, and they were given exact descriptions of Myles Prendergast. They were to observe his movements and make lists of those with whom he associated, but they were not to apprehend him. After each session Colonel Spiker ordered pens and paper to be brought to the room and set them out in front of the policemen. 'Now I wish you to make out a list of ten suspects in each locality you supervise. Begin with the most obvious. Leave the doubtful ones until last.'

He watched them at work, heavy backs bending over the pens. They wrote slowly and correctly. He observed them turning hostile, not towards him, but to those whose names they were writing on the page. He knew that they were getting their revenge upon those they disliked even if they owed no allegiance to the rebels.

The Queen has no more loyal servants, he thought to himself. Pick them from their own class and they will turn on their own for a meal and a uniform and position. They become a breed set apart. He watched one officer scratch out the tenth name on his list and place another beneath it. 'Why did you scratch out the final name?' the Colonel asked.

'I put down Gill the poet, but he is a drunkard and unreliable. He composes poetry of a seditious kind when he is with his own.'

'You mean to say the Irish have poets?' Colonel Spiker asked incredulously.

'They are rhymesters, sir. They write doggerel. But many say that Gill has written a poem which is on the tongues of all the peasants.'

'And has this man learning?'

'Oh, he can read in Latin and Greek – but who wishes to read in Latin and Greek among the peasants?'

'Do you know his poetry?'

'Oh, no. I heard some of it once but I'm not familiar with Erse.'

It was obvious to Colonel Spiker that he knew the peasant tongue but was too embarrassed to admit it.

'Before you go, gentlemen,' he finished off, 'I wish to tell you that I can place large sums of money at your disposal to buy important information. It must be important and accurate. Pay according to its value.' They were each given a leather

326

pouch full of money and ordered to count it on the spot and sign their receipts. They were surprised at the large amount of money they received.

Valuable information ended up on his desk: already he had a complete list of all the young men who were members of the historical society and had linked three of them with the French spy.

Periodically he made excursions through the small towns and the countryside in his carriage, accompanied by twenty horsemen. This served two purposes: first, it scotched the rumour that he was disabled; and, second, the unexpected appearance of cavalry struck fear into the people. He sneered at them from the window, disguising the pain which cut through his body as the carriage jolted over rough roads. Afterwards he had to be carried to his quarters, his body soaked in sweat. His officers were impressed by his ability to endure excruciating pain.

After some time Kenrick was recalled to his rooms for a further meeting. This time he was wary, wondering what was in Spiker's mind, but even so he was totally unprepared for the next move. The colonel placed before him documents proving that he had given the Burkes sums of money to buy guns. There was a moment's silence, then Kenrick jumped to his feet.

'These are forgeries! I know none of the names of the men who have put their names to this evidence against me! I have had no part in any of these activities!' He threw the sheets to the floor.

Colonel Spiker lost his temper, banging his fist on the desk. 'Pick them up! Pick them up!' he screamed. 'I will not have a lout behave in this fashion here!'

Kenrick crumpled, fear taking over again. The man before him seemed mad. He knelt on the floor and gathered them up and placed them before the colonel.

'Now, Kenrick, *you* sell your soul for high-grade whiskey; others sell their souls for meal. I can have any number of men brought into court who will perjure themselves for me in return for food. You have enemies all over this town, and this is the chance they have been looking for. There are many who wish you dead or transported. You have bled the countryside dry. Do I make myself clear? Do we understand one another?'

'Yes,' Kenrick whispered, white as a sheet.

'Yes, what?'

'Yes, Colonel.'

'You act above your station. Now, I will give you a firm directive. These Burkes have relations ten miles beyond Northport. I want them dispossessed. Whatever document you need for dispossessing people will be provided; you have my authority behind you.' He waved a white hand in dismissal. 'The sentry outside the door will see you to the barracks gate.'

'He is mad!' Kenrick told himself as he was led like a prisoner to the gate. 'He will have his revenge on those who whipped him at whatever cost.' For the first time in his life Kenrick was mortally afraid. The bent figure of the Colonel haunted him all that night. 'I will give them justifiable cause for rebellion,' he said to himself as he lay tossing and turning on his feather bed. 'When I am finished with them they will wish they had never been born. Not one will survive. I will hunt them like animals.'

The following day Kenrick called together the crowbar brigade, as his men were called. The veins in his cheeks and in his nose were raw from a night's drink, and his eyes were sullen and angry.

'We have one final clearance to make,' he told them.

'It's cold, Kenrick, and the snow has fallen in parts,' they objected.

'It has to be done!' he roared.

'Where?' asked one man listlessly.

'South of Clew Bay. We are moving against the Burkes.'

'We could end up dead, Kenrick,' they complained.

'I'll double your money,' he shouted.

There was a general discussion, and then a spokesman stepped forward. 'It is not enough for this time of year and for such dangerous work.'

'Very well, I'll give you five times your normal wages.'

They agreed reluctantly to the sum.

Kenrick moved with great rapidity against the Burkes. They were flanked by troops and taken by surprise. In two hours all that remained of Cashel was smoking thatches and ruptured gables.

When the news was brought to John Burke that evening he wept. His people had been on those lands as far back as anybody could recall, and now they were dispossessed. They would have to join the large crowds which made their way to the workhouse since they could not be sustained with food from Northport.

'On a black day he did an evil deed – oh, they have gone too far, the bastards! The Frenchman is right: if we don't fight now, we'll all go down one way or the other. Everything is falling asunder.'

He called the men aside and decided to arrange another meeting with Myles Prendergast. 'We'll use the revolvers on them. We'll see them in operation at close range. I can take no more.'

Myles Prendergast had been observed in Northport, and a report on the contents of his meeting with the Burkes was purchased from Kevin Healy for one hundred pounds, with the promise of three more hundred for further information.

When Colonel Spiker read the report he tasted the beginning of revenge. The fish were swimming into his net. 'And there is a lady caught up in the rebellion, too! Well, we shall deal with her and her heady ideals. I must open a file on this Gráinne Barrett. . . .' If his instincts were correct, the rebels would attack the military warehouses, which was precisely the move he wished them to make.

29

FRANK COSTELLO had made his decision the previous week. He did not have the grim determination of his cousin Seamus to hold on to the land and he did not have his sense of responsibility. Now, faced with failure, he decided to emigrate to America.

He walked his small plot of land and recalled the first time he had settled there with his wife. Now he had two children and four acres: a larger plot of land than that leased by his neighbours. He had made the fields fertile and dug drains; he had set the salley garden. Now one acre was blackened with blight, and a second acre showed only tawny stubble. The oats had paid the rent, but he had very little food and the money he had laid aside would be quickly consumed. He could hold on for one more year, but then he would be beggared. There was no point in going to the bank, and he would not go to a gombeen man. There was money to buy passage to America and, if he could sell their goods and chattels, they would have enough for a small start when they got there.

He set out early in the morning, his furniture heaped into a cart, and laid it out on Market Square like many others of his class. He waited for some buyer to come and sold the pieces eventually to a local huckster for a third of their value. He could lie on a floor for a fortnight, he thought, as he watched the double bed being carried to a store in Brewery Lane; a bed could be replaced, and he needed the money now. He left the market-place with his donkey and cart and made for a pub to reflect on his plans. Sitting down beside the small snug at the back of the bar with his whiskey, he felt relieved now that the decision had been made.

A quiet man himself, he listened at random to stray pieces of conversation around him. It was obvious that things were bad everywhere and nobody had any answers to the problem of hunger; many still hoped that the government would send wagons of flour to the towns. He recognised two men who came in by the side-door and sat in the snug as Kenrick the land agent and Hackett, Lord Lannagh's butler. They ordered a bottle of whiskey and then closed the hatch, but he could hear both voices clearly.

'How long has he been humping her, Hackett?' the conversation began.

'It started soon after he arrived. I wasn't certain when I went down to your house, but now I know. He humps her most evenings, and the maids tell me that the sheets are like ropes in the morning.'

'So Miss Horkan is the Englishman's whore!' He heard Kenrick smack his lips in satisfaction.

'Of course she is! Didn't I put my ear to the keyhole and them in hot passion? He's mad for her all right, let me tell you. I know it by the look in his eye.'

'I was wondering where the Costellos were getting their money to pay the rents,' Kenrick said idly. 'I'll wager it is from her, and I bet she's humping to get it!'

'Be careful of Lord Lannagh, Kenrick. She has a powerful friend.'

'I'll own his land some day,' Kenrick boasted. 'I've watched that bitch ride past my fields with her head in the air as if she were somebody. I'll bring her down through the Costellos. She'll have to sell everything she owns because I'll raise the rents so high they'll have to leave the place.' Kenrick's vindictiveness was joyful.

Frank Costello had heard enough. He left the bar and went in search of his cousin Seamus.

He found him in Geraghty's, sitting in a corner, gaunt with hunger. All day he had gone from merchant to merchant pricing grain. But all the prices were the same: the merchants

331

had done deals amongst themselves early in the morning. He had purchased enough food to keep his people from starvation for a week and now there was no money left. Outside the window four men were guarding the grain.

'I must talk to you, Seamus,' Frank said urgently.

Seamus Costello recognised his cousin and managed a strained smile. 'Sit down,' he directed. 'How are things going for you?'

'As badly as with any other. I'm not going to put another winter behind me – I'm selling out and going to America. I'm finished here. There is a curse on us.'

'We should have all gone years ago when we had the strength and a bit of money to spare. Now who knows what will happen?'

'Well, Seamus, I can tell you what might happen to you if you are not careful. I overheard a conversation in a pub that might be of great interest to you.'

Seamus Costello listened to the conversation which was told in full. 'So they call Eileen Horkan an Englishman's whore, do they?' he said eventually. 'Well, whore or not, she has kept us in food for many a month and I'll have nothing bad said about her. They have black souls and malignant mouths, Kenrick and Hackett. I'll not let them blacken her name. They consume the substance of the land, both of them.' They talked further until Frank left. Seamus Costello wished him goodbye as they parted and watched him walk up the street, some hope in his step. Then he fell into a brooding silence.

He had concealed from his cousin his shock when he heard that Eileen Horkan was now the Englishman's tally-woman. It explained how she could give him money to purchase food. He thought of her lying in the arms of an old man, her young mouth on his dissipated mouth, his body sated by hers. He checked his own sensuality and the lurid images which were pouring into his mind. These were strange times.

His mind turned to Kenrick. He knew the agent was bent on destroying him, and the thought of murder had passed fleetingly through his mind before. He had banished the temptation to commit the most primitive of all crimes, for the stain of blood would be never wiped from his conscience. He could forfeit his own salvation. He would murder Kenrick and face the consequences later.

He confided his thoughts to two other men of his village who

332

agreed to help him and he began to plan the murder. As he looked down the valley he could see Kenrick's house and barns. The small pockets of oats his village had grown had been taken to pay rents. Kenrick and his friends had not tasted the bitter humiliation of hunger. The far end of the valley would live, and those in the near end die. Kenrick, in drunken moods, had pronounced the death sentence on them in the public houses in Castlebar.

Seamus Costello looked at his thin worn hands. His life had been spent tilling poor land. He had given more to the land than it had given to him, and now it had failed him: it was a black afterbirth.

He waited until nightfall and then made his way up the small road out of the valley towards Eileen Horkan's cottage. He was cold, and the wind blowing through the vent in the mountains chilled his bones. He was overcome with humiliation. And now Eileen Horkan was a tainted woman. He had heard the whispers of Hackett. He had called her the Englishman's whore.

'If she is tainted,' he told himself, 'then she has sold out for meal and money. I am using a prostitute's money to save me from hunger.'

He was jealous of her attachment to Lord Lannagh and he reflected that he, too, had lusted after her. Now his feelings were not of lust but of desperation. His thoughts returned again to Kenrick. 'Should I kill him or not? Would I have the courage, or would I fear the damnation of hell in my soul for the rest of my life? Should one man live and crow over us while we die? Is life so sacred and are laws so firm that there is not an exception to them?'

He made vague plans in his mind. He knew exactly the part of the road which would be most advantageous to him and he had considered what weapon he should use. Old rusty guns were unreliable. He would split his head with a pike; it would be a direct and bloody act.

'Am I the man who five years ago went down the side of a cliff for an injured lamb which others would have left to die?' he asked himself bitterly.

He often thought of damnation. His imagination was filled with thoughts of hell. Murder was the most cursed of crimes, the first and the greatest, and it would leave its mark upon him. Yet, despite the prohibitions of conscience and imagination, he was drawn towards the act. He would no longer endure Kenrick's threats and laughter. The man was the cause of his own murder. He had set a bitter harvest and must reap its rewards.

He knocked on the cottage door. Eileen Horkan opened it and let him in. She carried a lamp, and her hair was loose about her shoulders, her skin delicate like cream. The features of her face were perfect. Even her voice had the gift of music.

'Come in,' she invited. 'I was thinking about you. I told you to come if you were in trouble.'

She walked before him in her long blue dress to the room at the end of the house where the fire was burning and where her books were arranged on shelves. As she walked before him he thought of her in the Englishman's bed, unchaste and wanton.

'Ah, look at you,' she said, stroking his face. 'Is this the young man who ran across the fields with me in summer and danced at night to Darby Hoban's fiddle?'

'No,' said Seamus bitterly. 'I am not that man. The times have changed me and sucked the juice from my soul. We have all changed. Hunger and starvation bring out the worst in us and kill the joy.'

'I'm sure you are very hungry,' she said. 'I will fetch you some bread and meat, and you must have a drink.'

He looked at her delicate fingers about the glass as she poured the drink. The nails were unbroken by labour, and the cuticles were clear. He accepted the drink and looked into the fire while she went to the pantry. She returned with meat and bread, and he looked at the plate placed before him. He wished to grab the meat in his hands and tear it asunder with his teeth, but some decorum prevented him from doing such a thing and he ate the food slowly.

It requires little to keep a man alive, he thought to himself. One meal a day is sufficient, and yet we cannot even have one meal in a week.

She left him to eat his food while she found something to do. She returned when he had finished eating.

'Tell me about the valley,' she said.

'There is very little to tell. Kenrick boasted in Castlebar that he would raise the rents further and that all our seed and breed would be on the road by January. James Fagan died two

334

days ago, and we buried him in the bog. He was old, but now the young are beginning to show the signs of starvation. There is not a berry left in the woods, and the few sheep we had have been killed. We have even eaten the flesh of wild goats, and now there are no goats left on the mountain. We sit all day beside the fire hoping that something will happen. The employment provided by the Board of Works is too far away, and the weather is now too cold for us to travel. A long journey takes the sustenance from a man.'

She was silent and contemplated the flames of the fire. 'I will make more money available to you,' she told him, 'but can you purchase enough meal with it now?'

'It gets more and more expensive at the markets. The merchants know that they can ask any price they wish.'

She realised that the money she could make available to him would not purchase the food they needed. She would have to beg for food. The lives in the valley depended upon her. 'Give me some days to arrange for food,' she said eventually. 'I will see if I can make some available.' Her forehead was tight with thought, and she did not look directly at him. He knew the decisions she was making in her mind. He was placing heavy obligations upon her: he had to beg from her, she had to beg from somebody else. Hunger brought desperation.

'You know the cost?' she said directly.

'No,' he lied, taken by surprise. It was an ambiguous statement, and he was without a ready reply.

'Then, Seamus, your eyes and your ears are not open. I'm sure you wonder, if you do wonder, where I can obtain money and food. I have no limitless supply. You have asked yourself the question many times?'

'Yes.'

'And you know the answer.'

This time he said nothing.

'Yes, you know the answer. You are saying in your mind that I am a whore. This woman lies with an Englishman – her money is ill-gotten. She has sold her body to obtain food. Well, so it is, if you wish to take that view. So it is.' Her voice was firm and clear as glass.

'For the love of God, stop!' he cried out. 'Don't talk like that! Don't be saying such things.'

'They must be said because I'm sure that everyone in the valley and at the great house has watched me visit there. Well, I'll tell you, Seamus Costello, I love that man and I cannot help it; and, if I'm his tally-woman, so be it. I accept it. *I* did not bring the famine about. You wanted for food, I gave it to you; I see no wrong in that. I have to beg for food. There is no ready source of food now but at the great house. If there is food there, it will be on your table. During better times, when you bring in proper harvests and when the weight of rents is lifted from you, you may call me a whore or a tally-woman. But I am a whore for the valley, and each child which survives the famine will curse me and will bless me.' Her voice was angry at her admission.

He did not look at her. He stared at the line of books above the mantelpiece. When she had finished talking he looked at her. There were tears in his eyes. 'I weep', he began, 'for all that has happened to us during the years. How the dreams we had are now ashes, and how this famine has broken me. Maybe I am jealous in my heart of the man who sleeps with you. And Hackett is no friend of yours. He is a friend of Kenrick's, and nothing happens at the great house but he does not carry to Kenrick.'

'They are two outcasts. Who else would befriend them?' she asked. Eileen became bitter when she thought of Kenrick and Hackett talking about her in some public house. She could imagine their raw language and their innuendoes. Her private relationship with Lord Lannagh was public knowledge. She must move against Hackett before he destroyed her. He would suffer for his disclosures.

'I will deal with him,' she said.

They talked further but they knew that their conversation was now becoming trivial. She gave him a small bag of sovereigns and told him to buy more meal. She told him to return as the need for food and money made it necessary.

He walked home thoughtfully. He was angry with himself and with Kenrick. The murderous thoughts which he had concealed from Eileen Horkan were raging in his mind again, and Kenrick was the cause of all his ills.

'I'll put an end to him! I will bear the weight of damnation on my soul for the deed.'

Three days later Hackett was called into Lord Lannagh's library. He entered, cap in hand, wearing a foolish grin. It had been a source of amusement to Lord Lannagh and a protection for Hacket.

'And what does the good lord wish of me today?' he asked.

'Mr Hackett,' Lord Lannagh began directly. 'You are dismissed from my employment. I can accept the fact that you are a thief and that you take from my larder and help yourself to my wine. But you will not blacken a friend's name in a public house in Castlebar and boast that you will destroy a visitor to my house. I do not wish to have myself described as an English bastard, when you are drinking with your friend.'

For a moment the implications of what Lord Lannagh had said did not register with Hackett. The announcement was too sudden. He held the foolish grin on his face. 'Ah, sure, my lord is mistaken! What reason would I have to call the great man such names? Sure, hasn't he been good to myself and my wife all the years? I'm the last one to say an evil word about anybody.' He was agitated now and made the foolish gesticulations which he believed Lord Lannagh found engaging.

'You did not hear me very clearly, Mr Hackett. You are dismissed!'

'But I'll die of hunger outside the walls! I have no land and no way of obtaining money. You would see me on the side of the road?'

'You should have thought of all these things before you carried your black gossip back to Castlebar. Now, I will give you two days to leave the estate. After that, the gamekeeper will order you off at gunpoint.' Hackett fled to the kitchen. His mind was thrown into confusion. He had watched the crowds making their way to the workhouse and had gloated over them. He knew that many people were dying of starvation.

'What has happened?' his wife asked as he burst in on her.

'The worst thing in the world! The worst thing in the world!' he babbled. Only later did he become coherent.

'You have destroyed everything, you fool,' his wife said in anger. 'You have destroyed everything. Where can we go now? Who will want us?'

'We must go to England. England is the only place to go.' He was a desperate and ridiculous figure now that his power had been taken from him.

'Kenrick will surely help me,' he said desperately. '*He* will give me the advice I need.'

He rode through the valley to Kenrick's and found him in the kitchen in a drunken stupor. He told him all that had happened and how he had been dismissed. Kenrick glared at him. Hackett was of no further use to him.

'You are a fool and you'll always be a fool, Hackett,' Kenrick sneered. He caught him by the back of his coat, dragged him to the door and threw him into the yard. Hackett lifted himself from the mud and looked bleakly about him.

30

Gráinne sat opposite Myles Prendergast. They looked into the deep fire, whose flames were reflected in the diamond panes of the library doors. The leather-bound volumes with their gold lettering brought a settled comfort to the place.

Myles Prendergast sipped the wine. It recalled memories of France and autumn in Paris with the leaves turning on the trees in the park at Saint-Cloud. Close by was the town of Sèvres with its wooded slopes and its country inns, and six miles south was Versailles, now decaying, the grass growing between the cobblestones. It was empty. It had been looted after the Revolution. All revolutions cost a price. Marie-Antoinette had been led from this regal palace to Paris. They had set her in a cart and jeered at her. She was ashen of face, they said, except for the blobs of rouge on her cheeks, when she stood trial. During less bloody and emotional times she might have been set free.

After the Revolution, Napoleon had lived for a while at Versailles, aping a royalty which had a blood-line of a thousand years. At Saint-Denis the coffins of the royalty had been plundered for lead and the bones of the kings and queens consigned to a pit. Were Napoleon's wars worth a million men? he thought. The cost of all revolutions and rebellions must be considered in the number of men who would be called upon to sacrifice their lives for a cause.

'What is passing through your mind?' Gráinne asked.

'Oh, mixed images,' he told her and went on to describe his autumnal walks at Saint-Cloud and his visits to Versailles and the choked gardens laid out by Le Nôtre.

'Your enthusiasm for the Revolution seems to have weakened. The wine and the warmth have softened you,' she said mockingly, looking up at him sideways.

'No,' he said, taking her seriously. 'I am aware that outside the walls of this great house there is cold and starvation. But I wonder if a small rising in the west of Ireland will in any way change things. Europe is too old and too settled. It is now returning to its old habits after the Revolution in France and the fever of the Napoleonic wars. It is weary.'

'Then what shall we do? I have a great deal to lose if we fail. This house would be easily destroyed and the people whom it sustains scattered.'

'Then, why would you forfeit everything?' He was curious why a beautiful and rich young woman would sacrifice herself to a peasants' cause.

'It has nothing to do with reason and much to do with feeling. The Wild Geese lost everything, and the O'Donnells and the O'Neills abandoned their territories and wandered down all the roads of Europe.'

'If that is how you feel and you are willing to pay such a cost, then I will stand with you. I have been brought up on revolutions and causes, and I am willing to take part in any reckless endeavour.' He spoke more jocularly than he meant to.

'Fate and the circumstances of the times are pushing us into something which will change all our lives,' she said fiercely.

'Then, these may be the last comfortable and civilised hours we shall have.'

She looked at Myles Prendergast. The light of the fire caught the lines of his face, tight with intelligence, and she realised she was falling in love with him. During the last months she had defined her position towards the house and her people, said farewell to her childhood and to the freedom she once enjoyed.

She looked at Myles Prendergast again, wondering what to do and what the months ahead would bring.

'Gráinne, Gráinne, come quickly!' a maidservant called. She

had entered the room without knocking. 'I think your father has taken a turn! He was asleep for about two hours, now he's awake and talks only in Irish. I tried to talk to him in English, but he does not understand.'

Gráinne left the room hurriedly and rushed upstairs. Her father was staring in front of him as if looking at some vision and muttering in Irish. It was incoherent talk; she knew that his mind was breaking up. His lips were sluggish. They had lost their grip on his sequence of thought. He spoke in sea phrases, remembering his youth. He was calling for the poet Gill and he no longer recognised her.

God, he's dying, she thought. I better send for the priest.

She rushed from the room and down the stairs and told a servant to saddle a horse to ride to Northport for the priest.

'What is wrong?' Myles Prendergast asked her urgently when she entered the library. He was standing with his back to the fire.

'It's my father. He's dying. Soon I'll be alone,' she told him, a hint of vulnerability in her voice for the first time. He came over to her and put his arms about her, and she placed her head on his shoulder and began to weep. She wept for a long time.

'I am with you now,' he said eventually. 'I have wanted to be with you since the first day I laid eyes on you. Take courage – you'll have to take charge of many things.'

'I don't wish to! I don't wish to! All this has come too suddenly.' She broke down again, a mixture of emotions pulling at her.

'I will be with you,' Myles said gently, stroking her hair. 'Can't you see that I am in love with you? It is a strange time to tell you.'

'Are you?' she asked in a whisper.

'Yes, through all which might happen.'

She rested on his shoulder for some time. Then she drew away, and he kissed her quietly, almost chastely. There was nothing he could say.

'I must go and prepare for the priest,' she said, brushing a tear from her cheek.

She went in search of candles and holy water. Her father's senses must be anointed with oil before death.

Myles Prendergast found himself isolated from the events

341

which were now taking place and sat down again, his mind in turmoil. Some time later he heard the sound of a bell. A servant beckoned him, and he joined a small procession upstairs, carrying lighted candles. He followed them into the room where Michael Barrett, his mind confused by memories, stared ahead of him. His eyes were deep in their sockets, his skin ashen and dry. Life was guttering in his weak body. The priest intoned the Latin phrases of Extreme Unction, moving to each sense, sealing it in oil against the influence of evil. Instinctively Myles Prendergast made the Latin responses. It was a ceremony of sad majesty, the ritual ending of life and the preparation for the departure of that in man which is immortal. The candles burned evenly about the bed, and the servants began to weep as they looked at the figure of a man who two months before had moved through the house irritable and lucid.

When the priest had administered the sacrament, he prayed for a moment, dried the wet chrism from his fingers on a cloth and made his departure. Gráinne and the servants remained for a while and prayed in Irish. Then she indicated that they should leave the room and that she would stay by her father's bedside. Myles chose to stay, too, and sat on a chair on the opposite side of the bed. They looked at the figure in the bed in silence.

'He grew old very suddenly,' she said, breaking the silence. 'In two weeks he failed.'

'His features are marked by heavy responsibility,' Myles said, with a sudden sense of the man's past power.

'In a sense he had a sad life. The plans he made for us failed: his wife died tragically; the famine took the people; he had no male heir to his wealth – he did not foresee these things.'

'If we were to foresee all that was going to happen to us, then we would wish that we were never born.'

'I suppose that is true.'

Michael Barrett was now sleeping. His breathing was regular. His eyelids were closed, mucus forming on them. Later Myles left the room and went for a rest, leaving Gráinne at the bedside of her dying father. She took his hand in hers and tried to rub warmth into it, but it could not receive any from her hands. She began to cry. Servant women came and took her place, and others led her to bed. Outside it was snowing:

the lights from the windows caught the flakes as they fell softly to the ground.

That night the news travelled quickly through the country-side that Michael Barrett was dying. Men sat in cabins or in taverns talking about him. The long ritual for a dying chieftain had begun. They traced his lineage and they spoke of his ships.

'It is the end of the great house, the end of the great house,' Gill lamented. 'It is the end of all things as I knew them.' He wept for the dying man, lonely that he was not with him to chant the 'Adoramus Te, Christe'. He had promised that he would come when called for and chant the sacred song for Michael Barrett, but he had not been called for and the snow was falling outside the tavern and he was drunk. If he tried to make his way to the great house, he would get lost in the snow or fall in a ditch and die, so he sat all night in front of a tavern fire in Northport drinking raw whiskey and weeping.

The morning gradually flooded in through the windows, and Gill, with puffed eyes, looked at the snow. As the light hardened he became more sober. 'I've a journey to make, and it's a sad journey and it's the last journey I'll make to Michael Barrett. There is something in my head which tells me that he is calling me.'

'You'll perish in the snow, Gill,' they told him.

'It's equal,' he said and he went out into the empty street. He scooped up handfuls of snow and rubbed them to his face and eyes. He noticed two corpses covered with snow; they must have died during the night.

He went up through the narrow streets of Northport and made his way out of the town along the coast road. The thin soles of his boots let in the wet, and soon his feet were cold. The trees were gaunt and black on either side of the road, and through them he could see the dark ocean. He dragged his feet forward through the snow until he came to the great gates of the house. Twice he had been dismissed from there and twice he had been invited to return. Timidly he looked up the avenue: it was empty, and the boughs of the evergreens were bending over with the weight of snow. The place was filled with the ultimate loneliness of death, and he emerged from the curved avenue with his mind sober and his eyes filled with tears.

'Michael Barrett was the only one who knew all my failings

343

and had some respect for me. Sure, where will Gill go now and no Michael Barrett to protect him?' he lamented.

The closer he approached the house the more he wept. He hoped that Michael Barrett was not dead. He had to recite the 'Adoramus Te, Christe'. It would be his final gesture of farewell and perhaps his last great moment of importance.

'Gill! You have no call coming today of all days,' the servants told him when he arrived in the kitchen. 'Last night the master was sealed with the holy oils. We want no drunks disturbing the house on this of all days. He's going down fast.'

'Can I see him once?' he pleaded.

'No, off with you, back to whatever shebeen you came from. Your power in the house is gone. You are filthy and could not be let into a clean room.'

Two of the men caught him by his gaunt shoulders and dragged him to the kitchen door.

'Just one prayer over my old patron and friend,' he cried.

'No, Gill. You should have said your prayers ages ago. You were always and ever a disgrace!'

He would have been thrown on to the snow but a voice behind them called: 'Stop! How dare you treat Gill in this way!'

Gill looked about him and saw the figure of Gráinne Barrett.

'Leave him be. He is always welcome at this house.' Gill began to weep. He sat on a chair and put his head in his hands and wept openly like a child. 'I came only to recite "Adoramus Te, Christe" for the master as I promised. I wished to say a final goodbye.'

'Patrick Gill,' Gráinne said, 'come with me and say your last farewell, for my father had a great love for you. You he loved more than all the others.'

Gill followed Gráinne Barrett upstairs, aware of his wet punctured boots which left marks on the carpet. When he entered the room and saw the shrunken face of Michael Barrett he fell beside the bed and prayed silently. Clearing the tears from his eyes Gill began to intone in his creaking voice the words of the 'Adoramus Te, Christe'. Myles looked intently at the rake in filthy and torn clothes chanting in Irish. He was a sad and tragic figure.

When Gill began the second verse of the poem, 'Harbour candles that lull to rest', a strange thing happened. Michael Barrett stretched out his hand towards Gill. The poet held it

344

in his and continued to chant. The two men were bound in some strange and mystical manner. Myles could not understand what was happening.

At the end of the poem Michael Barrett died. Gill, rake, poet and querulous man, had fulfilled his last promise. He crossed Michael Barrett's hands on his breast and left the room. He did not walk directly to the tavern, he went towards the sea. Looking out at the black islands and the waters about them, he wept both for himself and for Michael Barrett.

They laid out the body of Michael Barrett in the great hall. Two large fires kept it warm against the freezing weather. The snow had stopped falling the previous day and was now hardened by the frost. The trees were ink-black against the snow. The air was quiet, the cold intense. The year had entered its fatal month.

News of Michael Barrett's death had spread quickly. Frederick Cavendish on hearing of his death recalled him at the hustings. He had once been a Member of Parliament and he had spoken with an independent voice when others had held their peace; the House of Commons had been silenced by him. And there was the secret history of his life which he had shared with Frederick Cavendish a long time ago; it was almost a memory as he sat down to write the obituary. He wrote of his public life, and having delivered it to the printer he told him to bring out the edition of the paper rimmed in black.

All that day, people whose faces showed the strain of hunger, whose eyes seemed without hope, came and knelt at the great coffin. The Barretts and the Burkes who claimed direct blood relation stood for many hours in the great hall.

John Burke stood close to the coffin, his face serious and unmoved. It was evident to him that the power of the Barrett house was over for ever. Gráinne, despite her firm character, had neither the experience nor the maturity to continue its traditions. Its link with the Irish world would now be broken. Gill, half-sober and in the great black cloak given to him by Michael Barrett, thought of the same thing.

Frederick Cavendish, despite the ague in his bones, made the difficult journey from Castlebar to Northport. He was conscious of the desolation around him. The hard light from the snow hurt his eyes, and he drew the blinds of the carriage to banish the bleak whiteness.

He stood beside the coffin and looked at the face of Michael Barrett. The wide dome of his forehead was ashen, the cheeks netted with livid veins. He spoke to Gráinne for some time and was then ushered into the library. He sat in front of the fire and drank a glass of mulled port, reflecting on the times he had sat in this room over the years and discussed politics with Michael Barrett after days spent hunting in the mountains.

Suddenly he was aware of a presence behind him. He turned about and saw Myles Prendergast standing in an alcove.

'And so we meet again, Myles. Sit and talk to me,' Frederick Cavendish indicated.

They sat in the deep armchairs.

'Do you still think Ireland might be ripe for revolution?'

'Not for revolution but for rebellion.'

'Young blood is warm and reckless,' Cavendish sighed.

'And old blood is sluggish and will not take a chance,' Myles retorted.

'I prefer the comforts reserved for old age and the orderly habits age brings. I told you once that I thought such a rebellion would be a foolish expenditure of life. Well, life is cheaply expended at present. Men and women sit listlessly down and die.'

'The dead lie everywhere! Man has become valueless.'

'What plans have you made?'

'They are local and not on a grand scale.' Myles was reluctant.

'And guns?'

'They are ready.'

'Then choose your location with care. Remember, the eyes of the Castle are everywhere and if you got rid of some spies in Castlebar others have fallen into their place. Allegiance is easy to buy at present.'

'You know about my activities in Castlebar?'

'I guessed it was you.'

'It shows what a determined man can do.'

'Keep your counsels to yourself. I have been engaged in revolutionary acts in my time and I know what I am talking about.'

Frederick Cavendish looked at the tall young Frenchman, a mirror of himself in youth. He, too, had been caught up by the French ideals and ideas. That was a long time ago, and his memory became faulty when he tried to recall it. The Castle in Dublin had many secret files yet it had no files on Frederick Cavendish. He had disappeared into France as a young man and had fought in the revolutionary armies when the world was fresh with idealism. The rise of Napoleon had changed his mind about the progress of revolutions, and in 1804 when Napoleon crowned himself emperor he left France with his friend Michael Barrett. He returned to England as mysteriously as he had disappeared, the sword gash on his temple the only testament to the days he had spent in France.

They spoke of many things and did not notice the time pass. At four o'clock the Barretts and the Burkes came into the great hall. The coffin of deal was put into a shell of lead and placed in a larger coffin of oak. Each lid was sealed. A servant entered the library and told the two men that the funeral procession was about to begin. Frederick Cavendish rose slowly from the deep chair, and Myles wrapped his great cloak about the old man.

'Perhaps we shall meet again, Myles,' he said. 'But my good luck will be with you. You'll need it during these desperate times. These years will always be remembered as the blackest years the people of this nation have ever endured. It will be left weak and uncertain. And, remember, you never attack the enemy unless you are certain of your escape route.'

They made their way slowly through the door. In the main hall eight men had the great coffin on their shoulders. Before the coffin stood four priests. They began to chant the prayers in Latin as they walked forward through the front doors.

Outside, the ground was rigid. The crunch of boots on the frozen path seemed lost in the infinite stillness of the evening. The cortège wound its way through the woods of Eisirt. Once a fox ran across the path ahead of them and disappeared in the undergrowth. Gráinne Barrett walked immediately behind the coffin, weeping quietly, remembering her father following his wife's funeral along the same path. It had been in spring and a long time ago. Life was fragile, and death only certain.

Myles walked beside Frederick Cavendish. The old man was

347

breathing heavily and dragged himself forward in some pain. Behind them they could hear only the stamp of hard boots on the frozen path; ahead the priests chanted the penitential psalms, the sound of their voices re-echoing in the woods. Gráinne Barrett moved directly ahead of Myles, a hooded cloak made from purple velvet falling from her shoulders, its fur trimmings sweeping over the snow. Her bearing had a noble quality about it, which comes only from breeding and wealth. She now bore the responsibility of the great estate about them and she was mistress of the ships, but he could only think of her beauty as they moved through the winter woods.

Finally they reached the mausoleum which Michael Barrett had built to receive the remains of his wife and those of his family. It was a walled place surrounded by laurel bushes. The men walked down the steps leading to the great vault and laid the great coffin on a stone shelf. They withdrew and closed the inner iron gates. Later they would block up the door of the vault.

Just as the crowd was ready to disperse Frederick Cavendish moved forward and took some pages from his pocket. He looked at them for a moment, then he folded them and replaced them.

'I met this man in Paris during the Great Revolution. It was a summer's day, and the winds blew light through the great streets. It was a time filled with promise,' he began. His voice was deep with music. Gráinne Barrett listened intently to all that he said. She could not imagine her father as a young man. Once he had had ideals like Myles Prendergast and had been willing to lay down his life for them.

'I am old now, and our revolutions are over, and very little time remains to me,' Frederick Cavendish finished. 'Remember that Michael Barrett and I were once young and we attended the shaping of Europe. I hope that he lies at peace in Eisirt woods.' He wiped a tear from his eye and made his way slowly through the crowd.

Myles helped him back to his carriage and having wrapped a rug about his feet took his hand and said goodbye to him

'Remember that the world belongs to the young men,' Frederick Cavendish said and turned his head away in sorrow.

Myles walked back to the house and found Gráinne in the library standing by the fire, her head in her hands.

348

'I feel empty inside,' she told him. 'I feel that the spirit has left the house. There is something dark and ominous in my mind.'

He took her in his arms and looked down into her dark eyes. She kissed him again and again. 'God forgive me,' she said to the man from France.

'I will remain beside you,' he told her as he stroked her hair.

'I need you, Myles.' It was not an easy thing for her to say.

'And I need you also, Gráinne. I think I felt the need for you the very first time I saw you, on a fine summer morning. I listened to the sound of your voice as you spoke to the O'Hares – I was hiding in that dark cabin. Your voice was like silver in my ear, and I watched you race your horse on the shore close to the waves, your hair carried backwards by the wind. It seems such a long time ago, such a long time ago.'

He kissed her gently on the forehead, where the loose rope had torn her fine skin. Then he kissed her eyes and her lips. They were soft and delicate.

'I was full of my angers when I met you,' she said wretchedly. 'You watched me coldly, and I made a fool of myself.'

'I love your angers. Part of your great beauty is the fine anger and independence which you possess.'

'Where will it end, Myles? I bury my father and on the same day I confess that I love you. It is strange that I should lose somebody and find somebody on the same day.'

'I wish we could leave the great house now and take a ship back to France, but we cannot. I must remain and see all this out to the bitter end.'

'I have thrown in my lot with you, Myles.' She turned her head aside to avoid his eyes.

'You will always be in my thoughts during the next days,' he said.

'I will be sad when you leave and I will watch for your return. Hold me again,' she cried. 'I am gripped with fear.'

He held her for a long time. Her body was supple, and she excited him. He wished that he could be with this woman in Paris, walking through the great forests or riding through the Bois.

'Some day it will be over, and I will take you away from this place,' he whispered. 'I will bring you to France, perhaps. But do not be afraid – I am with you now and I think you should sleep.'

'I have no wish to sleep,' she protested. 'Let us remain here and talk with each other.'

They talked for a very long time beside the fire. When she fell asleep in the great armchair he took her velvet cloak and wrapped it about her. Then he sat in the other armchair and looked into the dying fire.

Frederick Cavendish did not sleep during the night. He feared the pain which would cut through his body. He opened a bottle of wine and sat before the fire, wondering if Michael Barrett was at rest at last. Would he carry punishment through an endless life? He recalled the horrible revelations of their last meeting when the old man was trying to salve his conscience. He recalled his final words.

'There were fifty Negroes chained on the deck, and I had the holds crammed with them as well. They fetched a high price in the south, and a man could make a fortune in a good year, so I overloaded the ship. I had done it before and I had got away with it. But then the storm came. What could I do? I held out as long as I could and, I tell you, if I had not done what I did we would have all perished. I ordered them to be thrown overboard, Frederick. They were chained together and they slipped over like a net being slipped into the sea. Their eyes bulged with fear, and as I looked back I could see them strung out across the waves, threshing the water. Then they disappeared, one by one. I had to do it.'

In his last days he had been continually confronted by the crime. Now Frederick Cavendish wondered if Gill the poet had brought him some comfort on his dying bed.

31

From his window Edward Silken watched the days grow shorter. Each evening the sun set earlier and cold began to increase. He had obtained turf for the workhouse, promising small farmers money he did not possess; the Board of Guardians could raise little money to sustain the workhouse.

Soon he would have to turn away the poor and starving from the gates. The numbers increased each week. Soon he would be faced with savage decisions.

'Mr Silken, sir. I once took great pride in my memory – I could remember the names of the great ships and their captains. But I can no longer remember the names of those who enter the workhouse. Soon there will be no timber to make coffins. We will have to bring the coffins back from the graveyard!' Jimmy the Sailor told him.

Jimmy the Sailor, with his sharp mind, knew more about the workhouse than Edward Silken. For Jimmy no world existed outside the workhouse, except the imagined land of America. He rarely visited the town and when he did he was uncomfortable until he returned; he was essential to the operation of that great gaunt building.

For Edward Silken, however, the world outside the workhouse was very real. He knew that money was circulating in the town; he knew that Kenrick, in a ruthless fashion, was bent on levelling all the villages for his 'great sheep-fields' as he called them. The rich farmers were emigrating: he had watched them sell their furniture in Castlebar. The famine was taking its full toll. The land could no longer sustain people. They would make their way blindly to the workhouse.

His mind was under a strain. Images of starvation came to him in his sleep, strange and distorted. There were images also of his pleasant childhood in Dublin, of gardens and apple-trees, and a punt on a river.

In October there was still some order in the town. The prison could contain the men who deliberately broke the law. Men and women had deliberately stolen Kenrick's cattle and driven them past the barracks so that they could be charged with stealing. They smiled when they were led away to prison.

'We'll have platefuls of gruel, your Lordship; and, sure, if you could give us transportation sentences to Australia we would gladly take them!'

Two women were given transportation sentences for stealing large sums of money. When the sentence was handed down they called to the judge: 'We go to a better place, my Lord, and may God grant you a long life and may you see your children's children.'

But these sentences were rare: the poor had no easy way out of this land of death. Some would make their way along the emigration path, which led directly across Ireland to Dublin. Some lived in hope that the British government would use the army to deliver food to them.

'They wait in expectation that the British government will bring wagons of free food to save them,' Edward Silken told Frederick Cavendish one evening.

'And what else can they do but live in hope? There is nowhere to turn. They live by this foolish hope. They are trapped.'

'But *somebody* must have compassion somewhere!'

'The Quakers have set up soup kitchens in Castle Street. But a rumour has got about that they will have to change their religion for a bowl of soup.' Cavendish was exasperated.

'And that keeps them from eating Quaker food?'

'Yes. To change one's religion is to mark yourself with the mark of Cain. You are cursed in the hereafter.'

'And what of the Quakers?'

'I have spoken to these people. They only wish to do good. Their charity is direct and without any obligations.'

352

'Are there no other charities?'

'The other charities are the charities of the merchants to themselves. One month ago those working for the Board of Works could buy food with their earnings. Now the money is useless. Money cannot purchase something which is not there.'

'What can we do?'

'Nothing. This is a tragedy of history like the Black Death in the thirteenth century. It is a dreadful and dark thing and must work its way to a logical end.'

'And where will this dark logic lead?' Silken asked desperately.

'Death. The old will be the first to die. Many of them have already died. Then it will be the turn of the young and the strong. That will be followed by the fever as malignant as starvation.'

It was gloomy and firm talk. Frederick Cavendish had rarely been so pessimistic. But he had seen the reports pour into his office, he had seen the villages clouded in despair. He had no illusions as to what might happen.

'Of course we must continue to print reports of the petty sessions in the paper and let people have news from abroad. Last evening I received an autopsy report – it helps to look inside the body and see what ravages the famine works there. Denis Kennedy was the subject of the report. Dr Fletcher, having carved open the body, made the following marvellous discovery: he reported that there was no food in the stomach or in the small intestines, but the large intestines contained some undigested cabbage mixed with excrement. Behold the noble body of man made after the image of God.' His tone was very bitter.

For Edward Silken, sitting before the warm fire in the drawing-room of Frederick Cavendish's house, the words turned his stomach and he wished to vomit up the dinner he had just eaten.

'Now,' continued Frederick Cavendish, 'that autopsy was done a month ago. If they were to perform autopsies now, they would find grass in their large intestines, or dog or ass meat. They have already slaughtered the asses to provide food. Notice how few there are about at present. Go back to Dublin, go back to London. You have friends there who will receive you. This is no place for a man of your sensibilities.'

'I could never walk out on my obligations!'

'And obligations will keep you tied to this impossible situation?'

'Yes.'

'I think it is time for you to leave. Remain on and you will fall into deeper depression – you were not reared to face a situation like this.'

That night, on his way home, Edward Silken reflected upon Frederick Cavendish's words. In the morning he could saddle his horse and within a week he could be in Dublin. He could stay at many houses on his way. But his humanitarian training always came up with the same tragic answer: 'You are obliged to stay. Only a moral coward would flee from such a situation.'

Frederick Cavendish, in his turn, reflected on the situation. Jimmy the Sailor, with his greasy captain's hat, was in a better situation to live through the famine. Hunger would not destroy Edward Silken; he would be destroyed by mental anguish and ideals not suited to the present situation. His mind would fail before his body.

Edward Silken no longer found pleasure in wine; he now drank whiskey. When he reached his room he opened a bottle of whiskey and placed it on the table beside him. He filled a tumbler and drank it. It was raw in his mouth, but he drank on through the night.

In the morning Jimmy the Sailor entered the room. He cleaned up the vomit on the floor, undressed Edward Silken and pulled the blankets about him. A half-tumbler remained, and Jimmy drank it. He enjoyed a glass of whiskey but he rarely had the opportunity to have one in the morning before he made his rounds.

At the end of October it turned cold. The fields were black and without sustenance. In the small woods and scrubs the leaves had fallen. The nuts had been eaten, the berries picked. In final desperation the people turned the dark earth in search of potatoes.

The peasants' minds were filled with confusion. They had been hungry before – they had sat huddled over fires during the dark winters stretching their resources until spring many times. But now no resources remained to them. They had eaten the seed potatoes which would have generated a new crop in 1847. Nothing remained.

At the beginning of November sleet and rain were driven down from the north-west on a hard persistent wind. The small wet fires were little protection against its severity. Edward Silken knew of these things through the starving who were permitted to enter the workhouse. They carried with them terrible tales of hunger and starvation. Men had fallen dead carrying stones to build useless roads.

Greyness covered the town. The earth was barren. The government was impotent. Edward Silken's mind could not endure the dark logic of history. Jimmy the Sailor was the first to realise that he was going mad.

December would be remembered as the blackest of months. In November the snow had lodged on the mountains, the winds from the north were honed, sharp and bitter, and they cried about the workhouse like wailing women weeping for the famine dead. In December the snows became blizzards stopping up valleys and isolating villages.

Edward Silken knew that he could no longer cope with the problems of the workhouse. His mind was taut with worry. He had pleaded with the Board of Guardians to increase the rates, but they would not. No money was available, and food was impossible to buy.

The sandstone walls of the workhouse seemed to have absorbed the cold. The high gaunt rooms were freezing, and men huddled about the fires with blankets on their backs. The rush beds upon which they slept were fetid. Silken calculated that by January the food supplies would have run out. Chaos would follow in the New Year. The workhouse was already a besieged fortress; outside, great crowds of people waited for admission each morning, gripping the bars of the main gates and crying out: 'Is there any room for us at all? Did anyone die at all last night? Did anyone die at all?'

Each morning at ten o'clock the tall gates would swing open and a huge cart, piled with corpses and covered with sacking, would make its way to the town graveyard. The corpses were buried in long shallow graves. Digging deep graves was a waste of energy.

For every one who died, one was admitted. The number within the workhouse was now at a steady thousand. As the days grew shorter and the cold deepened the crowds waiting for admission

355

began to grow. They could now be numbered in thousands. The workhouse was their last resort. Beyond the walls there was no hope and nowhere to go. On one occasion they had rushed the gates and had to be beaten back like animals.

Edward Silken now drank heavily. Every night he could hear the human wail outside the walls, sharp and shrill. In the morning many would be dead, their bodies rigid with frost. The grave-diggers would collect them and bring them to the mass graves where, unnamed and uncatalogued, they were buried.

'Oh, God, is there any end to this misery? Will this cloud which hangs over us ever be dispelled? What curse is upon the land?' he prayed in his drink. Pessimism had lodged in his mind. He no longer recalled gentle English lawns running down to river-banks or the white rustle of young women's dresses. All he saw in his mind were the emaciated hands clutching the bars of the great gates. His mind was infested with famine images. Life had become constricted to high brown walls and the workhouse which they enclosed.

Jimmy the Sailor often considered his position in the workhouse. Once it had been secure and certain. His hoard of money was now large enough to take him to England or America. He now no longer dominated the inmates of the workhouse: the rooms were crowded with people he did not know and upon whom he could not stamp his authority. One group of men was ganging up against him, and order was breaking down. They scorned the little authority he had and called him 'the cross-eyed sailor', envying his small room where he shut himself away for the night. He wondered if they suspected that he possessed money. He was always watchful of them and changed its location each day, for if they stole that his hopes would be destroyed.

He looked out at the snow from his garret: it would be a bad time to make his departure. He would wait until the weather improved, but now he wondered if it would improve. Soon he would have to make a decision: he would hasten to Dublin by coach. From there he would go to London. In the spring he would take a ship to America.

By mid-December the cold had become intense. The days grew short and helpless. The hope that food might be carried to the western ports by sailing ships had passed.

In the bay at Northport two Barrett ships were anchored close to the quay walls. John Burke insisted that every rigging be checked in preparation for the spring when they would take again to the high seas. After he had sent some men on board the ships with orders to look at the upper sections of the masts and the spars for damage, he made his way to the tavern. Men were gathered in from the cold weather. They always talked about the famine: it seemed to have left its mark on everyone. There was no one who had not lost some relation or other.

As John Burke sat in the tavern he thought of the ships. He wished at that moment that he was weighing anchor. The challenges of the sea he could understand, but the land was firm and limiting. Since his return from America he had been unhappy at all the events which had taken place, and the death of Michael Barrett had destroyed some final hope within him. He felt that Northport could now fail.

He had once felt protected in his own village, but Kenrick had moved against his relations and it was evident that he had been directed by somebody to destroy only the Burke holdings. It was a direct and obvious plan. After consultation with Jeremiah Egan, he discovered that Kenrick had been forced into action by Colonel Spiker.

John Burke could not feed his people. They would starve. 'Where are they now?' he asked his cousin, Brian, who came to visit him.

'Where can anybody go in cold weather, when the wind cuts the bone? They have made their way to the workhouse.'

'So the Burkes have accepted the foreign gruel?'

'Yes. Some have remained in the scailps they built, but most of them have lost heart. Some of the older ones have died on the long journey to Castlebar.'

'Is there enough food in the workhouse?'

'Barely, but I'm told that it will soon run out. They say that people sleep outside the walls in the hope that they may take the place of somebody who has died in the workhouse during the night. And from what I know the place is falling into disorder. There is no money left to buy food.'

'So the workhouse is finished?'

'Yes. The Burkes have been wiped out.' Brian Burke was bitter.

'We should have killed Colonel Spiker when the chance was

357

offered us. I do not think it will be given to us again. He has lived and I'm sure he is seeking vengeance. He suspects us for some reason or other. Why is he moving against us?'

'You know these things. I do not.'

'The Frenchman is right. There is nothing left but to rise out against them. Those of us that are left might as well put up a fight for it. I am not one to stand by and see my own starve. Things have come to a bad pass.'

'What will I do, John?'

'I will see to it that you have a few bags of meal when you leave Northport. And tell the men who remain that John Burke may be calling upon them one of these days to help him in a good cause.'

He left it at that, and his cousin, seeing that he wished to be left alone, left the public house.

John Burke settled down to plan coldly. The revolvers would be used in the event of an attack on the granaries. Already many of the men had practised with them and knew how to load them. They were accurate for close-in attacks. The fire was rapid and did not give the enemy a chance to reload. In his mind he had settled on a small uprising. He must have the ships provisioned in case they had to make their escape. There was always the danger of failure: at sea he would be safe from all enemies.

He thought of the Frenchman up at the great house and smiled. What a time to fall in love! he thought to himself. When the country is blighted and when all that we stood for is falling apart. Human nature must have its way.

Eventually he grew weary of his own company and the dark thoughts which filled his mind and he looked about. He saw Gill sitting by himself, drinking. Is he ever not drinking? he thought. Since the death of Michael Barrett the poet had begun to fail. He called Gill to the counter.

'Gill,' he told him, 'recite to me your great poem.'

'Oh, indeed, I will. Oh, indeed, I will, but my throat is dry. It needs something to wet it.'

John Burke placed a drink before him. 'Wet it,' he directed. Gill hawked phlegm from his throat and recited his great poem.

'Now recite me the revolutionary poems,' John Burke ordered.

'That I will, though my mind is faulty.'

358

'Never mind the excuses. Recite for me the revolutionary poems and see if I can obtain solace from inside them,' John Burke roared.

Gill pulled himself together and drew from his wide and faulty memory the poems which had been written by the dispossessed.

Jimmy the Sailor counted his money. He had enough in his purse to carry him to London and from there to America. He secured the money safely and suspended the purse about his neck, then he collected his few clothes and put them in his sailor's bag and made ready to leave the workhouse. He would wait a little longer, but if things became too chaotic he would depart quickly.

There was no break in the weather, no day of compassionate sunshine or blue sky. The county lay under deep snow, making travel almost impossible. Hunger and starvation had become general; people died more rapidly now. The fat on their bodies had been consumed by November; by December they were living off necessary tissue. In the valleys bound by snow, they died without the comfort of sacred oils.

They were pitiless days. The dawns and the evenings were grey. People lost heart. If December was so harsh, then January would be worse and so would February. The winds of March were never kind.

The villages fell strangely silent. Neighbours said their last goodbyes and went indoors. Then the families lay huddled together close to the fire. One by one they died, and as they died they were pushed aside. They had no protective heat left in their bodies. When they began to putrefy the others wished that death would come quickly. During the final days of death there was no fire on the hearthstone. Some had a strange exultation of mind before they died, but most died mutely, their minds empty of images.

Frederick Cavendish had suffered a chill at the funeral of Michael Barrett and was confined to his rooms. The compositors came up from the print works and took away his handwritten pages as soon as they were ready. He could no longer move through the town and he had to rely for his information on Joseph Foy.

'Now, what are your instructions for the day?' Frederick Cavendish asked him when he entered the room. Joe was wrapped up against the cold.

'I have to proceed through the town towards the workhouse. I have to count how many people are lined up outside the soup kitchen in Castle Street, I will count how many beggars are at the bridge and I will count how many are outside the county home. I will try to find out how many died during the night and I will use my own initiative to gather other pieces of information which may find space in our illustrious journal.'

'You are using words bigger than yourself, Joey!'

'My mother says that you can judge a gentleman by the length of the words he uses.'

'Good. Off with you now.'

The illness of Frederick Cavendish had given Joseph Foy a sense of importance which he had never before enjoyed. Some day he would be a compositor with the paper: with the aid of a dictionary his mother had purchased for him he would know the longest words in the English language.

There were no sounds of horses on the street when he left the archway and made his way into Spencer Street. People humped against the cold made their way down towards Castle Street. They were on the way to the soup kitchen.

When he reached the Mall he heard the sound of cart rims and the clatter of horses' hoofs. The evictions continue, he thought. Here is news for our illustrious journal.

He rushed down the street. Three carts, carrying the battering rams and tents, were on their way out of town. Five men sat on each cart. They were flanked by lines of soldiers. He recognised Gunner Darcy on the back cart, one of his friends. He was always drunk and he often gave Joe money, which he found with difficulty in the depths of his coat pocket. He ran alongside the cart.

'Where are you off to, Gunner?' he asked.

'Where are we off to?' Gunner asked one of the other men.

'Cloggernagh. There are three houses to be knocked and walls to be built.'

'We're off to Cloggernagh,' the Gunner told him. 'And how is your mother?'

'Great, Gunner. Great, altogether. She is salubrious.'

'I hope she gets better. I hope she gets better.'

The carts had moved forward with Gunner Darcy nodding from side to side. Joe Foy remembered the word Cloggernagh. Frederick Cavendish could write a whole column on this single incident.

'That man is not only a fine gentleman,' his mother told him, 'but he is also a genius with words. Remember them big words he uses. They might come in handy some day. You know quality by the big words they use and the voice in which they speak them.'

Castle Street was crowded with people. They lined up along the sidewalk with their bowls. They covered their faces so that they could not be recognised, and snow fell on their bent backs. He knew many of them; they were neighbours of his own. His mother would be interested to know that Mrs Reilly was now taking the bowl of soup.

'Ah, the mighty have been humbled,' she would tell him. 'I remember that one in silk and her going after the soldier boys. There is no road which hasn't a turning.'

He noticed Anne Fergus. She was a Protestant. Even the Protestants are feeling the hunger, he thought to himself. He believed that Protestants were all condemned to hell for following Martin Luther, the priest who married the nun in Germany. Anne Fergus was the first Protestant he had witnessed begging for food. His mother would certainly be interested in all these pieces of information. She loved pieces of information as much as she loved her pipe. She smoked her pipe with relish when he carried home choice pieces of information. 'Well, upon my soul, and is that true, son?' she would exclaim between satisfied sucks of the white stem.

He looked through the door of the soup kitchen. Three huge iron pots were on the boil, and the steam was coming out the door. He smelt it. It was full of meat, probably skinned sheep's heads. Andy Armstrong was stirring the pots with a large wooden spade. His sleeves were rolled up and he was sweating. Andy Armstrong was the drummer in the town band. He carried the large drum on his stomach. They said that he was the most important man in the band. If the drum-beat went wrong, then the whole band fell into discordance.

'Hello, Andy!' he called in the door. 'Are there more coming every day?'

361

'Yes,' he called, 'and push off from that door or I'll give you a cuff on the ear.' He looked very important stirring the soup with his large wooden spade.

He would have missed another story had he not delayed at the door of the soup kitchen. A crowd had gathered around Mulloy's door. The two Mulloy sisters had been dressmakers, small women half-blind from bending over their stitches in weak light.

People had formed a semicircle about the door, and Father Curley was arguing with some women. He was an old man and even during the good times he had a starved look upon his face.

'That man is a saint,' Joe's mother often told him. 'He'd give his last penny to the poor. Sure, look at him! His coat is green with age.'

'It's all right for you, Father Curley,' the women argued. 'You have neither chick nor child. If we went in there, we could become tainted. Fever is worse than hunger. There is no cure for it.'

'But they must have a Christian burial,' he told them. 'Wash their bodies and lay them out. I'll pay you for the service.' He took some money from his pocket, and two women who were drunkards entered the house, wrapping shawls about their faces and rushing in. They remained inside for about twenty minutes.

'It's the black fever,' they called through the door. 'Their faces are grey and turning black.'

'God protect us from all harm! The fever has reached the town!' the crowd said and fled from the door.

Father Curley arrived back with a cart and two long boxes. He carried them indoors. Later he emerged and asked for two volunteers to carry out the coffins with him.

'We'll catch the disease, Father,' they complained.

'But I have them confined. There is no danger,' he persisted.

'There is always danger,' they told him. 'They say the fever is in the air of the room where the victim dies.'

Finally the priest persuaded two men to enter the house. They later emerged with the coffins, pushed them into the back of the cart and fled.

Father Curley mounted the cart and drove it up the hill and out of the street. Joe Foy watched him turn the corner, his green coat covered with snow, almost too big for his meagre frame. He had hidden in the archway to observe the scene. He was delighted that Father Curley had not asked him to carry the coffins. His mother would never have let him enter their house. All the way down Main Street he felt that he might have caught the fever. But as he moved further away from the house he was convinced that he had not.

He did a quick count of the beggars in Main Street. There must have been five hundred of them, and that was two hundred up on the previous week. They gathered about the merchants' shops begging for grain. The shops were well guarded, and the crowds were pushed aside to make way for anyone who could purchase meal. They were up on the previous week.

Joe Foy always approached the workhouse with reluctance. The people lying about the walls and choking the road were strangers and they did not know him. He felt more comfortable within the limits of the town. Even as he turned off Linenhall Street and passed down by Sruffan he could see that the crowds were uncountable. People were everywhere. They lay in the snow and the slush, oblivious of the cold and damp. Sometimes when Joe thought that they were dead they stirred with life. He knew that they would be dead before the day was finished, so he counted them as dead.

Some asses, with creels on their backs, stood patiently among the crowd. He looked into the creels. In one set he counted six children, thin and starving. They tried to crawl up the wicker sides of the creels and look over the edges, but they fell back on each other. They reminded him of featherless birds he had seen in nests. They did not seem like the young of humans. He threaded his way through the bodies towards the gate and went to examine the long graves they had dug outside the workhouse. They no longer carried the dead to the graveyard. There were thirty bodies lying alternately in the trough of earth. They were fleshless and inhuman. The grave could take thirty more bodies. They were already filling in the far end. He watched the earth spread across the bodies and fall between the limbs, watching as they disappeared as further shovelfuls were thrown upon them. They were being sucked back into the earth.

'We are only dust, son. We are only dust,' his mother had

363

told him in one of her religious moods. These people will soon be dust, he thought. Well, the fleshy parts of their bodies would be dust. He was not sure about the bones. He had seen bones dug from graves, and they must have been fifty years of age.

Old women stretched out their hands towards him. He rushed from them and went to the main gates where he found a place at the lower part of the railings to look through. The narrow yard in front of the main building was empty. He waited for half an hour and then he saw Jimmy the Sailor emerge from the great main door. He could see that he was agitated.

'Jimmy!' he called.

Jimmy did not hear him. He called again, and Jimmy rushed over to him and knelt down so that they were facing each other.

'It's awful!' he told him. 'I couldn't believe my eyes!'

'What was awful?' Joe Foy asked.

'The sight I just witnessed. He was hanging from a beam!' Jimmy the Sailor was wild with fear.

'Who?'

'Edward Silken. Master of the workhouse. He had a rope around his neck and his tongue was out and he was staring at the roof!'

'Anything else?'

'Two empty bottles were broken on the ground. They must have fallen from the table, when he kicked it over. I don't know what we'll do. Somebody will have to come in and take charge. You better tell Frederick Cavendish.'

'I'll tell him immediately,' and Joe Foy turned and pushed his way through the crowd. He ran through the town. His head was filled with stories and observations.

Before he hanged himself Edward Silken had taken a final look at the white countryside, now so gentle and ordered under the deep snow. But he knew that beneath the snow the earth was poisoned. Outside he heard the thin wailing of the starved, and he had placed the noose about his neck and kicked the table from beneath him.

Jimmy the Sailor found him in the morning. He would always remember the look upon his face as he stared with large eyes angularly at the ceiling.

Jimmy the Sailor decided to leave for Dublin as quickly as possible. Next morning he left the workhouse, a purse of money hung from his neck, his possessions in his sailor's bag.

He never reached Dublin. At Mullingar, while he was asleep in a loft, he was attacked and his money stolen. One of his attackers hit him on the side of the head. He was unconscious for several hours.

32

No DOG BARKED THAT DECEMBER in the valley; they had all been eaten by the starving population. The single donkey which had survived now pulled the cart through the snow to Castlebar. The men had warmed themselves with poteen and did not feel the cold. There was a firm coat of snow on the mountains, and the white reflection made the air bright and hurt their eyes. They spoke only in fragments: their minds were troubled as they reflected upon what they were now about to do.

During other years they would have been thinking of Christmas and the rural celebrations to mark the season. No such thoughts passed through their minds. They knew now where Seamus Costello received the money to buy the food; they knew the rumours which persisted in the locality. If Eileen Horkan slept with the Englishman, well and good; it was no business of theirs. They had to survive. With the money Seamus Costello possessed they could buy enough food to tide them over for a week.

They took the long road to the town. Travelling across the mountain road drained their strength, and the cart could get lodged in the snow. They had not the strength to pull it forward if it did. In the cart, covered by rushes, lay the pike, the edge honed until it could slice bone. They had tested it on hard timber.

'Kenrick's head can't be more than half an inch thick. A direct blow could kill him,' one of them said brutally.

'Then, get him with the first stroke. If he escapes, then it is the end of us all. You have only one chance, so make it direct. We could hang for this.'

'Better hang than starve.'

'We barter our salvation for this deed.'

Kenrick, that morning, was not disturbed by the bleakness of the landscape as he passed across the mountain road on his way to Castlebar. He passed by several people dead in the snow, their bodies frozen, the limbs in tranquil postures. They did not give off a stench.

He carried his money in a purse. He would deposit it in the bank and, when added to what had already been lodged there, it came to a handsome sum. The valley had served him well, as had Spiker's recent offer. That evening he planned to spend with the soldiers' women.

When he emerged from the bank an officer was waiting for him.

'Kenrick,' he ordered. 'Colonel Spiker wants a word with you in the military barracks.'

'And how is Mr Kenrick?' Colonel Spiker asked when Kenrick was shown in. 'With all the money you have in the bank you will soon buy a great estate and a great house.'

'I have little money, Colonel Spiker. These are hard times for us all.'

'Sit down and have a glass of whiskey. It's not an account of your money I want. I called you here because you may be able to do a favour for me.'

'Well, if it is to our advantage, I'd be only glad to help you, Colonel Spiker. We all must help one another during these bad times.'

'Sip your whiskey and I'll tell you what I want.'

Kenrick drank some of the whiskey, feeling uncomfortable. Colonel Spiker meanwhile made a long speech concerning the state of the county and how he had information from the highest source that a rebellion was imminent and that land agents would be the first to suffer.

'If they burn the land agents' houses, then they will feel free and they will get others to follow them. The land agents will be the first to die. The whole county is riddled with secret

367

societies.' Colonel Spiker could see that this made Kenrick worried. He had a high regard for his own hide and no friends to protect him. 'Now, in an emergency you can come here for protection – no Whiteboy would dare trespass here – but in exchange I want a list of all the suspects in your area. You have a keen eye and you know who they are.'

Kenrick appreciated the reason for the friendly gesture, and it was in his own interest to give whatever information he had to this English colonel. It was also an opportunity to throw the Costellos under suspicion. He would have their names recorded in Dublin and make certain they were passed on to the police.

'Well, I have had my suspicions, Colonel Spiker, for a long time. The upper end of the valley, as we call it, is riddled with rebels waiting for a chance to move against us all.'

'Do they hold meetings?'

'Sure, they are always whispering and holding meetings. And they are not saying anything good about us.'

'Would you stand witness against them?'

'I would if it were in the interest of peace and law and order. I serve my sovereign to the best of my ability.'

'And you serve yourself first,' Colonel Spiker said directly, cutting across his pious pledges of loyalty to the Crown. 'Now, give me the names.'

Without hesitation Kenrick gave him the names of all the men in the upper part of the valley. He felt that each one was branded as Colonel Spiker wrote them down. He was going to add the name of Eileen Horkan but he refrained: she had too much power and she had destroyed Hackett; he must move cautiously in her regard.

'Well, our business is finished. We have no more to say, Mr Kenrick. I hope you will always prosper and enjoy your tumble in Shambles Lane.'

Kenrick realised that Colonel Spiker had used him and was planning to throw him aside. It was apparent that the colonel had a great deal of information about his activities.

The meeting had only taken twenty minutes, and as Kenrick made his way down the long avenue mulling over what had happened he grew angry at his humiliation. He had not enjoyed the drink. He would find out the soldiers and drink with them, and curse the colonel. He would drink and forget what had happened.

He made his way to the soldiers' bar. The soldiers entertained his company because he bought them drink and enjoyed their low company. Later in the evening he sang for them.

'And what will you do to the rebels, Kenrick?' they chorused when he had finished.

'I'll ram bayonets up their backsides and give a twist to their guts!' he cried drunkenly.

'And what else?' they called.

'I'll shove the muzzles of guns down their gullets and blow their backsides clean off them!'

Later he went with them to Shambles Lane, and it was dark when he sent to the stables for his horse. He was warm and satisfied. There was a clear moon above the town; it would brighten his path on the way home. He mounted the horse and moved sluggishly through the streets, dozing in the saddle. Outside the town the road began to ascend into the hills, which were now like the backs of sheep resting in flocks. They held a cold beauty under the moon. Soon the lights of the town were behind him and the hoofbeats of the horse were muffled by the snow.

Kenrick began to dream of Dublin whores. He shook himself awake periodically. Another half-hour and he would be home in bed.

All day Seamus Costello's palms had sweated. He rubbed them on his thighs, but the sweat of fear broke out again. At midday his resolution weakened, and he drank from the bottle of poteen he carried in his pocket. The town became a nightmare, and he felt that he was watched. Would some soldier notice that his eyes carried the thoughts of murder in them? The hours passed slowly.

'It must be done!' one of his fellow-conspirators said, 'and now is our chance. Don't jib now.'

'There will be a curse upon us. I don't think I have the stomach for it,' Seamus Costello replied.

'Well, think of all the empty stomachs in the valley. We will all take the blame. We will swear that you were with us on the lower road.'

Late in the evening they moved out of the town with their sacks of meal. At the fork in the road they parted company, and Seamus Costello made his way up into the hills with his pike. He continued to drink to keep himself warm and to exhilarate his mind. He found the spot he had picked, marked by a thick whin-bush, and concealed himself behind it. He began to get drunk as he waited. He looked at the countryside under the cold light of the moon: at another time it would have been beautiful.

In the distance he heard the horse, slow and dull, and the sound took him by surprise. He listened, swallowed the contents of the bottle and waited. Then he heard the heavy breathing of the horse. He gripped the pike firmly. His courage failed as he thought of the terrible deed he was about to commit, but he stifled his conscience and his imagination and rushed on to the road.

By instinct Kenrick jerked awake. He went for his gun. The startled horse took fright and reared. 'It's you . . .!' He tried to call out Seamus Costello's name but was given no chance. The pike was brought directly down on his skull. Seamus Costello felt the resistance of hard bone on the shaft of the pike. He wrenched it free. He prepared for another strike, but the horse bolted with Kenrick in the saddle. Seamus Costello ran from the scene, blundering across the fields to the village. He would find security there.

'I've committed murder! I have committed murder!' he kept repeating to himself. 'Will God ever forgive me?'

And then he realised that he was making tracks in the snow. They were leading directly to the village. He could be traced. He changed direction. He came to a stream. He entered the cold water and went home that way. The waters rushed about him and several times he fell into the dark pools, but forced himself to go forward.

Eventually he dragged himself from the stream and climbed up the bank on the edge of the village. Two men were waiting for him.

'Did you do it?' they asked.

'I think I did.'

'Did you splice him?'

'I couldn't say properly. The horse bolted carrying him on its back.'

'Then, we will have to sweat through the night and wait and wonder.'

The horse carried the body of Kenrick home. As the animal entered the door of the barn its burden fell off. The body was discovered next morning. His face had been eaten by rats.

The police discovered the murder weapon beside the whin-bush. There was an arc of blood on the blade, and blotches of blood diluted in the snow marked the direction taken by the horse. It was evident from the footmarks that the murder had been committed by a single person. The police, under Sergeant Huggins, followed the clear prints leading in the direction of a small village which appeared on the maps which they carried, but suddenly they curved away from it along the stream and disappeared. Sergeant Huggins sent several men downstream, but they could not locate the prints.

'He never emerged from the stream,' he announced to his men. 'I bet that he tried to destroy the marks he left behind with the same instinct as the fox. It is obvious that we move upstream.'

He checked the map again. There was another small village further upstream. It was clear to him that the murderer lived there – or had at least emerged from the stream at that spot.

They moved slowly towards the village searching the snow for marks, but they found only the prints of wild animals. They moved slowly forward, six men on either side of the stream. It was a crisp clear day, and the sky was intensely bright; only the scrunch of their heavy boots on the frozen snow broke the silence.

The police spoke only in disjointed phrases: they were large well-fed men, phlegmatic and dull. They had been drafted in from outside the county and they had no association with the people. They did their duty and received their pay and they knew that they would survive the famine.

By the afternoon they had reached the village. It consisted of twelve miserable hovels set irregularly to each other. The village was empty. Sergeant Huggins knew that everyone would be indoors, huddled together on rushes to avoid the cold. He looked at the chimneys where wisps of smoke issued from the stacks; like all other villagers they were starving slowly to death. The police moved up through the crooked muddy road, but there was no movement anywhere; not even a dog barked. Sergeant Huggins wondered, when he observed the

371

condition of the place, whether anybody here would have the motive or the strength for committing the murder. It had taken courage to do the deed; it seemed more than likely it had been organised by the Whiteboys.

Sergeant Huggins stood in the centre of the village and considered these things. But he knew in his mind that the murderer came from this village. He ordered a search of each house and was surprised to discover that they had reserves of food and money. He had checked with Kenrick's widow, but to her knowledge no money had been stolen from her dead husband and no food had been taken from the granary. She had been preparing for the wake when the policemen arrived on horseback and had showed little interest in their questions. For a moment Huggins thought that she might have arranged the death of her husband, but he stifled any suspicions.

Setting aside one house for his interrogations, Sergeant Huggins sat behind the only table in the village and began to question each individual. He spoke Irish to them, and this surprised them: they could not take refuge in the excuse that they did not know the English language. By the end of the day he thought he knew who had committed the murder. The men who had spent the day in Castlebar were the most likely suspects, but time and time again they were questioned separately and he could find no flaw in their story; it was too perfect.

He sat back and considered the problem. If he were to pick out one man from the whole village as the murderer, then it would be Seamus Costello. He was the obvious leader of this group of people and his eyes held intelligence, but they also held fear, and Sergeant Huggins was trained to recognise fear in a person not only by looking into their eyes but also by observing the movements of their fingers and their posture. The man was clearly under strain. It was only when he carefully checked two years' rents and those paid by the village and those paid by the 'lower ends' as they were called that the true reason for the murder emerged. It was obvious to him that Kenrick had rack-rented the village beyond their ability to pay him. No land could yield the amount of money handed over during the years.

'Why did you yield to this man Kenrick? Clearly with the amount of money handed over to him you could have emigrated to America. It is obvious that he wished you off the land,' Sergeant Huggins said to Seamus Costello.

'This land is ours. It was always ours as far as can be remembered. By some deed that I do not understand a lord in England buys it and sets Kenrick to collect the rents, and later he buys it himself. We were not always poor and hungry as we are today – I once had a dignified life and I enjoyed the pleasures of the hunt and the chase.'

Seamus Costello realised he had become too familiar with this policeman who had only one purpose in mind and that was to trap him in some way or another. He immediately withdrew into himself, and the brightness which had come into his eyes dulled.

Sergeant Huggins ordered his men to leave the room and eat the food they had brought with them. He was now left alone with Seamus Costello. The two men looked at each other. Seamus Costello knew that this man was suspicious of him; he saw that Huggins had more intelligence than the stolid policemen who dragged people from their cabins to be interrogated. With his subtlety he could achieve more than the others with their brutal heavy-handed gestures, and he must beware of him. He watched as the man picked imaginary dirt from beneath his fingernails. He placed a small silver article for cleaning his nails beside his papers and looked at him.

'They have all left now and so I have no witness to report our conversation. What is said between us will go unrecorded,' he began.

'I have nothing to say,' Seamus Costello told him bluntly, immediately breaking the easy confidence the sergeant thought he had established.

'Well, Mr Costello, let me put it straight to you. I cannot say that you are a murderer at this moment, but I can state that you are a thief.'

'I am not a thief!' Seamus Costello roared at him. 'All the money I have earned has been earned decently.'

'If you earned money decently and at the rates being paid by the Board of Works, then you would not be able to pay your rents. It is quite obvious to me that the money came from somewhere else. The only conclusion I can come to is that you are a thief.'

'I am not a thief!'

'The evidence supports the fact that you are.'

'I received it from a relation,' Costello blurted out and then realised he had made his first mistake. Eileen Horkan was now drawn into the web that this man was spinning, and in two more steps he would have her name and then all her private life would be brought out into the open. His assaults upon him were indirect.

'I must have the name of this relation. Obviously this could be some fiction. Everything has to be checked.' The sergeant poised his pencil.

'Her name is Eileen Horkan. Does she have to be dragged into this? She is a kind lady who has helped us during bad days.' Costello was ashamed.

'I am afraid that it is my business to ask questions, and sympathy is outside my domain. I have to see that the law is maintained.'

'Well, sir, you maintain a bad law if it permits people to die with the stores bulging with food.'

'I am in charge of law and order, not of food supplies. That lies with somebody else's conscience.'

'Conscience is dead, sir.'

'And is your conscience dead?'

That was the end of the conversation, and it had not gone well for Seamus Costello. The sergeant took up the silver instrument and continued to prise imagined dirt from beneath his nails; he knew he was questioning Kenrick's murderer.

Seamus Costello was not aware of the evening drawing in or of the cold as he returned to his cabin. His father and mother had prepared some warm gruel for him, and he ate it hungrily. His mind was racing forward. Only two men in the village apart from himself knew that he had committed the murder, and time and time again they had gone over the story they were to tell the police until they believed it themselves. He was satisfied with the story they had put together, but he wondered if they would break down under heavy questioning. Clearly this Sergeant Huggins was as sly as a fox and had none of the grossness of the policeman who guarded each cabin. He wished that he could speak with Eileen Horkan. Inadvertently he had drawn her into the investigation, and now she, too, would be subjected to questions and the private side of her life made public.

'Oh, but them policemen are well fed!' his mother told him. 'I saw the parcels of food they took from their leather satchels and it would keep three men going! Meat between bread. No wonder they are so big while the rest of us melt.'

'Stop your talking, woman,' his father said, 'and leave Seamus to his thoughts. He has had a hard day answering questions and is tired.'

'I was only remarking about the policemen's food. . . .'

'They are traitors, every one of them, and in the service to take the Queen's money. A soldier at least goes into battle – they just strut up and down the big towns and their eyes like the eyes of rats.'

His father and mother always argued. Eileen Horkan through her gifts had kept both of them alive, and they were unaware that he had committed murder to keep them in food.

'Well, I'll take my hat off to whoever killed that agent Kenrick. He was the devil's worst and he would have had us on the way to the workhouse come December,' his mother said.

'I hear the far ends are waking him. It won't be long until they realise that the threat of Kenrick is over and there will be no more licking up to him. Perhaps we will get a fair agent now who will give justice to all,' the father replied.

'Stop that soft talk!' Seamus said in anger. 'Don't you know that the job of any agent is to bleed the people dry? He will be replaced by another and, if he's killed, by another still. I'm going to lie down. I'm tired.'

He went to the back room and lay on the rushes. There was darkness about him and the room was cold. His imagination was in turmoil and he could not impose any order on his thoughts. Each time he banished the image of Kenrick from his mind and tried to think of something else, it returned again. Kenrick was always riding towards him, and he had always the pike raised to bring it down on the man's skull. He felt the shudder of iron on bone run through his arms and he was aware of hot blood on the blade. He could never clear the image from his head.

He had committed the first sin. Man had not changed since Adam was banished from the garden. The first sin had been murder, and he had committed it and would carry the mark of it for ever. He thought of Castlebar prison: he had passed it many a time and once he had witnessed a public hanging.

375

Now he saw his own head in a noose and the hangman placing the bag over his head. Justice was summary in Castlebar, and there was little time given to a man between conviction and hanging. Sergeant Huggins would be the person who would finally catch him in some way or other.

'It is only a matter of time,' he said to himself. 'It is only time he wants. He knows that I did it. I could see it in his eyes and in the way that he dug under his nails with the silver knife as if there was no injustice and no anger. He knows I did it. He will have me swing for it.'

He slept little during the night, and if he did sleep it was only intermittently. Always the face of Kenrick returned to haunt him. He began to sweat. It was the cold primal sweat of fear and it ran down his shoulder-blades and between the cleft of his backside.

Outside, the policemen kept guard of the cabins. There was no communication between people, and they wondered what was happening. The two neighbours who were party to the murder also had nightmares. They wondered why Seamus Costello had spent so long with Sergeant Huggins. Had he betrayed them? Had he implicated them in the murder? They were innocent – they had not killed Kenrick, it was Seamus Costello who had first put the idea into their heads. If he had left them alone, they would never have thought of the idea. Their allegiance and their confidence began to weaken. They went over the story they had given to the police. It was evidence now against them. They wondered if it had any flaws. They began to question it in their minds. Could they recall the details as they had been set down? They were not certain. If only they could speak with Seamus Costello. They paced up and down the mud floors of their cabins. They could always save themselves by going directly to the sergeant and telling him the true story – he seemed a compassionate type of man. They would get free transportation out of the country for giving king's evidence and they would live. They would be fed while they gave the evidence and they would be fed during the voyage to Australia or to America.

Sergeant Huggins called aside his men before he left the village. He told them that no one was free to leave the houses and that there should be no communication between people before the investigation ended. They only understood part of his intentions. He knew that at that moment the men who had been party to the murder were in turmoil. The presence of a uniformed force in the village would have its effect upon them, for nothing terrorised the peasantry as much as men in uniform. In his opinion he would have solved the murder in a week.

When his horse had been brought around by the long road, he set off to interview Eileen Horkan. He would have to make his report to Colonel Spiker in the morning.

He felt secure as he rode out of the valley: his large cape kept out the cold and he had time to reflect. With this case solved he might get promotion to Dublin. He would bring his children to that city and perhaps give them the education which he lacked. There would be openings for them in the law offices and the banks. He had no intention of spending the rest of his life in an overpopulated county, where Irish was the common language of the people and where there was no opportunity for anyone.

Sergeant Huggins was surprised at the poise of the woman who opened the door. He knew by instinct that he would not overawe her and that he could not clean his nails in her presence.

'Good evening, my dear lady,' he began in his most obsequious voice. 'Excuse me for calling at this late hour but I wonder if I could have a few words with you?'

Eileen Horkan retained her calm disposition. 'Certainly,' she told him and directed him to an armchair by the fire, taking one opposite him. As he looked at her by the lamp-light he became aware of her great beauty. He was also aware of the books lining one of the walls, and realised he was in the presence of someone of culture; it always put him in a weak position.

'Well, sir,' she said formally, 'what can I do for you?' She looked directly into his eyes.

'I have reason to believe that you have handed over sums of money to one called Seamus Costello?' he said, taking out his notebook and flicking through it. It gave him a sense of importance to flick through a notebook.

'And what business of that is yours, sir? I can dispose of my money in whatever way I like.'

'I know that, ma'am. I know that. But he mentioned your name with regard to large sums of money he paid over to the murdered land agent, Kenrick, and we were quite surprised that such sums were made available to him.'

'And why do you ask these questions?'

'People are rarely so generous.'

'Your people are not so generous, but I bear blood relationship to the man.'

'And where, ma'am, did you acquire such sums of money?' He thought that this question might break this rigid coldness she had towards him.

'Sir! You outstep yourself. You imply that I am some sort of thief, that I do not possess that type of money?'

'No, ma'am. I did not imply that you were a thief.' He was nervous now. He had handled this badly and began to seethe with anger and a sense of humiliation.

'Sir, you did! Suffice it to say that I handed him the sums of money. I do not think that we have any more to say. Good night!' She rose directly, took the light and directed him towards the door.

Eileen felt ill when she returned to her room. There had been rumours of Kenrick's murder all over the countryside. Many had said that the Whiteboys had committed the crime, but she knew in her heart that the organisation had not been strong enough to carry out such a deed. Then she thought of Seamus Costello. He was so filled with hatred of Kenrick that he was capable of doing it.

She began to cry: she was certain that Seamus Costello had committed the murder. The world that had once been full of joy and promise was ugly and falling apart. Soon her pregnancy would be obvious to all, and she wondered if she should follow Lord Lannagh's advice and go to England. He would protect her there, and she would live in the delightful house he had promised her. The famine was now in full spate and the evils of the world were loosed.

She left the house and saddled her horse and rode down towards the village. There was a bonfire burning in the village street. Policemen had gathered about it and were warming their hands. She rode up to the fire.

'Could I speak to some of the people?' she asked.

'No, ma'am. Our orders are to let no one out of the village or into the village. Be on your way or we may hold you as a suspect.'

'Suspect?' she asked, holding herself rigid.

'Yes. I'm afraid that the murderer came from this village.'

'Have you proof?'

'No, ma'am, but we soon will have.'

She turned her horse and rode away from the fire and up through the valley which had now become the scene of a tragedy far greater than the death of Kenrick. She wondered what perverse news the following weeks would bring.

33

THE NEWS OF KENRICK'S DEATH began to spread through the county. Fear gripped the agents. They no longer moved openly through the countryside. Even the large farmers and the merchants barricaded themselves into their houses at night and slept with guns primed.

Colonel Spiker was aware of the rumours. Landowners had come to him quietly during the evenings or sent letters to him seeking protection. He was impressed by the sense of power he now generated; the landowners no longer looked to the scattered forces of the police. Spiker had hand-picked Sergeant Huggins to deal with the crime – he had read a report on his work in the county and he knew that he was both shrewd and devious. The combination of the two qualities attracted him.

He sat in his room and decided what course of action to follow. He could have extended the net of suspects and drawn in every revolutionary sympathiser in the county, but this would not have served his own overriding purpose. He must draw the Burkes and the Frenchman into open conflict and settle his old score with them. This recent murder must be kept local; it must be seen as an agrarian crime and the culprit must receive summary justice. Agrarian crimes were usually local and brutal.

Sergeant Huggins visited him as soon as he arrived in Castlebar. His face was unshaven, and he was obviously tired after his journey. Usually he presented himself at the barracks in an immaculate condition.

'You need sleep, Sergeant,' the colonel said immediately.

'You told me to come straight away with any information I had,' Sergeant Huggins reminded him wearily.

'And have you discovered the culprit?'

'I think so. But it will take time to break him.'

'And how do you propose to do that?'

Sergeant Huggins explained how he had set his men to guard the village and how he had isolated each house. 'They cannot consult each other, and this gives us the advantage. I have seen men break under such isolation. They will be brought to Castlebar within the next two days and kept in separate cells. If necessary, we can use some rough methods upon them. A few of my men know how to get information from men that they would not normally give.'

Colonel Spiker did not ask for the name of the murderer. Instead he took out a map of the area and spread it in front of him. He studied it for some time.

'Believe it or not, I have a statement here from Kenrick on the day he was murdered. Do not enquire how I obtained it, but I have men everywhere. I would hazard a guess that the murderer is a man called Seamus Costello.'

Sergeant Huggins was taken aback. There was a look of surprise on his face when Colonel Spiker raised his eyes from the folio on his desk.

'That is correct! How did you guess?'

'It was not a guess, it was an assumption. And we are dealing not with a political murder, but with an agrarian one. We must keep it local. I want that man broken within the next three days. I do not wish to have these rumours continue. Daily I receive letters from landlords and landowners for protection. This man must be brought to justice and he must be hanged. Do you think you can do it?'

Sergeant Huggins thought for some minutes. He would have to use some rough tactics, but he knew he could obtain a confession within three days. 'What is done to these men in the cells must be kept secret,' he said slowly. 'I do not wish to have my name associated with rough justice. I would be a marked man. And if I do succeed in bringing him to justice I wish for a transfer to Dublin – I do not think that I could continue my work here.'

'Bring this man to justice and I will recommend you for a transfer,' Spiker said, almost carelessly.

Sergeant Huggins left the barracks. He walked down the long walled avenue and reflected upon what he had now to do. His whole career depended on the outcome of this investigation. A quick transfer to Dublin would advance his ambitions more rapidly than he had planned.

His wife was waiting for him when he returned home. They were firm in their ambitions for their children, the source of the rough love they had for each other. She was as ambitious as he was and as secretive of what went on in the county. She was the only person he could trust. He sat in the kitchen and talked with her, and watched the delight flood her face as he told her the bargain he had struck with Colonel Spiker.

'We'll be out of here yet! I've come a long way from the village of Crom and not without your help.'

'You had it in your head, Dan. I always said that you had it in your head. Given a chance you would be sitting on the bench handing down the law instead of standing cap in hand waiting to be called on to give evidence.' She was excited at the prospect of leaving for Dublin. It would be the fulfilment of her wishes. She had worked as a servant at one of the Protestant houses and she had picked up the manners and the behaviour of her superiors. This she intended to put to good use in the future when her sons and daughters were growing up.

'And there will be no word of Irish in this house. It kept people back too long and kept them ignorant,' she told him a long time ago. She had never permitted her husband to speak Irish in the house. She had banished the tongue for ever. It was her hope that none of her children would ever know a word of it. To her it was the stigma of the poor and the peasantry.

'Here, Dan. Mrs Greevy brought me four eggs this morning and I put them on for you. She said she would never forget the favour you did for her.'

She placed four soft-boiled eggs in front of him and watched as he unbuckled his thick belt so that it would not impede his enjoyment. He knocked off the top of the first egg with a deft stroke. He dropped a blob of butter on it and watched it melt over the yolk. Then with two scoops he ate the egg.

'We'll make it yet, Dan,' his wife whispered.

He did not hear her. He was concentrating on the enjoyment of the second egg. Later he ate some bread and drank two large mugs of tea. His body was warm and comfortable, and when he was ready he asked her upstairs. Outside it was a cold day, but in the comfort of the bed and with the warm body of his wife beside him he forgot that his men were standing guard about the village and that three men were almost sick with apprehension in the small cabins. He was fortunate that he could lock out the harsher aspects of his work when he lay in bed.

At the far end of the valley news was passed quickly from house to house. Some had ventured to the top of the valley to observe the policemen, but a shot fired over their heads had dispersed them and they had rushed home. It was evident to them that the Costellos must be suspected of murder.

'Well, they will all hang and there might be more land to go about. Kenrick once said he would destroy them, and it's strange that his own death will be the cause of their downfall.'

They had hated Kenrick as much as the Costellos, but it was in their interest to be subservient. They had been his workmen and his tools, and he had abused them in his time. But they had suffered his injustice patiently. Now they could take delight in his death and in the trouble he had brought to the Costellos. The next agent would be more careful.

They were not yet finished with Kenrick. Now that he was dead he owed them a turn. Now that he was dead he would pay back some of his blood money. They laid their plans.

Very few came to Kenrick's wake. Candles burned about the coffin in the large kitchen. Kenrick's head had been bandaged, and only the lower part of his face could be seen. It was significant that the rats had got him, they thought to themselves. Every man gets the end he deserves, and the rats had had their own wake about his body.

His wife, who was from outside the valley, had been an ineffectual figure during his life and was now an ineffectual figure after his death. She sat at the head of the coffin and stared in front of her. She was still in a state of shock. She had discovered the dead body and was the first to look down upon the half-eaten face. She had been a chattel most of her life and she had little love for the man who was dead, but she wondered how she would make out now that she was alone. She was confused about his money and his possessions.

Very few of the men who had worked in the yards and in the fields came to pay their respects. When some of them did come it was only to remain for a few minutes and then depart. They had not the charity to pray for the repose of his soul in death. Now that they were certain that Kenrick was dead, the grip of fear in which he had held the valley was loosening, and they wondered how he had gained control over them so that they woke from dreams at night calling out his name.

The women from the lower end of the valley sat with Bridie Kenrick all night. They cried over the dead as was customary and drank his whiskey and made his widow drink to kill her grief. The sound of their wailing filled the kitchen and could be heard in the yard.

Bridie Kenrick drank the whiskey to forget the image of the half-eaten face. She became sleepy during the vigil and nodded by the coffin. And all night, while the women so noisily waked Kenrick, the men from the lower end of the valley broke into the granary. Furtively they crept up the outside stone stairs and took the bags of oats and barley, carrying them on their backs to their homes. It took them eight hours to remove them. Later they muzzled the pigs and carried them away to be killed and salted. The blood was drawn away and mixed with gruel. The entrails were boiled and eaten. They secreted the barrels of bacon in bog holes. Finally they took Kenrick's horse. This was the horse which had carried the dead body to the cobbled yard. It, too, was killed and the hide buried in a bog. The horse meat also was salted.

'It will see us over the worst months of the famine,' they told each other at morning light when the night's work was finished. 'But we're not finished with him yet,' they said.

In the morning the women suddenly left, and Bridie Kenrick was left alone. She awoke from her drunken sleep to see eight men standing about the coffin. They were from the lower end of the valley. She thought they had come to carry the coffin to the graveyard.

'Have you come to bury him?' she asked.

'Why should *we* bury the bastard? He's dead and he can't give us orders any more.' They had sullen hateful faces.

'What will I do?' she asked.

'You can sit beside him until he rots if you like, or you can pay us to dig his grave and carry him to the graveyard. But we won't do it without silver and gold crossing our palms.'

'I don't know where he kept the money,' she said desperately.

'Well, you lived with him long enough to know. If you want a burial, you will pay hard for it as he made us work hard for anything he gave us.'

'How much?'

'A sovereign a man, and there are eight of us. Four to dig the grave and four to coffin and carry him.'

Her mind was in confusion, and she felt shame at her humiliation. 'I'll see if I can find it.'

She recalled that the clock on the mantelpiece had often been a little out of line in the morning-times when she rose to clean the house. He had told her not to touch it, and she never had. Now she realised that he had kept his money there. She went over to the mantelpiece and pushed the clock to one side. There was an opening in the wall. She put in her hand and took out a soft leather bag with a thong about the neck. 'I'll have that,' one of the men said and snatched it from her hand. Sovereigns flashed from the mouth of the purse and scattered over the corpse and the floor. Quickly they collected them, digging down between the body and the side of the coffin to find those which might have lodged there.

'Put him out on the floor,' one of them ordered.

They took the body and placed it on the floor. They searched the lining of the empty coffin until they had recovered the lost sovereigns.

'It's no use burying them with him – he'll have no use for them where he's going!' they said, laughing. They took the body and threw it back in the coffin and counted the money. The bag had contained twenty-four sovereigns.

'We are charging three sovereigns each for the burial,' they told her.

At midday the coffin was brought out of the door of the kitchen. The four men lifted it on their shoulders and they moved forward towards the graveyard.

'He's a light bugger,' one of them said as they moved forward. Bridie Kenrick followed her murdered husband's body. Women who had cried over the corpse the night before now cursed her from their cabin doors.

'May he burn and rot in hell!' they called. 'And may his bastard children spit on his grave!'

Bridie Kenrick was an outcast now, and she wondered what she would do. Later she only recollected part of the journey to the cemetery and some of the curses that were hurled both upon her and her dead husband; she had not earned the humiliation she was now enduring. Not even the policemen who had come to question her on the morning after the murder came down from the far end of the valley to give her their sympathy. Somebody threw a stone at the coffin. It made a dull thud on the timber and fell at her feet.

With little ceremony they placed the coffin in the grave, shovelling the soil down on it as if they were burying a diseased animal. They did not even pat the mound of clay into shape when they were finished. They took their spades, turned their backs on her and left the graveyard. She looked at them as they left. These were the men who would have crawled on the ground at her husband's wish.

She returned home. At least the women were not at the doors of their cabins to curse her. She entered the yard and realised immediately that the pigs were missing. The granary door flapped freely in a small wind. She mounted the small stairs and looked in. It was empty.

'They have stolen everything,' she repeated to herself. 'They have left me with nothing.'

She went indoors and sat over the fire. She recalled the sad features of her life. She had never known either love or affection. Her father, in all respects, had sold her to Kenrick. She had cost him thirty pounds, the price of a good horse. She had been beaten and abused in the empty kitchen in which she sat and she had been humiliated on the way to the graveyard.

Later, she stirred herself. She considered what she might do. Kenrick's clothes were lying in a bloody bundle in the pantry. She would burn them and rid herself of his presence, but before she threw them in the fire she searched his pockets. They contained only small coins. Then she felt something oblong in one of the sleeves. She found a hidden pocket, put her finger in it and took out a notebook. She brought it over to the window and looked at it. It was a bank-book. She had never seen it before. She could only read English with difficulty, but she was not interested in the words, only in the figures which ran down the right-hand side of each page. She flicked to the final page. It carried the date of his death. Above the date was the amount of money lodged to him in the bank in Castlebar. She examined the figure twice and she knew at that moment that she was a rich woman.

'They can have their pigs and meal,' she said out loud, 'and may they choke upon them.'

Next day she walked the back road to Castlebar, passing the spot where her husband had been murdered without offering a single prayer for the repose of his soul. She walked up the town and went directly to the bank. The manager told her that she was the rightful heir to the money and that it would be made available to her.

'I want enough to keep me in comfort for a week in Castlebar,' she told him.

With the money she took lodgings and never returned to the house in the valley. She showed little interest in the news which quickly passed through the town on Wednesday. A man named Seamus Costello had been accused of the murder of her husband. He was in Castlebar prison awaiting trial.

The night was long and fragmented for Seamus Costello. Several times he had gone to the small window and looked at the great fire in the centre of the village. The policemen wrapped in cloaks stood about it, shadowy figures half-realised by the flames. The snow on the roofs was turned livid by the light.

His mind was empty. The doubts which nagged him and the images which flooded his mind had exhausted him and he felt limp and spent. During earlier days when he was robust and had not been ravaged by hunger he could have sustained his mind against depression. Now it was not so. His face was haggard, and he felt that his neighbours would break down under the isolation now imposed upon them. The heavy sergeant with the white nails knew his work. There was a sly look in his eyes.

Meanwhile in the other cabins the isolation was taking its effect upon his two neighbours. One of the policemen had knocked upon the door of Pete Costello at twelve o'clock and asked to see him alone. He was the weakest character of the three, and the policeman was following Sergeant Huggins's instructions when he called. There was fear in the man's eyes, and he knitted his fingers nervously.

'I have nothing to say! I have nothing to say! I'll stand by the story,' he blurted out, without being asked.

'Well, I hope the others hold to the same story or *you* may swing in Castlebar shortly.'

'What do you mean? What do you mean? They haven't changed the story?'

'I'll say nothing. We have our suspicions. I think we know what happened that night.'

'The three of us came straight home from town, that's what happened.' Pete Costello looked wildly about him.

'That's what you are supposed to say happened. But now we know that one of you broke away and headed into the hills. That was the one who committed the murder. Very soon his name will be known and he will be brought to Castlebar.'

'I had no hand, act or part in whatever went on.'

'That's not what the other two said.'

'Have they made statements?'

'They have.'

'What did they say?'

'I have to keep my mouth closed in these matters, but I'll say this: you have few friends in the place.'

He left the house. Pete Costello called to his wife: 'They have split on me, Sal. The two have split on me,' he cried.

'What do you mean?'

'They have changed the story. I'd swear they have ganged against me and named me as the one who committed the murder!'

'What about murder?' Sal asked.

'Seamus Costello killed Kenrick. Sure, he didn't come home with us at all that night!'

His wife shook him. 'What happened?' she asked.

He told her the whole story. It had been boiling in his head, and he had to tell somebody.

'The three of you will surely swing for this,' she told him.

'I'll give evidence against them.'

'Hold your tongue! How do you know they have put the blame on you?'

'I know it, I know it! They are out to save their own skins.'

'Tell me the whole story again,' she said.

He controlled himself and told her the story. She listened carefully. She had held a grudge against Seamus Costello ever since she married into the village, but it had remained controlled until now.

'Confess to what happened,' she urged, seizing her chance. 'Make a deal with them. There is no blood upon your hands. Make a deal to get out of the country. It has been done before – both of us can leave and have a decent life in America if you make a deal!'

'No, I'll make no deal. I'll not say what happened that night. They are getting at me.' He recovered his composure. The other two would not change the story. They had set a trap for him, and he had almost walked into it. He must remain calm.

It was a cold dawn. There had been frost during the night, and the snow was crusted. The policemen let the fire in the village street die. They marched up and down to warm their feet. The ring of their heavy boots echoed off the gables of the houses. They whispered amongst themselves.

At ten o'clock the first cart arrived in the village. Pete Costello was taken from his cottage with his hands tied and brought away.

'I didn't do it! I had no act or part in it,' he called as the cart trundled away. Soon his voice was lost in the vastness of the snow. He began to shake with fear. No words were spoken to him by the driver or the policeman who sat beside him.

'They have split on me,' he told himself. 'They have split on me.'

He felt isolated. He had never been out of the village alone. He felt intimidated by the white and empty landscape created by the snow. He tried to talk to the policeman, but he only looked stolidly ahead.

'Am I the only one they are bringing in? Are there others?' he asked. He did not answer him.

They moved up through Castlebar. The houses seemed to crowd in upon him. This was a foreign place with foreign ways. He wished he were at home.

They made their way up Church Hill and did not stop until they reached the gaol. The huge gates creaked open to admit

389

the cart, then they closed behind him. A large courtyard stretched out before him, covered with snow, footprints showing the dividing paths. He stared at the grim barred windows, and fear tightened his heart. He was weak and hungry. The men beside him held their silence. He was taken from the cart by two warders and brought through a series of corridors. He soon lost his direction.

'I did no wrong!' he called out. 'I'm no murderer. Look for another.'

They stopped in front of a narrow iron gate. The warder unlocked it with a great key, pulled the bolt back and pushed Pete into the darkness of the cell. His mind became prey to doubts as he sat there: the police had not taken the step without evidence; they knew something more than the story the three men had fabricated. He went back upon each word the policeman had said in the kitchen.

A small window at ground level and above him let in some light as his eyes became accustomed to the small damp cell. 'I could walk out of here to the scaffold,' he told himself. 'I'm party to the murder.' He wrung his hands in anguish. He wished that he had died from the hunger.

An hour later Peader Costello arrived at the gaol. He had been grim-faced during the journey. Doubts also assailed his mind, but he held firmly to his silence. He spoke no word as they led him through the corridors and when they closed the iron door upon him. He would hang rather than betray Seamus Costello.

Eileen Horkan stood at the window and watched the road leading out of the valley. She recognised the first figure in the cart as it passed by, the wheels sliding in the snow. She waited for the third cart. Before it passed she knew it carried Seamus Costello to gaol. She saw his figure bent between the driver and the policeman. Then, as it passed the house, he turned towards the window as if he knew she was looking at him. His face was haggard and worn, the face of an old man. Penury and hardship had destroyed him.

Now that the men had been taken to the prison, Sergeant Huggins returned to the village. The old men and the women were brought to the house to be interviewed. He sat calmly behind the table, well rested and his mind alert. He wished to see if the isolation of the night had yielded any fruit.

The people passed through the room, tight-lipped and hungry. He knew when Sal Costello entered the room that his first break in the case had come.

'Well, good woman,' he began. 'You are the wife of the prisoner, Pete Costello. He is now in solitary confinement in Castlebar.'

'Will he be hanged?' she asked, trembling.

'They may all be hanged. The evidence is against them. Of course, they don't *all* have to hang. Clemency can be shown on occasions. In fact we can sometimes offer more than clemency. We can offer good money for information.'

'How much?' she asked quickly.

'Enough to get a prisoner and his wife to America to start a new life there.' The sergeant's eyes were wily.

'How is one sure of that?' she asked warily.

'I can write out a guarantee,' he told her.

She considered the position for some moments. She must get her hands on money, but she could not rely on the word of the sergeant. 'I'll not give evidence here,' she said eventually. 'I want to be taken to Castlebar and I want to see one of them solicitor men. They know all the tangles of things.'

'Do you wish to be taken to Castlebar?' he asked in surprise.

'I do, for I'm finished in this place and I don't belong here any more. I never belonged here.'

'Is your evidence worth money?'

'I can tell you what happened on the night, and that is surely something you want to know, but I won't do it without a solicitor man with me and money on the table.'

Sergeant Huggins considered his position. He was anxious to close the case and bring the murderer to justice. This woman with her evidence could give him the small details which would break the confidence of the three.

'Very well. I'll have you brought immediately to Castlebar. Go to your house and collect whatever you wish. I do not think you will be returning here.'

With her cloak drawn about her head, Pete Costello's wife went to her cabin and bundled her few belongings into a bag. A cart drew up beside the cabin door, and she threw them into the back. She mounted the seat beside the driver, and he drove the cart away from the village. Instinctively the people knew what was happening. They rushed from the cottages, gathered stones from the village street and threw them after her. Their curses followed her down the road.

The solicitor listened to Sal Costello's story in his office. He understood Irish and he also understood the offer she had made to him. She would give him a quarter of all she could obtain from Sergeant Huggins.

In the meantime Huggins had visited Colonel Spiker and told him that he could come into the possession of valuable evidence but that he would have to purchase it.

'How important do you think it is?' Spiker asked.

'As far as I can judge I can break two of them with what she has to offer. The one that I suspected broke. His name is Pete Costello. He told his wife what happened the night we isolated the village.'

'And she has a lawyer who is drawing up legal documents?'

'Yes.'

'These peasants are cunning.' And treacherous when they turn on themselves, Spiker added silently. 'I will place one hundred sovereigns at your disposal. Let them make the offer. And remember the promise I made to you.'

'Yes, Colonel. I'll be on my way immediately.'

The lawyer and Sal Costello faced Sergeant Huggins and another police officer across a table. Before him the lawyer had a signed confession with Sal Costello's mark at the bottom of it. He knew that the sergeant had been in communication with Colonel Spiker: he had sent his young assistant after him and he had followed him to the barracks.

'We can break the case without this evidence, of course,' the sergeant began, but the lawyer did not let him pursue his statement.

'The very fact that you make such an admission means that you may not break the case, so let's assume that this is the best evidence that is going to come into your possession. Let us also assume that you wish to establish that this is an agrarian murder and not a political one. It will put paid to the rumours which are circulating about the town. This evidence is worth two hundred sovereigns – take it or leave it.' The solicitor sat there with a placid face and watched Sergeant Huggins. Clearly he had not expected such a figure to be mentioned.

'No, I cannot make such an offer,' he said at last. 'I could offer you perhaps a hundred. Two hundred I could not offer.'

'Then, there is no bargain. This woman's future and the future of her husband depend on whatever money she receives. It is my business to ensure that my client receives her just reward.'

Sergeant Huggins wondered what deal they had worked out between them. It was certainly in the lawyer's interest to obtain the largest sum he could. 'Excuse me, I must leave the room and take counsel.' He returned much later with an offer of one hundred and fifty sovereigns. 'But I must hear the statement before I part with the money,' he insisted.

'No,' said the lawyer. 'It is my legal opinion that it is worth the sum mentioned.'

'Very well, then,' Sergeant Huggins said. He brought the money, which was counted out on the table. The signed document was handed to him. Sergeant Huggins left the office immediately.

'It was a good day's work, sir, on your part,' Sal Costello told the solicitor when they had divided the money.

'Good day, ma'am. Our business is finished,' he said without emotion and showed her to the door. He had got what he could out of this woman and wanted no more of her presence.

She walked out into the street with a great amount of money in her possession and with little knowledge of the world about her.

That night Pete Costello broke. For five hours he had been threatened and cajoled. He knew now that his wife might have signed a document in the possession of the police. In the presence of three witnesses he confessed to all that had happened on the day and the night of the crime. He wept as he put his mark to the confession document.

'I have no dignity left. You have taken it from me. It would have been better had I died. Where can I go to now? I'll always carry the mark of the traitor on me.'

They left him to weep. Two days later the papers carried the news that Seamus Costello was to stand trial for the murder of the agent Kenrick. He was described as a small cottier who lived in a valley named Glen Cullen.

34

MYLES PRENDERGAST remained on at the great house. The house, firm and classical, which Michael Barrett had built to be the residence of his descendants, was now quiet. At night the lights glowed in the windows, and it had a warm and comfortable appearance in the darkness. The lights falling upon the snow turned it into soft gold.

The house had revolved about the life and humours of Michael Barrett, and the Christmas season had always been celebrated with great joy and much noise. For two weeks before the great Christmas meal in the dining-room, the servants had dusted and cleaned the house, polishing the silver and hanging chains of holly along the walls. During December each fireplace, burning oak from Eisirt wood, kept the house warm against the cold and the damp. On St Stephen's Day there was a continual stream of visitors to the house. In former years there had been a hundred small rituals to attend to; now the house was strangely silent. There was no excited flurry amongst the servants.

'The place is like a dead house,' Mrs Jennings told her son. 'Not a visitor has called since Michael Barrett died, except that stranger – and nobody seems to know why he's here and what he's doing, except bewitching the young mistress's heart.'

'Won't we have no big Christmas like we had last year when I got drunk?' her son asked Mrs Jennings.

'That depends on the lady of the house. I don't think that she is in any humour for parties. I approached her the other day, and she snapped my nose off. How can we have parties and the whole countryside starving?'

'I think she's taken by this stranger, Mother. They walk a lot in the woods, and one day I saw him putting his arms around her and squeezing her hard. I thought he was going to strangle her!'

'The man who will soften Gráinne Barrett's heart, son, has yet to be born. You have seen her ride a horse and you have heard the stories of her voyage to America. She climbed the mast during a storm and went out along a spar to reef a sail – and the wind at sixty miles an hour! The master of that woman has yet to be born.'

'Well, Mother, judging by what I saw in the wood, the stranger has mastered her.'

'And did you see anything else, son?'

'I'm ashamed to tell you, Mother.'

'Tell your mother, son.'

'He was kissing her, and cuddling her like you would cuddle the infant.'

'Or did she kiss him, son?'

'I don't know. You are confusing me, Mother.'

It was a time of lassitude for Gráinne Barrett. Her mind was exhausted by the responsibilities of the house which lay heavy on her. She had a fire set in the map room each morning and she spent her days looking out of the window at the sea and the islands. Sometimes she took down a map from the racks and spread it out before her, but she soon lost interest and returned to her seat at the window. The days were aimless, the seas about the islands sluggish.

She was disturbed by the experience of love with its summer qualities. When she reflected on the death of her father, she also thought of Myles Prendergast, who had come into her life so unexpectedly. Sitting by the window she would listen for the sound of horse's hoofs on the snow, and when she heard them she would look expectantly to the avenue to see if Myles was returning from one of his journeys, wrapped in his great black cloak. He was always cold after his travels, and his mind was disturbed by the starvation and death he saw about him. He was angry at the little he could do.

The hours they spent in the library before the great fire were the most idyllic she had spent in her life. It was an unreal world, and she knew that it could not endure. She drew Myles Prendergast's mind away from the immediate thoughts of the famine, and he told her of his travels through Europe. He had visited Germany and Italy and had a feeling for the political changes taking place in men's minds.

'There is a new spirit growing all over Europe,' he would say, taking her hands between his. 'The Germans take greater pride in their myths and their native music. The myths stir them and give them an undefined unity. The Italians have no such myths, but they have the sun and the warmth and open hearts. The Germans are more inward and mystical, and mystics can be dangerous people. I walked through Germany and I walked through Italy, staying at the small isolated villages where life has not changed since the Middle Ages. They are pleasant untroubled places.' The conversation was not always so political. Sometimes, when he was warmed by wine, he sang the songs he had learned in the villages where time had stood still. They had been unaffected by all the revolutionary changes. Europe was an old place. Great armies had marched across it in each century, and each field and furrow had been drenched with soldiers' blood. It was old and mature and settled.

'That is why I often think I should go to America. Imagine setting the plough to land which has never been turned before! Imagine the clean air blowing across a thousand miles! The human spirit would be renewed there.'

'My father, too, had dreams of America,' Gráinne said. 'He, too, was weighed down by the poverty and the hardship of the people. He built the warehouses at Northport in the hope that the town might bring employment and dignity. This, he said, was the land of the dispossessed. All the great families were once driven across the Shannon to be imprisoned by that great stretch of water. Connaught is an impoverished place. That is why he thought of building a great mansion in America beside some great river and beginning his life all over again.'

'Why do you not pick up your belongings and leave?'

'Because I feel I owe some obligation to the people,' she said fiercely.

Their conversation always returned in the end to the famine.

'It is difficult to realise that outside the walls of this estate people lack the necessary food to live. And what can I do?' she asked. 'Can I sell the house and give the money to the poor? If I put it up for sale, who would buy it?'

'That is not the answer. People will have to emigrate. The land cannot sustain them.'

The heavy days ended with the news of Kenrick's murder. The kitchen and the pantry were rife with rumours. Some said that the Whiteboys were to account for it, others that he was shot several times; others maintained that he had been felled by a sudden blow. The gory details soon appeared in the paper.

The county was in panic for many days. The agents travelled under heavy escort, and the landlords demanded that the culprits should be immediately traced. Decent people assumed that this was a single incident and not the signal for a general rising.

'What does this mean to your plan, Myles?' Gráinne asked.

'It may help a great deal. It has shaken the authorities, and Spiker has given orders that he wants an immediate arrest. In fact, despite his crippling disability, he has visited many of the big houses to assure the landlords that they are safe, and he has billeted soldiers in the outhouses. He has been seen, too, in the towns in his coach.'

'If this fear grows, then Spiker will have to draft in troops from Galway surely,' said Gráinne.

'That would make for greater unease. The whole province could be affected. No, the murderer will be quickly caught and quickly hanged. It is obvious from what I heard that it was the work of one man. He left his traces in the snow.'

The next day as they sat in the great room overlooking the avenue they saw a coach approaching, flanked by four horsemen.

'Good God, Spiker!' Myles said, jumping to his feet.

'You should fly, Myles. You can escape through the court-yard and make your way through the woods.' Gráinne paced the room wildly.

'No. That would draw attention to myself, and it would place both you and the house in danger. I will sit here and make no move. If we have to fight them, you know where the new revolvers are and you know how to use them. I cannot endanger our plans.'

Myles watched, fascinated, as Spiker descended from the carriage. One of the soldiers tried to help him, but he brushed his hand aside. His body was bent, and he walked with great pain. As he made his way up the steps one of the soldiers knocked on the great door.

'Colonel Spiker to see the owners of the house,' he announced when a servant opened it.

Gráinne was waiting in the hall. She invited Spiker into the library.

'My cousin, Edward Barrett,' Gráinne said, introducing Myles to the colonel.

'It is my pleasure to meet you, Mr Barrett,' Spiker said with elegance and sat down. It was evident that he was embarrassed by his injuries and found that the great armchair he had chosen concealed them. There was a cold glitter in his eyes as he looked at Myles as if observing every detail of his person. Myles looked at his enemy. A small nervous twitch on his right cheek made his face sinister.

'I believe that you had a bereavement in the house recently,' he began, turning to Gráinne.

'Yes, my father died.'

'So I heard. He had reached a great age and died peacefully. Not everyone is granted the gift of dying peacefully in their bed during these uncertain times,' Spiker commented, turning towards Myles Prendergast. 'Would you not agree, Mr Barrett?'

'Are the times uncertain, Colonel?' Myles asked.

'Not in England and France, but they may be uncertain here. However, I can assure you that we have the situation under control. At this very moment a suspect is being questioned for the murder of the agent Kenrick. I expect it will reassure you. I came to reassure you,' he told Myles.

'It is gratifying to know that the British government is protecting our interests and that all the great houses are protected against the smell of starvation,' Myles said with a shade of sarcasm.

'We protect all our interests. You live in Mayo?' Spiker asked abruptly.

'No, Galway. I am a merchant there.'

'Have you travelled abroad much?'

'To Spain and France to buy wines.'

'Then you have picked up a slight French accent?'

'I had not noticed.'

'Had you not noticed, Miss Barrett?' Spiker asked, turning towards Gráinne.

'No.' Gráinne was uncertain of his intention.

'I distinctly thought there was a slight suggestion of a foreign accent. However, let me turn to more serious matters. If necessary, I can place soldiers here for your protection. Be assured that Colonel Spiker will trap all our enemies. I am sure that gives you reassurance.'

'It does, but I think we do not need the protection of soldiers. Very little of any political significance happens in this region,' Gráinne said.

'One never knows,' Spiker drawled. 'However, I am sure you have drawn up your own plans for any emergency. I must be away. I have several other houses to visit.'

He rose slowly from the great chair, his eyes never leaving Myles. Myles thought that he could detect controlled hate in the pupils.

Colonel Spiker walked slowly to the door, his back curved, his head a little towards the side. He looked like an old man. He turned at the entrance and waved to them.

'Have confidence in Colonel Spiker,' he said. 'He is a determined man. That is why you have no reason to worry.'

They watched him drive away. Gráinne turned to Myles.

'Does he suspect who you are?'

'I am not certain. But I have a feeling I should move rapidly.'

They closed the great door and returned to the room.

Meanwhile Colonel Spiker was making his own plans as he went down the avenue. He was certain that he had been speaking to Myles Prendergast, the man who had flayed him. He would not only destroy him and his friends, but he would also destroy the great house he had just visited.

One morning Myles strode into the library. 'Today I go to Northport,' he announced. 'Fear has gripped the landlords and the agents after the death of Kenrick, so perhaps this is the spark which will ignite the powder-keg! Something has to be done to draw attention to the plight of the people. I have made the decision and now I must follow it through to completion.'

He turned and left without a word, her bright image scored in his mind.

She watched him ride down the avenue, wrapped in his great cloak. He was a black mysterious figure against the snow. She watched him until he was out of sight and knew that something desperate was about to happen. Some fatal intuition stirred within her, and she realised the quiet nights they had spent in the library were over.

All that day he drew plans of the granaries and of the hills about the quays. He counted the soldiers on guard and the hours when they changed their watch. They could attack the warehouse without difficulty, but their escape routes would soon be cut off and they could be hunted down and slaughtered. The bare mountains offered no cover. If all failed, they could escape only by sea, so a Barrett ship must be anchored by the quay and the tide must be filling when they attacked. He remembered the warnings he had been given: 'Do not attack unless you are certain of your escape routes.' They could escape by the sea if they failed.

Myles Prendergast did not suspect that all his movements were watched. Colonel Spiker had dispatched soldiers disguised as civilians to Northport, and they looked down on him from the granary windows as he sketched the buildings. Reports of his activities were immediately dispatched to Castlebar. 'He is falling into the trap,' Colonel Spiker said when he heard the news. 'He thinks the granaries are the weakest chink in our armour.'

Two carts left the barracks the following day. To the casual observer they were carrying bags of meal. By midday they reached the quays of Northport. The great doors of the warehouse were swung aside and the carts entered. When they left the warehouse much later the carts were empty.

In the upper storey two soldiers ripped open the bags, took out the guns and stood them against the wall. They put the powder in a dry place. Eventually forty guns rested against the wall.

'What's the plan?' one soldier asked.

'I don't know. I've just been told to deliver the guns here, stand guard over them, and not to put my nose outside the door. Just got to stand here.'

'It's cold here. Think we will have an invasion?'

'Don't know. It's not the time for invasions. No Frenchman would set out to invade us this time of year. Anyway, aren't we at peace with the French just now?'

'Yes. That's right, but there must be some reason for all this, though.'

'I never ask questions. I just stand guard over the guns. Smells nice here, like a haggard at home. I always liked the smell of a haggard.'

They made themselves comfortable. Later they cut their tobacco and smoked their pipes. They wondered again if there was an invasion in the air, but could find no answers. 'Still, we've got to obey orders. You never know what's going on in the colonel's mind.'

Myles Prendergast decided to call a meeting in preparation for the attack on the warehouse. The plans were final in his mind: they must go ahead.

35

Seamus Costello knew that when he entered through the great gates of the prison he would never return to his village again. He had forfeited his life when he murdered Kenrick and would hang for this action. In the clear pitiless courtroom they would not listen to the emotional reasons which led to the murder.

The sergeant showed little feeling when he entered the cell on a cold Wednesday morning. He had official documents in his hands. He was unaffected by the events which led to Seamus Costello's conviction. He simply stated that he was due to appear in court to stand trial. He told him of the evidence that had been gathered against him and then he left. They brought him food. It was wholesome and warm, and he ate it without thought.

'Now that they are ready to hang me they fatten me. When I was hungry and innocent they did not bring me warm plates of food to the village,' he told the warder ironically.

'I am sorry for your troubles,' the warder told him. 'We live in bad times. I'll be close at hand if you want me.'

'There is little you can do for me now. How are the others?'

'Oh, Pete Costello has a warm cell. He is the prime witness. That wife of his visited the prison. She kept telling the warders that she was a rich woman now and that she had done her duty.'

'The only duty she ever did was to cause bother and trouble. I put food on her table, and she complained that others got a greater share. Pete Costello was always a weak man and he married a shrew of a woman whom no other would have.'

'Eat now and try to sleep. You will want all your senses about you.'

'I'll need them for a week and then I'll need them no more,' Seamus replied bitterly. 'They say hanging is a fast form of death.'

'Don't think about it.'

'But they say it is a fast form of death,' he persisted.

'Yes, it is very fast.'

'Will the body be returned to the village?'

'No. It is laid to rest here.'

'I'm told there is a murderers' plot here with no markings over the grave.'

'Don't think about these things. You will need sleep now. I'll call in to you later.' He was a fat warder, his eyes and his skin white as if they never left the underworld of half-light, but he had the mark of compassion.

As soon as he heard the evidence against him, Seamus Costello began to take his leave of life. Many times the image of the gallows would rise before his eyes, but he began to have other thoughts. He recalled his youth in the valley in the thirties when there was less hardship and when he would walk across the mountains in search of game. He thought of the stream, through which he had waded on the night of the murder in the hope that he would throw off his pursuers. It had sparkled with life, and the music of water falling across brown plates of stone had had a hundred voices. In spate and in drought it had filled his ears with sound. He had plunged his feet into the deep sandy pools to cool them; he had watched for the trout with his fingers in a circle and then thrown their shimmering bodies on to the puffy bank.

In the dank cell warm memories flooded into his mind. He thought of Eileen Horkan and knew he would not see her again. She had warned him against murderous thoughts. Her mind had been always quiet and thoughtful, and during his desperate hours she had found food and money for him. Now she was mistress to Lord Lannagh; he no longer thought her flesh was tainted. Who was not weak? His hands were stained

403

with blood, and he wondered if there would be some charity towards him in eternity.

He paced the cell from wall to wall. Four paces carried him across the floor. He felt the hard iron of the door, which had been painted green; the paint sweated on to his fingers. The light entered the cell through a small semicircular window. The ledge sloped inwards, so he could not draw himself up to look at the light and the snow.

Outside the prison walls the course of justice was moving rapidly. Sergeant Huggins, now that he was certain of a conviction for murder, visited the barracks each evening.

'I've written to Dublin to bring the sessions forward. I want a conviction as soon as possible. Already the newspaper articles on Costello have allayed some of the fears of the people. A hanging will convince the peasants that there is nothing to be gained from murdering agents,' Colonel Spiker told him.

'Will it be a public hanging?' Sergeant Huggins asked.

'Of course it will be a public hanging! Men have been hanged before outside the prison. Nothing better to send a shiver down a man's spine than the sight of a man dangling from the end of a rope.' There was pleasure in the colonel's voice. He dragged himself up and down the room trying to burn the excitement in his body. He had vowed that he would have his revenge on the malign landscape and the peasants who had cut his back to shreds, and this hanging would satisfy this in part.

'The hearing is in five days' time, Huggins. Have everything in order for the judge. Make sure that he is well accommodated.'

'Yes, sir.' Sergeant Huggins waited for further instructions.

Colonel Spiker limped up and down the room, his hands behind his back and a grim smile of satisfaction on his lips. He seemed to have forgotten that Sergeant Huggins was still there. He finally looked up at him. 'You may go. You are dismissed, Huggins,' he said directing him with a casual gesture of his hand towards the door.

On his way from the barracks and between the two high limestone walls which bordered the entrance to the barracks, Sergeant Huggins was having his first misgivings about Colonel Spiker. His attitude towards him had changed. He had dismissed him today as if he had been a batman or an underling. He wondered if he would keep his promise and have

404

him transferred to Dublin. The doubt began to grow in his mind.

In Molly Ward's pub the talk centred on Seamus Costello. Everybody seemed to have forgotten for the moment that a famine raged in the countryside, and there were no accounts of whole villages wiped out by starvation.

'Kenrick deserved what was coming to him!' Molly Ward said. 'He was like the gombeen man, fattening on other people's misfortunes. He was a low type and one of our own, and that makes him black.'

'Easy, Molly. You will be brought up for sedition. Seamus murdered a man and must hang for it.'

'But we have had no hanging for five years,' she protested. ¿

'Well, we'll have one now. Colonel Spiker will have his revenge for the maiming he got. They say that they castrated him with a whip.'

'There was a good motive for the murder. Kenrick had roared enough in Castlebar that he would have the Costellos out of their village and on the way to the county home.' Molly was flushed with anger.

'Well, he's dead now and a man must swing for his death. That's the course of justice for you,' the soldiers said and continued their conversation. They had little interest or care for Costello. They were fed and paid, and it mattered little to them who died. Molly Ward held her patience. She knew they would hang Costello like a dog; it was an old pattern. She had seen men hanged after the '98 rebellion.

Gill, the poet, read the first account of Seamus Costello's arrest in the local newspaper. It was one of his functions to translate the substance of the newspapers to the men in the shebeens. He had already heard the rumours that there would be a hanging. He knew as many gaol poems in Irish as he knew the poems of migrations and of love, and sad feelings rose in his heart for this man now incarcerated in the cold damp cell in Castlebar and the anguish of mind which he now suffered. He imagined him during happier times, playing hurley or cutting the first sod of land for the spring sowing. He thought, too, of the hempen rope which he would wear like a tie or a scarf about his neck; it was not for a wedding but for a wake.

405

The shapes of the poem like forms in a mist were in his mind; if only he could find the correct words.

He wondered where he had had the courage to look for correct words before. He had borrowed all the old rhyming schemes and images from useless poems. And then the first line came to him. He could not account for its origin: it was on his lips, and he did not know where it had come from.

'The winds cannot sing,' he repeated to himself. It was like the touch of a soft new silver coin, and he hoped it would not leave him, for his memory was defective. He repeated it again and again until the harmonies were ringing in his mind. And once he had set up the harmonies the other lines followed.

'The winds cannot sing
On the sere grass,
On the dead man's bones.
Weep in Invar and Ivagh by the sea,
The winds can only cry.'

His instinct when he had finished the first verse was to rush to the bar of the shebeen and call for more drink. He refrained. Instead he tapped out the rhythm of the lines on the floor and listened for the voice in his head again.

'The people cannot sing
On the edge of a winter sky,
Cannot weep over a dead man's bones
In Inch and on the islands.
Only the winds cry.'

Once he had obtained the second verse he repeated it again and again so that he would not lose one syllable. He must hold on to the gift from the gods. He must not lose the words.

And then, when the third verse was rising in his mind, a drunk who had been urinating in the back garden entered the shebeen and hit him on the back, knocking him forward. He almost fell into the fire.

'Well, if it isn't Gill the versifier! The man who can run up a poem like a tailor runs up a trousers or sow a litter of bonhams!'

Gill broke from his ecstasy. He shook his head and remembered where he was. 'You drunken fool,' he roared. 'You have destroyed a great poem.'

'*Aragh*, Gill, you only wrote one good poem in your life,' the drunken man told him and went back to his friends.

Quickly Gill recalled the lines which had come to him. He remembered each word. He tried to take up the strands of inspiration, but they had been cut from the loom of his imagination. He wondered if the gods of poetry would ever visit him again; if he would ever have the chance to finish the poem.

Eileen Horkan knew that she would soon not be able to conceal that she was carrying a child. She wondered if she should have taken Lord Lannagh's advice and gone to England. There was very little reason to stay on at the house and the farm.

She wept as she looked into the fire. Her memories were filled with recollections of the past. She thought of Seamus Costello in Castlebar gaol. He was like a caged eagle. Once he had ranged the mountains in search of game. He had been an outstanding athlete whose physical presence drew admiration from the crowds. Now he was a common criminal. The papers referred to him as a peasant and to the murder as the act of a small cottier jealous of a land agent. She no longer took pleasure from the books about her, for her mind was arid, her heart without emotion. She felt that something had snapped in her mind.

She heard the sound of a horse in the snow as a rider stopped at her gate, and some minutes later there was a knock upon the door. She wondered who would visit her at the dead of night.

She opened the door to Lord Lannagh. He was wrapped in a heavy cloak, and there was snow on his grey hair. He had never visited her house before.

'May I come in?' he asked.

He followed her to the room at the end of the house where she had set a fire and which contained her books.

They stood and looked at each other. Then without removing his cloak he put his arms about her and she began to cry.

'Why did you not come to the house? I have been worried about you. Day after day I have paced the library floor wondering if I should come to see you.' He held her from him and looked at her face. 'You are tired,' he said. 'Your face is drawn. Do you sleep well at night-time?'

'I have not slept well for a long time, Edward,' she told him. 'My mind and my heart have been torn by many things.'

'Then, you should have come to me. You should always come to me when you are disturbed.' His face was agitated and concerned. He stroked her hair as he spoke. 'Oh, but you are beautiful, beautiful,' he repeated.

'I do not think that you should have come here,' she said. 'I do not wish to draw you into what is happening.'

'What is happening?' he asked, gazing into her face.

'My cousin will be brought on trial for murder,' she told him bleakly. 'I do not know if I will be called upon to take the witness stand.'

He was clearly confused by all that she said. 'Sit down and tell me all that has happened,' he directed her.

It took her two hours to tell all that had happened during the last two weeks. She went into detail to explain to him her relationship with Seamus Costello and the blood-bonds which bound him to her. He listened to her intently, interrupting her only when he needed some point clarified. When she had finished he thought for a moment.

'Then, there is no reason to remain here – it will not be very long until your time has come. I wish to bring you to that house in Kent which I promised you. It is close by the sea, and the seasons come early there. You are tired and depressed. Your mind is hard-pressed. I have stayed on here only to be with you. Come with me now.'

She considered all that he said to her. 'I will go after the hanging. I will go after the hanging, I promise you. My life has grown empty here and I wish to be in a place where the breezes are gentle, where the wind does not moan in the chimney, where the landscape is not bleak and where the smell of blight is not on the air.'

'I will take you with me.'

'Then, I will go, but I have one favour to ask you. I am always asking you for favours, but could I obtain access to Seamus Costello at the gaol?'

'That will be arranged indirectly. I cannot be seen to be associated with you during the next few weeks, but I will place money at your disposal.'

'And then I will leave with you. I wish to be with you now.
I am tired.'

He placed his arm about her, held her to him and gave her
quiet comfort. Then he left in the darkness.

Seamus Costello could not recall in sequence all that happened
to him in the short space of a week. He was brought chained
to the court in Castlebar. The courthouse was like a theatre,
with rows of faces looking down at him in the dock. He had
smelt the sweating bodies, and seen the reporters writing
down each thing he said. He spoke in Irish and then in English,
but the judge could not clearly understand him, and asked
him to speak in his native language so it could be translated
by the translator. Ranging over the hostile faces, he saw Eileen
Horkan above him and their eyes met.

His mind was tired, and he felt that he could not follow all
that went on. Huggins gave evidence, and it was strange
how respectable Kenrick could be made when they added
his Christian name. Several of the man's acquaintances in
Castlebar were brought forward to prove that he was a man
of the highest respectability. Sal Costello stood out from the
mass, looking at him malevolently, dressed in garish town
clothes with rouge on her cheeks as if she were a soldier's
prostitute. She was brought forward as a witness, and her
evidence alone was sufficient to condemn him to death. Her
husband had told her every detail of what had happened on
the night.

He did not recognise Pete Costello when he arrived in the
witness-box. He had been washed and shaved and had on a
new suit in which he seemed strangely uncomfortable. Now
that he had decided to give evidence aginst him, he was voluble
in all that he had to say. Some of his descriptions and remarks
translated into English caused the audience to laugh.

'You were always a fool, Pete Costello,' Seamus Costello
shouted at him, 'and never more so when the county is laughing at you. May you have some peace of mind when you come
to die.'

Finally the pike was produced. A doctor acted out the killing
for the jury. It was dramatic and detailed, and he explained
what had happened in heavy medical idiom. It was clear to
Seamus Costello that the jury would bring in a verdict of

guilty for him and one of transportation for his neighbour. He was led away to his cell at five o'clock: the court would resume the next day and give its verdict. He wept when he returned to his cell; all during the day he had heard no kind word in his defence.

As the early evening came on and the light faded in the semicircular window above him, the door was unbolted. He did not look to see who had entered; he was too confused with the process of law to understand what was happening.

'Seamus,' a voice said behind him, and he turned around in disbelief. Eileen Horkan had entered the cell.

'How did you get permission to enter the gaol?' he asked abruptly.

'Do not ask questions,' she said. 'I am here.' The fat warder had brought a light and placed it on the table and then left.

Seamus was ashamed of his prison garb. 'Look at me,' he said, 'and how low I have been brought. All day my mind has been confused. I will be condemned tomorrow. Did we ever dream a long time ago that it would come to this?'

'No. Last night I was thinking of our youth together.'

'I will hang, Eileen. I deserve to hang.'

'No. I sat in the court all day. I did not watch justice at work, but injustice. They did not hear of how much you suffered before you made the decision.'

'There is blood on my hands. The blood of Kenrick is on *these* hands. I do not fear what they will do to me but I fear the eternity out there which will never end. I know I'll be damned in hell.'

'Have you gone to confession?'

'No, not yet. I'm sorry for what I have done, but I wonder that if given the circumstances I would not do it all again.'

'I cannot deal with these questions, Seamus, but mercy is on your side. What else could you do in such desperate circumstances?'

'I must confess. I suppose that this will be part of what happens. It is like the plays you read for me. Now life is catching up with them.'

They sat and talked for a long time. On the eve of his sentence they talked about trivial things, and memories of what had happened a long time ago came back to them.

'Strange, on the eve of death we talk only of sunshine and

410

distant summers. I suppose the valley will soon be emptied of Costellos,' he mused.

'Yes. The lower half stole everything that Kenrick possessed.'

'I saved the wrong people!'

She left the prison late that night. Next day she was in the courtroom when the verdict was given. Seamus Costello was to be brought to the gaol from whence he had come and he would be hanged in public three days later. As he was led from the courtroom in chains he felt that the tragedy was entering its last act.

Silence now descended upon the prison. The thought that a man was to be hanged on Saturday muted noise and speech. A priest had been brought to the cell by the governor, and Seamus Costello had confessed his sins, weeping as he told each detail of the murder.

Colonel Spiker was satisfied with the verdict and had a rare bottle of claret opened for him as he took his evening meal: the net was tightened about those who had deformed him. He sent immediately for the hangman who lived in Athlone.

The administrator of the prison was shocked by the hangman's direct manner. He paced the front of the prison and directed where the gallows should be set up. 'Bring it forward towards the road where everybody can see what is happening. I am giving a performance and I wish the audience to see each dramatic move. Have the hour of the execution announced and keep all reporters away from the scene. I hate reporters. I have always hated them: they are always abusive towards me.'

He directed the construction of the scaffold. Several times he tested the trapdoor. It was too rusty, he complained. 'I did not come here to do a botched job,' he told the warders.

Then on the eve of the execution he went to the administrator and asked for his fee in advance.

'How much?' the administrator asked.

'Ten pounds,' he told him. 'The price of food is dear, the price of drink is dear and it is not every day that I have a hanging. In my time I have hanged seventy people. This will be my seventy-first.'

'And do you relish the thought of hanging?' the administrator asked, appalled.

'The man is condemned. I do a necessary job of work. This is my business. If you are not willing to give me ten pounds, then I'll be on my way.'

'Oh, I'll give you the ten pounds,' the administrator said and he took the money from the safe.

'Good,' said the hangman, counting it. 'I must sleep now. Tomorrow is a busy day for us all. I can assure you I am the best hangman in Ireland and, when the trapdoor drops, the criminal will be dead as soon as the rope jerks.'

Next morning a curious crowd began to gather outside the prison. Children pushed their faces close to the bars to get a good view. Women in shawls gathered behind them, curious also. Many men had left the shebeens to witness the event. It gave them some consolation to know that they would be alive that evening and the Costello man dead. They had listened to the papers being read to them, and clearly this Costello was a brutal murderer. It would be a lesson to all future murderers.

On the scaffold the executioner, with a mask drawn over his face, directed the final arrangements. The crowds asked him questions which he eagerly answered. The hour of the execution approached.

'Is it the hour yet, Eileen?' Seamus Costello asked. Cold sweat poured down his face as he waited for the final call.

Eileen Horkan had been with him all morning giving him consolation. She had arranged with the priest for a final confession and that water should be brought to the prison so that he could wash himself before the hanging. He found the soap strange and scented on his hands and upon his face.

'It is like the preparation for a marriage!' he told her as she dried his face and combed back his hair. 'God, Eileen, I wish I was running free through meadows or had gone to America a long time ago and this would not have happened to me.'

'Don't think, *allanagh*. Life is short, and some day we will meet in the fields of eternity.'

It approached three o'clock, and the administrator of the prison knocked at the door. He was accompanied by two monks from Errew monastery in their brown habits.

'It is time to go,' the administrator said quietly. Seamus Costello broke down and wept, and Eileen Horkan put her arms about his body.

412

'I don't wish to die, Eileen! I don't wish to die.'

They prised his arms from her body and led him away. She waited in the cell.

The monks began to chant the litany of the dead. The procession did not lead directly to the scaffold. In all the yards the prisoners were drawn up by the officers, and at the appearance of Seamus Costello they knelt down to pray for the repose of his soul as he passed. Seamus Costello had refused his breakfast, otherwise he would have vomited his food on the snowy path. The main gate appeared and was drawn slowly open. He raised his eyes and saw the gallows and began to tremble, and then lost control of his body and urinated in his prison garb. He drew backwards, but the prison officers grabbed him by the arms and dragged him forward up the wooden steps and set him on the stage. The crowd cheered. He gazed at them, but his eyes were glazed, unseeing.

'Take heart, my boy. Take heart, my boy. It will be over in a second!' the hooded executioner told him.

Seamus Costello's face and hands turned black. He fell forward on his knees on the trapdoor and began to pray in Irish. The executioner pinioned his arms behind his back, then drew him upwards and put a mask on his face. The gaping faces of the crowd were blotted out. Expertly the hangman put a noose about his neck and immediately pulled the bolt beside him. The body shot downward. There was a jerk and the hangman knew from the sharp snap that the job had been expertly done. The crowd set up a cry when the body fell through the trapdoor. It was left to dangle for some time. Then it was cut down, placed on a shelf and carried away for anonymous burial.

After the cry, Eileen Horkan waited on in the prison cell with the iron door ajar, praying for the soul of her friend. Later she left the prison and made her way homeward. She had no strength left in her body, and the horse carried her forward sluggishly. Her mind was heavy with the thoughts of what had happened during the day.

On her journey home from the prison Eileen Horkan changed her mind on many matters. She had been with Seamus Costello just a few minutes before his fine life was destroyed by a hangman who had been paid ten pounds for his service. She

413

remembered Seamus Costello in his youth before poverty and hunger had broken his manhood.

The trial had been a travesty of justice. She had not sat in a courtroom before and she recalled vividly the judge with his ornate robes and his British voice which so smoothly set out the case before the jury arrived at their verdict. Kenrick's character was shown by the witnesses to be one of integrity, devoted to the good service of the State; Seamus Costello, in the eyes of the law, was a vengeful peasant. He was humiliated further by the fact that the court proceedings were carried out in a precise legal English in which he found it difficult to express himself.

She was certain that he had not been given a fair trial. 'He should be alive today!' she cried to herself. 'There was no reason why he should have died. If Kenrick died, he deserved to die.'

The legal sytem was weighted against the poor and the dispossessed, she thought. She had followed the course of justice for two days, and now a hatred began to grow in her for all that the system of government stood for. Her father's words returned to her from the past. 'Do not trust them,' he had said. 'Never forget that we are a different race. We have been disinherited, but there is something proud and noble in us. The day they destroy the language is the day they destroy what we are.'

She had been blind during the last few months. She had abandoned her people and her reason, using her body to obtain food to keep the village alive. Lord Lannagh had obtained a permit for her to enter the prison and he had given her money, but he had little interest in saving Seamus Costello.

'He has committed murder, Eileen,' he told her when she made a final visit to the house in order to seek his help. 'He will be brought to justice. Nothing I could do would help him.'

Now she was angry. Lord Lannagh lived in a world which was cut off from the hardship of the peasants or the immediate events of history. The hunger held the whole county in its grip, yet he spent his days in the glasshouses and his evenings reading in the library.

She had been blinded by love. They were true when they called her 'the Englishman's whore'. The trial and the hanging had awakened in her the realities of the famine and above all

414

her allegiance to the people who were dying in the small villages or making their way to the workhouse in Castlebar. She had been deaf to the pleas of her conscience.

Her heart was now empty of feeling as she thought of Seamus Costello and how he had cried like a child in the cell before they brought him out to be hanged. She recalled the long lines of people on the way to Castlebar along her way home from the house of Lord Lannagh where she had satiated her body with food and love.

She wondered how Lord Lannagh had spent the day of the hanging. He had probably potted an exotic plant in his glasshouses and later read some book or other which had been sent from London.

She began to question her love for this man who was part of the system which had brought about the death of a man who had been decent and upright.

She no longer thought of the house Lord Lannagh promised both her and her child in Kent. She thought rather of the people in the valley who could starve to death. Should she now abandon them in the hour when they needed her? It would be too easy to lock up her house and move to England.

When she reached her home it was very dark. She unharnessed her horses and went indoors. She lit the lamp in her room and placed some kindling on the bright embers. Soon she had a warm fire burning in the grate and only then did she realise how cold she had been.

Later she recalled the nights Seamus Costello had visited her secretly at the house. He must have been hungry for many months. His life in its final years had been sad: he had lost a wife in childbirth and he had watched Kenrick impose rents upon him that he could not pay. He should have left the valley many years ago, but he felt that he owned the land and that some day he might come into legal possession of it. Now he was dead and so was Kenrick who had brought about so much of the trouble which had shattered all their lives. She slept uneasily that night and next morning she saddled her horse and went to see the ravages caused by the famine.

It was a journey through an empty landscape. Whole villages had been abandoned and no sound broke the winter silence. The fields, where the potato had failed, were now covered by snow.

She entered one village. It was silent. Then a dog barked before a cabin. She dismounted, and the dog fled and continued to bark at a distance. She entered the dark, low cabin and the stench of putrid flesh filled her nostrils. In the corner, heaped together, were several emaciated bodies, breast ribs holding collapsed flesh; they had been dead for several days. In every cabin she visited she was greeted by the same rotting stench.

She mounted her horse and left the village, her mind filled with the sights she had witnessed. No passages in the great books could describe the horrors of the famine.

During the last few weeks she had felt the child stir within her. Now she must think of its future. She would not flee to England: her child would be born in this landscape and it would be trained to rise out against all the injustices with which the country was burdened. The next generation must enjoy a life of prosperity and freedom, but they would have to take up arms to obtain it, for nothing could be achieved through the present process of law she had seen.

Two nights later, Lord Lannagh came to visit her. When she opened the door he stood there in his cloak and she would have thrown herself into his arms, but she controlled herself. There would be no love shared between them again.

'I expected a note from you during the last few days,' he told her when he had taken his seat. 'You know how much I think about both you and the child.'

She looked at him directly. He was a handsome man, like one of the rare plants in his glasshouses. He did not belong in the landscape, and all the phrases she had prepared for this occasion seemed hollow now. She forgave him for his ignorance of all that was happening in the country: there was something unreal about his house and his library and his gardens. Perhaps he was not to blame for all that had happened. He was just a small figure in a vast tangle of things.

'I shall not visit you any more, my Lord,' she said formally.

He was taken aback at her cold voice. 'But I love you! I will take you to Kent. I will take care of both you and the child.'

'It is no longer a question of love. I was with Seamus Costello before they took him out to be hanged. He did not deserve to die!' she cried. 'He was my blood and my flesh, and at the end there was nothing I could do for him. He wept like a child – he should not have wept but he did, for he was saying

416

goodbye to a life that he once loved. When men like Seamus Costello are forced to kill savage agents like Kenrick, then there is something wrong with the political system which brings that about.'

'I know. I understand,' he told her.

'You do *not* know and you do *not* understand! You say you understand, but you don't. Do you know that Kenrick kept his battering rams and his tents in your farmyard? Do you know that he slept in your bed while you were in England? Do you realise that he *hated* you and boasted that he would one day possess your land?'

'Nobody told me about these things! I thought Hackett kept the house in good order while I was away. Mrs Rance never drew my attention to these things.' Lannagh was clearly shocked.

'She was afraid for herself and her crippled husband. And do you know that the great open lawn in front of your house once housed several families? Kenrick had them evicted so that the house would have an uninterrupted view of the lake. *That* is the reality beneath your lawn!'

He was taken aback by her anger. A part of her character to which he was not party was unleashing all the pent-up hatred within her. 'I did not bring about these things, Eileen,' he told her.

'You may not have brought them about but the system to which you belong did. I am sorry if anger boils within me but I have seen too much during the last few days to remain silent or inactive any more. Feelings for the land and its history that I have stifled during the last months have returned, and I am afraid, my Lord, our affair is over. Had it happened at another time and in other circumstances I might have gone with you to Kent. Now I cannot.'

'But you may die here! The child may die.' He was pale in the lamp's dim light.

'Others have died. I am unimportant.'

'You are important to me.'

'I cannot love you further, my Lord.' She stood unsteadily. 'It is time our talk came to an end. We must say our goodbyes.'

'No,' he cried. 'I will not easily walk out of your life. I ask you once more to come with me.'

'No. That is final.'

'And the child?'

'I will rear the child according to my best lights. I may even marry in haste so it will not carry the mark of bastard on it.'

'You are cruel to me,' he said in anguish. 'You blame me for things outside my control.'

'Perhaps I do. I suppose some day when I am old, and time and history has taken their toll on me, I will remember pleasant days with you.'

'They were pleasant, and you know that I love you. I always will. I will close the house and I may not return again. I will have nothing to return to.'

'And the flowers and shrubs?'

'They will die. Everything in this landscape seems to be dying.'

'Then, it is time for you to leave,' she said bitterly.

'Will you write to me when the child is born?'

'Yes.'

'You know I will leave aside a large sum of money for its education?'

'You may be educating a rebel.'

'I may, but I am educating my own flesh and blood.'

'You must go now. I thought our final words would be angry and I had planned it so, but you are a gentleman and we *did* enjoy the delights of Paradise.' She began to weep.

He rushed over to put his arms about her.

'No!' She shrank from him. 'Don't touch me or it will all start again. Go now!'

He left the room, and she heard the door close. Now she would have to face the bleak months ahead alone; she had made a hard choice.

36

IT WAS APPROACHING the shortest day of the year. Of all the years which people could recall, none could be compared with it for the severity of the weather. There was no break in the cold: day after day it continued, hardening the earth, chilling the bone.

The dead were no longer counted outside the workhouse. They were buried without blessing or decorum in long narrow graves. All during December starving people continued to make their way to the high sandstone walls and the tall locked gates in the hope of obtaining some food, but the workhouse was full. There was nowhere else to turn. Everything had failed. They lay down on the stiff frost-hardened ground and died, and there was no pity towards the dead.

Whole villages were deserted. The wind blew through the small rooms and began its subtle work of destruction. There was silence over the land and no animal moved across the snow-covered fields. They had been killed to provide meat. Even the rats were hungry: the final predators were dying.

There was food in the towns; it was hidden away and eaten in secret. It was no longer possible to buy meal at the market. In the ports the ships had cast anchor for the winter. Very few captains would take on the dangers of the sea.

But in the military barracks the soldiers were well fed and always on the alert. Troops had been rushed to Mayo to deal

419

with any rebellion. Men looked jealously at the lights in the barracks at night-time.

'The soldier boys have enough in their bellies to feed families. If we could have a quarter of the food they eat, we could live.'

For the constables it would be a good Christmas. They, too, had been well provided for and they would even have beef on the tables. It would be doubly tasty knowing that the country was in the grip of the most severe famine on record. Their orders were clear: they were to be on the alert until the potato crop of 1847 was ready. The government had abandoned any hope of feeding the hungry, and now only the soup kitchens provided food during the winter months.

For John Burke the time had come to make a stand. He and Myles had discussed the attack on the warehouses in Northport. They intended to blow the large doors from their hinges and let the townsfolk have all the food they wanted.

John Burke suggested that they should at least use one of the ships in the attack. 'We are safe at sea, Myles. The army would cut us down if we retreated inland or to the mountains. No man would be secure or safe in this weather. We will have a ship anchored close.'

That night, in Barrett House, Myles told Gráinne his plans. He put his arms about her as they lay in the great bed, and brushed her hair when she wept for the danger he now exposed himself to.

'It is so cold to set out on such an adventure! The guns will freeze in your hands!' she cried.

'Now is the time, when it is least expected. If we wait until spring, then more will have died. It may prompt the government to throw open the depots and the warehouses. And if we fail, then it will be a glorious failure and I will have done the thing that any man would have done whose heart has not gone hard during these awful months.' His voice was firm and determined.

'I hope nothing happens. I do not wish to see you killed or thrown into prison! Take the two ships if necessary and make sure that you can escape. We have enough food left to take the two crews to France.' She spoke hesitantly, as if unsure of his love.

'If we fail, we cannot go to France. The British ships will be on the seas immediately, and we would stand no chance. We must sail directly to America.'

'At this time of year?' she asked in horror.

'Yes. John Burke has sailed across the Atlantic in winter.'

'Then I will have both ships provisioned for you. One will be at the Barrett section of Northport waiting for news, ready to sail. I shall go with you.'

'Oh, no.' He turned towards her. 'Your place is here in the great house,' he said gently.

'No, not any more.' Her voice was muffled in his arms. 'My father had a great dream and great plans for this house, but they never lived up to any promise. I will sail with you if necessary.' She was crying now.

He looked around and lifted his eyes to the great room, with its ornate ceilings. He had spent many happy hours in this house. Here he had told Gráinne he loved her and promised her that some day he would bring her to France and they would walk together through the woods of Saint-Cloud. He thought also of the map room with its large expensive maps secured in their brass tubes, and his mind wandered to the woods and the walks.

'You would leave all this?' he asked wonderingly.

'I want to be with *you*, Myles Prendergast,' she said fiercely. 'I want to go where you go. I can return to the great house at another time. It is an empty place since my father died.'

'No, you must stay here. It is too dangerous. You are getting yourself into something which could lead to great trouble, and I will have brought it all upon you.'

'I have chosen. I have brought it upon myself,' she told him, and the strength of her conviction drew him to her and he loved her with a passion she had not known before.

John Burke had called a final meeting to tell his men of their plans. They were issued with revolvers and told how they would assemble for the attack.

'In the event of a retreat I will call on you to follow me. Follow me blindly, for your safety depends on it!' He would not be more specific.

Late that night a rider set out from Northport carrying with him the date of the attack and the hour. It was the news which

Colonel Spiker had been waiting for and he drew up his final orders. He knew exactly now what he must do.

'So they will put forty men in the field? No Burke will escape. I will follow them across every mountain until I bring them to justice.' He would have revenge for the welts on his back. Barrett House would stand as a charred reminder that he had left his mark upon the landscape. He called Captain Ormsby to his rooms and gave him his instructions.

Gill was drunk in the Sailors Tavern. He slept intermittently in a corner, but he was sharp enough to hear many of the whispers about him. He knew that there was going to be a rising in Northport and he knew the very hour. He had often composed poems of imagined rising and now he would witness a real one. He decided to stay close to the Burkes – there would surely be a free drink in it for him if he were in the right bar.

The shortest day of the year dawned brightly, filling the mists with silver and turning the countryside white and bloodless. Men began to move towards the granaries in twos and threes. They were tense. In the pockets of their greatcoats they carried their revolvers, primed for the attack.

Gráinne Barrett said goodbye to Myles Prendergast in the great hall. 'I wish this day were over,' she said.

'We will see what the night will bring,' he told her, a gleam in his eye.

She threw her arms about him, not wishing to see him go, but he left quickly, mounted his horse and rode down the avenue.

She set quickly about her plans. She called the servants and told them to bring the carriage around to the front of the house then went upstairs and opened her father's cabinet. She took out the documents he had shown her and put them in a leather case and then went to the map room and took some of the maps.

The carriage set out for the quays where two men were waiting. They emptied the contents of the coach into a boat and rowed towards one of the ships. Altogether the coach made three journeys.

'Is it to America you are going?' one servant asked Gráinne, a grin on his face.

'Keep your mouth closed or it's the worse for you!' one of the others told him sullenly.

Gráinne called everyone together in the library. Some of them had been in the house since she was a small child. She looked at their faces. For a moment she wondered if she should remain in the house and not leave for the ship.

'I may be away for some time,' she said. 'Take care of Barrett House for me. I have arranged that you will be paid during my absence.'

'You are not going to leave us, surely, Gráinne?' Mrs Jennings asked. She burst out crying and threw her arms about her. 'It's that Frenchman that has turned your heart, love! I know it.'

'The Frenchman has turned my heart, Mrs Jennings,' she agreed simply.

The evening was coming on, and Gráinne Barrett looked at the sky. Soon they would be attacking the warehouse. A horseman hidden in the woods above the warehouse and on the far side of the cut away from the fire would bring news to her.

Towards dusk, more men began leaving the taverns and making their way along the quays. Two of them were dragging Gill with them.

'Oh, I have no taste for blood!' he cried. 'I have no taste at all for it.'

'You brought it on yourself, Gill. You always turn up where you are not wanted.'

'Oh, it was a bad day that you ever thought of taking on the British arms. Couldn't you have left me drinking?' he pleaded.

'You brought it on yourself, Gill. Going round the bar telling people that the great revolution was going to take place and that the town would run red with the blood of redcoats!'

'It was my imagination. It ran away with me. It runs away with me when I'm drunk.'

But they would not listen to his pleas. He should never have come with them. His stomach tightened as they approached the warehouses, running along the quay: he had no taste for battle and no gun to protect himself.

The men took up their positions quietly as they had been told. They stood in groups of fives and sixes before the great

423

doors. Two soldiers guarded each door. They seemed unper-
turbed and did not appear to take notice of them.

The men noticed that a Barrett ship had sailed across the
harbour and was tied up by the quay wall which jutted out
into the sea. They knew that if they had to retreat it must be
in that direction.

'It looks too easy, far too easy,' Myles muttered to John
Burke as they looked out at the warehouses. 'But, whatever
else, they cannot cut off our retreat to the sea.'

Up in the woods the horseman, cold now, looked at the men
assembling on the quays.

From his position in the upper storey of the warehouse Colonel
Spiker looked at the ship across the harbour.

'Why was I not informed about the ship?' he asked one of
the men standing beside him. He could not move from his
position and watched the men gather in groups on the main
quay.

The line of soldiers running down the long storeroom had
their guns primed. At a signal they would approach the windows and open fire. Inside the great doors other soldiers were
drawn up, waiting for the doors to be thrown wide.

'Make every shot count,' Colonel Spiker told them. 'We may
not have a second chance.'

All day Spiker's agents had moved through the villages on
the north coast buying drinks in the shebeens for the starving
people.

'I see you starve and the great house filled with food,' they
said. 'Do you know that the Barretts have outhouses stuffed
with meal that would see you all through the winter?'

'The Barretts would never see us ill done by,' the people
said.

'Well, we have heard in Northport that the house is filled
with food. It's even stacked in the great rooms. They brought
it from America in September. There is plenty for everyone.'

The men got quickly drunk. Word passed through the villages that the Barrett house was as full of corn as a warehouse.
There was enough food there to feed them all: they would not
have to die if they acted quickly. Now that Michael Barrett
was dead they had no fears of the great house.

They banded together and began to move along the road to

the Barrett House. On the journey they continued to drink from the bottles provided by Spiker's agents, and courage ran high in their minds. As the darkness fell, they lit torches to guide their way.

Gráinne Barrett saw the long line of people making their way up the avenue and soon she could hear their drunken voices. The servants gathered about her in the main hall and watched them approach.

Myles Prendergast signalled to his men. They drew the heavy revolvers from their pockets and stormed across towards the warehouses. It was dusk, and images and shapes were becoming doubtful. Before they could discharge their first shots Colonel Spiker ordered his men to the windows above them. They took quick aim, and a ragged round of fire shattered the evening quiet. Men fell on the cobbled quayside crying out in pain. As the main doors were drawn open, the Burkes managed to discharge the revolvers into the dark mouth of the warehouse and soldiers fell forward on to the pavement.

'Keep up the fire!' John Burke called to his men. He was bleeding from the shoulder.

They continued to fire the rounds of shot into the dark warehouse, and cries of soldiers cut the air. By now the soldiers in the upper storey had charged and primed their guns again. They sent another round of shot down on the men.

'Retreat towards the ship!' Myles ordered, his voice ringing out above the sound of gunfire.

'Hold your fire! Keep the final shots for close range. Retire to the ship! We have been led into a trap! Make for the ship! Carry all the wounded men you can with you.'

The men retreated in confusion, Myles and John Burke bringing up the rear. Five of their men were dead. They did not know how many soldiers lay wounded inside the warehouse.

Colonel Spiker saw them retreat and ordered his men to move down the narrow winding stairs. They rushed down the steps, their boots ringing on the iron, trampling on several of their colleagues as they pushed out through the doors.

Gill had whimpered like a child when the balls cut up the puffs of snow and mud around him; he had no idea of what was happening. He heard Myles Prendergast call out the retreat but hesitated, not knowing what to do. Too late, he decided to follow the retreating men. When he emerged from behind the bales he saw a British soldier bearing down upon him. He cried out in Irish: 'I am a poet! I am a poet!'

The soldier discharged his gun, and the ball caught Gill in the throat. He grasped his shredded gullet and tried to stanch the flow. His voice was gone. He could not call out.

'He's one of the rebels!' another soldier cried out. He took careful aim and shot Gill through the heart. He fell forward on to the bales of ropes, held on to them for a moment, then slipped to the ground. Gill, rake and poet, was dead.

Colonel Spiker mustered his men into an orderly line on the quay. Then, drawing his sword, he moved forward with them after the retreating figures.

'I'll put paid to the bastard this time!' John Burke roared in anger. He discharged the remaining two shots into the soldiers. Two of them fell forward and while the rest regrouped he drew two more revolvers from his belt. Too late Colonel Spiker saw his move and rushed forward with his sword raised above his head. At close range and with deadly aim John Burke blew off the side of his head, and he fell forward at his feet.

'Now we are square, Colonel!' John Burke looked at the soldiers priming their guns. 'And here's to you, you red bastards!' he cried out and fired his revolvers into the group of soldiers. With all the chambers discharged, he threw down the useless revolvers, took up the colonel's sword and holding it firmly in his hand he retreated.

John Burke held the soldiers at bay for five minutes. During that time the others had clambered on board the ship and were casting off the ropes. The wind was catching a sail. If he did not hurry up, the ship would be drawn away from the harbour wall. Men held grimly to the ropes.

'Hurry up, John Burke! Our arms are nearly torn from us,' they called.

'Always complaining! Always complaining!' he told them as he was drawn on to the deck.

'Keep ready for a final shot at them,' he said. 'It's not every day you get a chance like this, lads! Hold steady and firm.'

The ship eased its way along the quay wall. The soldiers ran along beside the ship unable to take proper aim.

'Now, men!' John Burke called, waving Spiker's sword above

426

his head. 'One final blast and it's off to America with us!'

The men picked up the guns from the deck and trained them on the running soldiers. Fifteen shots rang out. Soldiers fell forward.

'It was too easy. The woodcock and the plover would have more sense!' John Burke shouted. He looked backward into the gathering dusk, taking his leave of Northport as the ship slid out to sea through the islands. He would not visit it again. Myles Prendergast lay on the deck covered with a blanket, bleeding from the chest.

'Where is the food?' the crowd roared. 'Where is the food?'

Gráinne Barrett stood on the steps, the light from the torches burning about her. 'There is no food stored in the house. We have only sufficient for ourselves,' she shouted.

'Lies!' cried one of Spiker's men. 'Out of the way!' The men rushed forward up the steps and into the house, the servants fleeing before them to the kitchen and out into the yard.

'Oh, God!' they cried. 'They will surely set the house on fire! They are drunk.'

Gráinne could see them in the torchlight pulling down the curtains and pushing the books from the cabinets. She rushed to her horse and mounted it, moving some distance from the house.

The curtains caught flame. Seeing the fire, others rushed through the rooms in search of food, but there was none. As they left each room they set it on fire, a mad frenzy gripping them. Gráinne wept as she watched the house burn and the men rush from room to room, black figures against the fire which raged in the main hall. It seemed far away, like a dream, too horrible to be real. Then the windows exploded and the flames shot outwards. Fed now on the inrush of winter air the fire began to rage like a beast of many tongues. The house was being consumed.

Gráinne turned the horse away and rode towards the port, the reflection of the flames on the snow before her. When she reached the quay people were streaming through the town out towards the great house. They had seen the fire over Eisirt wood.

'It's over, Gráinne. It's all over. They walked into a trap,' the waiting horseman told her.

427

'How many are dead?' she asked.

'It was hard to see, for it was dusk.'

'Then, quickly get the ship ready. We must sail to meet them in Clew Bay.'

When she reached the ship the small crew were ready to take her orders. They would have to take the two ships to America. It was the end of all things.

She looked up at the woods of Eisirt as the ship made its way out through the islands. The great house was now glowing in the darkness, huge flames licking the sky. With a crash, the roof fell in and a huge shower of sparks issued towards the sky.

'The house is dead,' she said simply.

John Burke knew that Barrett House was burning when he saw the flames in the sky.

'It's been a wicked and bad day,' he said. 'But maybe at the end of all the reckoning it was the best we could have done. The spirit of the people is broken, and it will take another generation for it to stir again.'

Myles Prendergast was now lying in the cabin. He drew himself up and, looking out of the porthole, watched the great house burn. 'I have brought destruction on a great house,' he said to himself. He lay back and worried for the safety of Gráinne.

Soon he heard voices on the water as the second ship approached. Gráinne was rowed across and she climbed the rope ladder on to the deck.

'Is he wounded?' she asked in a low voice.

'Yes,' said John Burke. 'It's not dangerous. He will recover. He took a ball in the chest.'

She rushed down to the cabin. Myles was lying on the bunk, his face ashen. She put her arms about him.

'I am sorry about the great house,' he said. 'It was a beautiful place. It should not have been put to the flame.'

'It is gone now and, although I weep for it, we will build another one in America. My final attachment has been broken, and they will never catch us on the high seas.'

'You will have no regrets?' he asked.

'No, I will have no regrets. Rest now and I will return later. I think I should be with John Burke now.'

The ships moved forward through the darkness, with only the lanterns indicating their position. Gráinne walked towards John Burke. He stood beneath a light and looked towards the great house as it entered its final hours. Tears ran down his face, and he remembered the vault of his old dead friend in Eisirt wood.

There was a final shower of sparks as the second storey fell in, and then the fire became a steady flow. He knew that Gráinne was beside him and put out his arm and placed it about her. They wept together for the passing of all they knew and loved, and they watched the glow of the burning house until it fell below the horizon. It was cold now at sea. The stars were bright in the wide arc of the heavens. A wind was rising in the sails.